Praise for *New York Times* bestselling author
Allison Brennan

Stolen

"The evolution of Lucy and Sean's relationship has been a critical piece of what makes these novels so compelling. Brennan is a true master at providing byzantine plotlines that keep readers guessing as the danger amplifies."
—*RT Book Reviews* (4½ stars, Top Pick)

"All the excitement and suspense I have come to expect from Allison Brennan."
—*Fresh Fiction*

Stalked

"Once again Brennan weaves a complex tale of murder, vengeance, and treachery filled with knife-edged tension and clever twists. The Lucy Kincaid/Sean Rogan novels just keep getting better!"
—*RT Book Reviews* (4½ stars, Top Pick)

"The novels featuring Lucy Kincaid and her cohorts are marked with deep characterizations and details of the workings of investigations by private eyes, the police, and the FBI . . . Catch the latest in this series as Lucy continues to evolve in strength and wisdom."
—*Romance Reviews Today*

Silenced

"Brennan throws a lot of story lines into the air and juggles them like a master. The mystery proves to be both compelling and complex . . . [A] chilling and twisty romantic suspense gem."
—Associated Press

Titles by Allison Brennan

COLD SNAP

SNAP

Allison Brennan

St. Martin's Paperbacks

This is a work of fiction. All of the characters, organizations, and events portrayed in this novel are either products of the author's imagination or are used fictitiously.

COLD SNAP

Copyright © 2013 by Allison Brennan.
"Reckless" copyright 2013 by Allison Brennan.
Excerpt from *Notorious* copyright © 2014 by Allison Brennan.

Cover design for "Reckless" by Ervin Serrano
Cover photographs for "Reckless" by shutterstock.com

All rights reserved.

For information address St. Martin's Press, 175 Fifth Avenue, New York, NY 10010.

ISBN: 978-1-250-03800-5

Printed in the United States of America

St. Martin's Paperbacks edition / November 2013

St. Martin's Paperbacks are published by St. Martin's Press, 175 Fifth Avenue, New York, NY 10010.

10 9 8 7 6 5 4 3 2 1

FOREWORD

I've received many letters from my longtime readers wanting to know what all the Kincaids are up to. Because Lucy's story will be moving to San Antonio when she starts her new career with the FBI, I won't have many opportunities to revisit her family. I wanted to write a thriller while also bringing readers up-to-date on where the clan is and what they're doing. Here's a list of key characters to refresh your memory.

Lucy Kincaid: My series protagonist. Seven years ago Lucy was kidnapped and raped by a man she met on the Internet; since, she's been determined to stop sexual predators and help give victims and survivors peace of mind. The youngest Kincaid by ten years.

Sean Rogan: Lucy's boyfriend and a computer genius. Has a checkered past of computer hacking, but has also helped the FBI on complex cases. Until recently, he worked as a partner in Rogan-Caruso-Kincaid Protective Services, based in Sacramento, California, and Washington, D.C.

Jack Kincaid: Enlisted in the army directly out of high school and later became a mercenary headquartered in Hidalgo, Texas. Estranged from his family until seven years ago. Married to FBI agent Megan Elliott.

Dillon Kincaid: Forensic psychiatrist, fraternal twin brother to Jack. Married to FBI Quantico instructor Kate Donovan.

Kate Donovan: FBI agent who went rogue to search for her partner's killer. Helped Dillon and Jack locate Lucy after she was kidnapped. After a reprimand and demotion, she returned to the FBI.

Connor Kincaid: Former cop turned private investigator in San Diego. Married to Julia Chandler, a prosecutor. Now partnered with brother-in-law, Nick Thomas, as private investigators.

Carina Kincaid: San Diego PD detective. Married to Nick Thomas, former sheriff of Gallatin County, Montana. They met eight years ago when Nick's brother was accused of murder. Her longtime partner is Will Hooper.

Patrick Kincaid: Former San Diego PD and most recently partners with Sean Rogan at RCK East, based in Washington, D.C., until Sean left. Seven years ago, Lucy's attacker set a bomb to explode that left Patrick in a coma for nearly two years.

Nelia Kincaid: The oldest sibling in the clan, a former corporate attorney who became a recluse after her seven-year-old son, Justin Stanton, was murdered eighteen years ago.

Andrew Stanton: San Diego district attorney, Nelia's ex-husband and Justin's father.

Colonel Pat Kincaid, Sr.: Retired army colonel and family patriarch.

Rosa Kincaid: Cuban who escaped to Florida; rescued by Pat. They've been married for forty-five years.

New readers may want to know a bit more about my characters. I created a special page on my Web site, allison brennan.com/LucyKincaid, if you want to catch up on past and future stories. I even brought back some secondary characters, like SWAT team leader Tom Blade from San Diego, and included some fun trivia, like which characters were supposed to die (but didn't!) and which characters died that I didn't expect.

I hope you enjoy these stories, as the Kincaid kids travel home to San Diego for a Christmas reunion—only to encounter murder and mayhem along the way.

Allison Brennan
Northern California

PART ONE

San Francisco

Saturday, December 22

CHAPTER 1

Patrick Kincaid had a problem: he couldn't say no.

Whatever was asked of him, he did it, usually without complaint. He was amicable that way, and his friends and family knew it. He didn't mind helping out; if he could do something for someone, why not? He had a challenging job he liked, a family he loved, and a few good friends who had stuck around even during his two-year stint in the hospital sleeping off a coma. Life was too short to be stingy with it.

But this time, as he circled the arcane San Francisco streets, which seemed to have no methodology, looking for a parking place in a dense fog, he wished he'd said no.

He would have, if anyone else in the world had asked him to drive two hours out of his way (which took three because of the inclement weather) to hunt down a family friend he hadn't seen since he graduated from high school, except at her father's funeral. He'd have found an excuse or found a replacement. Except it was his mother who had called. And Patrick had never, not once, said no to his mom. His older brother Connor had told him—often—that he was Mom's favorite because he was her yes-man.

His job was to bring Gabrielle Santana home for

Christmas. Gabrielle Santana—the girl who'd staged a sit-in sophomore year in high school to protest the expulsion of three students who she thought hadn't had a fair hearing with the school board. The girl who'd been arrested at seventeen for organizing a rave in an abandoned warehouse in downtown San Diego. The girl who'd been suspended for skinny-dipping in the high school pool. Patrick was three years older than Gabrielle, but she'd done more her freshman year—both good and bad—than he had his entire four years of high school.

It didn't help that Patrick had dated Gabrielle's older sister Veronica during their senior year and Gabrielle had often tagged along with Veronica to his baseball games and even on a couple of would-be dates.

The problem was that Gabrielle had called her mother two days ago and said something had come up at work and she couldn't come home for Christmas. Now, she wasn't returning her mother's phone calls, or those from anyone else in her family. They were worried, and because the Santanas were worried, Rosa Kincaid was worried. And if Rosa Kincaid was worried and called on one of her children for help, the worry fell onto them. In this case, Patrick.

"You're already in Sacramento," his mother had said. "It's not that far out of your way to help the Santanas."

She had to have sensed the hesitation in his tone because she gave him the hard sell—and the guilt. Irish Catholic guilt compounded by the fact that he had a Cuban mother. No one said no to Rosa Kincaid.

After fifteen minutes of driving around in widening circles because there seemed to be no street parking in the vicinity, he finally squeezed the rental car into a spot four blocks from Gabrielle's loft in a converted warehouse off Howard Street. At least he was driving in a flat area and not the insanely steep hills that made up so much of the city.

Patrick pulled up the collar of his jacket against the cold, damp air as he walked briskly down Howard. Lighted garlands wrapped around light posts were the only visible reminder of the holidays. This was a business district, and the thick fog made visibility next to nothing. Some of the apartments above storefronts were more jovially decorated—colored lights framing the windows and small, decorated trees, but Patrick had to strain his neck to look up, and honestly he wasn't in the holiday spirit.

His phone vibrated in his pocket and he pulled it out reluctantly. He hadn't brought gloves. He'd packed for San Diego—where it had been a respectable seventy-eight degrees today—not cold, wet San Francisco. He glanced at the text message from his sister Lucy.

> Be glad you're in Sacramento—we're stuck in Denver. Airport shut down. Blizzard. Won't get out until tomorrow night, if then. Love you! —Lucy

He responded that he was on an errand for their mom in San Francisco and would be delayed as well, then pocketed his phone and continued up the hill.

Maybe this side trip had a silver lining. He wouldn't want to be the third wheel stuck in Denver with Lucy with her boyfriend, Sean. It would have been doubly awkward. While he'd grown to accept her relationship with his best friend and former partner, Sean Rogan, she was still his little sister. There were some things he didn't want to think about.

The fog was so heavy a layer of moisture quickly coated his jacket. Driving here, he'd thought of all the reasons why Gabrielle could be incommunicado. Off with a boyfriend. Working. Drinking with her girlfriends. It was selfish and cruel not to respond to her mother's calls for two days, but it didn't mean anything was wrong. He'd already checked hospitals and called her employer. Nothing. The only odd thing was that her employer said she would be out of the office until after the holidays. Patrick couldn't get any other details from the snippy receptionist.

Again, not being in the office didn't mean something was wrong. In fact, that she'd informed her employer she would be out told Patrick there was nothing to worry about.

Except . . . he had to talk to her. Find out what she was doing and give Mrs. Santana peace of mind. Give Gabrielle a piece of his mind, too. He would never needlessly worry his mom; he hadn't as a kid and not as an adult, either. He'd been a cop for more than a decade, and now worked for the private security firm Rogan-Caruso-Kincaid. When he was going to be unreachable for more than a day, he made sure his family knew his plans. It was common courtesy.

He rounded the corner of Gabrielle's narrow street, not wider than an alley. One car could barely squeeze through. The buildings were a mix of very old and newly renovated. Mostly businesses with apartments upstairs. In Gabrielle's converted warehouse, the heavy metal door was accessible only by a keypad. A sign indicated that the lobby was open from 6 A.M. until 6 P.M.

Patrick rang her buzzer. No answer. He tried her cell phone number—she didn't have a landline in her name—again, no answer. He looked around for an external security camera and didn't see any. He easily hacked the keypad and the door opened.

Sean had taught him a lot of tricks over the years, and the former cop in Patrick winced at breaking and entering. Though, as Sean would say, he wasn't breaking anything.

It took Patrick a few moments to get his bearings. First, he was surprised at the quiet. Even the traffic from the interstate a few blocks away had dimmed once he stepped inside. Music faintly played from somewhere upstairs. The lobby was a small square with a flocked Christmas tree in the center covered with blue and green glass balls. It looked fake. Christmas had always been Patrick's favorite time of the year because his parents went all-out. They didn't have a lot of money growing up, but Christmas was the time for making presents, eating far more than was healthy, and spending time with family. Decorating the Kincaid family Christmas tree—which they cut down themselves every year—was a party in itself.

You'll be home for Christmas. This is a just a small delay.

Sixteen mailboxes were built into the wall. Eight of them were larger boxes labeled with business names—a Realtor, an interior decorator, and similar white-collar professionals. The other eight were narrow and had last names only. Bruce. Carmichael. Santana, in unit 12.

Though the warehouse had been completely built out, the industrial feeling remained, cold and sterile, like the fake tree. The polished concrete floors and modern metal staircase might be seen as hip and trendy, but they contributed to the lobby's icy interior. The building seemed lonely, if a building could feel anything.

On the second landing he found unit 12 in the far back corner. He knocked on the door and silently swore, shaking out his sore knuckles. Solid metal. He rang the bell.

No one answered.

Patrick tried the door, not expecting it to open, but it did. Gabrielle left her apartment unlocked? Even in a semi-secure building, he'd never leave his door open—especially in the middle of a major city.

He pushed open the heavy door and glanced around before entering. The entry was small and narrow, only the light from the corridor casting a glow in the dark. He called out, "Gabrielle? Hello?" then felt along the wall and found a light switch. The entryway and living room brightened. A short staircase led to the large central room with lush, bright throw rugs tossed haphazardly over the cement floor. The exterior walls were brick; one was embedded with small, square warehouse windows; the other was dotted with bright and wild contemporary art. The raised, galley-style kitchen included a long, low bar with two benches. The ceiling was more than thirty feet high. A spiral staircase led to a loft above the kitchen. Small, but the towering ceiling and wall of windows made it seem much bigger.

Standing in the middle of Gabrielle Santana's apartment, Patrick felt like an idiot. Nothing appeared out of place. Two mismatched couches that looked comfortable. Several bean bag chairs. Scuffed coffee table covered with books and magazines. He tilted his head. One side of the table was definitely shorter.

"Gabrielle?" he called out. "It's Patrick Kincaid from San Diego. Your door was open."

Nothing.

The living room was just that, no work or desk area. He smiled as he approached a small tree on a corner table. It was a Charlie Brown tree, spindly and half dead, a string of lights draped across and plugged into the wall, tinsel and a popcorn string. A star, too heavy for the tree, leaned precariously on the top.

He didn't want to roam through Gabrielle's home. He went into the kitchen and rummaged through a couple of drawers before he found a sales flyer. He turned it over, pulled a pen from his pocket, and started writing a note. What was he going to say? To phone home? To call him?

He jotted down his name and number and put it under a magnet for Chinese takeout on the refrigerator.

Still, the unlocked door made him nervous. He went upstairs to the loft to make sure there was no sign of foul play.

The loft was divided into two long, narrow rooms, both

of which looked down into the living room at different angles, with a connecting bathroom. One was Gabrielle's bedroom, one her office. Gabrielle's bed was unmade, clothes strewn all over a chair in the corner, makeup and other girl things covering the long, scratched dresser. In the den was a couch. A pillow and sleeping bag were tossed to one end. Company?

But there was no blood, no sign of robbery, no sign of anything amiss.

He went back downstairs just as Gabrielle—wow, she'd gone from stunning to gorgeous, but he'd have recognized her anywhere—was running up the short staircase from the entryway. She glanced at him, dark eyes wide with shock, then turned and ran back out the front door.

"Gabrielle! It's Patrick Kincaid!"

His words were cut off by the metal door sliding shut.

Damn, damn, damn! He'd scared her, and that made him feel like shit.

He ran after her.

As soon as he opened the door, something hit him on the side of his head, and he stumbled. Something hard pressed against his back.

On instinct born from years of training, he kicked his legs, rolled over, and flipped his attacker. His hand grabbed the wrist that held the weapon he knew wasn't a gun.

It was a cell phone.

"Dammit, Gabrielle! It's Patrick Kincaid."

She stared at him blankly. He jumped up, holding out his hand for her. She didn't take it.

"A cell phone will protect you better if you call nine-one-one."

Recognition finally replaced her stunned expression. She got up on her own and grabbed her phone from his hand. "Patrick? *Kincaid?* What the hell are you doing here? In my apartment?"

"The door was unlocked."

"So you just walked in?"

"Your mother sent me."

"My mother?"

He rolled his eyes and brushed off his slacks. "Can I come in?"

She glared at him. "You already have." She turned and walked through the doorway. She started to slide the door shut, but he caught it with his hand and followed her inside, closing it behind him.

Gabrielle had always been pretty, like all the Santana girls. But Patrick remembered her as Veronica's tagalong little sister—annoying, opinionated, and wild. She might still be opinionated and wild, but he no longer could think of her as a little sister. She was, simply, stunning. He had a hard time not staring.

"Gabrielle—I'm sorry, but—"

"Elle."

"Excuse me?"

"Only my family calls me Gabrielle. As soon as I went to college, I changed my name. It's Elle."

"Like the letter *l*."

"Like the last syllable of my name," she snapped.

"Elle, I'm sorry. I didn't mean to frighten you. Your mother was worried because she couldn't reach you—"

"And you came all the way from San Diego? No—wait—you don't live there anymore, do you?"

"I live in Washington, D.C., but I was in Sacramento for the week."

"So you drove two hours just to check on me?"

"Your mother is worried—" he said again.

"Because I said I couldn't come home for Christmas? Jeez!" She tossed her hands in the air, then scratched the back of her head as if she were still confused.

"Because," Patrick continued, "she's left a dozen mes-

sages and you haven't called her back. And your employer said you took vacation time."

"I'm thirty-two years old and my mother is sending a cop after me because I don't answer my phone."

"I'm not a cop anymore."

"Tell her I'm *fine*. Thank you. *Good-bye*."

Elle seemed agitated, over and beyond her irritation that Patrick had been in her apartment.

"What's wrong?"

She gave him a puzzled look. "What's wrong?"

"Why do you do that?"

"Do what?"

"Deflect. I ask questions. You don't answer them."

"I have a lot going on, Patrick." She spread her arms wide and spun in a circle. "Take a good look. Tell my mother I'm alive and well."

"Call her."

"I will."

"Now."

She scrunched up her nose. "I haven't seen you in, like, ten years, and you break into my apartment and order me to call my mother?" She laughed, but it sounded strained.

Patrick didn't want to get in the middle of a family squabble, because he was getting the distinct impression that this was mostly about family, and family—even a close-knit clan like the Kincaids or the Santanas—could drive anyone crazy.

When she realized that he was serious and that she was still holding her phone, she made a production of punching the buttons. A moment later Patrick could hear a loud *"Gabrielle!"* on the other end of the line.

"Mama, I can't believe you sent Patrick Kincaid to track me down. I am so embarrassed!"

She didn't look embarrassed; she looked pissed.

"I told you, I have to work. It's an important case, I can't take time off."

Patrick raised his eyebrows, but Elle wasn't paying attention. She listened to her mother talk, then both of them started speaking rapidly in Spanish. Patrick wasn't as fluent in the language as his younger sister, but he'd been raised by a Cuban mother and had a basic understanding. The conversation was rapidly deteriorating as Elle explained why she had to spend Christmas preparing for a case, and why it was important, and that she couldn't do it in San Diego because she needed access to her law office.

And the entire time, Patrick had the strong impression that she was lying.

"I love you, too, Mama. I'm sorry—I'll visit as soon as I can. I know it's not the same as Christmas—I know it's been two years—Mama, *please,* I feel bad already. Yes. I promise." She hung up. "There," she said to Patrick. "Satisfied?"

"I did my job," he said. "But why did you lie to your mother?"

"What?" She blinked rapidly. She was an awful liar.

"Your law firm said you were on vacation."

"I don't need to explain myself to you—look, Patrick, I *really* have to go."

"You just got home."

"Because I needed to get some things."

The buzzer rang and Elle briefly looked like a deer caught in headlights. She ran to her front door and pressed a button on the panel. A screen with a black-and-white image popped up. An Asian woman in jeans and a long wool coat was at the door. She rang the buzzer again.

"Shit, what's she doing here?" Elle backed away from the door as if it were about to attack.

"Who is she?"

"A social worker. Damn, now I have to wait until she leaves. This is the worst day in my life!"

Patrick knew he was going to regret it, but he said, "Can I help?"

"No!"

"What does she want?"

"Something I can't give her." Her cell phone rang and Elle looked at it. "She's calling me now. Dammit!" She then glanced at Patrick and said, "Tell her we're not here."

"We?"

"She's going to ask about Kami. Tell her Kami and I went out and you don't know when we'll be back. Look, I can't lie to her, but you can!" She tossed Patrick her phone.

Skeptical, and wholly uncomfortable with what Elle was asking him to do, he answered the phone. "Santana residence."

"Is Elle Santana there?"

"I'm sorry, who's calling?"

"Sandy Chin, I need to come up."

"I'm sorry, I'm not supposed to let anyone inside when Gabrielle isn't home."

"Who's this?"

"Who's this?"

"Sandy Chin. I'm with the San Francisco Department of Child Welfare. I need to inspect the apartment, and Ms. Santana has been avoiding me. Where's Kami?"

Elle had leaned close to him to hear both sides of the conversation better. Sandy Chin had a much softer voice than Elle's mother.

"Not here, either."

"And you are?"

"A friend."

"Ms. Santana didn't inform us that a man was living with her."

"I'm just visiting."

"Tell Ms. Santana that I expect to hear from her by ten P.M., or Kami will be placed in custody until the hearing." She cut off the call.

Patrick had no idea what that conversation was about. "Elle, what just happened?"

She glanced at her watch, then took her phone back from Patrick. "I have two hours to find Kami. I've been looking for her since noon."

"Who's Kami?"

"A fifteen-year-old who's in deep trouble and will be in deeper trouble if she doesn't show up in court Wednesday morning. Something spooked her when I went out for groceries. She wouldn't just leave. She knows how important this is!"

Elle ran into the kitchen, opened the freezer, and removed a can of coffee. But there was no coffee inside—only money. Roughly a thousand dollars in fives, tens, and twenties.

"I've never known anyone who keeps money in her freezer."

"My mom," she said. She counted out three hundred dollars, divided it between two different pockets, then put the can back. She ran upstairs and came back a minute later with a bag filled with clothes, and a heavy jacket with a hole in the elbow. "Thanks for covering with Sandy."

Patrick was going to regret this. He said, "Let me help."

She stared at him as if surprised by the offer. "Don't you have someplace to be?"

"My flight doesn't leave until tomorrow."

"It's nice of you, but no one is going to trust you. You look—well, I know you're not a cop anymore, but you look like one. I know where Kami hangs out. They don't like cops. Especially cops who dress like rich kids from a prep school."

Patrick glanced down at his khaki Dockers and leather loafers. Rich prep school kid? Really?

He said, "You've been looking for her all day and couldn't find her."

"I have to convince the right people that they can trust me." She didn't sound optimistic, just determined.

"You need help. I have the time. And the training."

Her expression showed her inner battle as much as her fidgeting. The woman couldn't keep still as she shifted her weight and played with a string on her jacket. Finally, she said, "Okay, fine, thanks. But just trust me out there, okay? Don't do anything, well, coplike."

"I'll try." They walked out. He motioned to the door. "Aren't you going to lock it?"

"Kami has the downstairs door code, if she comes back she needs to be able to get in." She waved her hand dismissively. "It's not like I have anything valuable in there, except my computer."

They walked down to the lobby. "Are you going to tell me what's going on with this kid?"

"There's nothing to tell. She's a witness and I need to keep her safe until Wednesday morning."

Warning bells rang in his head. "A witness? Why aren't the cops watching her?"

"Because no one realizes that she could be in danger. They wanted to 'protect' her by putting her in juvenile hall, and that's exactly where Lorenzo's crew could get to her. I promised the judge that she'd be in court on Wednesday morning to testify—it's required for her plea agreement—and everything was going great until this afternoon. I gave her a phone, but she's not answering it." Elle turned down a hallway opposite the front entrance and through a door marked FIRE EXIT. No alarms went off. "It's disabled," she said dismissively. "If Sandy is hanging around, I don't want her to see me."

Patrick realized then that something much, much bigger was going on. "Why not call the police? They can help."

She spun around. "Look, you're going to have to trust me on this. If I tell anyone she ran away, they'll put a bench warrant out for her and she'll not only go to jail before she testifies, but her plea deal is off. She's fifteen. She's been on and off the streets since she was eleven. I got her a great arrangement, and if she testifies she'll be put in a group home that can protect her, send her to school, make sure she has a real shot at a future. And that's why I'm not going to San Diego. Because her hearing is the day after Christmas, and she needs one person around who cares what happens to her."

Patrick had a dozen questions: Was Kami a client of hers? What kind of law firm did she work for? Why would she agree to bring a client to live with her? Who was the girl testifying against? Had she left the apartment willingly? Had she been taken?

Elle led the way to a carport in the building next to hers. "I don't have my own spot, but my best friend is a flight attendant and she's gone half the time and lets me park in hers." She glanced back at Patrick as she headed for her car. "I'm going to retrace my steps, but she's probably hiding out in the Haight."

"The infamous Haight Ashbury?"

Elle rolled her eyes as she stopped next to an older blue Honda Civic. The city's salt air hadn't done the paint any favors. She put the bag of clothes in the backseat, which was packed with blankets, boxes of granola bars, and Gatorade bottles. "Just get in."

"Santana!" a voice shouted from behind them.

Patrick turned and saw two men running toward them.

"Get in!" She was already turning the key to the ignition before she'd closed her door.

Patrick did. "More social workers?"

A gunshot rang out.

"That's a warning, bitch!"

Elle pulled out of the carport and sideswiped one of the guys. He shouted profanities at them and his partner fired another shot, this time at the car. It missed.

"How did they know where I live?" Elle glanced over her shoulder, eyes wide, knuckles white on the steering wheel. She turned onto Howard from the alley and sped up.

"Who are they?"

"I think they work for Richie Lorenzo."

"Who the hell is that?" Patrick was getting testy, because he really hated being shot at—especially when he didn't have his gun.

"A drug dealer. Kami used to work for him. That's what got her in trouble with the police."

"Is that who she's testifying against?"

"No," Elle said in a tone that made Patrick feel like he'd missed several conversations. But she didn't clarify as she turned onto another street and started winding through hills.

"Elle, talk to me! Who is this kid testifying against? Who's Lorenzo?"

"He's a twenty-three-year-old punk who uses runaways to sell his trash."

"And the case? The trial?"

Elle hesitated, then said, "Kami is testifying against a prominent businessman who Lorenzo sometimes works for. The bastard has a teen center over in Dogpatch, an area desperate for revitalization, and a factory a bit south of there, near the old Candlestick Park. He hires kids from the teen center to buy their loyalty. But he's into serious shit. No one will speak against him. Without Kami, the guy walks." She bit her lip and glanced at Patrick. Though there were tears in her eyes, her jaw was clenched in anger. "I have to find her, Patrick. I can't lose another kid to those bastards."

CHAPTER 2

Until Lorenzo's boys started shooting at them, Elle had planned to get rid of Patrick Kincaid. She'd considered losing him in the streets of San Francisco, an easy enough job for her considering she knew the city and he didn't. But now? She was scared, and she didn't like being scared. Not just for herself, but for Kami.

Elle figured she could protect herself well enough. She put aside the threats Lorenzo had leveled at her when he found out she'd been the one who'd convinced Kami to turn against him and Christopher Lee. It infuriated Elle that Lee received accolades for his good works when he was really a criminal bastard bringing in drugs from overseas. Lorenzo provided Lee with the network of street kids to both buy and sell the poison that ended too often with prison or death. She'd been trying to nail him for over a year.

A brief, painful memory broke Elle's concentration. She shook her head, but not before her eyes burned with rage-filled tears she refused to shed.

Lee was a killer. She knew—in her heart—that he'd killed Doreen, a teenage girl who had learned about his involvement with drug shipments. But Doreen had been buried as a victim of a drug overdose. No one, not even Elle, knew her last name.

After Doreen was murdered, Elle had snapped and acted without thinking. She regretted confronting Lee without hard proof of his crimes, because at that point she'd lost any chance of turning public sentiment in her favor. Worse, she nearly lost everything she'd fought so hard to earn since she'd become an attorney. She was reprimanded by her boss, ridiculed by the press, and ostracized by her colleagues.

Elle hadn't been able to get close to Lee again after her very public verbal attack on the so-called philanthropist. She'd seethed quietly, keeping her nose clean but never ending her search for proof. When one of her pro bono clients, Kami Toland, came to her with information that pointed to Lee's involvement in the drug trade, Elle told her to steer clear. Yet Elle feared she hadn't been emphatic enough with Kami because of her own deep-seated need to expose Christopher Lee for the predator he was.

Kami hadn't listened—maybe because youth gave these kids a sense of invulnerability, or maybe because street kids faced danger on a daily basis—and she'd gone on her own quest for answers. Which landed her right back in Elle's world when Kami was arrested for possession with intent to sell. Kami would have gone to juvie because it wasn't her first arrest, but Elle intervened. Kami told Elle she had physical proof of Lee's drug running, and Elle cut a deal with the prosecution.

But Elle had to be sneaky to avoid tipping anyone off. Kami associated with Richie Lorenzo, a known drug dealer in the city. She cut the deal for Kami to reveal Lorenzo's suppliers without naming the supplier in the paperwork, because she feared Lee's friends in government and law enforcement would alert him to any sting operation. Kami would name Lee and reveal the proof in front of a judge in a closed hearing on Wednesday. Then she'd be sent to live in a group home in a different county, away from those who would want to hurt her. She'd be given a chance to survive the shitty life that had been handed her by her worthless parents. Elle couldn't save Doreen, but she'd damn well save Kami.

Now Kami was missing. Something—or someone—had scared her and she'd bolted. If Elle didn't find her before Lorenzo or Lee, Kami would be dead. Elle was certain of that.

And Elle couldn't have another death on her conscience.

She glanced at Patrick, who looked like a cop even if he wasn't one. Tall, long, angular face—he didn't look half Cuban, like his sisters; he took after his Irish father, with his light eyes and conservatively cut dark hair. Elle had been around enough cops in her life to know Patrick thrived in a law-and-order environment. Yet, having an extra set of eyes and hands would help as she sorted out this mess.

But Patrick Kincaid? Dear God, what had her mother done?

She'd had the biggest crush on Patrick for years. She had begged Veronica to take her to Patrick's baseball games in high school. He'd never noticed that Veronica spent all her time talking and socializing, while Elle was the one who had watched Patrick play. He was the first boy she'd found truly hot. He'd always had a terrific sense of humor and was so easygoing and kind, even to Veronica's little sister. He'd gone to college, and then his nephew died and he became a cop. She went off to college and never looked back.

Patrick had a sharper edge now, quieter but still sexy. She could much better appreciate his sex appeal. But dammit, she wasn't a child anymore, and she'd had enough of the Kincaids.

Her entire life she'd heard about the Kincaids *ad nauseam* as if they were damn saints. As her sisters had married and started their own families, they bought into her mother's mantra. Why can't you be more like Carina Kincaid? She's a police detective, one of the youngest women to make detective in San Diego. And now she's married! Or Dillon Kincaid—he's a doctor, and now he's married, too! Connor Kincaid, private investigator, and look at this! He married a prosecutor. A lawyer, like you, but she puts bad guys in prison. And even Jack Kincaid, big bad special forces army guy, is—yes, you guessed it—married.

Elle tried marriage. It had been a mistake. They'd both known it was a mistake—except for the sex part. That was really good. But neither she nor Dwight had been ready for marriage, they were both stubborn and opinionated. They divorced before they ended up hating each other. Which was a good thing, because Dwight was a prosecutor and she worked with him all the time. They had drinks on occasion, sometimes had sex when they were both free, and they didn't argue anymore. Much.

When she told her mother they were getting divorced, you'd have thought she'd admitted to murder. Was it any wonder Elle didn't want to go home for Christmas? She was the only Santana who wasn't married (remarried) yet—even her baby sister, Marissa, had married her high school sweetheart and they were so sickly-sweet in love Elle needed an insulin shot whenever she spent five minutes with them.

And her mother sends the only unattached Kincaid to San Francisco simply because Elle hadn't returned her phone calls for two days.

She was going to give her mother a piece of her mind. After she found Kami.

Elle needed to figure out what to do with Patrick. She wanted his help, but she didn't.

"You're not talking," Patrick said.

"What do you want me to say?"

"Start at the beginning."

"In the beginning when God created the heavens and the earth, the earth was a formless void and darkness covered—"

"Dammit, Elle, I need information if I'm going to help you."

"Look, this is a bad idea. Where's your car? I'll drop you off—"

"I already told you. I'm here, I'm helping, or I'm calling the police about the shooting. In fact, why didn't you?"

"I'm sure one of my neighbors phoned it in." She turned off Howard Street and headed toward the Haight. "If the police know Kami isn't with me, they're going to arrest her."

"What did the girl do?"

"What hasn't she done? She's a street kid, has been for four years. Tossed out of her house by her father and his girlfriend when she was eleven because they didn't want her around anymore. She's been in and out of the system. Shoplifting. Grand theft auto. Lorenzo took her in when she was thirteen and had her pickpocketing tourists at the pier and museums. I met her six months ago through the pro bono work my law firm does and helped arrange a plea agreement to keep her out of juvie. She picked the wrong pocket, the mark was a cop on vacation from Bakersfield who nailed Kami. When the cops picked Kami up again last week, this time possession with intent, she called me. Swore she wasn't selling, she didn't know what was in the package she was delivering, but the D.A. wasn't going to budge because Kami hangs with Lorenzo, a known dealer." Elle hesitated, then added, "Kami wants to change. We've kept in contact, I've been helping her study so she can get her GED.

She has information about a bastard named Christopher Lee, a philanthropist."

She rolled her eyes. That's what the press called him.

"Philanthropist?"

"He just got some stupid plaque from the city for building that new teen center mentioned, near Dogpatch, a depressed area of the city."

"Sounds like a rotten bastard," Patrick said sarcastically.

Elle bit back a snide comment. "Well, on the one hand he gives homeless and runaway teens minimum-wage jobs in his garment business, and built them this great place where they can do their homework and apply for colleges and hang out. On the other hand, he's importing drugs that are distributed all over northern California and Nevada. The DEA raided him—once. But they found nothing, and he ended up suing the government. It was settled out of court as far as I know, but he has everyone snowed. If anyone speaks out against him, they end up dead." *Like Doreen.* "He has to be stopped, and Kami can do it."

"If you really have even a hair of proof, the feds will start an investigation. You don't need to put yourself in the middle—"

Elle groaned, and out of the corner of her eye she saw Patrick frown. "Are you really that naïve?"

"I'm not an idiot," he said. He was pissed, and Elle didn't blame him, but he didn't understand what they were facing here. He was part of the system. The system was broken.

"Lee has inside information. He's been raided before. He was nailed for minor OSHA violations, paid a fine, but the feds haven't been able to prove he's breaking any laws. The child labor laws are complex, and Lee keeps detailed records. The borderline sweatshops he's running are more or less legit. But he makes kids disappear when they make waves. No one is going to turn on him."

"Still—"

"Look, I had a girl inside, and she turned up dead last year when she was about to bring me physical proof of Lee's operation."

"And Kami?"

"She says she has proof."

Elle shut up. She couldn't reveal everything about Kami, and she didn't want to admit that she didn't know exactly what proof Kami had. She was an eyewitness to Lee's drug trafficking, but the D.A. had made it clear that Kami's statement alone wouldn't fly. Lee was too powerful and had too much money and had spent too much money in the city—the D.A. wasn't going to prosecute anyone on the word of a teenage criminal. The only reason Elle had gotten as far as she had was because of her friendship with her ex-husband, Dwight Bishop. If she screwed this up, she'd ruin that relationship as well.

Patrick asked, "What evidence?"

Elle didn't say anything. They were nearing the Haight and she looked for a place to park.

"She has nothing," Patrick said. As if he just knew the truth.

"Of course she does." Elle pulled into a slot on the street.

"But you don't know what it is."

Elle turned off the car and glared at him. "I believe her, and that's all I need. But even if she's lying, Lee thinks she has something, and that puts her in danger. There's a leak somewhere—otherwise why would those men have shot at us? Someone knows Kami is staying with me, and that she can take Christopher Lee down. I need to find her—and I don't need you."

Elle wished she had shut up. Her mouth constantly got

her into trouble, and the truth was she needed help. Her boss had told her to leave this case alone. Dwight had told her she was walking a fine line and had gotten too close to Kami. But she couldn't leave it alone. Not after what happened to Doreen.

"You're a smart woman," Patrick said. "You know this is a bad situation; you could use the police on your side."

"If Kami goes to jail, I lose her. She'll never trust me again. Or worse, she'll get killed. Lee is not to be underestimated. I've—"

She cut herself off.

"Tell me."

"Let's go." Elle jumped out of the car before she said anything else. Family friend or not, she didn't know Patrick well enough to confide in him about everything, at least not yet. She didn't have time to chat while Kami was missing. She was a smart girl, but if Lorenzo turned her over to Lee, she'd be dead.

Why'd you run away, Kami?

"Clark Grayson is a friend of mine from college," Elle said. "He's a social worker for the city, and also volunteers some nights with Granny's Kitchen, which serves primarily homeless kids and kids who aren't getting fed at home. It's not the largest youth services program, but it gets by. He's a good guy—Kami might have gone to see him if she was worried about Lorenzo or if she thought they'd found her at my place." She paused. "Which they might have, considering they shot at us."

"Which suggests she was warned," Patrick said. "If you're telling me everything you know. Which you're not."

She stopped on the street, turned and poked a finger at him. Damn, his chest was hard as a rock. He didn't look at all muscle-boy, but he definitely had them under his tall, lean frame.

She pushed aside the memories of her crush and focused on the here and now. "Look, Kincaid, I told you all the important stuff. I don't have time to hold your hand through every damn detail. I need to find Kami before she's killed, and get her to court on Wednesday. End of story."

Elle opened an unmarked door. The walkway was narrow and poorly lit. Downstairs was a low-ceilinged room, which by the noise was full: video games, television, chatter. Granny's Kitchen's offices were on the main floor, all locked at this time of night except for the library in the front of the building where kids could use the Internet and study. Upstairs was the kitchen where they made hot meals daily. This wasn't the newest or most modern youth facility in town, but the people who volunteered truly cared, which is why Elle had a soft spot for the place.

Now that the new teen center had opened, Granny's Kitchen wasn't as popular as it used to be. Kids who weren't tied to the Haight for other reasons had migrated to Dogpatch, and that made Elle angry. She'd promoted the new teen center to many of the kids she'd met through either her pro bono work or volunteering. The teen center should be a safe place to keep them off drugs and give them tools to succeed; knowing that Lorenzo was using it as a base of operations for Lee made Elle furious.

"Hi, Elle." Two young boys walked up the stairs toward the kitchen. They were brothers and inseparable.

"Deej, Tom," she said. "Don't make your mom worry. She gets home from work at eleven."

"I know," Tom said, "we're getting a to-go plate for her. Clark said we could."

She smiled. They were good boys. She hadn't met them because they'd gotten in trouble; she'd met them through her friend Clark while he was tutoring Tom in reading. The kid had graduated eighth grade without being able to read. Elle had helped their mom find a second job. They lived a couple blocks from Granny's Kitchen and ate dinner here almost every night.

She and Patrick followed them upstairs. Because it was nearly nine, most of the kids had already eaten. The hot food was gone, but the volunteers would make sandwiches for anyone who came in late. She spotted Clark talking to three boys while they ate. He saw her and waved, but she didn't miss that he looked twice at Patrick.

Clark motioned for Elle to come over. "What's up?"

"Do you have a sec?" she asked.

"Of course."

Elle didn't say anything, and Clark said to the teenagers, "Go back downstairs. I'll meet you at the Xbox in ten minutes."

The kids left, all about sixteen and rough around the edges. That wasn't unusual, but Elle hadn't seen these three before.

"Sit down," Clark said, motioning to the vacated chairs.

Elle introduced Patrick. "He's a family friend from San Diego." Better than saying a cop or private investigator or whatever Kincaid was now. "I need some help, but you have to keep it confidential."

"Of course," he said, concerned. "Is it about Kami?"

Elle was surprised. "Yes, why?"

"I heard that she got arrested again, figured you'd take her case."

"I need to find her."

"She's not in juvie?"

"No. I'm responsible for her."

"Elle, I've warned you about that—you're going to get in trouble with the bar if you keep this up."

"There were extenuating circumstances."

"Like what?"

"Like stuff," she said vaguely. "Has she been in here tonight?"

"No, but I didn't get in until eight."

"If you see her, please tell her to call me. She's in danger."

"How so?"

"I can't say, she's my client," Elle said, "but I need to find her. You understand, right?"

"No, but I trust you. I can ask around—"

"No, don't do that. But you can help me—where's Lorenzo tonight?"

"Stay away from him," Clark said. "I shouldn't have to tell you that." He paused. "Is that why Kami's in danger? From Lorenzo?"

"Possibly. She got picked up for possession with intent. She said she wasn't selling, that she didn't know what she was carrying." Elle didn't believe it. The not-selling part, yes, but Kami had known what she was doing. She probably thought it would help her get the goods on Christopher Lee. She hadn't *told* Elle that, but it seemed obvious.

"I don't feel comfortable sending you out there—"

"He's at the new teen center? Really?" Why was she surprised? If Lorenzo and Lee were tied at the hip like Elle thought, of course Lee would let him use the new center as a base. It simply confirmed what Elle suspected.

"He has an apartment near the center, but I don't know exactly where. It's one of those better-that-I-don't-know situations."

"Thanks." She got up.

"Don't do it."

"Whose side are you on?"

"The kids', always. And the best way to stop Lorenzo's power is to educate these kids and give them opportunities and hope."

"The best way to stop his power is to put him in jail," Elle snapped. She and Clark had gone around and around on this. While Elle didn't care much for the police, she knew they were the only ones who could truly stop the drug dealer. Yes, others would fill his shoes, but if people like her and Clark were there to help the kids transition from being victims—throwaways, homeless, emotionally and physically abused—to becoming productive, clean-living citizens, they could perhaps take on future leadership roles and prevent people like Lorenzo from gaining power over the desperate. There was no easy solution and the problem would continue as long as Elle was alive. But she looked at it one kid at a time. Save Kami. Save boys like Tom and Deej. Keep them from running the streets or getting killed through violence or drug abuse or prostitution.

Sometimes, it was so overwhelming she wanted to scream. Usually, she managed okay. Until things happened—like today.

"I know of two more places she might be," Elle said. "I'm not going to do anything stupid with Lorenzo."

"Good. Be careful." Clark glanced at Patrick and frowned. Patrick stared back at him. God, *men*. Testosterone. *Impossible*.

She stood, then said to Clark, "I'm going downstairs to see if some of Kami's friends are here. Okay?"

"Go ahead."

She walked out and turned to Patrick, who started to follow her. "You want to wait here?" She gave him a look that said her question was actually an order.

"I'll go to the car. I need to call my sister anyway."

She handed him her keys. "Thanks." She turned and headed down to the basement.

Patrick watched Elle leave, then returned to the dining hall. Clark wasn't at the table they'd just vacated, but he saw the guy in the kitchen with a phone in his hand. As soon as Clark saw Patrick, he pocketed his phone.

"Kincaid, right?" Clark said. "Can I get you something?"

"Why did you lie to Elle?"

Clark's expression darkened. "I don't know who you are, but Elle and I have been friends for a long time."

"That makes lying to her worse."

Clark sneered. "Who are you to sit there glaring at me for the last ten minutes, then accuse me of—"

Patrick cut him off. "You know more about what's going on with Kami than you told her. Lies of omission."

Patrick wasn't wrong about this, every instinct he had told him Clark had been fishing for information—subtly, but clearly. Elle didn't realize it because they were friends, but it was in his body language, how he worded his questions, the way he let it "slip" where the drug dealer Lorenzo was hiding out. Elle might be in danger because of someone she trusted.

Clark made a move to leave and Patrick stepped in front of him. Patrick was several inches taller and in much better shape than this weasel. Out of the corner of his eye, Patrick saw the kitchen volunteers look both wary and suspicious.

Clark said, "Are you a cop?"

Elle hadn't introduced him as anything more than a family friend, and Patrick didn't want to fill in any gaps. Let Clark think what he wanted. And by the look on Clark's face, he didn't like cops. "I care about Elle, and I don't trust you."

"I honestly don't give a fuck what you think of me, asshole."

Patrick smiled, though he didn't take his eyes off Clark. "I'll find Kami, I'll find out what you're hiding, and Elle will know you're one of the bad guys."

Clark leaned forward and poked Patrick in the chest. "Tap her ass while you can, because when I'm through with you, she'll never speak to you again. Elle and I have been friends for years. She trusts me a lot more than some domineering prick from—"

Patrick grabbed Clark's finger as it came down on his chest a second time. He applied pressure on a critical nerve, mentally thanking his brother Jack for teaching him some tricks of the trade.

"Don't be crude."

Clark's eyes watered as Patrick continued the pressure, but he practically growled when he said, "You certainly don't know her well, do you?"

"Hey!" Elle's voice came from the doorway. "What the hell's going on?"

Patrick dropped Clark's finger and stepped back. He wasn't prone to temper, but right now he knew if he had been a cop, he'd have arrested this bastard just on general principles.

"Let's go," Patrick said. Elle's confused expression silently asked him a myriad of questions, but he wasn't going to explain. She was holding back on him, he didn't need to share his unproven suspicions about Clark Grayson. "Anyone see her?" he asked.

She shook her head. "There's another place I want to go, over by—"

"Great," Patrick interrupted. He didn't want Clark hearing where they were going. He needed to do a background check on Elle's friend.

He steered her out. He'd been concerned after the near-miss attack at her loft, but now he knew something else was going on—and Elle had tunnel vision. All she wanted to do was find Kami, and maybe that was the first step, but there was more to this situation than one street kid who might have information on a drug dealer.

As soon as they were at Elle's car, she took the keys from Patrick and said, "What was going on between you and Clark?"

"Guy talk."

"Oh, please."

Patrick weighed keeping his thoughts to himself, but decided to tell her. "I don't trust him."

"You don't know him!"

"I was a cop for a long time, I've been a PI for years. I don't have to personally know him to understand him."

"What the hell does that mean? You have some super-cop power that lets you instantly judge someone as being a good guy or a bad guy? Geez, I thought you were better than that."

"He was fishing for information—he wanted to know what you knew."

Elle rolled her eyes. "I swear, every cop I've ever met is either paranoid or has it out for people."

"That's not fair."

She shrugged. "Sure, you're the only cop who cares."

"You have a chip on your shoulder that's blinding."

"Mixing metaphors now?"

Patrick wanted to throttle the lawyer.

"I guarantee that he knew Kami was missing before you walked in. He didn't ask the questions he should have, and he's steering you toward this Lorenzo guy."

"I asked *him* about Lorenzo! If Lorenzo has Kami, I need to get her away from him."

"And this Lorenzo guy is just going to let you walk away with her?"

"I'll figure it out when I find her." She peeled out of her parking place and whipped around the corner.

Patrick closed his eyes and pinched the bridge of his nose. Trying to remain calm, he said, "We need a plan. We can't go into a potentially dangerous situation without knowing what we're facing."

"I want to check out her dad's place," Elle said. "If

Kami really wants to hide, she might go there. It means she's really scared—and desperate."

"Swing by my car—it's about four blocks from your place, on Howard."

"Why?"

"I'm going to pick up my gun, which I left locked in the trunk. I didn't think I'd need it, now I fear I will."

"I don't like guns."

"Most drug dealers do."

Patrick also wanted to pick up his laptop computer so he could run a deep background check on Clark Grayson as well as Richie Lorenzo. Patrick had always been an information guy. When he was a sergeant in the San Diego Police Department, he'd been in charge of the e-crimes unit, back when most police departments didn't even have an e-crimes division. What he learned there, what had only been strengthened since joining RCK Protective Services, was the military motto "intelligence, planning, execution."

They didn't even have basic intelligence now, let alone a plan that wasn't riddled with holes.

"Patrick," Elle said in a soft voice, and he immediately thought she was attempting to manipulate him. "I know this city and these people very well. I can handle this."

"You need help, and I'm willing—against my better judgment."

"Why?"

"Because I don't want to go home and face your mother if you get yourself killed because I walked away."

"I've faced worse," Elle said. By her tone, she was fibbing. Again. "They weren't trying to kill me. You heard them, it was a warning."

"A warning means back off or they *will* kill you."

Her jaw clenched and she didn't say anything. Because she couldn't. Patrick was right.

He said, "I'm going to help you, and for now I'll keep the police out of it. But if there's any reason to call them in, for the health and safety of you or Kami, I will do so."

"All right," she said reluctantly. "First, we go to Kami's dad's house. Then, we go back to your car for your stupid gun."

CHAPTER 3

"Stay here," Elle told Patrick when they arrived at a run-down narrow house up a steep hill. In the dark, Patrick couldn't tell whether the house was divided into apartments or one large unit, but he guessed the former. "I don't want to overwhelm Kami's dad—I need his cooperation."

It was obvious Elle expected an argument, but Patrick didn't give her one. He wanted a few minutes alone to call RCK.

"Okay," she said with a nod and got out of the car.

Patrick watched her walk up the stairs to the door, then he called Jaye Morgan, the computer guru for RCK.

"You know it's nearly ten o'clock on a Saturday night, right?" Jaye answered in lieu of hello.

"Did I interrupt something?"

"No, but you could have."

"I'm sorry, but I really need your help."

"Anything for you, PK," she said happily. Patrick honestly didn't think the girl slept; she seemed to have endless energy.

"I don't have access to my laptop right now, and I need you to run a couple names for me. One is a social worker who might look squeaky clean on the surface, but I know he's dirty. The other is a known drug dealer."

"E-mail me their names and any other info you have and I'll see what I can find."

"You're an angel."

Jaye snorted. "Remember that on my birthday."

Patrick laughed and hung up. He kept an eye on the house while he sent Jaye the information she needed to begin the background. He added Elle and her law firm to the list as well. She was keeping something from him, and that irritated him.

Elle was still the impulsive, compassionate teenager she'd been fifteen years ago, but there was far more at stake here than a suspension or detention.

He used his phone to look up the company Elle worked for, Feliz, Hochman, and Fellows. They were a full-service law firm that handled a variety of cases including civil litigation, estates, and criminal defense. Elle was listed as "Gabrielle J. Santana, Esq. Pro Bono Division." Did that mean she only handled pro bono cases? Didn't all attorneys take a few freebies? How did she get paid? Salary? Was that common? There were only two attorneys with that designation on the rather generic law firm Web site, Elle and Madeleine Starr.

Generic Web sites for lawyers were common, and a cursory search in the news told Patrick that Feliz and company was more respected than not. The criminal defense they handled was predominately on behalf of criminal neglience for the city and county of San Francisco, nothing high profile like drug dealers and murderers.

How had Elle gotten hooked up with them? Why did she take only pro bono cases? Was it more profitable for the law firm to hire young and idealistic lawyers and pay them a salary rather than billable hours?

Again, this was an area Patrick was only marginally familiar with.

Elle had an almost obsessive need to help people, and the fact that she hadn't seen the subtle manipulation by her so-called friend Clark Grayson told Patrick that maybe she couldn't see the truth about Kami. What if she had used Elle's goodwill and trust in her to run from the drug charges? Disappear because she didn't want to go to juvenile hall? In Patrick's experience, criminals ran because they were guilty. Of course there were exceptions, but they were few and far between. And Kami was a street kid with a criminal record. It would be easy for her to disappear, and Elle, no matter who she knew or where she looked, wouldn't find her if she didn't want to be found.

Elle walked back from the house. She pulled open the door, jumped into the car, and slammed it shut. "Fuck!" She banged her fist on the steering wheel. "What a bastard! Not only does he not know where Kami is, he doesn't care. He doesn't care about his own daughter. Actually said he told her mother to have an abortion, it's not his fault she didn't. Can you imagine?"

Patrick could. He'd been a cop for a long time. Too often, families were a percolator of violence. Husbands who abused wives, mothers who abused children, extended family who did nothing to stop it, or even contributed to it. The cycle of violence seemed like a slogan, but it was far too real to be dismissed. So when he heard of stories like Kami's, they were too familiar to shock him.

He'd had an idyllic childhood—an army brat until he was almost a teenager, when his father was assigned to a permanent post in San Diego shortly after Lucy was born. But even with the moves and having little money for extras, his parents were always there for him and his siblings. They'd had family game night more than once a week, shared nearly every dinner, and supported each

other. Problems with homework? He had brothers and
sisters who could help. Wanted help on his batting? Dillon drove him to the batting cages, or took him to the
park when Patrick didn't have money for the cages. Without Dillon, Patrick would never had made varsity as a high
school freshman.

Elle had had the same upbringing. Other than her father's sudden death ten years ago, the Santanas and Kincaids could have been clones. She chose this career because
she saw injustices in the world—so why was she surprised
that Kami's father didn't give a damn about his own kid?

Elle glanced at him. "Why are you staring at me? Have
something to say?"

"Just thinking about how lucky we were growing up."

That obviously surprised Elle, and she turned the ignition rather than respond. "We're going to the teen center.
I will find Lorenzo and he will tell me where Kami is."

"My car first."

"You think a gun is really necessary?"

Patrick pulled his phone from his pocket. "Or I can
call the police."

"You can be a jerk, you know." She made an illegal
U-turn and sped back toward her place.

Patrick's phone vibrated. Jaye sent him a message:

Lorenzo has a long record, and an active bench
warrant from two weeks ago for missing a court
hearing on a misdemeanor possession charge.
Grayson has a sealed juvie record, clean as an
adult. Want me to dig?

Patrick immediately responded: Don't do anything
illegal.

Like his former partner Sean Rogan, RCK computer
master Jaye Morgan could (and would) hack into any

computer system to get information. Patrick had learned early on working for RCK that he had to make clear he didn't want Jaye—or Sean—to break laws to gain information. Too often Patrick found himself wanting to cross the line—and taking a step across when he was pushed—but he didn't want a cloud hanging over him, wondering if he'd gone too far, trampling over privacy rights and worse. He'd been a cop first, dropping out of college when his nephew was murdered. He realized that while he loved baseball, and had had major league scouts looking at him since high school, he wanted to do something with his life that meant something, that helped people. Being a cop had satisfied him for a long time. Now he felt the same about his work with RCK.

He glanced at Elle. They weren't all that different. "Why do you do this?"

"Do what?"

"Pro bono work for teens."

"It's not all I do."

"But it's your passion."

She didn't say anything for a minute. "When I started working for Feliz I was still in law school. I lived with three other girls because I had no money. I had scholarships and loans for my classes, got paid next to nothing for the internship, and worked the late shift at a twenty-four-hour gym. It was a good deal, because I could study. I don't think I slept more than three hours a night during those years . . . anyway, between the gym and my BART station, there was a large group home. I never thought much about it until one night there was a shoot-out inside, two kids were killed, and the police swooped down and arrested everyone. The other kids were automatically put into the system. No one competent was there to protect their rights. It wasn't even someone in the house who'd gone in shooting, it was a gang who wouldn't let their members leave. The group home was a second chance, but even when kids want the opportunity, others try to stop them.

"I realized that these kids, through little fault of their own, had been dealt a shitty hand. They were doing what they could to survive, but if there wasn't someone there to help—help legally—they would learn that no one cared. They'd become the future criminals, the drug addicts, dying young because they lost all hope.

"I can't live knowing that there are so many kids who are without hope. You're right, we had an amazing childhood. I hate myself sometimes because I used to complain that I had to wear my sister's hand-me-downs, which were themselves secondhand clothes. I had to share my bedroom my entire life with two of my sisters. Three hotheaded Cuban girls in the same room? It was hell . . . but nothing compared to what these kids go through. They'd be happy to have hand-me-downs, a warm jacket, a hot meal. My mom never let us go hungry. We were always tight for money growing up, but we always had a home and dinner on the table, fresh fruit in the refrigerator, a library card, and shoes that fit."

She stopped at a red light. "So I went to Gary Feliz, whom I had interned for, and told him we needed a pro bono division. He put Madeleine Starr in charge of the program, and I became her intern, then worked for her when I graduated. Maddie is just like me, but cares even more. Because she had been one of those kids."

Patrick pointed to his rental sedan on the next corner. She illegally double-parked, and said, "Be quick."

She didn't look at him, and Patrick had the distinct impression that she regretted spilling her guts. But he was glad she had. Now he understood Elle, and that gave him the information he needed to get them out of this situation without bloodshed.

He opened his trunk. He threaded his holster through his belt, then holstered his Glock. He slipped a backup clip in his pocket, then grabbed his laptop. While he was at it, he pocketed his jammer. Back in Elle's car, she said, "I hope you have a permit for that."

He ignored the hostility in her voice. "We need a plan, and don't tell me to wing it. I want to know why you think Lorenzo will help you."

"I don't."

"Then what are we doing?"

"I'm going to the teen center. It's Saturday, it's open until midnight, so we have a little time. I'm hoping to spot one of Lorenzo's kids, someone we can follow to his place. Once I know where he is, I can sneak around and see if Kami is there."

"That's an awful plan."

"You have a better one?"

He didn't, because he didn't know the layout of the teen center and he had to assume that a drug dealer like Lorenzo would have armed thugs. They often used underage kids because the system dealt differently with fifteen-year-old killers than eighteen-year-old killers.

"When we get to the center, you can look for Kami and ask around, but don't follow anyone. There's an active warrant for Lorenzo. If we—"

"How do you know that?"

Patrick glared at her. "You knew and didn't tell me?"

"He's a drug dealer. There's always a warrant for him."

"You didn't answer my question."

"It's irrelevant."

It wasn't, but Patrick let it slide—this time. "If we see him, we tell the cops where he is. We're not confronting a guy who knows the cops want him."

"If I turn him in, he won't tell me where Kami is!"

"And why would he tell you now? Why do you think he even knows? Dammit, Elle, what aren't you telling me?"

"Nothing."

"Bullshit."

Her jaw clenched and unclenched. "I plan to offer Lorenzo my help. Help him with the bench warrant. It was a misdemeanor charge; even with his record, I can get him community service if he agrees to testify against Christopher Lee."

Patrick almost laughed, but Elle was deadly serious.

"And you think he'll do that? Testify against his supplier?"

"Yes, with the right motivation."

"Elle, he won't."

"You don't know that. You don't know him. I have to give him a chance to do the right thing."

"He's more scared of his supplier than he is of the police. I guarantee you he will not turn. Have you considered that his supplier told him to silence Kami because she was going to testify?"

"Yes, but he wouldn't."

"Why?"

"He's been protecting her for years. I don't think he'll hurt her." She bit her lip.

Patrick shook his head. "He doesn't have to do it. He can turn her over to someone who will."

"I can't believe that."

But her voice said the opposite. Elle drove white-knuckled through the city. Patrick would be lost if he had to find his own way back. "Kami could be in hiding herself," he said. "Or run away, out of the city, because she didn't want to testify, knowing what could happen."

"I promised her she'd be safe."

"How good are the promises she's received in the past?"

"I've always done what I said I would do," Elle said. "She knows she can trust me."

"What if she thinks she's protecting you? What if she's scared and just wants to disappear? Sacramento. Stockton. Even Los Angeles. She doesn't have to stay here."

"She wants to stop Christopher Lee, too."

"Why?"

"Because she was friends with Doreen."

Patrick had no idea what Elle was talking about. "Who's Doreen?"

"Shit," she mumbled.

"Is this what you've been keeping from me?"

She didn't say anything.

"Stop the car. Let me out."

"Patrick—"

"Now."

What was Elle supposed to do? Tell Patrick everything? He would never understand. Or . . . maybe he was the only one who could. He'd seen shit, as a cop.

She pulled over to the side of the road, but she didn't turn off the car. "Don't go," she said quietly. She hated asking for help, but even she recognized when she was in over her head. "Please."

He didn't make a move to get out. Instead, he asked, "Is Doreen the girl who died of a drug overdose?"

Elle closed her eyes and nodded. "It's my fault Doreen is dead," she said quietly.

"Why? Because you gave her the drugs?"

"Of course not!" Why was Patrick doing this? Pushing her to lose her temper?

"Tell me, Elle. Tell me how this started and who Doreen is to you."

She hadn't told anyone about Doreen. Not the details. Not even Dwight, though he suspected she had a personal reason for wanting to take Christopher Lee down.

"A year ago, Doreen came to me because she thought that Christopher Lee was supplying drugs to Richie Lorenzo. She knew I'd helped some kids get out from under Lorenzo's thumb, and she knew how I felt about drugs. Doreen was sixteen, had watched her mother turn into a drug addict and her father go to prison for dealing. She recognized the signs when others didn't. She knew who Lorenzo was, and found out something that made her suspicious about Lee.

"I didn't want to believe her. I was helping Lee raise money for the teen center; it was already under construction. I admired how he gave jobs to kids who had no other way to feed themselves or who could learn a skill that would help them later in life. But I agreed to follow Lorenzo to meet his supplier—and it was Lee. I saw it with my own eyes."

"Why didn't you turn the information over to the police?"

"I did! I used all my clout with law enforcement and they raided his business, TK Clothing, and found *nothing* other than minor OSHA violations. He was clean, according to them, and he paid his fine and all was well. But it *wasn't* good, and Doreen was so disillusioned by the system that she planted a recording device in Lee's office. She told me after the fact. I would have stopped her."

But Elle wasn't certain she would have. She wanted Lee as much as Doreen did.

"I don't know what happened, but Doreen disappeared. I was frantic, searching for her just like now . . ." Suddenly, Elle saw the parallel and she clutched her stomach.

"What happened?" Patrick asked quietly.

"Someone—one of Lee's men, I know—dumped her body outside my apartment. She was barely alive. I tried to save her. But—" She drew in a deep breath, forcing herself not to cry. Forcing herself to control the rage that she constantly fought whenever she remembered Doreen dying in her arms.

"Sorry," Doreen had said. Elle could barely hear her. "I—I failed."

"No, no! Hold on, Doreen, please."

Doreen's petite body was shaking uncontrollably. Elle took off her sweater and put it over the girl as she tried to hold her. Where was the ambulance? How long did it take to get here in the middle of the fucking night?

"It's worse," Doreen whispered.

"Don't talk."

"It's worse than I even knew."

Doreen didn't speak again, and by the time the ambulance arrived three minutes later, Elle knew she was dead.

"Elle?" Patrick's hand was on her arm.

She took a deep breath. "Kami knew Doreen. I didn't know it at first, and one day I said too much. Told Kami that I knew Lee had killed Doreen and that's why I was so focused on learning everything about him and his connection with Lorenzo. Kami started snooping, she wants to take him down just like I do, but she's young and reckless. She doesn't understand she can't do it alone."

"That's the pot calling the kettle black," Patrick muttered.

"I'm not reckless."

"Yes you are, but I understand why." Patrick touched her cheek and turned her to look at him. It was dark, but she didn't mistake the determined set of his square jaw. She wanted to turn everything over to Patrick, to let him fix this mess, but she'd always cleaned up her own messes.

"Patrick—"

"You have to trust me, Elle," he said. "You're in a dangerous game with dangerous people who have already proven they will kill to keep their drugs moving. If you don't trust me, listen to me, you're going to get hurt—or worse."

"You're a Kincaid, right? Truth, justice, and the American way."

She was being sarcastic—it was a defense mechanism—but she couldn't stop herself.

But instead of being angry, Patrick smiled. "I like it."

He dropped his hand and Elle breathed easier. Who could have imagined she'd still have a crush on Veronica's boyfriend?

Ex-boyfriend. Veronica is married with two kids.

"Drive," Patrick said, "and tell me more about this teen center."

"Christopher Lee donated the land and a public-private partnership built the facility. It's sixty thousand square feet, with an indoor basketball court, a library, computers, games, a meeting hall, and more. There's four full-time staff members and several part-time staff and volunteers. They're good people . . . but they all have bought into the myth that Christopher Lee is this wonderful and caring philanthropist. It's a beautiful facility, much needed. During really cold or stormy weather, the city lets us open it as a youth shelter. It's open from six A.M. until midnight on the weekends, and until ten P.M. during the week.

"Lee's garment factory is walking distance, and many of the kids work for him part-time. That's how Doreen got in, and how she found out that he was dealing. She came to me, and—I went to the police. But they found nothing, because Lee is smart. He probably has one or more of them on his payroll. He became suspicious, and Doreen paid the price. That's why I can't just call the police. I don't know who I can trust inside."

"And he knows about you."

"Why do you say that?"

Patrick chuckled in amusement. "Because you're not someone who can keep her emotions to herself. If you had to see him after that, he'd know just by looking at you."

"You sound like that's a bad thing. I can't lie. I can't hide what I really think about people. If that's a fault, sue me." She paused. "Lee ordered his people to throw Doreen out of a car in my alley the night she died. I know it and I will prove it. Somehow."

This was personal for Elle, and now he knew for certain. The story about Doreen dying, Lee's involvement, and now Kami missing—Elle blamed herself, and she wasn't thinking ahead.

Patrick was going to have to do that for her.

He needed to talk this out with her. If revenge was in her heart, Patrick had to find a way to stop it.

CHAPTER 4

They parked at the far end of the parking lot adjacent to the teen center. There were only a few cars, but Patrick wanted to assess the terrain before they went in, and the end of the lot provided him with the best visual of the entire grounds, even with the fog.

He liked that someone had taken the time to decorate the center for Christmas. White lights trimmed the front windows, and a tree in the front was decorated with large plastic ornaments and green and white lights. There were basketball courts on the other side of the center from the parking lot, and a lot of open space. The streets that framed the center's boundaries weren't as clean and bright— warehouses, decrepit apartments, and boarded-up businesses.

He asked Elle, "How many entrances? Exits?"

"Two entrances, one that goes straight into the gym, and the main entrance. The gym entrance is closed after six P.M. The other exits are alarmed."

"I'm more concerned about safety issues."

"There haven't been any major problems since it opened. These kids know that if a few rotten apples get in, they'll mess it up for everyone."

Patrick wasn't sure that was true, but he didn't comment. "I'm going to let you go in alone," he said, "because as you said, I look like a cop."

She gave him a genuine smile. "Maybe if you let your hair grow a bit, replace the conservative Dockers with faded jeans, and get a nice tat on your arm . . ."

"No way in hell am I getting a tattoo." Two of his brothers had them, but Jack had been in the army and Connor had been an undercover cop. Patrick had never had the urge to inject ink under his skin.

When Elle's eyes sparkled, Patrick said, "You have one."

"Two."

"Where?"

"That's for you to find out." She winked and got out of the car.

Patrick decided to ignore Elle's flirtatious comment. She was trying to divert his attention from the seriousness of the situation and he wasn't sure what to make of it. The brief connection they'd made when she told him about Doreen was gone, and this was Gabrielle Santana, after all, the girl who had the ability to appear wholesome and sexy at the same time.

Besides, her mood changes threw him for a loop. First she was driven and worried, then angry at Kami's father, then grumpy that he insisted on retrieving his gun. Her anguish about Doreen was real, of that he was certain, but she had a well-honed defense mechanism that kicked in whenever those emotions hit her. He didn't know if she was flirting with him to throw him off guard or because she was relieved he was helping her.

Maybe a little of both.

Patrick watched her cross the parking lot and enter the building. Elle was a bundle of energy, a spitfire his mother would have said—and that could be taken as a compliment or an insult.

Elle was beginning to grow on Patrick.

He looked around the area. There were no street decorations to signal that it was Christmas, only the tree and lights in front of the building, visible through the thinning fog.

To the north of the entrance, a group of young men played basketball on a lighted, outside court. Two on two, three black kids and a tall, skinny white guy. The fog wasn't as thick as earlier, but the air was still damp. He got out and walked over to them. They eyed him warily. Patrick was six foot three, but except for one scrawny black kid, the others were as tall or taller.

He made eye contact. "Up to taking on an old guy?"

"You?" The short kid snorted.

"Baseball's my sport, but I also played hoops in high school."

"You a cop?"

"No."

They didn't believe him, but he couldn't help what they thought.

"You want something."

"I do."

The short kid nodded. "You and me against them."

"Three on two?"

"Yep."

Patrick put his hands out and was thrown the ball. "What's your name?"

"Jazz."

"I'm Patrick, but in college they called me K."

"Just 'K'?"

"Special K."

Jazz snorted again. "And you're a cop."

"I'm not a cop."

Patrick didn't know whether Jazz believed him or not. He'd earned the nickname long before the moniker referenced a drug.

"Then what are you?"

"Private investigator." Patrick bounced the ball. "Ready?"

Almost immediately, Patrick realized he was too old to be playing basketball with teenagers. Against Sean, one-on-one, he could hold his own, but Jazz was fast and the other guys were good.

Still, he read Jazz and they developed an unspoken communication. The kid should be playing varsity. He wasn't tall, only about five nine, but as a point guard he'd rule the court. They scored the first basket on a dunk, and Jazz high-fived Patrick.

Fifteen minutes later, it was 20–14 against him, but Patrick cried uncle. "I'm getting too old."

"What are you, thirty?"

Thirty-six. He'd always looked younger than his age. "Close." He needed water. "Good game."

"Not bad for an old cop. But you should know, I'm not a rat."

"I know."

"How?"

"Because I know you."

He snickered. "Never seen you before. You're not from the city."

"I live in D.C."

"You're a fed?"

"No. I told you, I'm a private investigator. I'm visiting a friend. Elle Santana."

The kids immediately recognized the name, and the white kid said, "Elle's friend? Why didn't you just say it? Or are you trying to jam her up?"

"I'm helping her." Patrick spoke to the group, but focused on Jazz. He was the leader; the others deferred to him. "We grew up together, so when this thing went down with one of her clients, she asked me to help. And—between us—I used to be a cop, until seven years ago."

"And they still let you carry a gun?" Jazz gestured to his holster.

"I have a permit."

"Can I see it?"

"No."

Jazz grinned. "So why you helping Elle?"

"Her client Kami's in a jam."

"Kami's in trouble?" the white kid asked. But by Jazz's expression, he knew. They all knew who Kami was, but Jazz knew what had happened. The kid didn't fear much, but Patrick could see in his old, dark eyes that he was worried.

"Have you seen her tonight?"

They all shook their heads, except Jazz, who hesitated.

Patrick said, "Maybe you didn't see her, but know where she is?"

Jazz ignored Patrick but motioned for his boys to walk across the court, and they talked, unmindful of the cold through their thin hoodies. Then Jazz returned alone and the other three went into the building.

"I don't know where Kami is, but you know Lorenzo?"

Patrick dipped his head.

"He's looking for her."

"Is she in danger?"

Jazz shrugged. "I'm only telling you this because Kami's a good kid, and I don't want her hurt. I haven't seen her for days, but Ace"—he gestured toward the building where his friends disappeared—"thought he saw her at TK at closing today."

"TK?"

"The clothes shop. You know, where they make T-shirts and shit. They hire out of here. Ace is sixteen, so he has good hours and shit. I'm too young."

"How old are you?"

"Fourteen."

Patrick would have guessed older, just from the way the kid held himself. "Thanks for your help, Jazz."

"Eyes open, it's been a weird night already."

Before Patrick could ask him what he meant, Jazz slipped away.

He walked back to the car and pulled out his laptop. He sent Jaye a note to dig as deep as legally possible into Christopher Lee and TK, a clothing manufacturer in San Francisco, focusing on finances. Any business that regularly imported or exported could easily run drugs. Patrick had seen it quite a bit in San Diego because of the proximity to the Mexican border, but any city with a port was particularly vulnerable.

On the map, TK was only half a mile from the teen center. It was definitely worth checking out the facility. He closed his laptop and put it under the seat.

He considered going there without Elle, except that he didn't know what Kami looked like, and she had no reason to trust him. He didn't want to spook her. At least he had a viable lead to share when Elle came out, instead of trying to find the drug dealer who might want her dead.

As Patrick watched the teen center, he saw several male youths approach the entrance, then lurk. Jazz knew about the situation with Elle and Kami; there could have been others who did as well. Someone could have tipped Lorenzo off that Elle was inside the building, alone, asking questions. Jazz and his friends knew Patrick was here; no one else did.

He turned off the overhead light in the car and slipped out, quietly closing his door. The center itself was well lit, and the thugs didn't seem to care if they were spotted. They were definitely waiting for someone. Patrick could see six, but because visibility was low, there could be more out of his sight. Jazz and his friends hadn't come back out. It was eleven-thirty, and the center would close soon.

Patrick decided he needed to be bold. He didn't know if one of these kids was Lorenzo, but he doubted it. No one seemed to be a leader, they were all just . . . waiting. Patrick strode toward the doors without saying a word as he passed. They remained silent as well, but watchful. Patrick opened the door and went in with purpose.

A twentysomething black girl with a nose ring and tight braids manned the front desk. She had a stack of textbooks next to her, two of which were open and marked up. "We're getting ready to close, sir. Are you here to pick someone up?"

She said it in a tone that implied she'd be shocked if he had a kid here.

"Elle Santana."

"Oh."

"Where is she?"

"I don't know. She came in about forty-five minutes ago."

"Can I look around?"

"The facility is for young adults under twenty-five."

"Elle's thirty-two."

Elle stepped around the corner and said, "It's not polite to talk about a girl's age." She smiled at the nose-ring chick and said, "Thanks, Mikayla, I got what I needed. And don't forget, if you see Kami, text me."

"No problem," Mikayla said, still looking suspiciously at Patrick.

Elle brushed past Patrick and was about to walk outside when Patrick grabbed her arm and pulled her to the side.

She glared at him and shook off his grip. "Dammit, Patrick, I don't like to be manhandled."

"There's six guys loitering outside."

"This is a teen center. There are *always* kids loitering. It's not a crime here."

"In this weather?"

"Are you always so suspicious?"

"They arrived thirty minutes after you did. And they're waiting. For you."

"Paranoid, too."

"You've got to trust my instincts because it's pretty damn clear you have none of your own," Patrick snapped. "I have a lead on Kami."

"You? From your trusty rusty computer?"

"From the basketball players outside. She was seen earlier this evening at TK."

"No, she wouldn't dare go there, especially since Lee suspects she's turning evidence against him. She wouldn't risk it."

"Unless she's trying to find the evidence she told you she already had."

"Two girls told me they saw her at an apartment building not far from here."

"You're being set up."

"Maybe the basketball players were playing you."

"You're impossible."

"TK is closed—unless you want us to go our separate ways? I'll check out my lead and you check out yours."

"I'm not letting you out of my sight." Though he was growing more irritated by the minute.

"What, you're my personal bodyguard now?"

He ignored the sarcasm. "Do what I say."

She was about to argue with him, but his attention shifted to the door. Two of the thugs were coming in. They spotted Elle and sauntered over, their jeans hanging low on their hips. "Miz Elle, we hear you looking for Kami."

Elle eyed them. She spoke without her usual friendly tone. Maybe her instincts weren't as bad as Patrick thought.

"Word gets around fast," she said flatly.

"We'll help find her."

"Thanks anyway, but I have help."

"We'll look, just the same."

"I'd rather you didn't," Elle said. "I'm sure you're just looking out for Kami, but I need to talk to her."

"So you bring the cops in here?" one of the guys said.

"I'm not a cop," Patrick said.

The two punks glanced at each other and snorted, smirks on their lips. "Right."

Patrick eyed them closely. One of them was definitely packing.

"It's nearly midnight," Elle said. "Go home."

"It's Saturday night," one said. "Early."

"The center closes in twenty minutes. Do I need to call Gerald?"

They both scowled.

"Bitch."

"Go."

They grumbled, talked to Mikayla for a minute, then left.

Elle walked over to Mikayla. "Don't let them back in. If they come in, buzz security."

"Who's Gerald?" Patrick asked when Elle walked back to where he waited in the corner of the lobby.

"Gerald Duncan, a former football player with the Niners. Or Raiders. Or . . . some team in California. He was raised on the streets, and he's here every week, mostly to play basketball or football with the boys. They listen to him, and he takes care of kids who don't want to play by the rules. Doesn't always work, but since he helped build this place, he's invested in making it succeed."

"Like Christopher Lee?"

"Totally different."

"And does your friend Gerald think Lee is corrupt?"

"I'm not going to talk about this here. Time's running out. I need to get to the apartment before she bolts again."

Patrick didn't want to follow Elle's lead, but like she said, he didn't know that he could trust Jazz. He thought he could . . . that's what his instincts told him.

"Those kids were part of Lorenzo's gang, weren't they?"

She hesitated a fraction of a second. Was she going to lie to him? Then she said, "Yes. I know who they are."

"Are you ready to accept my help without fighting me every step of the way?"

"I'm not fighting with you."

They walked outside. Lorenzo's boys were still there, but they didn't approach. Patrick had Elle walk slightly in front of him so he could keep a better eye on their surroundings. The boys kept their distance, though they moved in the same direction they did. Keeping an eye on them. Per orders, it appeared.

"Trust me, Elle."

"I do."

Patrick had a feeling he was going to regret letting Elle take the lead.

CHAPTER 5

Elle didn't want to let on to Patrick that Lorenzo's guys had gotten to her. Maybe he knew, because he got all caveman protective of her when they were outside, herding her like cattle. Except . . . she wouldn't admit it to him, but his presence did make her feel safer. Great, now she was acting all helpless female waiting for the big, brave man to save her.

Please.

Real heroes didn't exist. She'd learned that the hard way, watching so many kids suffer and die. If they weren't physically dead, they were emotionally crippled, hopeless and broken by a callous system that didn't have any real solutions to real problems. It was overwhelming at times, but she pushed on, because the only solution that ever worked was for a person to care, and if she stopped caring, then she might as well just give up everything. What she really did was help kids of parents who were jackasses—basically, the kids whose parents were in prison, or drunks, or drug addicts. And unfortunately, a lot of those kids grew up to be just like their parents, to become criminals, abusers, and addicts. She wanted to stop that. Help them before it was too late and they killed themselves, or someone else.

She drove several blocks to a row of dilapidated apartment buildings that probably should have been condemned years ago. She was about to pull over when Patrick said, "Drive around the block."

She did, but frowned. "Why?"

"Lorenzo's boys followed us."

She'd thought they might have, but she hadn't been sure. How did Patrick know with such certainty? Had the police academy handed out psychic skills at graduation? "I have an idea," she said. She didn't drive around the block, she kept going straight.

She drove half a mile, then took a major road to the highway. She merged onto 280, going north, and got off at the next exit. No one was behind her. She still spent a good ten minutes driving around in circles before she ended up back at the apartment building.

"Good job," Patrick said.

"High praise from you."

Elle needed to stop being so sarcastic. He was trying to help; why was she being so bitchy? "I'm sorry," she mumbled.

He reached over and took her hand. "It's okay. Elle, we've known each other ever since I moved to San Diego when I was still a short, scrawny kid. You don't have to apologize. I know this is stressful, so we'll take it one step at a time."

Why was he being nice when she was so antagonistic? "Thanks. My attitude gets the best of me sometimes."

Her phone was ringing again. "Dammit, it's Sandy Chin again. She's called, like, three times since ten."

"You need to talk to her."

Elle shook her head and sent the call to voice mail. "I have to find Kami first. If I can't find her by tomorrow morning—well, I'll figure out what to say to Sandy then."

"If we can't find her, we need to bring in the police. She's in trouble."

"She's in hiding." She had to be. No one had found her body—Elle would have heard. But that didn't mean she wasn't dead.

You can't think like that.

She focused on what she could do and gestured toward the buildings. "This is Section 8 housing. One of the girls at the center said she saw Kami walking across the courtyard after dark. When she called out, Kami didn't turn around, and she thought she hadn't heard her. Another girl said that one of Kami's friends has an apartment on the ground floor, with her mother. It's late, but I don't see an alternative to knocking on the door."

"Except?"

How had he sensed her skepticism?

"I learned that Lorenzo's new place is also in one of these buildings. Which confirms what Clark told me." It irritated Elle that Patrick didn't trust Clark. Was that a guy thing? Or a cop thing? Either way, he didn't know Clark like Elle did, and therefore should trust her judgment. And while she may have known Patrick longer than her college friend, she saw Clark nearly every day.

"How far is TK from here?"

"Down the next street a couple blocks, toward the bay. Light industrial area."

"I don't feel comfortable letting you go in there alone," Patrick said. "But I'll make myself scarce. No one will know I'm watching you."

She raised an eyebrow. "What, you have an invisibility cloak?"

Patrick laughed before stepping out of the car.

At first, Elle knew exactly where Patrick was, then suddenly, he wasn't there, and she couldn't see him. Wow, neat trick.

She went to the apartment that belonged to Mia Jones and her mother. Elle didn't know Mia, but she had names to drop.

She couldn't tell if there were lights on in the apartment, but she heard a faint laugh track from a television sitcom. She knocked on the door. There was no answer. She knocked a little louder.

A young black girl answered the door. She wasn't older than thirteen. "Mia?" Elle asked.

"Who are you?"

"Mia?" a voice from another room called. "Who's there? Not a boy!"

"No, Mama," Mia called. She looked Elle over. "You're Kami's laywer friend."

"I am."

Mia glanced down the hall, then motioned for Elle to come in. She closed and bolted the door behind her. "Who told you she was here?"

"I need to talk to her. She's in danger." Elle glanced around the small apartment. Kami wasn't in the living room. There were two doors off a short hall.

"She left. A couple hours ago. I told her she could stay, my mom never leaves her room except to go to work. But she said she had something to do, just wanted to hide here until it got dark."

"What was she doing?"

"I dunno." But Mia didn't make eye contact.

"Please, Mia, if you don't help me, I'm afraid she'll get hurt. Bad people are looking for her."

Mia frowned. "I don't know exactly what she was doing, but she said she was going to TK. She was waiting until everyone was gone."

This was worse than Elle had expected. Why would Kami risk herself like this?

"Thank you. And don't tell anyone I was here."

"And don't tell anyone I said anything. I don't need to be on Lorenzo's bad side. But Kami helped me once. I couldn't just tell her to go away."

Elle left. Patrick had been right—Kami had been seen at TK. Why had she insisted on following her lead instead of his? Had she put Kami at greater risk because she was so stubborn? Maybe she just couldn't accept that a bunch of basketball players would trust someone like Patrick enough to tell him the truth.

She looked up and down the dimly lit interior hall, but didn't see Patrick. She walked to the end, then stepped out into the central garden of the complex and walked briskly toward the gated exit. The gates had no locks, hardly any barrier to keep out people who shouldn't be here. As she reached the gate, two young men approached her. They were the same two who'd been talking to her inside the center.

"Richie wants to talk to you," one said.

She kept walking until the other kid stepped in her path.

"Move out of my way," she said in a voice that sounded stronger than she felt.

"After you talk to Richie."

He stepped forward, she took two steps back. The kid smirked, knowing he'd scared her. She hated that, that this hoodlum got his jollies out of making her afraid. She didn't like being afraid, and she glared at him.

His eyes flicked to her right, and Elle glanced over her shoulder. Patrick, right behind her. How had he snuck up on them?

"Let Ms. Santana pass, Ringo."

The kid glared at him. "How do you know my name? Who's been talking?"

"I have a lot of friends in law enforcement. When I

called in to say I saw Raphael Clinton, aka Ringo, they were very interested, considering there's a warrant for your arrest."

"Bull-fucking-shit."

"About my friends or that you have a warrant for robbing a liquor store on Third last month?"

Ringo's eyes went to his friend.

Patrick continued. "You may have enough time to disappear before the cops arrive, but they're on their way. Now we're going to leave."

He put his hand on the small of Elle's back and almost pushed her forward. She started walking, trying not to shake, but the tension in the courtyard was thicker than the fog.

Patrick didn't hesitate, he kept them moving to her car.

"Get in and drive," he said.

She complied. "When will the police be here?"

"I didn't call them."

"You lied?"

"Bluffed."

"There wasn't a warrant? Then why was he so worried? How did you know his name?"

"There's definitely a warrant. I took his picture, and the others', when we were at the teen center and had RCK run their faces. ID'd four of the six, all with records, all under eighteen except for Ringo. He's twenty. I'll let the locals know where he can be found. Right now I just wanted to get us out of a sticky situation without having to pull my gun."

Elle took several deep breaths. "You were right."

"About?"

"She went to TK. She's planning to break in, but her friend didn't know why."

"But you do."

Elle was angry and upset and she didn't know if she

was to blame for everything. "Doreen did the same thing, and got killed. Kami knows that! Why is she doing this? Why would she risk her life?"

"Why are you?" Patrick asked quietly.

"Why am I what?"

"You're doing the same thing. Risking your life to find Kami before something happens to her."

"You are, too," she said, averting the question.

"I'm trained for this. You're taking risks without even realizing it."

"If not me, then who? This world is fucked up enough because people pass the buck or turn their back. Not me, not on Kami."

Not when it's my fault she's in trouble in the first place.

Patrick took her hand and squeezed it. She stared at him, wanting to let him do everything because she was scared. But she also knew what she was getting into. She knew the people and the players.

Patrick said, "If Kami is there, we'll find her."

Elle voiced her real fear. "What if she's already dead?"

CHAPTER 6

Patrick told Elle not to drive directly to TK. He wanted to make sure that Ringo and his goon didn't follow them. His phone vibrated and he answered.

"Kincaid."

It was Jaye. "Christopher Lee is squeaky-clean on the surface. Too clean. I dug into his financials—"

"Jaye—"

"All legal, pinky swear. What he really needs is a good audit, because it feels fishy to me."

"That's not going to get anyone to look at him."

"Hey, my word should be good enough."

"It is with me, but I need something solid. Or did you call just to chat?"

"Solid. He does a lot of business with another squeaky-clean company in Stockton, which works with a shipping company that isn't so squeaky-clean. Peeling back the layers and that not-so-squeaky-clean shipping company is actually owned by one of Lee's holdings, but he buried it well."

"Not well enough, if you uncovered it in an hour."

"I can't take credit for it. Chi Sun Shipping is on the RCK watch list."

"What watch list?"

"Oh—right, you don't do international. The human trafficking watch list."

Patrick's blood ran cold. "Are you sure?"

"Of course," she said, sounding offended. "I wouldn't have said it if I weren't."

"Can you do one more thing?"

"You know it's after midnight, right?"

"Are you going to bed?"

"No."

"Then please? Pretty please? Pretty please with a triple espresso on top?"

She giggled. "God, Patrick, you owe me big-time."

"We all do."

"What else do you want?"

"Our contact with DEA, can you find out if Lee or Chi Sun Shipping is under watch for drug smuggling?"

"Not until the morning—it's three A.M. in Washington."

"Right. Sorry. Thanks again."

"Be careful. Jack said if you need help, call him."

"I'm okay for now."

"And JT wants an update if you uncover anything connected to Chi Sun Shipping."

JT Caruso was the *C* in RCK. "You told him before me?"

"He pays me. But just so you know, I e-mailed him while we were talking, and he just responded. So technically, I told you first."

"You're a gem."

"A diamond. I want to be a diamond."

He laughed and hung up.

"You're laughing," Elle said.

Patrick sighed and rubbed his eyes. "Sometimes, Elle, you have to laugh, otherwise we'd be depressed all the time."

"Did your people learn anything important?"

"Maybe. Chi Sun Shipping, owned by one of Lee's holding companies, is on a watch list for human trafficking."

Elle didn't say anything.

"Elle?"

"That can't be right."

"You're defending him now?"

"No! But—shouldn't people have known? I mean, you waltz into town and six hours later you've connected my nemesis to trafficking in people?"

"RCK was started by two ex-military who specialized in hostage rescue. Since then, we've grown to do primarily corporate and personal security, but we still have one guy who works south of the border whose primary job is finding Americans who have disappeared—and likely were kidnapped and forced to be sex slaves. So RCK keeps tabs on human trafficking and forwards information to the appropriate governments. We can't stop it all, but we do our part."

"Which sounds like more than most."

"I work with some good people. My brother Jack is one of them."

"But—human trafficking. You'd think I would have heard something, sensed something." She wasn't sold on his information. And, truth was, Lee could have his fingers in a lot of illegal activities. Criminals like him—those with legitimate business and public ties—often had multiple illegal venues. Maybe he was running drugs in San Francisco—and running people out of Stockton. But in Patrick's experience, it was likely connected. His legitimate business was the perfect way to launder money. And working with the teen center gave him access to throwaway kids.

"They prey on runaways—kids no one will miss."

"Do you think they took Kami?" Elle's voice turned panicky.

"We don't know anything—we don't even know if what's going on here has anything to do with his shipping company. We just need to be aware that this could be a lot worse than drug trafficking."

"It's worse," Elle mumbled.

"Excuse me?"

"That's what Doreen said to me before she died. She said, 'It's worse than we thought.' I didn't know what she meant. I didn't understand—I should have."

Patrick reached over and took her hand again. "You had no reason to think that Lee was trafficking in slaves when you had proof he was tied in with a local drug dealer. Let's go to TK. It's nearly one in the morning, we should be able to snoop around."

"He'll have security, I don't know how we're going to get in—"

"There is no 'we.' I'm going in, if I can. And I promise, I won't trip an alarm."

"How can you promise that?"

"Because I know how to bypass virtually any alarm system ever made." He squeezed her hand, then let go and took out his cell phone. "And if I can't, I have someone who can."

"And he's just going to meet us here?"

"No, he'll do it remotely." He sent Sean a text message. How late was it in Denver? Two hours ahead?

Sean responded:

Yes, I'm awake. We have a dead body here. At least, we think we have a dead body. There's a lot of blood, no body. What do you need?

Patrick blinked at the message. He decided not to ask questions.

Can you be on call for the next thirty minutes? I might need to tap into your expertise.

Though Patrick's phone was secure, he didn't want to explicitly type that he might need Sean to hack into a security system.

Sean replied:

I'm going to start charging RCK for my services. But since you're Lucy's brother, I'll give you a freebie.

Patrick shook his head.

Thanks, pal, you're all heart.

"We're good," he said to Elle.

"I don't even want to know what that was about."

Patrick directed Elle to park halfway down the street from TK Clothing. He didn't want her car to be caught on external cameras. The building was dark, except for faint security lighting, dim through the heavy mist.

"No one's here," Elle continued, looking around.

Visibility was next to zero. The fog was so thick, the security lights simply provided a lighter color to the eerie mist. There were two cars parked around the side of the building, but that didn't mean anyone was there. There were no external windows so no way to tell if anyone was inside.

"I'm going in. Under no circumstances are you to follow, understand?"

"You're bossy."

"If you see anything, text me." He sent her a quick message so she'd have his number. "If I don't return in thirty minutes, or contact you, call the police."

"And say what? My friend just broke in to TK Clothing?"

"Whatever you need to say to get the police here."

"Fine." She pouted, but her brows were creased with worry.

Patrick zipped up his jacket against the cold and walked along the street across from TK Clothing. There were no security cameras on the outer gates, but several were attached to the building. He took out the jammer he'd grabbed from his car, which would interfere with the cameras if they were digital. Unfortunately, he couldn't tell from this distance and would have to take the risk. He pulled his hood over his head to obscure his face if he was, in fact, recorded.

The gates were locked, but they were electronic. He didn't even need to call Sean for help. He decoded them in less than a minute using an app on his phone that Sean had originally written. The gate released, and Patrick slipped in. He didn't close it all the way, in case he needed to get out fast.

He made sure his jammer was set on high, pocketed it, and stayed close to the building. He walked around to where the cars were and touched their hoods. Both were warm, but not hot. An hour? Maybe. But it didn't matter: people were definitely inside.

He snapped pictures of their license plates and sent them to Jaye for identification.

Patrick assessed the door. It, too, was a keyless entry, but different from the gate and like nothing he had hacked before. And he couldn't risk going in without knowing the layout of the building.

He decided to circle the building and see if there was another entrance or windows. First, he downloaded an app from the RCK server that would turn his cell phone into a listening device. He put a wireless transmitter in his ear.

His phone vibrated. It was Elle.

Status?

He responded:

Be patient.

He almost laughed. "Elle" and "patience" didn't belong in the same sentence.

He set the transmitter on high and held his phone in front of him. There were voices coming from inside. He walked toward the rear of the building and the voices grew louder.

He turned the corner and noted that there were several windows on the back facade of the building, two lit bright. Venetian blinds covered the windows, but it would be easier to pick up the conversation through glass. He hit Record.

Through a narrow crack in the blinds he made out three distinct people, but based on the voices, there were at least four in the room. He took several pictures.

It was the female voice that threw him off guard. She spoke English, but in a thick Chinese accent.

"I need your assurance, Mr. Lee, that you can deliver per our agreement."

"Yes, of course."

"Jonny tells me there's a problem."

"There is no problem."

"That woman, she's been a problem, no?"

"She's an annoyance, not a problem. I've been searched, I'm clean."

A male voice said, "Yet she brought a cop around."

"That has nothing to do with this," Lee said.

"Don't be so certain," the woman said. "I want you to find out everything about him. Who he is, what department he's with. If I lose my merchandise, you will pay."

"I told you to stay off the river, but you didn't listen."

The woman answered in rapid Chinese, and Patrick had no idea what she was saying. Lee, whose English had no accent, also spoke in Chinese, and the two argued until the third person said, "This isn't getting us anywhere."

The woman said, "Jonny is right. I'm leaving tonight. I expect my merchandise to catch up with me on schedule."

"My trucks will be ready tomorrow night."

An arc of a very familiar light cut across the wall on the building opposite him. Patrick shut down his phone and pocketed his equipment.

He knew that light. It was a police searchlight, from the top of a squad car.

At first he thought he'd been busted, but he didn't hear any commotion from inside. He ran around to the corner of the warehouse, keeping low, and looked across the street to where Elle was parked.

She was standing next to her car talking to two cops.

Shit.

The spotlight didn't come across the TK Clothing parking lot, so Patrick ran along the fence and out the gate. He crossed to the other side of the street, then approached opposite of TK. Elle was arguing with the cops.

Never a good thing.

Patrick came up to them. "Hello, Officers, I'm Patrick Kincaid. Is there a problem here?"

They looked at him with suspicion. "Sir, we need to see your identification."

"This is ridiculous!" Elle said. "This is a public street, there's no reason to—"

"Gabrielle," Patrick said, forcing a smile but giving her a stern look. "They are only doing their job." He turned to the senior officer and handed him his wallet. "I'm a private investigator and have a license to carry a firearm. I have a Glock holstered on my belt. My permit is in my wallet as well." It was always best to immediately inform law enforcement when he was carrying.

His wallet also had a card that identified him as a former sergeant with the San Diego Police Department. It meant nothing officially, but when he dealt with locals he found they were much nicer if they knew they were talking to a fellow officer, even one no longer on the job.

The senior officer handed the PI license and ID to his younger partner. "Run him." But when he looked at Patrick, he had relaxed. "Your girlfriend hasn't been as cooperative."

"Because you're harassing me for no reason!" She glared at the cop. "And he's not my boyfriend."

"She won't even tell us her name."

"Gabrielle Santana," Patrick said automatically. "She's an attorney for Feliz, Hochman, and Fellows. We were at the new teen center earlier, and I wanted to see the area, but nature called. I walked over to those trees over there"—he gestured—"then saw you drive up."

"Patrick!" Elle said. "We haven't done anything wrong! They shouldn't be—"

"They're doing their job," he said, and caught her eye. *Keep your mouth shut!*

She took a deep breath and bit her lip.

The other cop returned. "He checks out."

The senior cop handed Patrick his wallet. "Just to let you know, the city and county of San Francisco requires you to report in if you're here carrying concealed. We recognize permits from other counties and states, but only if you report in."

"I'm sorry. I'm only here for a couple days, and not on an official job. I stopped by to visit Elle on my way to my folks' house in San Diego."

"Must be much warmer down there."

"It was seventy-eight today."

The senior cop sighed with longing. "I'm retiring to Arizona. Not sure where yet, my wife and I are going down to visit this spring."

"There's some nice areas. Scottsdale, of course, but also some of the communities in the hills. I worked a case down there, a threat assessment for one of the colleges that had a foreign dignitary coming in to speak."

Patrick removed one of his cards and handed it to the cop. "If you need to contact me, here's my card."

"Thanks. Sorry to bother you, but there's been a lot of break-ins down here. We're trying to lock it down."

"I understand. No apologies."

Patrick noticed that one of the cars at TK was leaving. He didn't want Elle to be seen by Lee. "Thank you," he said, and got into the passenger seat, as a signal for Elle to start driving.

Elle hesitated, as if she wanted to say something, but she wisely bit her tongue and said, "Thank you, Officers," through clenched teeth. She then got in her Honda and drove away.

When Christopher Lee saw the cops on the street and a car driving away, he first thought it was a traffic stop.

But with this deal so close to completion, and all the problems he'd faced in the last two days, he couldn't risk it. He told his bodyguard to pull over and Christopher rolled down his window. "Officers? I'm Christopher Lee, I own TK Clothing." He gestured.

"Of course, Mr. Lee. I recognize you. I'm Sergeant Dunn."

"Sergeant, has there been any trouble here?"

"No, sir."

"I just saw a car drive off."

"It wasn't an incident. Locals, who just made a quick stop. We're being extra cautious because of the recent thefts in the area."

"I appreciate that."

"You're working late."

"End-of-the-year inventory," he said with a tired smile.

"We'll be patrolling the area regularly, sir."

"Thank you. I appreciate your diligence, and the department's." Lee rolled up his window. He called his contact in the San Francisco Police Department. "A Sergeant Dunn ran the plates on a car within the last thirty minutes. I need to know who it belonged to, and anything else about the traffic stop."

He ordered his bodyguard to drive. He had planned to go to his other warehouse, but now he was worried that someone might follow him.

Instead, he called his partner to go over and check on the girls.

Five minutes later, his contact in the police department called him back.

"The car belongs to Gabrielle Santana."

He knew it. That woman had gone too far.

"Anything else?"

"Dunn's unit also ran the identification for Patrick James Kincaid, a licensed private investigator from Washington, D.C. He also holds a California PI license."

"I need everything you can get on Kincaid."

"I'll try."

"Just do it." He hung up. "Our friend was wrong. It

wasn't a cop Ms. Santana brought to snoop around, it's a private investigator."

"That's good, boss, right?"

"That's worse. Who's paying him? Why's he here? We need answers. If he's investigating me, I'll have the answers beaten out of him before I kill him."

No one snooped around Christopher's business. The ones who did paid the highest price.

CHAPTER 7

Kami had fucked up many things in her life, but now, for the first time, she really thought that she might die.

Elle had told her that if she wanted a real life bad enough, and worked hard enough, that she could have it. That Elle would always be there to help her, no matter what. And Elle had done everything she'd promised, and more.

So the big lie Kami told her—that she actually had evidence of Christopher Lee's association with Lorenzo—made Kami feel especially guilty. Elle had never lied to her. She'd told her life was hard, but Kami was a survivor. Kami wanted to be a survivor. She wanted a life. She wanted to show Elle that the faith she had in her was warranted.

And she wanted to punish Christopher Lee for killing her only other true friend, Doreen Day.

The only reason she'd carried drugs for Lorenzo was to convince him that she wanted into his operation as a full member. She'd been running drugs for him for months, but never told Elle. Elle wouldn't have approved, and might not have helped her if she got caught. Like she finally had been. She'd been so close! Lorenzo trusted her, and then . . . well, it was her own fault she'd gotten caught before she had the evidence against Lee that she needed.

She'd known for over a month that Lorenzo was turning street kids over to Lee to sell. Sell, like they were drugs. He picked kids that no one would miss, usually runaways who weren't from the city, who were new in town, picking mostly white and Asian girls because, as he said, "Men paid more for them, the younger the better."

She hadn't let on that she was interested in any of that. She focused on the money Lorenzo paid her. That she was from the city, that she had friends and people knew her, helped. She thought she would be safe.

She waited until Lee's goons left for some meeting, and went to the warehouse where he did his real business. Elle had been angry that the DEA hadn't found anything at TK Clothing last year when she tipped them to Lee's operation. But now Kami knew why—he had another building, not under his name but some business that no one knew he had. She didn't understand how it all worked, but she'd been following him so long, she knew this was the place.

She knew it because he'd taken girls from the warehouse to his penthouse apartment. Kept them overnight. Returned them the next day, barely able to walk. And Kami never saw them again.

She should have gone to Elle sooner, but she didn't have proof. She only had her eyes, and who would believe her? She had a record, she was a known thief. Only Elle believed in her.

And then you lied to Elle. Lied to the district attorney. You have nothing to show for all your work.

Now, she would get proof. She had her camera. She knew that the guards had left. Two had gone with Lee, the other two had taken one of the girls to another room.

She couldn't think about what they were doing with her, only that she could stop them when she had the pictures.

The warehouse was near both a port and a side road that went directly to the highway. Private, secluded. The businesses were all industrial, but most were shut down and boarded up.

Kami was dressed all in black, her dark blond hair hidden under a Giants baseball cap she'd taken from Elle's closest. Elle knew nothing about sports, except baseball, and she'd taken Kami and some of the other girls to the games when she got tickets from her ex-husband or her boss. Kami needed to return the cap, because it was Elle's favorite.

Because if she could return it, it meant she wasn't going to die.

Death scared Kami. She'd seen kids die on the streets. Of exposure. Of drugs. Once, a guy bled to death in front of her and she didn't know what to do. That night, after six months of being on her own, she'd gone back to her dad's house and begged him to let her stay. He said if she could pay rent, she could stay. She stole enough money each week to pay him, but after two months she found out her dad and his girlfriend were using the money she stole to buy drugs and hire hookers. She was sick and disgusted and didn't understand why her mother had to die so young and leave her with that bastard.

She never went back.

She managed on the streets just fine until two guys, crashing off drugs, attacked her. Richie stepped in and saved her from being beaten and raped. He wasn't all bad, but he wasn't good, either. She and Richie had an okay relationship, she guessed, until she found out some of the truly sick shit he was doing with Christopher Lee. How could he save her but sell other girls?

She swallowed heavily as she slipped in through the

main entrance. When the two goons left, they didn't reset the alarm. They never did, when they were planning on returning. She didn't know how much time she had, but she didn't need a lot.

All she needed was a picture.

She didn't know exactly where the girls Lee took from the streets were being held in the building, but she'd followed Lorenzo when he made the last delivery. A girl he'd snatched right off the bus. Obviously a runaway. Kami had met her at Lorenzo's apartment, briefly. She knew her name was Ashley, that she was from Colorado. Ashley had told Lorenzo she'd left home because her mother was a bitch, but when Kami talked to her alone, she didn't think that was true. Kami thought there was much more to the story than a bad mom, but Ashley looked so sad and lost and defiant . . . she looked the way Kami felt.

Then Kami overheard Lorenzo telling his goon squad that blondes went for twice the regular price.

Kami had mixed feelings about turning on Richie. He'd protected her more times than she could count. He'd given her a place to live, a bed to stay, and he didn't try to get into her pants. She knew it was because he was gay, though he didn't advertise it. She really thought that the only bad thing he did was sell drugs, and she didn't think drugs were all that bad . . . she didn't do them, but hell, if rich prep school kids wanted to buy an eight ball, why the hell not make some money off them? It wasn't like anyone was forcing them to snort their allowance or pop pills.

But Richie had a mean streak, and he didn't like girls. Really didn't like them. Kami was the exception, she knew, because she was from his old neighborhood. But Richie didn't care whether he handed over girls to Lee to be sold to rich men in foreign countries as if they weren't human.

Deep breath. *You can do this.*

She slipped inside the warehouse and listened.

The two men left behind were making noise in the office. A girl was crying. Kami blocked out the sound. She had to. She walked slowly through the wide-open, dimly lit warehouse. There were truck bays here, but not much else. It used to be a meat-packing plant, but that was long before she was even born.

She didn't know exactly what time it was, but it was well after midnight. Last night at this time she and Elle had stayed up eating popcorn and drinking Diet Coke while watching Elle's favorite movies, romantic comedies. Kami had never heard Elle laugh so much, and that made Kami feel even more guilty because she'd already been planning on skipping out.

She listened and could hear quiet sobbing coming from someplace below. She hadn't known that this building had a basement. She found the stairs. A rusted sign on the wall identifed the space as COLD STORAGE.

Kami walked quickly and quietly down the stairs.

She wasn't prepared for what she saw.

On both sides of a long narrow walkway were jail cells. At least, that was her first impression. Locked bars. More than a hundred girls, between the ages of twelve and twenty, filled the space. If they all wanted to lie down, they couldn't. Many huddled in corners, wrapped together for warmth. There were thin blankets that barely covered thin women wearing thin dresses. Most were Asian, but about a dozen were white, all blondes.

And Ashley.

Ashley saw her at the same time Kami recognized the Colorado runaway. Her eyes were hollow, as if she hadn't processed what had happened to her. Or maybe she had, and she'd shut down.

Kami went over to her. "I'll get you out of here." She took pictures of the women, trapped and dirty. She walked down to the end and saw that there was a shower room, and a storage room filled with new, clean dresses. She had no idea what this was.

"Kami."

The plea was small, quiet.

She turned and saw that Ashley had walked from one end of the cell to the other, to where Kami stood staring, unbelieving.

"I'll get you out," she whispered.

"Help me. Help us."

"I will."

She ran back the way she'd come, away from hands and arms reaching for her. Their voices rose, speaking in a language she didn't know, she didn't understand.

"Shh! Shh!" she begged them. If Lee's people found her down here . . . She couldn't think. She ran and their voices grew.

She ran up the stairs, past the rusted sign, heard a commotion in the room where Lee's men were raping a girl, to the door. Outside. Into the fog. Free.

"Kami."

She stopped and stared at the man in front of her. He had a gun.

Her blood ran cold.

He smiled, but it was as evil as Christopher Lee himself. "I had a feeling you'd be here."

CHAPTER 8

By the time they arrived back at Elle's apartment, they were both tired and on edge. Elle had been ignoring calls from Sandy Chin and Patrick knew the situation was bad—if the child welfare chick pushed it, Kami would the subject of a bench warrant and Elle would be in trouble with the bar. He hoped that, since it was the wee hours of Sunday morning, they could find a way to smooth things over if they found Kami soon and child welfare could see that she was safe and sound.

Patrick himself was torn about what to do. He understood Elle's concern about a possible bad cop. He'd faced a few of them in his former career. His brother Connor was forced off the force when he testified against his corrupt partner. No one in uniform wanted to admit some in law enforcement were on the payroll of organized crime and drug lords. It was a constant battle, but Patrick also knew more cops were ethical than immoral.

Yet all it took was one bad cop in the right place and people died.

Patrick didn't feel confident about the entire situation. If he were from San Francisco, if he knew the cops and the players, he would know who to go to. But he was operating blind; he didn't have a contact and he wanted desperately to protect Elle—and find Kami.

While Elle listened to the recording Patrick had made at Lee's business, Patrick scrambled up some eggs and cheese—about the only thing edible she had in her apartment. They ate and listened, then Elle listened a second time.

"There's nothing here that says they're selling people. Merchandise can be anything, including drugs."

"You're right."

"But this is good—this proves they're doing something illegal."

"This proves nothing except that Lee and this woman are involved in a business arrangement. Everything they said could be construed as completely legitimate."

"And they were meeting after midnight? Right."

"A business meeting after hours isn't a crime, Elle," Patrick said. "What I'm more concerned with is the fact that they know what you're doing. You've become a liability to them."

She dismissed his comment. "He said I was an annoyance, not a problem."

"They thought I was a cop."

"Everyone thinks you're a cop."

"No, only Clark Grayson."

"Don't even go there."

"He assumed I was a cop, and I didn't correct him."

"All the kids at the center who saw you—Lorenzo's thugs—they—"

"No. I told them specifically that I wasn't."

"Maybe they didn't believe you."

"Elle," he said, forcing his rising temper to stay buried.

"Why are you so willing to think I'm an idiot?"

"I don't—"

"Kami is missing and all you can think about is that my

good friend Clark is involved? He's done nothing to make me think he's a criminal, and he's done a lot of good with these kids."

"Do you know how human trafficking works?"

"Don't talk to me like I'm stupid."

"Elle, you keep saying that, and I haven't been. I've given you the lead on this. I've helped against my better judgment. But Grayson is in the perfect position to help Lee find the right girls."

"Don't. Maybe—maybe—I can see Clark turning his back on Lorenzo's drug network. Not being involved, but not stopping it. But kidnapping young women? No. There's no reason. No."

Elle was getting agitated and even more upset, and that was something Patrick did not want, but maybe that's what it was going to take to convince her that *maybe* her friend was involved. If not directly involved, quietly complicit.

"Maybe Grayson got in over his head—"

"No."

Patrick tried another angle. "Human traffickers pick on girls who have no support system. Girls who have run away, are probably not even from the area, or if they are they have no adult who is looking for them. They want girls off the bus, so to speak, so that if they disappear no one is going to miss them. They drug them, imprison them, break them until they don't fight anymore, then ship them out. Most go out of the country, but there are plenty of perverts in the U.S. who will pay for their own sex slave."

Elle didn't want to believe Patrick. She didn't want to listen to him, especially about Clark. She and Clark had been friends since college. She saw him all the time. They went to the movies together, had coffee on the weekends; he'd always come when she needed help with a kid. He had infinite patience with homework, and she'd seen him dole out tough love to some of the rough teens who didn't believe anyone cared. He'd helped more kids than she could count get their GEDs; if there was a chance they could make it in college, he helped them with the applications and paperwork. He pulled money from his own pocket for admissions fees and books.

People like that—generous with their time and money—didn't abuse the same kids they were trying to help.

"You are wrong about Clark," she whispered.

"All right."

She was surprised Patrick didn't continue to argue. "Okay," she said.

She turned and faced the wall, not wanting to look at Patrick, not able to think about what might be happening to Kami right now. The compassion on Patrick's face, so different from the hard edges when he confronted Ringo and the others. It was like there were two men in Patrick: the hard, angry cop and the kind, funny kid she'd known who'd dated her sister and played baseball.

But Patrick was right about one thing. People were cruel. She had seen what adults did to kids, what kids did to each other, and it tore her up inside. Parents and guardians who abused their kids, who hurt them emotionally and physically, who killed them, who didn't care what happened to them, kicked them out on the street, made them suffer because their own lives weren't what they'd planned.

"Elle," Patrick said softly. "You care too much."

"No one can care too much."

"It's tearing you up inside."

"And you don't care about these kids?" She turned to face him, searching his face for a connection, for understanding.

"I do," he said. "Maybe it's because I was a cop for so long, but I have a separate place for the pain. I get just as angry as you. My sister—Lucy—was brutally gang-raped on her high school graduation day, and I nearly died searching for the man who was responsible for setting it up."

Elle had known Lucy had been attacked and that Patrick had been in a coma, but she hadn't known any of the details, and it was so long ago and she'd already left San Diego by that time, she'd been in law school, worried about her own life and future. She hadn't thought much about it, other than it was horrible.

She may have been wrong about Patrick. Maybe he did understand.

Patrick continued. "The pain I felt then is just as powerful now, and it forever changed me. But I have to keep it locked up or it would be unbearable. There was a time I couldn't look at my sister without seeing what she had suffered. But I couldn't continue to do that, for my own sanity and her own healing. Pain is black as revenge. It's powerful and constantly trying to eat you up from the inside. If you don't contain it, it will destroy you. Pain, guilt, anger . . . they feed on each other until they consume you. You need to care, but don't turn it into darkness. Don't turn it against what makes you so amazing."

He stepped closer to her, and Elle didn't think. She reached out and pulled Patrick to her, so hard her back hit the wall. She held his head to hers, kissed him hard, passion ripping through her body so that even if she wanted to stop, she wouldn't. Elle was a physical person. She touched. She craved contact. She wanted Patrick and wanted him to want her, at least for tonight.

The kiss was everything she'd always thought it would be. Her teenage crush exploded into grown-up lust. She could lose herself with Patrick, and she wanted to be lost right now. She was overwhelmed, but his body cured her pain and fear, at least at this moment. And that was enough for her.

Patrick was shocked when the deep desire for Elle hit him all at once, and then he was kissing her back, hard against the wall, his hands on her face, as he recognized that their mutual attraction was mutual lust.

He pulled back, but Elle held tight.

"Don't go," she said. "I've had a crush on you since I was fourteen. I never thought—" She kissed him again, hard. Then she pulled back, her eyes melted chocolate, her face flushed, her chest rising and falling as her breathing sped up. She was the sexiest woman he'd ever seen.

"Elle—"

"I never thought it would be as good as my fantasy, but if that kiss is any indication, sex with you will be better than anything I've imagined."

He shouldn't be doing this, not here, not when Elle was emotionally on edge. Her dark eyes drew him in, the energy that vibrated in her body breathed a love for living, a passion for life that he hadn't seen in a long, long time. He wanted her.

"You had a crush on me?" he asked, trying to lighten the mood because he was quickly reaching the point of no return.

"Had, have, will have." She leaned forward but her lips didn't touch his. She whispered. "I want you. Do you want me?"

Yes.

Patrick grabbed her wrists and held them on either side of her head, pinned against the wall, while his mouth devoured hers. Though he had her hands restrained, her body didn't stop moving against him, stirring him up. He kissed her neck, the back of her ear, used his teeth to pull back her shirt so he could taste her shoulder.

His teeth skimmed her breasts through the thin T-shirt she wore and her breath hitched as she said his name.

"Don't. Stop."

He pulled back and smiled down at her. "You want me to stop?"

"No."

"No, you don't want me to do this?" He kissed her. She grabbed at him, but he pulled back. "Or this?" He put his hands up her shirt, underneath her bra, and held her breasts. Teasing her was driving him as crazy as it was her.

She didn't answer him, but curled her fingers around the top of his pants and pulled him close. Her hands went down his pants, rubbing his penis until all thought of teasing and game-playing went out the window. He groaned and pulled off her T-shirt, tossing it behind him, putting his hand down the front of her jeans. "Two can play that game," he whispered in her ear as he slipped his fingers inside her panties and found her sweet spot.

Elle's knees buckled as Patrick rubbed her, and there was no more waiting. She'd screw him up against this wall if she had to. She pulled at his shirt and he used his free hand to help her pull it over his head. She unclasped her bra and pressed her breasts against his hot chest. She was about to take off her pants when he pulled his hand out and picked her up.

"You can't carry me," she said.

"Watch me."

Patrick had muscles that she hadn't seen under his conservative clothes. Muscles sharp and well defined and perfectly capable of carrying her. He took her up the stairs with an ease that surprised and thrilled her.

He dropped her to her bed and she grinned. "Well, Pat-
, it's all or nothing." She reached into her nightstand

and pulled out a condom, mentally thanking herself that she had them. She tossed it at him.

He caught it and dropped his pants. "All," he said.

Elle was happily lost for the rest of the night.

CHAPTER 9

The door buzzed and woke Patrick up before Elle. He blinked, but it didn't take him long to remember he was in Elle's apartment—in her bed—and Elle was sprawled naked next to him. She sighed as the buzzing continued, stretched, but didn't wake up.

Patrick grabbed his gun but he, too, was naked. He found his pants in a corner and slipped them on, sans boxers that he didn't take the time to locate. It was nearly seven in the morning, but the last time he looked at Elle's bedside clock, it had been four.

He went downstairs and peered through the security peephole. White male, mid-thirties. Looked like he'd just gotten out of bed. Patrick pressed the speaker. "Who is it?"

There was a pause. "Dwight Bishop."

Dwight. Elle's ex-husband.

Patrick opened the door. Immediately, Dwight took in Patrick—both that he was shirtless and that he was carrying a gun.

Patrick assessed the guy. He didn't look like a threat—in fact, he looked like he was worried and hadn't slept all night.

"I need to talk to Elle," he said.

Patrick motioned for Dwight to go to the living room in front of him.

Elle was at the top of the stairs in a long shirt and nothing else. Her dark hair was messy from sleep and she was just as gorgeous as she'd been the night before. She caught Patrick's eye and smiled, just enough to have Patrick remembering every moment of last night. And wanting to repeat it.

Patrick was going to have to put Elle and sex out of his head. It had been a bad idea to go to bed with her, but he didn't regret it. How could he? It was like she'd given him a much-needed jolt to feel again, to enjoy a physical connection. Sex had become rote, a function of dating; he hadn't felt connected to any of his girlfriends ever since he recovered from his coma.

Sex with Elle was anything but ordinary.

Elle turned her gaze to her ex, and Patrick slowly released a breath he hadn't realized he was holding.

She said, "Dwight, what are you doing here?"

"Freaking out. I heard you were lurking outside Christopher Lee's garment factory. What the hell? That restraining order means something."

"What?" Patrick said.

Dwight looked at him. "Who are you?"

Patrick put his gun on the kitchen counter and extended his hand. "Patrick Kincaid."

"Kincaid—Kincaid—why is that name familiar?"

Elle said, "My mom's best friend is Patrick's mom. We were neighbors half my childhood." She walked into the kitchen and started making coffee.

"Elle, what restraining order?" Patrick asked. Jaye hadn't told Patrick she'd found anything on Elle, and he'd asked. She had a sealed juvenile record from San Diego, but Patrick suspected that was about the rave she'd organized when she was seventeen.

"There's no restraining order." She glared at Dwight.

Dwight said, "No, but there is an agreement that you stay away from Lee."

"Back up," Patrick said. "Is this a legal agreement?"

"Private. Maddie Starr, Elle's boss, arranged it with Lee that Elle would stay away from Lee's businesses, other than the teen center."

"Why?"

"Because Elle doesn't know how to keep her mouth shut!"

Elle slammed a coffee mug on the counter. "He's not who everyone thinks he is!"

"But there's no proof, and he's going to destroy you and your career. He knows you were there. He came out of TK after you left, and asked about why the police were there."

"And they told him?"

"You were trespassing."

"No, Patrick was trespassing. I was waiting next to the car. And Patrick thinks Lee's not only running drugs, but people."

Dwight looked like he'd been slapped. He stood there stunned, unable to speak.

Patrick winced. He wished Elle hadn't said anything. Dwight was a prosecutor. "It's better if you don't know," he said.

Dwight ignored Patrick and said to Elle, "You've been trying to get proof on Lee for running drugs and have nothing. Now you're saying he's smuggling people?" He shook his head.

"Kami is missing."

"The girl you got out of juvie on Friday?"

"Yes. She disappeared yesterday afternoon, and Patrick and I tracked her down to TK but lost her trail there. Lorenzo's people are looking for her, and that means Lee is looking for her. She's hiding, and they'll kill her if they know she has evidence on Lee."

"Why didn't you tell me?"

"Because your office negotiated this arrangement, and you'd have to tell them she ran from me!"

"Elle, maybe because she's one of them."

"She isn't."

"You're going to get your heart broken, as well as your license to practice law pulled by the Bar. You've always been on the edge, but I think you've really gone over now."

"At least I'm willing to take risks to help people!"

"That's not fair, Gabrielle," Dwight said.

Patrick had to step up. This was getting them nowhere. "Maybe you should leave," he said.

"Just because you're sleeping with my ex-wife doesn't mean I'm the one who should leave, buddy. Is this your idea? Putting Elle at risk? Waving a gun around like you're some sort of macho soldier?"

"Like I would let anyone tell me what to do," Elle snapped.

"Knock it off, both of you," Patrick said. "This isn't helping. Kami is in trouble, and if you can't help us, Dwight, then you need to leave."

Dwight stared at him. "Which Kincaid are you? The mercenary? The doctor?"

Patrick was surprised that Elle had even talked about the Kincaid family with Dwight, since she'd already moved to San Francisco before she met and married him.

"I'm the former cop, current PI. I'm not here officially." Though, Patrick thought, that might change if RCK decided that they had a better shot than law enforcement at taking down this human trafficking ring. "I'm here because I heard Elle needed help, and I was in the area."

"Made yourself right at home, too," Dwight said.

"Oh, shit, Dwight, we've been divorced for five years."

Elle and Dwight exchanged a look and Patrick wasn't quite sure what to make of it. Then, suddenly, Dwight said, "I'll take off my prosecutor hat for five minutes. Tell me what you have."

Patrick didn't know if they could trust Dwight. It wasn't that he was part of any conspiracy, but he was an officer of the court, and legal people took that oath seriously. His former brother-in-law was the district attorney of San Diego, and he was Mr. Law and Order if there ever was one. He'd never go off book for any operation, even for five minutes. There were police investigations where he might take a judicious water cooler break just so he wouldn't know about certain details, but beyond that, he wouldn't have risked his career—or a conviction.

Dwight seemed sincere and worried about Elle. And he was clearly still in love with her. Patrick had walked into the middle of something.

Elle looked at Patrick and said, "It's up to you."

"I'm not the one risking my career."

"I trust him," Elle said.

"You also trust Clark Grayson."

Her face reddened and she said, "I told you Clark is fine. Do what you want. I'm taking a shower."

She went upstairs.

Dwight stared at Patrick. "Wow. I didn't see that coming."

"What?" Patrick snapped. He ran a hand over his face and helped himself to coffee. It was strong, which he needed. He hadn't wanted to piss off Elle, but she had to see the truth before she was hurt by it.

"I never liked Clark," Dwight said. "But he and Elle have been friends since college, before I even met her, and he was always off-limits."

"She's going to be devastated when she finds out he's

one of the bad guys." Patrick wished he wasn't going to be the one to prove it to her, because she would hate him for it. But what was he even thinking about? If she hated him, that was life. He lived in D.C., she lived in San Francisco, and last night notwithstanding, they didn't have a future.

For some reason, that realization made him angry. He'd never been an angry person, even after his nephew had been killed when Patrick was in college. It was the attack on Lucy—watching it online, unable to stop it—that had affected him in ways he hadn't been able to process at the time. Only a day later, he'd nearly died in an explosion, and then after brain surgery, he'd spent nearly two years in a coma. He'd woken up with the pain and rage of what had happened to his sister, not knowing if she was dead or alive, while the world had continued to function without him. While Lucy had healed, he had not.

What happened seven years ago couldn't have helped but change him. He'd always been the most easygoing of the Kincaids. Even-tempered like his brother Dillon, but more of a joker. He used to love to play pranks on his siblings, but he hadn't done anything, not even an April Fool's gag, since he woke up in the hospital racked with guilt and anger he didn't understand.

Patrick compartmentalized his anger and asked Dwight, "What do you know about Grayson?"

"I think he's a phony."

"But what do you know about him?"

Dwight frowned. "Nothing. It's just a feeling. Elle always told me I was jealous because she and Clark used to go out, but that wasn't it." He glanced at Patrick. "If I were the jealous type, I'd be more jealous of you."

"You divorced her."

"Because we can't live together. We drive each other crazy." He glanced toward the stairs.

"But you love her."

"What's not to love? She's beautiful, with a heart as big as the bay. She'd give you the shirt off her back. She's loyal, and she's smart. But—"

"But?"

"She lacks common sense. I swear I wanted to throttle her when she'd walk right into dangerous neighborhoods. She knows self-defense and all, but still—she thinks she's made of Teflon and bullets and knives will just avoid her. Did she tell you she was stabbed last year?"

She hadn't said anything, but Patrick had found the scar on her stomach, right next to one of her tattoos. She'd dismissed it, made a joke about a psychotic tattoo artist, but Patrick knew a knife wound when he saw one.

"Outside the BART station," Dwight continued, "when she was coming back late from helping one of her clients. A guy jumped out and demanded her purse. She gave it to him and still he stabbed her. Would have killed her if she hadn't been smart enough to kick him in the balls and run. Then surgery and stitches, and three days later she's back at work."

"Did they find the guy?"

"No." Dwight poured himself some coffee and dumped a liberal amount of milk in it. "Elle always makes it too strong." He turned and faced Patrick. "Okay, five minutes, starting now."

"I work for Rogan-Caruso-Kincaid Protective Services, a private security company that has its fingers in a lot of areas. It's not my specialty, but RCK initially began as a hostage-rescue company working with for-hire soldiers to rescue Americans and others from captivity in countries south of the border. One of the offshoots of that was human trafficking. There were villages decimated by rebels and drug lords where all the adults were killed, the girls sold as sex slaves, and the boys forced to go to war. So

RCK keeps their fingers in the business, providing federal law enforcement with information we obtain through our work. And, often, we work with or for the government to stop it. But human trafficking, it's a multibillion-dollar industry—plug one hole and ten more pop open."

"I've heard it's only getting worse."

Patrick nodded. "RCK has extensive information, and our database spit out one of Christopher Lee's companies, Chi Sun Shipping in Stockton, as a cover for human trafficking. Elle thinks Lee is involved only with Lorenzo's drug operation, but I overhead a conversation last night that made me think they were talking about people, not drugs. That, coupled with his shipping company, makes me think his criminal enterprise is far bigger than supplying drugs to a local distributor. I made a recording of the conversation—it wasn't explicit, but something is going down tonight."

"I can't listen. It's not legal."

"It might be. I sent it to my office because part of the conversation is in Chinese. They'll translate it. And I took a picture of the people, hoping to get IDs, but the photo is low quality and taken from a distance."

"And where does Kami fit in?"

"My guess? I think she left here because either she thought she was in danger or she'd put Elle in danger, or she didn't have any physical proof against Lee like she told Elle. But now . . . I think she definitely has something that Lee wants, or he thinks she has something. It might just be information, but if it's the information about his shipments, he wouldn't want her talking. Everyone is looking for her—Lee, Lorenzo, and us. Elle refused to let me call the police last night because of the deal she made with your office about Kami's testimony—I was a bit unclear on the details, but there's also a social worker breathing down her neck."

Dwight swore under his breath.

Patrick continued. "I met Grayson last night. He's the only one who thought I was a cop, and I let him believe it. When I talked to some of the kids at the center, I specifically told them I was a private investigator. Yet when Lorenzo's people came in and tried to harass Elle, they said they'd heard about the cop from out of town. That had to have come from Grayson. Elle doesn't believe it—she says I look like a cop, so any of the kids I spoke to could have assumed it."

"But you don't think so."

"He's manipulative. He was trying to get information out of her, but I'll admit he's good. Very subtle. I know he has a sealed record."

"When I brought that up with Elle years ago, she had a fit. How can young people who make mistakes ever be able to get beyond their pasts, yada yada. Elle had her own record as a youth." Dwight glanced at Patrick. "You probably know that."

"Yes. But disturbing the peace and organizing a rave is a far cry from drug dealing or assault."

"Is that what Grayson did?"

"I don't know. It's sealed. Elle knows?"

He nodded. "And she doesn't care."

Patrick assessed the situation. "Okay, I'll make sure she keeps Clark at arm's length. But this is what I need from you—how close are you with law enforcement?"

"Good."

"Something is going down tonight, but according to Elle, Lee has elected officials on the payroll, and she implied some bad cops as well."

"If Lee's guilty, he would. He has the resources. I just—why would he? He has successful businesses all over town, owns several multimillion-dollar properties, why would he need to do this?"

"I have people at RCK looking into his finances, but it's going to take time to pull together." Legally. "But human trafficking is about money and power. Where did he get his money in the first place? How did he amass so much wealth? Is he using his businesses to launder money? RCK dealt with a case a few years ago, before my time, where the FBI shut down a major human trafficking network in Sacramento by tracking their financial crimes."

"Like Al Capone."

"Exactly." Maybe Dwight did understand. "If I need help, from good cops, can you get the message to the right people?"

"Yes. I know who to call."

"Thank you."

"Why not bring them in now?"

"Because if Lee's moving a shipment—of drugs or people—tonight, and they have someone inside, it'll tip them off. We're also trying to get ICE involved, but they have no active investigation into Lee. That means I need something more to give them. Like this." Patrick showed Dwight the fuzzy picture of the people who'd been meeting with Lee last night. "The woman was clearly in charge," Patrick said.

"I have no idea who she is. Can they even get anything from the photo?"

"RCK is working on enhancing it, and we have a contact at ICE. If any of these people are involved in human trafficking, we'll know soon enough." It was nearly eight. Dwight had been here almost an hour.

Elle came downstairs. Her hair was wet and she was dressed in jeans and a T-shirt. She looked ten years younger than her age. Dwight walked over to her and hugged her tightly. "Listen to Patrick, okay? I don't want you hurt. I'll let you know if I hear anything about Kami."

"Thanks," Elle said, a quizzical expression on her face. She walked Dwight out, then turned around and questioned Patrick. "What was that about?"

"It was about our concern over tonight. We have a lot to do today."

"Like find Kami."

"Like figure out what's happening tonight."

"You promised."

"Yes, we're going to look for Kami. But we have preliminary work to do. I need information about the people Lee was meeting with, and I'm waiting for a call back from my contact in ICE. Just give it a couple hours."

"I can go out now, you can meet me later—"

"No. You heard the recording—Lee sees you as a threat. You're not safe."

"He's not going to hurt me. But what about Kami?"

Patrick stepped closer to Elle. He didn't know if these protective instincts were from training, or because of something more . . . but he dismissed the emotion. Emotion was dangerous in an operation like this; he needed to focus on protecting Elle and finding Kami. "Trust me, Elle. I know people like Christopher Lee. He will kill you if you interfere."

She nodded slowly, and Patrick relaxed. He kissed her. It was spontaneous, but felt right. She wrapped her arms around his neck and held him tight. "Thank you," she whispered.

He didn't want to let her go. He'd been craving emotions again, emotions other than the anger and pain that had driven him for the last five years. With Elle, he'd found the part of himself that had been buried since Lucy's attack. He finally remembered who he'd been before his coma, before his life had been irrevocably changed.

She tilted her head back and frowned. "Are you okay?"

He nodded. He wanted to say something more, something about them, but for now, he was going to have to be satisfied with feeling again. The rush of complex emotions was dizzying.

"I'm going to take a quick shower," he said. He smiled. "I'd ask you to join me, but you'd be a distraction." He glanced at his watch. "I'm hoping Dean will call before nine, and then we can make a plan."

"Dean?"

"Dean Hooper. He's the assistant special agent in charge of Sacramento FBI, and a good friend of RCK. He also used to run one of the white-collar-crimes divisions in Washington—if anyone can follow a money trail, it's Dean." At least legally.

"Okay. I'll make some breakfast."

"You don't have to," he said.

"I want to. You earned it." She smiled and kissed him. "Towels are in the closet behind the bathroom door. And if you really miss me, just call."

Elle waited until Patrick was in the shower, then she hastily wrote out a note. She didn't try to explain. Either Patrick understood that she had to find Kami, or he didn't.

She'd let Doreen down last year, she couldn't let Kami down. While she trusted Patrick, she couldn't just sit around and wait. She had to get them herself. Once she found Kami, she'd do anything Patrick wanted. Once she knew Kami was safe, she'd be able to breathe again.

While the shower was running, she called Clark. "Can you meet me at the coffee shop around the corner from Granny's Kitchen?"

"Of course—what's wrong?"

"I need your help to find Kami. You'll help me, right?"

"Of course I will. What happened to your friend from San Diego?"

"He's doing something else," she said, and glanced up

the stairs. Maybe she shouldn't do this. Maybe Patrick was right.

He was right about a lot of things, but not Clark. She'd dated Clark for over a year. They'd been best friends forever. Guys like Clark didn't sell people. She would have seen it.

But she would definitely keep her eyes open. She added a PS to her note as she said to Clark, "Twenty minutes."

"I'll be there."

She heard the shower turn off as she slid the door closed behind her and left.

CHAPTER 10

Kami woke up, not from the cold, wet concrete, but from the sobs in the cell next to hers. She opened her eyes. Blinked, her head aching. The one bare lightbulb didn't help her see much except a crowd of girls. The stench of urine and vomit penetrated her pores, worse than any night she'd slept on the streets. She'd have preferred a cardboard box next to a Dumpster to this basement full of despair and hopelessness.

"Kami, thank God you're alive." It was Ashley. She was holding her hand, but Kami was so numb she didn't feel it.

"I'm fine."

"He hit you and I thought he'd killed you."

The night before came back to her in a rush. She hadn't forgotten, but she wanted to.

She'd tried to run, but they caught her. Hit her over and over, and she thought she was going to die. Like Doreen. She only vaguely remembered being carried into the warehouse, past the COLD STORAGE sign, into the basement with a hundred young women, locked in this cell, a prisoner. Or an animal. She felt disoriented, unable to understand most of the women around her because they must not speak English. Except Ashley.

"We have to get out of here," she said.

"Impossible," Ashley said. She lifted her shirt and revealed an ugly bruise. "I tried, once, when they were feeding us. It still hurts."

"I'd rather be dead."

"No. Please help me. I don't want to die."

"What's going on over there?" Kami gestured to the crying women in the cell next to hers.

"I'm not sure, but I think someone is hurt."

Kami frowned. She shuffled over to the side, stepping over sleeping women, until she could see into the adjoining cell. A young girl was crying over an older girl who lay on the floor, her eyes open. The younger girl was repeating something that sounded like a name. Something like Flower, but that wasn't exactly right. Flower wasn't moving. Her eyes looked unnatural.

Kami turned her face. She was dead. Kami had seen dead bodies before, and Flower was dead.

Ashley whispered, "Several of the girls are sick."

"What else have you heard?"

"They're going to move us tonight, when it's dark."

Kami frowned, looked around at all the women, the hollow eyes, the defeat.

She didn't want to die, either. "Okay."

A crashing noise upstairs preceded the rumbling of footfalls on the metal stairs. Three men entered, all thugs Kami recognized from Lorenzo's gang. Ringo approached her cell and sneered. "You should have stayed out of business that doesn't concern you."

She spat in his face.

Ringo reached in and grabbed her by the neck, slammed her face against the bars. She grabbed the bars, trying to pull free. She couldn't breathe.

Another guy hit Ringo on the back of the head. "Knock it off."

Ringo dropped her, and she fell to her knees.

Ringo said, "Clean them all up and make them ready. Open the cells, one at a time, order them to line up for showers and clothes. We don't have a lot of time."

Ringo turned back to Kami. He said, "You do what you're told or you're dead. You'll get no other warning."

All three men had guns. They started with the cell closest to the showers. Kami watched as the girls were walked through, ordered to strip, and sprayed with soap and water. There was no steam, no warmth coming from the open shower room, and the girls came out cold and shaking. There were a couple of towels, but after the first few dried off, the towels were too wet to be effective. They were each handed a shapeless dress and no underwear. After they dressed, right ankles were tied together as they lined up down the hall. The girls shuffled back into their filthy cells. It took thirty minutes, and then they opened the next.

"Shit, Ringo, I think this one's dead."

"Flower," the younger girl wailed.

"Well, fuck me," Ringo said. "I'll take care of it. Start the next cell. Lee's going to inspect them this afternoon, they need to be ready for the trucks. We're moving up the schedule, no fucking around this time."

Kami's cell was opened. The girls lined up, quiet, resigned to their fate.

Kami couldn't let herself get tied up. But the third guy with the gun was at the base of the stairs. There could be more upstairs. Maybe this was her only chance.

Ashley grabbed her hand. Looked at Kami, as if Kami had all the answers.

"How old are you?" Kami whispered. "Don't lie this time." She'd told Richie she was sixteen.

"Thirteen," Ashley said. "I just want to go home."

"Shh," Kami said.

The young girl sitting over Flower's body started screaming and kicking, and Ringo hit her so hard her body slammed against the cement wall and collapsed, unmoving.

Some of the other young women started crying and shouting, and Ringo took out his gun and shot two of the girls who were sick in the corner. "Nobody move!" Ringo said. "Tell them, Jonny!"

The man guarding the stairs came down the hall, towering over all of them, shouting in Chinese. The girls cowered and cried.

Kami squeezed Ashley's hand and they both ran up the stairs.

They heard more gunshots in the basement below, and Kami didn't know if the gunfire was directed at them or if Ringo had just lost it and was going to kill them all. Kami hated leaving all those girls, but if she didn't run and try to get help, she'd suffer the same fate.

"Come on," she urged, then noticed that Ashley was in pain. She must have been hurt far worse than either of them had thought.

"We have to keep going," Kami said. No one was guarding the top of the stairs so she ran straight for the door. Ashley's hand slipped from hers. Kami grabbed it again, pulling her along.

She pushed open the door. The bright sunlight nearly blinded her. Where was the fog? The rain? It was cold, but the sky was so clear she wanted to cry.

"I can't see!" Ashley said.

Ashley must have been down in the basement for days—ever since Richie turned her over to Lee. How could Richie have done it? How could he be so cruel that he'd sell runaways to Christopher Lee to be forced to do unspeakable things? Kami knew Richie Lorenzo was a cruel drug dealer but he'd always looked out for her. How could he turn on her like this? Because he had to know that she'd been locked up, too. Right?

"Stay with me," Kami begged Ashley. "Please, just stay close."

Kami made sure she had a good grip on Ashley as she pulled her through the cracked parking lot. Rocks and broken glass cut into her bare feet. She heard shouts behind them and they ran harder. Her vision was clearing up. She knew these streets as well as anyone; she just needed to get to Elle's apartment. She hoped and prayed Elle was there.

Lee's men were going to follow them. They had cars. They also knew this town.

But Kami had one ace in the hole. The money she'd stashed under a rock near the teen center. If they could get there, only half a mile away, they could hop on BART and go anywhere.

Ashley was slowing down. One look at her pale face and Kami knew she wasn't going to make it.

Kami half dragged, half carried her toward an abandoned warehouse down the street from where they'd been held captive. Though it was fenced off, there was a hole in the chain-link fence from scavengers who'd picked the place clean of cans and bottles to earn a few bucks to buy beer and crack. Kami had crossed paths with the mentally disturbed homeless who puttered about, barely surviving.

Kami pulled Ashley through the hole and wished she could find a better, safer place to hide.

Behind the boarded-up warehouse were piles of garbage, broken machines, and boxes. Kami positioned Ashley between the Dumpster and a doorless refrigerator. "Stay here. I'm going to get help. No matter what you do, don't leave."

"Promise? Promise you'll come back?"

"I promise. Just be very, very quiet."

Ashley nodded and lay down. She was not well. What if she had a broken rib or something? Couldn't that be dangerous?

But Kami couldn't sit here and wait for Ringo and the others to find them. She peered around the building and didn't see anyone.

She bolted.

Christopher Lee listened to the report from his men and was proud that he resisted the urge to shoot them all.

"The two girls who should never have been allowed to escape, escaped?" Lee shook his head.

"We found the blonde," Ringo said. "She was hiding behind a Dumpster."

"Where is she now? In the Dumpster, I hope?"

Ringo glanced at Jonny, and Jonny said, "Blondes are worth too much. I drugged her. She won't be waking until she hits the border."

Marginally better.

"And the little bitch who was spying on me? Why didn't you kill her outright?"

"Boss, you said we were short on girls," Ringo said.

"You should have dumped her on that bitch lawyer's doorstep like the last one," Lee said.

Jonny spoke up. "We're on a tight schedule because of all the mistakes with your shipping company, Mr. Lee. Playing games with a two-bit lawyer wastes time."

Lee didn't like Soldare's man. He didn't treat Lee with the respect that he had earned. He was constantly watching, waiting for a screw-up. To report him to Soldare? To cut him off? Neither of them knew how important he was to their operation. One call and he could shut them down and walk away clean.

He said, "You know where that little girl is going, don't you?"

"Yeah, but we may have a solution," Ringo said. "We had a guy watching Santana's apartment. She left thirty minutes ago."

"Did you follow her?"

"Yes, we have eyes on her. If the girl contacts her, we'll get them both."

"You'll kill them both. I'm tired of that lawyer interfering with my business. For years I've worked under the radar, and she comes in like a bull in a china shop." He closed his eyes and forced himself to be calm.

"Where is the private investigator?"

"Still in the apartment, we think."

"Think, or know?"

"He's there," Jonny said.

"I want eyes on Ms. Santana and eyes on her apartment. That little tramp Kami is the only real threat to our operations. She's the only one who knows where this place is. She's the only one who might have evidence against me. Find her then kill her. She may very well go to Santana's apartment first."

"I'll do it," Ringo said.

"No. Jonny, you're in charge now." As much as Lee didn't like Soldare's people, they were effective. "Ringo, you get the rest of my merchandise ready for transport and move them to the backup facility."

"Isn't that risky during the day?"

Lee didn't like his orders questioned.

"Jonny knows what to do," he said quietly.

"Yes, sir," Jonny said. "Find the girl and the lawyer and kill them both."

Effective. And long overdue.

CHAPTER 11

Patrick
I'm really sorry, but I have to go out and look for Kami. She may have gone back to Mia's, or she might be at the center. Forgive me—but I waited too long last time, and they left Doreen dying on my doorstep. I can't wait for them to kill Kami, too.

You have my number. I turned tracking on. I'm sure that's something you can work with, considering.
Elle
P.S. I hope we can repeat last night. XOXO

Patrick wanted to throttle her. She knew she was in danger, and yet she walked out of her apartment without backup, without a bodyguard, without anything but her wits.

And right now, he wasn't thinking too kindly about her wits.

His phone rang and he immediately thought it was Elle. But the caller ID was in Sacramento.

"Patrick? It's Dean Hooper."

"You have something for me?"

"You may have broken an ICE case wide open."

Dean Hooper was one of the top-ranked FBI agents in Sacramento. He specialized in white-collar crimes, particularly money laundering, and his wife, Sonia, was an ICE agent who specialized in human traffickers. Between the two of them, they'd shut down more trafficking pipelines in northern California than any other interagency task force.

"Sounds great. Tell me what I did."

"That woman you photographed is Margret Chin Soldare. Her father was British, her mother Chinese. She was raised in Hong Kong and married a businessman with a penchant for underage girls. She would procure the girls for him, then dispose of them by shipping them overseas. China is still the number one exporter of sex slaves. And Soldare is one of the top sellers.

"No one knew she was in the country. Sonia's team shut down her pipeline on the Sacramento River and severely damaged her network. We translated the Chinese conversation—essentially, she was railing against the problems that destroyed her network and forced her to work with Lee who, apparently, she does not like. She turned over one hundred thirty girls to him last week—girls that were supposed to be on the boat—and he must guarantee that at least one hundred twenty of them make it to the border where she has a buyer."

Dean Hooper certainly sounded excited, but Patrick was lost. "I don't understand. Where did these young women come from? China?"

"I'll backtrack a bit—last month, Sonia learned of a shipment of underage girls from China who'd landed in Vallejo. They were being transferred from the main ship to a smaller ship, using Lee's shipping line, but someone tipped them off and when ICE got there, the girls were gone. From what we've determined, Lee—we didn't know for certain, but after the conversation you recorded we have it confirmed—stored the girls for Soldare. We suspected they were waiting until ICE backed off unscheduled inspections, but because ICE essentially shut down Lee's shipping company, they came up with an alternate plan. Moving them by truck, knowing we're focused on the Sacramento River."

"So these girls from China have been locked up for a month?"

"Yes, we think so." Patrick's stomach turned, but Dean continued. "ICE is mobilizing a team. I need a location."

"The girls aren't in his factory—I didn't see any sign of them. But Elle is out looking for her contact."

"Elle?"

"Gabrielle Santana, a lawyer. Long story, but I think she's in trouble, as well as a young girl named Kami who claimed to have proof of Lee's illegal activities."

"Margret is ruthless. We've already alerted Homeland and she won't be getting out via plane or train, but she has contacts we don't even know about. Look, I'll have the ICE team leader contact you directly. No need to have a middleman. I'm going through Lee's finances; he's good, but I'm better. I'll find out how he's laundering his money and exactly where it is."

"What would help is a list of his businesses—anything he owns, or that one of his shell companies owns."

"I'll pass everything on through Homeland. And you'll be looking for a facility with a truck bay."

"Why?"

"Chi Sun Shipping doesn't operate on water, it's all tractor-trailer rigs. They're putting the girls in trucks, not ships, which means the destination is somewhere in the U.S., though they might have a spot to cross into Mexico through Imperial County."

"That makes me sick."

"Join the club." Dean hung up.

Patrick pulled out his phone and called Elle. She answered on the second ring. "I know what you're going to say."

"Get back here." He set his phone to trace her GPS.

"I'll let you know if I run into trouble."

"You're already in trouble, Elle."

"It's Sunday morning, it's bright and sunny outside. I'm not going to do anything stupid."

"You already have." He winced, then tried to backtrack. "Look, Elle, there are a lot of people working on this. You're safer here." *Where I can keep an eye on you.*

"I'll keep in touch." She hung up.

"Dammit!" He slammed down his phone. He monitored the app that was tracking her GPS. It wasn't a trace program, but since she'd turned on her GPS and made it public, he could follow her.

So could anyone else, for that matter.

He was going to have to catch up with her. She really irritated him. He didn't like operating without a game plan, and now he was being forced to react instead of act.

He checked his gun, holstered it, and then his phone rang again.

"Kincaid."

"It's Jack."

"I might need you—I'm in San Francisco."

"I know all about it. I'm downstairs. Buzz me in."

Patrick went to the door and buzzed the lobby door open. A minute later Jack was at Elle's door. He gave Patrick a brief hug and slapped him on the back. "Good to see you."

"You must have left at dawn."

"JT got an ID on that Chinese chick and I knew we had a situation, so I came."

"Thank you." He showed Jack his phone. "Elle skipped out when I was in the shower and I'm tracking her. I need to bring her back. She's not thinking."

"What the hell's she doing?"

"Trying to find Kami, a missing girl she feels responsible for. We tracked her to Lee's main business, the garment warehouse, last night, but had no leads after. How did you know Soldare's identity when Hooper just called me about it?"

"Where do you think he got his information? Probably told you *his* people ID'd her." Jack half smiled. His smile looked almost sinister. "You go get Elle. I'll work with Jaye to narrow down locations where Lee could be holding the girls. She's been running through all businesses owned by Lee or any of his companies. The FBI is working on it too, but I'm putting my money on Jaye. By the time you get back, we should have a good list."

"Thanks, Jack."

"Be careful."

Patrick opened the door, then halted when he heard a sound on the stairs. He looked around the bend and saw a teenage girl in a baseball cap limping up the stairs. She spotted him and froze.

"Kami?" he asked.

She turned and started back down the stairs.

"Kami! Wait!"

She didn't stop.

Jack was right behind him. Patrick ran after Kami and easily caught up with her before she could open the door.

He grabbed her and held her from behind.

"Kami, I'm a friend of Elle's."

"Let me go!"

"Stop! You can call her. She's out looking for you right now."

Jack checked the door, made sure it was secure, then

gave Kami the once-over as Patrick held on to her arms. "Where've you been?"

"Who the fuck are you?"

"Jack Kincaid. This is my brother Patrick." He looked at her bare feet, the dirt caked onto her jeans and T-shirt. "The first thing they take from the girls they kidnap are their shoes, so they can't easily run away." He grabbed her arm and looked at her wrists. They were red and swollen from being tied. "You escaped."

"How do you know that?"

"It's written all over you. Do you know where they're keeping the girls?"

She glared at Jack, scared and suspicious, but curiosity won. "You know?"

"We know a lot of things." Jack looked at Patrick. "Let's get her upstairs so she can clean up and give us a location. We end this now, not tonight."

Patrick led Kami upstairs. "Elle is going to be relieved to know you're safe. We looked most of the night, then she left early this morning. She's worried."

"I have to go back. I left Ashley—"

"We'll get her and everyone else."

"We escaped, but she was hurt and couldn't run, so I hid her so I could find a car, and when I went back they had her. And I just—I just left."

"You did the right thing," Patrick said. "If you exposed yourself, they'd have you, and we wouldn't know where they were." He picked up his phone to call Elle. "Jack's going to contact Immigration, who are all set up to help. I'll get Elle back where it's safe." He picked Kami up because she was struggling to walk and carried her directly to the couch in Elle's apartment. Her feet were cut up and bleeding. Jack saw and his face hardened.

"You call Santana, then Hooper, I'll look for a first-aid kit and a map."

Patrick sat on the table across from Kami. She was still wary and confused, and he didn't blame her. Elle picked up. "Patrick, I'm at Mia's. She's not here."

"I have Kami."

"What?"

"She just walked into your apartment. Get back here now."

"Yes—let me talk to her."

Patrick handed Kami the phone. Kami immediately started crying when she heard Elle's voice.

"I'm so, so sorry. I didn't have any proof, and I went to find it, and I'm so sorry. He has so many girls, some younger than me, they don't speak English, and Ashley— Richie found her at the bus station last weekend. And then said she'd gone back home, but she didn't. He sold her. Sold her! And she got hurt real bad, I had to leave her. What if she dies and it's all my fault because I left her?"

Patrick wanted to reassure her, but Elle was talking and Kami was quietly crying, and nothing he could say would make her feel better.

The only thing he could do for her was find Ashley. He prayed she wasn't already dead, but Patrick knew how those people operated, and if she was a liability, they'd kill her.

Jack came back downstairs with a hodgepodge of bandages and sprays. "Santana is a slob," he said. "But at least she has everything we need." He sat on the table in front of Kami and waited until she was done with her phone call. Jack was a hard person to read, had always been that way even as a kid. But Patrick saw his well-controlled anger locked in his jaw. Patrick moved his own mouth up and down and heard his jaw crack.

Kami hung up, eyeing the first-aid materials with suspicion. "Elle's on her way back," she said. "She has to drop Clark off at his car."

"What?" Patrick said. "Clark Grayson?"

"You know him?"

"Yes."

Jack looked at Patrick. "You have a problem with him?"

"I don't trust him. I think he's involved."

Maybe he was wrong. Patrick knew he wasn't wrong that Clark was a criminal, but maybe he wasn't involved with Lee's human trafficking operation. Maybe it was something else altogether.

"Trust your instincts, bro," Jack said.

"She also told me I need to call in to the social worker in charge of my case. Sandy Chin."

Patrick found Sandy's number and handed the phone to Kami. Kami listened, then said, "Voice mail," to Patrick.

"Leave her a message," Patrick said. "Tell her you're fine and to call Elle later."

Kami nodded, and into the phone said, "Um, Ms. Chin? This is Kami Toland. Elle Santana told me I needed to call because I came in late last night. It was totally my fault, I'm sorry. I'm fine, promise. Call Elle and she'll tell you I'm good. Thanks." She hung up and handed the phone back to Patrick.

Jack inspected Kami's injuries. "This is going to hurt. But if we don't clean you up, the cuts will get infected."

He used tweezers dipped in rubbing alcohol to remove small rocks and glass embedded in her feet. She winced, but didn't flinch.

"When are we going to get Ashley?" she asked.

"Soon," Jack said. "How did you escape?"

"They took us out of the cells to force everyone to shower. One of the girls—she died last night. Two others were sick. I think . . . I think they shot the sick girls. Killed them. And everyone was crying and screaming and I took Ashley's hand and we ran. Ashley has a huge bruise on her side, and couldn't run far; she was coughing and the sun hurt her eyes—she'd been down there for days. Maybe a week, since I last saw her at Richie's place. I hid her behind an empty warehouse and stole a car a couple blocks away, but when I got back, they'd already found her."

Jack nodded toward a map on the table, and Patrick laid it out on Kami's stomach. "Where?" Jack asked.

It took her a couple minutes as she oriented the teen center on the map, then TK Clothing, and then moved her finger farther south. "I think it's here," she said, and pointed to a dead-end industrial area near the Bay. "I'd recognize it."

"It's safer for you here."

"I don't know on the map! I'm not sure!"

"That's okay, we will be. We have people running through all Christopher Lee's properties, and knowing it's in this area will narrow our search."

"Cold storage," she mumbled.

"What?" Patrick asked. "Cold storage?"

"We were kept in a basement that had an old sign that said 'cold storage.'"

Patrick said to Jack, "That could be a restaurant or meatpacking or processing plant."

"Good," Jack said. "We'll—"

Pop! Pop!

Kami jumped at the loud sound that came from downstairs.

Jack immediately had his gun in his hand.

Patrick pulled his own gun and ran to the balcony. Keeping clear of the windows, he cautiously peered out. Two cars were blocking the rear entrance, four goons—including Ringo—were outside.

"I have eyes on four," he told Jack.

"Get her upstairs. Call 911."

Patrick picked Kami up off the couch. She was shaking. He carried her up to the bathroom and told her to lock the door. "Do not open it for anyone, until Jack or I tell you it's clear."

He closed the door, made sure she'd locked it behind him, and called 911 as he ran back down the stairs. He put the phone on speaker near the rear windows as he watched the group out back. The balcony was long and narrow, and the small windowpanes were set in metal, easy enough to break through. A narrow door on the left provided access to the balcony.

Jack was at the front door looking at the small security screen. "They took out the camera. They're going to need small explosives to get in through this door, which they may have."

"They're scaling up to the balcony."

"Those pops were explosives. They took out the door downstairs, but this one is stronger. They're going to try to force us out the front." Jack came over to the windows. "They're not getting through that door anytime soon—it's solid."

The 911 operator finally came on. "Please state your name and the emergency."

"Patrick Kincaid. Four or more armed men are attempting to break into this location." Patrick gave them the exact address and apartment number.

"Sir, I will dispatch a patrol officer to check out the address."

"Send six cars, Code 3."

The dispatcher said something else, but Jack cut her off. "They're coming up." He glanced at Patrick. "You ready for this?"

Patrick knew what Jack meant. It had been a long time since Patrick was in the trenches, but they ran drills every month at RCK. He nodded. "Hell, yes, I'm ready."

Jack ordered Patrick behind the kitchen counter, and

Jack took cover by pushing the couch onto its front and sliding behind it.

Patrick sent Dwight a text message:

Elle's apartment under attack. Four to six armed men. Send cops now.

Between Dwight and 911, the cops should get here soon. Patrick hoped it was before they were all dead.

Two thugs were on the balcony. Through the sheer blinds, Patrick could see them fumbling with the narrow glass door. It was locked. One used his elbow to break the glass, then opened the door by putting his hand on the inside.

Jack fired at the hand, hitting it. The guy screamed, stepped back and held his hand to his chest.

The second guy moved out of their line of sight. They were shouting orders, and the other two thugs scaled up to the balcony while the injured guy sat down on the ledge. It visibly sagged under the weight of four grown men.

One man exposed himself to kick open the glass door. He had a gun in hand and looked around, his eyes wide but his hand steady.

Jack shot at the guy's gun hand, and winged him. The bastard turned toward the couch and fired repeatedly at Jack's position. Patrick shot the guy with three bullets to the chest. He went down. He wasn't moving.

The other two didn't show themselves, but they were still on the balcony.

Using the outer wall as a partial shield, one of guys on the balcony took an illegal semiautomatic gun and fired indiscriminately into the room. Both Jack and Patrick took cover flat on the floor as bullets hit the bricks and furniture, spraying debris everywhere.

As soon as the bullets stopped, Jack was on his stomach, his gun out and trained on the broken glass door as the two men walked in through the dust, smug as if their wild shooting had done the job. Jack put a bullet in each shooter's forehead without hesitation. They were dead before they knew what had happened.

Sirens were very close, and no one remained on the balcony except the first guy Jack had injured in the hand. Jack motioned for Patrick to check the vitals of the three men in the living room, while he went to the balcony and trained his gun on the sole survivor. The guy was more like a kid, maybe nineteen, cradling his arm.

"You killed my brother," he said, shaking with pain.

"You try anything, you'll see him in hell," Jack said, his gun aimed at the teen's face.

Though the three men were dead—young men, Patrick thought with a deep sadness—Patrick kicked their guns across the room.

Jack called back to Patrick, "The cavalry has arrived. You deal with them. I'll check on the girl."

Elle drove Clark to Granny's Kitchen. "Thank you so much for helping. I'm so glad Kami is safe. I owe you one."

"I'll collect on it now."

She glanced at her old friend. "What do you need? I don't have a lot of time."

"You're right. You don't. Keep driving."

Elle stared at Clark. Then she looked down to his lap and saw that he was holding a gun on her. *A gun*. "What the hell?"

"Drive. By now Kami should be dead."

"Kami is safe. She's with Patrick."

"Then he's dead, too."

She couldn't move. Patrick was not dead. Neither was Kami. Clark was just trying to scare her.

"You bastard." Elle was just as angry with herself for

defending Clark as she was for his betrayal. Patrick had met him for five minutes and knew what he was. She'd known him for twelve years and had never figured it out. What must Patrick think of her judgment? Who could she believe? Was everyone in her life a phony? A criminal?

Dwight had always told her she was too trusting. But she never saw herself that way, until now. Now she felt used and manipulated.

"If you don't drive the damn car, Elle, I will shoot you. You're collateral."

"You're helping Lee and Lorenzo sell drugs to the kids you claim to want to help."

"This has nothing to do with drugs. That's all Richie."

"So Patrick was right. This is about human trafficking."

"He's been using you. Did you think of that? I did my own research. His employer had to have sent him here to get close to you, so they could get intel on Lee. He had no reason to think that I wasn't who you told him I was, yet he acted all big macho cop or whatever." Clark laughed. "You're so damn gullible, Elle. You always have been."

Elle didn't want to believe Clark, but Patrick did seem to know a lot about Christopher Lee and his shipping company—things that Elle had never put together. Had Patrick used her own family to gain access to her information? Maybe her mother hadn't sent Patrick, maybe he'd used that as an excuse. Was he involved in an undercover operation? Could she trust her feelings about him?

She was gullible, trusting, and stupid. What mattered now was getting out of this mess.

Her phone was ringing and Clark grabbed it from her pocket. He threw it out the window.

Was that Patrick? Had he survived? Maybe all Clark's talk was intended to distract her, to get her to act instead of think.

Idiot. All you do is react. You never think!

Kami wasn't dead. Patrick wasn't dead. Clark was lying. She had to believe that or she'd fall apart.

But he wasn't lying about hurting her. She could see it in his eyes. It was as if their twelve-year friendship meant nothing to him.

She slowed down at a green light, frantically looking around for a cop, for anyone who could help her.

Clark hit her on the head. "Drive." Her vision blurred for a moment, but she was more angry than hurt. "Toward the teen center, then keep going."

CHAPTER 12

Patrick tried Elle again; it went directly to voice mail.

She should have been here by now.

He looked at his app to see where she was; nowhere. Her phone was not only off, it wasn't functional. Either the battery was completely dead, or someone had taken it out.

He reviewed the history on her GPS. She'd driven from Mia's to Granny's Kitchen, then left Granny's Kitchen. She must have dropped Clark off. Maybe Patrick had been wrong about him, and he wasn't involved, or at least not involved in human trafficking.

But right after she left Granny's Kitchen, her phone went dark.

Who had told Lee's people Kami was at Elle's apartment? They hadn't followed her, she'd been here more than thirty minutes before the gang showed up.

Elle knew. And Elle had been with Clark at the time. And Kami had left a message on Sandy Chin's phone. Either of them could be guilty.

Patrick carefully examined the GPS map. It was accurate within five hundred feet, and he could clearly see that Elle had made a U-turn and started back the way she'd come, past Granny's Kitchen again and moving away from her apartment.

Right after Patrick called her and she didn't answer, her phone went dead.

Something was wrong.

"Jack," Patrick called to his brother.

They'd already given a preliminary statement to the authorities, but three dead bodies—even when they'd obviously been the aggressors—were going to cause a huge headache for RCK. JT Caruso was already on his way to San Francisco from Sacramento to work with local authorities so Patrick and Jack wouldn't be detained. Dwight Bishop had arrived a few minutes ago and was talking to the assistant chief of police, and paramedics were upstairs treating Kami. She had more cuts and bruises than those on her feet—injuries that suggested she'd been beaten up, which she hadn't mentioned to them.

Jack said, "The feds are on their way. ICE and DEA and probably the FBI. It's a fucking alphabet soup." Though Jack was married to an FBI agent, he still preferred to keep law enforcement at arm's length. He was used to doing things his way. "JT and Hooper will smooth things over, but this situation isn't helping any."

"Elle's missing."

"Define 'missing.'"

"She should have been here thirty minutes ago. Her phone is dead. She was last with the asshole I think is working with Lee. I need to find her."

Jack glanced around. "Go."

"I can't—"

"I'll cover for you. Go get her."

"What about ICE?"

"They're sending Kyle Tucker. Former Delta," Jack said, as if that explained everything. So was Jack, and military stuck together, especially special forces. It was a brotherhood Patrick understood even though he wasn't part of it.

"Let me know the plan."

"Same here. Holler if you need backup."

Dwight approached them, and Patrick introduced Jack. "This is a fucking mess," Dwight said. "Where's Elle?"

"I'm going to find her," Patrick said.

"You can't leave," Dwight said. "They have more questions, and the assistant chief of police isn't inclined to let you keep your weapons."

Jack stared at the prosecutor. Dwight fidgeted and said, "There are three dead bodies."

Neither of them said anything.

The paramedics were bringing Kami downstairs. Patrick walked over to them. "What hospital?"

"Mercy."

"She needs a twenty-four-hour guard." Patrick approached the assistant police chief. "Sir, Kami Toland is a witness to a major human trafficking ring and needs a guard posted at her hospital room."

"Mr. Kincaid, we don't know what the hell is going on here except that you and your brother shot and killed three armed intruders, and this isn't your apartment. We don't know what Ms. Toland thinks she saw or didn't see, we'll investigate it in due time."

"There is no time!"

As the paramedics were about to leave, Patrick said, "Don't go anywhere yet."

Dwight stepped in and diplomatically explained to the paramedics that it would be best for Kami Toland to have an armed guard, but the senior cop was being unnecessarily argumentative.

Patrick couldn't leave to find Elle until Kami was under protection. Christopher Lee had sent at least six men to kill her; she was still a threat to him. He would be angry, cornered, volatile. She was a witness. Just like Doreen had been a witness. Patrick had never met Christopher Lee, but he knew criminals like him didn't leave witnesses alive.

A broad-shouldered black man entered the room. He was shorter than both Patrick and Jack, but his presence was immediately felt. He showed his badge to the cop at the door and said, "Special Agent Kyle Tucker, Immigration and Customs Enforcement. Sorry I'm late to the party, looks like ya'll got to have fun without me." Tucker had a slight Southern drawl, as if he was born and raised in the deep South but hadn't been home in a while.

Jack's lips twitched and he approached Tucker. At the same time, Tucker grinned and gave Jack a hug, then they did a complicated handshake. Patrick watched with curiosity. Jack wasn't usually so warm.

"When JT told me you were coming, I knew we'd get this job done right."

"Damn straight, Kincaid. Hooper in the fucking FBI—sorry, I heard you married one of them—briefed me on the way over. Hooper gets a pass, since he married one of mine, but damn, the Fibbies are like an octopus, getting their tentacles in every damn pie."

"They are," Jack concurred.

"When I saw Soldare's name on the list, I took the job right off the ticker. The bitch is mine. I've been chasing her for two years. Sonia Hooper and I shut down Soldare's Stockton operation last month, had her running, but she skipped the country. Or so we thought. When your brother—" Tucker looked around, then pinned his eyes on Patrick. "You're Jack's brother."

"Good call," Patrick said. He and Jack didn't look much alike, since Jack looked Cuban and Patrick looked like their Irish dad.

Tucker slapped him on the back. "Damn, boy, you gave me a hard-on when I saw Soldare's picture. She's a fucking snake, can't wait to cut off her head and watch her body wither and die."

The local cops were staring at Tucker as if they'd just walked into a bizarre play.

Tucker continued. "Soldare is wanted for more than twenty thousand individual counts of trafficking in persons—and those are just the ones we know about. That she's here makes me glow with excitement."

Patrick said, "Did Hooper send you the tape?"

"Of course. You're thinking that she's already gone. She might be, but she won't be getting out of the country if my people do their job right. Now, let me do my job so you boys can get out of here and catch some bad guys."

He sauntered over to the assistant police chief, and Patrick leaned over to Jack and whispered, "I expected him to say, 'I love the smell of napalm in the morning.'"

Jack cracked a rare grin. "I'm sure he does."

The paramedics started moving Kami again, and Patrick stopped them at the door. "Don't leave."

"Sir, you need to step aside."

"You can't take her unless a police officer goes with her."

Tucker looked over at them arguing and said, "Kincaid, what do you need?"

"She's an eyewitness. Lee and Soldare sent those men to kill her. She needs twenty-four-hour police protection."

"I agree." Tucker turned to the assistant chief. "Your people or mine?"

The assistant chief motioned to two patrol officers, spoke to them, and they joined the paramedics. "We'll stay on her," one of them said. "One of us will ride in the ambulance."

"Thank you," Patrick said. "I'll walk out with you."

He glanced at Jack, who nodded. His brother would cover for him so he could find Elle.

Patrick trailed behind the paramedics until they reached the ambulance. As they loaded Kami inside, Patrick said, "You'll be safe as long as you stay in the hospital. You have to promise me, Kami—stay put. I don't want to worry about you while I'm looking for Elle."

"You'll find her, right?"

"I promise."

"I'm sorry."

"None of this is your fault. Got it?"

She nodded. He didn't know if she believed him, but he squeezed her hand and turned to the officer who would be guarding her. "Protect her as if she were your daughter," he said.

"Of course."

Patrick handed Kami his backup phone. "For emergencies."

"Call me when Elle is okay? Please?"

He nodded, then kissed her on the forehead. Kami was a brave kid. Kid? She'd been through hell and back, and not just in the last few days. She hadn't had an easy life. Yet her character was stronger than that of many adults, than that of many privileged kids he'd grown up with. When it came down to it, she'd done the right thing. She'd tried to save her friend. She came to get help. Street instincts should have sent her deep into hiding; instead, she'd risked her life to give them information to stop Christopher Lee and save lives.

Now he understood why Elle risked so much for Kami. She saw Kami as she truly was, not how she appeared on the surface. And in Kami, Patrick also saw Elle. They both were reckless, but they both acted to help others, caring about what was right above what was safe or expedient.

As soon as the ambulance left, Patrick slipped past the police and then hightailed it to his car.

He didn't know where Elle was, but he knew where to start looking.

After Tucker was done taking over the investigation from the San Francisco PD and pulling in a team of ICE agents to process the scene and interrogate the lone prisoner, Jack told him about Elle Santana's sudden disappearance. "Patrick is looking for her."

"Off the record, good. I don't have the resources at my fingertips to run two operations, and right now the priority is the meatpacking warehouse. I have a team mobilizing as we speak, they'll be ready in ten minutes for a location."

"I got one. Kami Toland, the girl, gave us enough information about the structure to run through property records, and we are confident that the women are being held in an abandoned food processing plant between Dogpatch and Bayview."

"Lay it out." Tucker pushed debris and clutter off the kitchen counter, where it crashed to the floor.

Jack opened his laptop. He wasn't a tech guy; in fact, he hated the overreliance on technology and gadgets, but information traveled faster.

Between RCK and the FBI, they'd compiled photos of the building and blueprints. "Kami said they were locked in cells in a basement marked 'cold storage,' and the original plans show that the cold storage room is here, on the east side of the building. There are three truck bays on the south side, entrances on the north and west."

"They most likely moved the women after the girl escaped, but that takes time and manpower," Tucker said. "Or they killed them."

Both Jack and Tucker had seen situations where mass

murder was a better solution than capture for criminals like Soldare and Lee.

"I'm voting that they moved them—Kami said that the girls were being prepped for transport, showered, given clean clothes—so my theory is that they had the means to move the girls."

"Optimism from you, Kincaid? Marriage is good for you." Tucker grinned. "So, manpower? What are we looking at here?"

"Unknown. According to Kami, she saw three men with guns at the facility, but one of those men was shot and killed here in the apartment."

"None of the deceased, or the prisoner, are part of Soldare's known crew."

"We suspect they work for a local drug dealer who supplies runaways to Lee. An asshole named Richie Lorenzo."

Tucker nodded. "Soldare uses locals extensively, keeps her own crew small but lethal. Her right hand is Jonny Wong, one of the four people your brother recorded last night. Not to be underestimated."

"Are we hitting the facility, Tuck?"

"We have to start somewhere." Tucker made a phone call. He looked at the map Jack had on the computer, and said, "I have a potentially hot location, I'll send you the target. I'm on my way. Let me know where you're staged. We do this fast, boys, or not at all." He hung up. "Let's roll."

"My gun?" Jack nodded over to where the assistant police chief was watching ICE process the evidence with rapid efficiency. He'd taken Jack's weapon that had been used in the shooting; Jack had slipped Patrick his backup piece when he left with Kami.

Tucker reached behind his back and pulled out Jack's Sig and Patrick's Glock. "Sorry, almost forgot."

Jack smiled. It was good to be working with an old friend.

"Now let's go and nail these bastards," Tucker said.

Patrick thanked Jaye for the information and parked in front of Clark Grayson's condo in Russian Hill, a wealthy San Francisco community. Jaye had also told him that Grayson paid more than five thousand a month for the place, though his gross income was less than that. She couldn't find either a family money connection or trust, but she did learn that he was also on the payroll of TK Clothing, where he brought in twice his salary for the city. That, coupled with any under-the-counter money he got from Lorenzo or Lee, would keep him in a nice, secure building like this.

There was no doorman, and the door was electronic and easy for Patrick to hack, though he didn't have to. He held the door open for a mother pushing a bulky stroller, then slipped inside.

Grayson lived on the top floor of the nine-story building. Patrick knocked. There was no answer, no movement inside. Patrick slipped on gloves and picked the lock, then slipped in.

Grayson's unit was in the corner, with two windows exposing an amazing view of the Bay and Golden Gate Bridge.

Patrick did a quick search and didn't see anything out of place or that pointed to where Grayson might have taken Elle. Jack had the food processing plant covered, and if Elle was there, he'd find her. Would they get there in time? Or did Lee have a backup plan? Another location to move them?

It would take a lot of work—and time—to move that many young women, especially without being seen.

Patrick was worried and not thinking like a cop. He

pushed aside the complex emotions the last twenty-four hours had stirred up, and focused on finding a fugitive with a hostage.

The desk was clean. There were cords for a laptop computer on top of the desk, but no computer. The bottom drawer was locked. It was easy to pop open with the right tool, and within a minute, Patrick was looking through files Grayson wanted to keep private. Banking records. Files on homeless kids—who was working for Lorenzo and other criminals in the city. It seemed that Grayson was the recruiter, he found the right kids for the right jobs.

Bastard. He was not only contributing to the problem, he was growing it.

But there was nothing in the drawer that would help him find Elle.

He slammed it shut. This was getting him nowhere. He searched Grayson's bedroom, not taking any care to put things back where they belonged. In the day and age of modern technology, criminals didn't leave directions lying around on little pads of paper—they kept the information on their phones and laptops.

He already had Jaye trying to trace Grayson's phone, but either it was off or he had security protecting it from being tracked.

It all came down to Richie Lorenzo. Patrick had his mug shot, but didn't know where to find him. But that kid would know where Grayson was—and possibly Christopher Lee. Patrick needed help. He knew exactly who to ask.

Patrick quickly took pictures of Grayson's files and left the condo, heading toward the teen center to find the scrawny black kid who went by Jazz.

Jack had the same feeling Tucker did about the food processing plant.

"They're not here," he said.

"Guess you don't want to take my bet then," Tucker grumbled.

The parking lot was empty. No cars or big-rig trucks. The heat sensors showed no bodies inside, but the basement was harder to read because of the type of Sheetrock and metal used in construction. Tucker ordered the team to secure the building and be aware of potential booby traps.

"I lost two men in an operation near the border," Tucker said. "Went into a coyote's den and they had it rigged to explode."

"That's not like you, Tuck."

"We all make mistakes, Kincaid, and it was a long time ago. I wasn't using my head. Now focus."

They split into three teams of three. One team, with two explosives-sniffing dogs, secured the bays. Two went in through the main entrance. The first team fanned out into the main warehouse to search, and Jack's team went immediately to the basement.

He saw the sign that Kami had seen, COLD STORAGE.

He also smelled the feces, urine, blood, and death that rolled up the stairs in the icy air.

Jack had seen death up close: enemies, friends, innocents. There was no need for civilians to die.

Three girls, two naked and one clothed in a stained, torn cotton dress, had been shot on the floor of one of the cells. Another girl lay bloated in the corner. There didn't appear to be any blood. She'd been dead longer than the others.

Tucker motioned for Jack and one of his people, Agent Young, to continue moving forward and search the remaining cells and the room in the far back. Everything was as Kami said. The cells, the showers, the storage room with sack dresses and paper shoes. No toilet facilities, no windows.

In the storage room Jack saw a slight movement in the corner. He motioned for Young to halt and gestured to the corner. Guns raised, they aimed their flashlights toward the movement.

Two Chinese girls were huddled in an impossibly small shelf, both naked.

Even victims could be a threat. Jack told Young to cover him, and he lowered his gun. He didn't know more than a few words in Chinese, but he managed to get out, "We're friends. Help. We're help."

He said into his mic, "Tuck, we have two survivors."

Tuck came in and motioned for Young to guard the stairs. Tuck spoke to them in Chinese. It took a few moments, but then the girls responded and came out of their hiding spot. Jack handed them dresses that were on the table, and they put them on. Still clinging to each other, one of them spoke to Tuck. He asked questions; she responded, gaining strength as she spoke. Her arm was around the smaller girl. They weren't older than fourteen.

Tuck led them out, Jack took the rear. Before they stepped outside, another team greeted them. Tuck snapped his fingers, pointed to the girls, and two men handed over their sunglasses. Tuck handed them to the victims and said something in Chinese. The girls put them on.

"Ambulance ETA is five minutes," the other team leader said.

"Stay with them. They're witnesses. If Soldare knows Lee left behind witnesses, she'll come back for them."

"Yes, sir."

Tucker stepped outside with Jack. "They don't know where Lee went, they don't understand English. They said the girls that were shot were sick. One had died last night, and they didn't want to transport any sick girls. When they were killed, there was chaos, and Min Su, the taller girl, took her little sister into hiding."

"Any idea on the time? Two hours? Ten?"

"It's a guess, but she said very soon after they brought back the white-haired girl."

"Ashley," Jack said.

"You know her?"

"Kami escaped with her, but she was injured."

Jack mentally ran through the timeline based on what Kami had said. "Three hours," Jack said. "They have a three-hour lead."

"I have my people working on satellite footage and security cameras in the area. The FBI is canvassing, but so far no one saw or heard a big rig this morning in this neighborhood. My guess is that they moved them out in vans—there's fresh oil in one of the docking bays—to a secondary facility. We need to find it."

"They're not going to wait until dark," Jack guessed.

"I doubt it. They know we're here."

"I have a list of all Lee's properties in a fifty-mile radius."

"Let's split up the list and I.D. possibles." They walked back to the command truck, which was set up with computers and satellite equipment. "Those girls were eleven and twelve. Told me their orphanage sold them." Tucker kicked a tire and went inside the truck. "I swear, Jack, I want blood."

Jack knew exactly how his old friend felt.

CHAPTER 13

Patrick was sitting in his car outside the teen center watching the kids going in and out when Jack called him.

"Four dead, two survivors. The girls were moved about three hours ago, based on the witnesses and the timeline Kami gave us. About the same time we were being attacked at Santana's apartment."

"Gone? How the hell did they just disappear?" But Patrick had had a sick feeling in his gut that they'd be too late. He was out of options.

"We don't think they've packed them for long-term shipping. There's evidence that they moved them in vans, likely to a secondary spot until the trucks can get here. ICE is on top of it and we're sorting through Lee's holdings looking for a likely spot, as well as any street cams near the building."

"I have an idea. I'll let you know if it pans out." Patrick hung up before Jack asked him what. He knew his plan was risky, and Jack would want to back him up. But it was better for Jack to be with ICE where they could find Ashley and the other girls.

Finally he spotted Jazz walking down the street with two of the guys from last night, toward the teen center.

But they didn't turn into the complex. Instead, they continued down the street. Patrick got out of his car and followed. Jazz immediately saw him and frowned. Patrick held back and nodded, then circled around and walked back to his car.

He hoped he was right about the kid. If not, he had no other ideas.

Five minutes later, Jazz slipped into the passenger seat of his car. "Drive," he said, "or I'll be jammed up."

Patrick complied. "I need your help."

"Figured that's why you started following me. Don't they teach you guys stealth?"

"I wasn't trying to be discreet."

"You should. Everyone here is nervous. They know something's going down. It's fucked."

"I'll tell you what's fucked. Clark Grayson from Granny's Kitchen kidnapped Elle and I have no idea where he took her."

Jazz didn't say anything.

"Did you know?" Patrick's anger started to bubble to the surface.

"No, but I know Clark works with Lorenzo."

"I need to find Lorenzo. Now."

"I can't do that. I gotta live in this town."

"No one will know you told me."

Jazz snorted. "Right."

"I give you my word. Six armed thugs broke into Elle's apartment this morning and tried to kill Kami."

"You found her?"

"She found me. They're selling girls, Jazz. Black, white, brown, don't matter—if they're young, they can sell them. Do you want that on your conscience?"

"Not my problem. You think just 'cause I'm black I care about it?"

"I think you pretend not to care. What if it was your

sister? Your girl? You think you can just walk away and let them be sold as sex slaves? They'll be dead before they turn twenty."

Jazz didn't say anything.

Patrick drove by Mia's apartment building and slowed down.

"What you doing, Special K? You think you can scare me into talking?"

"Just give me an apartment number."

"He'll take you out. You think he's there alone?"

"Three of his boys, including Ringo, are dead," Patrick said. "One is in police custody."

"No shit?"

"No shit."

"Drive around the block."

Patrick did.

"Top floor."

"Number?"

"No number. He moves around, no roots. If he's in there, there'll be a NO PARKING sign on the door."

"Tell me something," Patrick said as he drove to drop Jazz off farther from the apartment. "Does Lorenzo care about anyone? Kami?"

"He don't care 'bout anyone but Richie. He don't like girls, don't much like boys, either. One thing about Richie you gotta know: he ain't afraid of no one. You want him to help you, he only cares about one thing." Jazz put his fingers together and rubbed. "I guarantee, Lee put a price on Ms. Elle's head, and Richie wants to collect."

"He's working for Clark."

"Clark works for Richie. Everyone does. Even Lee don't control him."

Patrick let Jazz out of the car. "Keep your head low."

"Stay loose." Jazz gave him the hang-ten sign and walked away, hands in his sagging pants. He didn't look back.

Patrick circled back to the Section 8 housing and checked Jack's gun. Four bullets gone, but he had an extra clip. He didn't want to shoot anyone else, but he knew this was risky. He still didn't have a plan as he took the stairs up to the third floor. For a beautiful Sunday afternoon, there was no one out enjoying the day.

Did everyone know something evil was happening in their neighborhood?

Patrick found the door with the NO PARKING sign and listened. No sounds. Then he heard clicking on a keyboard, followed by silence.

He tried the door. Locked. Without debating with himself, he drew his gun and kicked open the door.

One lone man was sitting at a computer. A gun was within reach. Patrick recognized him as Richie Lorenzo.

"Don't," he said, nodding toward the gun.

Richie glared at him, but there was no fear in his eyes. Only an underlying humor. "Don't you need a warrant?"

Patrick closed the door, not taking his eyes off Richie. "I'm not a cop. Your pal Clark Grayson kidnapped Elle Santana, and I want her back."

"Clark's not my pal, and neither is Santana. If you don't want to be on a slab, get lost."

He turned back to his computer. He had no fear that Patrick would shoot him. And Patrick wouldn't. He couldn't kill a man in cold blood, not like this.

He walked behind him. Richie reached for his gun, but Patrick grabbed his wrist first and slammed it on the table so hard he heard a bone crack. He pocketed his own gun and pressed his thumb on a pressure point in the back of Richie's neck. "I don't give a fuck what you're doing, Lorenzo. I only care about Elle. And you're a smart guy to have gotten away with selling shit on the street for so long, so you know that Grayson kidnapping a do-gooder attorney who's been married to one of the top prosecutors in the city is going to bring down the law so swift and hard that you won't be able to slip away. And if anything happens to Elle, my brothers and I will make your life hell. We'll dry up every one of your suppliers. We'll make sure the word on the street is you sell little girls to perverts. Then, when you get tossed in prison, and I know you will be, I'll hack into the Department of Corrections files and alter your records so everyone there thinks you're in jail for being a pedophile. Pedophiles don't do well in prison."

"You don't scare me."

"Then you're stupid."

Lorenzo attempted to get out of Patrick's grip, but he pressed his thumb harder on the pressure point and Lorenzo involuntarily moaned. "If you'll help me, give me a location, I'll hack into the Department of Corrections right now and give you a clean slate. Your file will disappear. If you keep your nose clean, it stays disappeared."

"You can't do that."

True, but Sean could.

"Watch me."

"I want to see it."

Patrick let him go, but told him to sit. He called Sean and put Sean on speaker.

"Rogan."

"It's Patrick. I have a pal here, who doesn't believe that I can make his criminal record disappear."

"Plug me in, buddy."

Patrick plugged his phone into Lorenzo's computer and at the same time launched an app that would allow the phone to be a conduit and clone Lorenzo's hard drive onto an external server that Patrick could later access.

"Set it up, but don't delete it until he realizes I am serious."

"Got it."

Sean was working on his laptop, but mirroring what he

was doing on Lorenzo's screen. Watching how fast Sean worked always amazed Patrick, but he'd stopped praising him because it only served to grow his already inflated ego.

"I'm in. Social."

"Give him your Social Security number," Patrick told Lorenzo.

The kid was glued to the screen, impressed. He told Sean.

Sean plugged it in and almost immediately Lorenzo's lengthy record was displayed. Assault, possession with intent to sell, assault, assault, possession. He'd done time in prison when he was eighteen. He was only twenty-three now.

"Ready to purge," Sean said.

"Do it," Lorenzo said.

"Hold it," Patrick said. "Give me the address."

"How do I know you'll really delete it after I tell you?"

"How do I know you'll give me the right address?"

Lorenzo thought on that a moment.

Over the phone, Sean said, "Watch."

The first assault charge disappeared. The screen refreshed and it was gone.

Lorenzo grinned. "I wish you worked for me."

Sean laughed. "I don't work for anyone, and I like it that way."

"I gotta tell you, I had nothing to do with Grayson's stupid-ass plan. That was all Grayson and the Chink."

"Would 'the Chink' be Lee?"

"Bastard."

"You sold him that blond girl."

"Me? Fuck, no. Is that what he said? Fucking prick. That's all Clark. I might have known about it, but I wasn't involved. I stay out of that shit."

Patrick wasn't certain he believed him.

"Address."

"Okay. I'll do you one right. I heard that Lee was moving a shipment tonight out of the old food processing plant."

"We were already there. They're gone."

"They had to change plans because Kami ran. Gotta love that girl. She's a hard-ass bitch. They'd planned on moving them out at nine tonight, but moved it up to three this afternoon."

It was already after two.

"Where?"

"An abandoned warehouse near Candlestick Park. It's owned by the city so you'd never find it just looking at the Chink. It's one building surrounded by an empty parking lot. One large trucking bay with three doors. Lots of tags. Ask any pig, they'll know where it is."

"And Elle?"

"Don't know why she wouldn't be there with them. Clark wants to get rid of her, he'll turn her over to Lee." Lorenzo pointed at the computer screen. "Now do it."

"Go ahead, bro," Patrick said to Sean.

Lorenzo's record disappeared. He grinned widely. "That's cool."

"And if you lied to me, we'll put it right back. And more."

Lorenzo tapped the digital clock in the corner of the terminal. "Better hurry. It's nearly three."

Patrick unplugged his phone and left. Once he was out of Lorenzo's hearing, he said to Sean, "Thanks."

"I saw you copied his hard drive."

"Do you have time to go through it? I want everything he has, and if he's lying—"

"I'm on it. And you really did mean for me to delete his record."

"Yes. I gave him my word. But you have a copy, right?"

"You didn't even have to ask. Be careful, buddy."

"Always."

Patrick filled Jack in on the details he learned from Lorenzo, and hung up when Jack started chastising him for confronting the drug dealer alone. Then Patrick called Dwight Bishop and described the structure.

"I know exactly where that is," Dwight said. "I'll send directions. Do you want me to call the police in on this?"

"ICE is taking the lead. It sounds like the facility is isolated and easy to defend."

"They'll be able to see from any direction. It used to be an off-site storage warehouse for events at Candlestick. The city owns the property and leases it out when they can, but it's been vacant for months."

"Could Lee have gotten a lease?"

Dwight considered. "Very possible. I'll dig around and see if we can tie him to the facility. Elle's okay, right?"

"I'll do everything to ensure that."

He hung up and sent Jack the information, then drove to check it out.

Dwight was right; it was not only exposed, but the road was closed off. Lee's people would be able to see them coming at any angle. That put Elle and the other women in even greater danger.

If Elle was inside. There was no reason to think that she was, but no reason to think she wasn't. Unless Clark Grayson already killed her, Patrick didn't have any other option at this point except to keep moving.

He went back to his car, which he'd hidden among a bunch of abandoned cars in the lot next to the warehouse, then called Jack.

"We have a problem. There's no tactical way to approach the building without being seen."

"Our ETA is four minutes."

Patrick heard rumbling on the street leading up to the warehouse. "Four minutes?"

Using the old cars for cover, he got as close to the street as he dared. Three identical big rigs lumbered up the street. Three? The girls they had could fit into one. It wasn't like Lee and Soldare cared if they were comfortable. But at night they would blend together, providing cover for each other, decoys.

"Jack, I see the trucks. There's three." They were early. He eyed a cluster of trees by the side of the road, several with branches that jutted out into the street. He could make it. "I'm going in. Trojan-horse style. You need someone to disable their eyes and ears."

"N—"

Patrick cut his brother off. He pocketed his phone and scaled the tree before the trucks rounded the bend. He crawled out to the end of the smallest branch that he thought could hold his weight. The leaves were sharp and scratched his skin, but he slid forward and prayed this would work, or he'd be splattered all over the broken pavement.

He had to wait for the first two trucks to pass to minimize the chance of the drivers seeing him.

The first truck hit the branch immediately beneath him, causing it to crack. As the tree shuddered, Patrick dipped precariously. He held on tight. The second truck went through, so close he could have reached out and touched the top of the container.

His heart raced and he wasn't certain he'd be able to do this. He hoped the scratching of the tree branches against the top of the big rig would mask the sound of his body falling onto the roof.

He didn't have time to think about it. The third truck moved into position.

Patrick jumped as lightly as he could, only two feet from the tree to the container. He flattened himself onto the top, put his head down, and closed his eyes against the dust and bugs that flew into his face.

When they turned into the lot, the truck hit another clump of leaves and it was all Patrick could do to stay on the roof.

The truck slowed and soon stopped. Patrick ventured a look, but couldn't see much.

Then he heard a rumbling, and a large metal door rolled up. Patrick couldn't see anything inside; he was the last truck. The other two maneuvered so they could back up. Though there appeared to be only one truck bay, the door was so wide that the three trucks could be lined up side by side. Once the first truck was inside, the second truck backed in.

As soon as his truck began to move, Patrick sent Jack a text letting him know he was inside and he would have the security system disabled in ten minutes.

He hoped he could do it in time.

CHAPTER 14

Elle had been separated from the other women shortly after Clark brought her to the old event warehouse near Candlestick Park. Elle remembered driving by this place many times, taking the back way home after baseball games, before they opened AT&T Park. She never paid it much attention. There would be boat shows here, RV shows, used-car discounts, and once a craft fair that didn't do well with the sudden gusts of wind from the Bay. Now the pavement was broken with weeds growing in the cracks, and while the city might maintain it, they were rarely here. This particular back road had been shut down for well over a year.

It was a perfect place for criminal bastards like Christopher Lee.

And Clark.

She was still furious with herself for trusting him, but more than that, she was angry with Clark for being a two-faced bastard himself. The kids trusted him, and he used them. Buying and selling people? Kids? It was as horrid as it was cruel. Elle had never wanted to hurt anyone, but right now if she'd had a gun—and knew how to use it— she would shoot Clark. She didn't want to kill him, she wanted to make him suffer.

What did that make her? Just as bad as they were? Because she had this driving need to hurt Clark?

She closed her eyes and listened to the young women murmuring and sobbing quietly in a walled-off room in the back of the warehouse. No windows, one door, crammed in like cattle. Clark had wanted to put her with them, but some creep named Jonny grabbed her and tied her up in a small office to the side. She couldn't see anything, either, but she could hear. Their voices, how they planned to move the Chinese girls to Los Angeles, where they would be forced into the sex industry. The other girls, the ones Clark and Lorenzo had brought to Lee, were being taken farther south, to a Central American country where they were already sold to a brothel owner who only wanted blondes.

That she'd overheard all this information meant for certain that they planned to kill her. She had to find a way to escape and get help.

The large, metal door rolled open, making the entire structure rattle. Elle tensed, fighting her ropes, then winced in pain as her already chafed wrists burned.

She heard idling trucks slowly driving in, drowning out all other noise.

The office door opened and a gust of diesel exhaust filled the room. Clark entered with the big thug named Jonny.

"Showtime." Clark was smiling. "Finally things are going right. Trucks ahead of schedule, we'll be out of here before your boyfriend knows you're missing."

Jonny glared at Clark. "The whole job is fucked. You'll be lucky to walk away with your head."

Clark swallowed uneasily, his Adam's apple bobbing, but he didn't sound scared when he said, "Without me, you'd have nothing, so shut the fuck up."

Jonny didn't say anything. If Elle had to choose,

she'd rather stick with Clark. Jonny scared the hell out of her.

A cry in the small room next to theirs made Elle jump. "What are you doing to those girls?"

The men ignored her and walked out. The cry hadn't come from the main holding pen, but from the other side of the wall. Elle didn't want to think about what these barbarians were doing; she kicked at the ropes around her ankles, but couldn't get those off, either.

"Dammit, Clark!" Elle shouted.

Nothing. She surveyed her surroundings again and eyed the desk. Maybe she could open the drawer and use the edge to cut through the nylon ropes. It was worth a shot.

The trucks masked the sound of her sliding her chair back two feet until she reached the desk. She ignored the pain and maneuvered her fingers to pull open the heavy metal drawer. She didn't know if this would work, but she had to try something.

The trucks all shut down, one by one, until her ears rang in the silence. She moved her wrists, which were tied behind her back, back and forth against the metal edge, but didn't know if she was making any progress. The heavy main door slid closed. The cargo doors of the trucks opened.

The sobs started up again. They were moving the girls. It was now or never.

She pulled at the ropes. Nothing. They didn't break; they didn't even loosen.

Tears of anger burning her eyes, Elle kept sawing.

She had to get help. Somehow.

Jack was angry with Patrick for going into an unknown situation alone and without backup. Tucker wasn't happy about it either, but he also saw the potential.

"If he can take out their security without alerting them, we can approach and circle the warehouse before they're aware of it," Tucker said. "Wait until they reopen the doors. They won't do that until the girls are in the trucks, and that gives us a modest degree of security that the hostages are at least marginally safe."

Bullets could penetrate the trucks, but it would take both force and time. If the traffickers turned on the girls, Tucker and his team could take them out before they could do much damage. Minimize losses. But both Tucker and Jack knew that at the first opportunity, the traffickers would target whoever was shooting at them. They wanted to make the trade work, and without the girls, they had nothing.

One of Tucker's men came over with an iPad. "Here's the map of the area. There's a drainage system that goes out to the Bay for runoff, and there's a sewer lid just behind the building. We can access it here"—he pointed—"and it'll take three minutes to get to the warehouse if we book it."

"Good."

"We have eyes on the building. There's security cameras at each corner. There's also a generator next to the sewer access panel."

Jack said, "If we take out the generator, they'll know we're here."

"We have to time this to the second," Tucker said. "Grant, take your team into the sewer and let me know when you're in position. Greene!" He snapped his fingers. Another team leader approached. "I want your men here and here." He pointed to the two best sniper positions. "On my command take out the generator and keep eyes on the building and surrounding area. Go."

To Jack, he said, "We don't know how many are inside, but there's a minimum of five, more likely eight to ten. There could have been reinforcements in the trucks. I want as many taken alive as possible. If Soldare is smart—and she is—I'm sure she left the city immediately after her meeting with Lee last night. I have everyone who's free checking leads. But I know where she's going—and I'll catch up with her. I will nail her, Kincaid. But first things first."

He pointed to Jack and Young. "The three of us will go in on foot as soon as we know security is down. How many more minutes?"

Jack looked at the timer he'd started when Patrick told him he was inside. "Four minutes, twenty seconds."

"We're cutting it close. Can he do this?"

"Yes," Jack said. He hoped. Patrick used to be ahead of the curve on security systems, until his coma set him far back. RCK relied on Sean for computer security issues, but Patrick was still one of the smartest guys Jack knew.

"Let's get in position."

As quietly as possibly, Patrick slid off the top of the truck and fell to the ground. It was a much longer drop than he expected, and his shoes echoed in the large chamber. He slid under the truck to assess how many people were inside.

The doors rolled up on the back of the trucks, and suddenly, the cries of women broke through.

From Patrick's hiding place underneath the big rig on the far side of the warehouse, he could see dozens of bare feet walk behind the trucks. The girls were tied with nylon rope around their right ankles, some so tight he could see bruising and blood. A male voice barked orders in Chinese, and Patrick saw two pairs of black boots flanking the captives.

It appeared that the girls were being loaded into the

truck farthest from him, which made it difficult for Patrick to get to that side, where he could see unfinished Sheetrock walls and at least one closed door. Security panels would be near the truck bay door or in an office.

He glanced at his watch. Less than five minutes before Jack expected security to be disabled. Patrick couldn't let him down—too many people were counting on him.

He looked west—the outer wall. The truck was close to the edge, which might give him a shield. Except he would be too exposed making his way to the makeshift office. There was really only one viable option.

Patrick rolled under all three trucks, stopping under each to check if anyone could see him. Only one driver had exited the truck cab. Other than the two pairs of boots with the girls, he only saw two more hostiles. Finally, he reached the last truck.

Three and a half minutes.

He waited for a man to pass who, based on his loafers, might have been Clark Grayson. That meant Elle was likely on-site.

If she wasn't already dead.

He pushed the thought from his mind and focused on the job at hand.

When it was clear, he took out his gun and left the protection of the truck. He crawled to the office door and slipped in, hoping the room was empty.

It wasn't.

A blond girl was lying on the dirty concrete floor, seemingly unconscious, her face pale. Patrick tried to lock the door, but there was no lock. Instead, he went to her side and checked her pulse. She cried out when he touched her.

"Shh," he whispered. "I'm here to help."

She moaned, and Patrick knew she was in a bad way. He couldn't see any visible injuries other than cuts on her hands and bare feet.

"Are you Ashley?"

Her eyes fluttered open, blue and far too bright. Her skin was cool to the touch.

He put his finger to his lips.

There was a computer on the desk hooked up to a small box with red blinking lights on the wall. Patrick opened his phone to text Sean, then realized it would take too long to bring Sean in to help. He had less than two minutes to disable the cameras.

He drew in a deep breath and assessed the system. It was simple. Outside movement would launch a program in the computer that would turn on each camera and trigger an alarm. Four cables. He almost pulled them out, but considered there might be a fail-safe that would set off an alarm.

He typed on the keyboard. A basic program ran the security system, and it was simply a matter of shutting it down. He almost smiled as he exited the system, powered down the computer, then pulled out the cables.

No alarms.

He was about to send Jack a message that it was done when the door opened. Patrick dropped behind the desk and squatted there. Two men were arguing. If anyone came around the desk, he was trapped. He glanced over at where Ashley lay, half conscious. If they went for her, they'd see him.

He had his gun in hand. He could take them both, but the sound of gunfire would bring in the others he'd heard in the main warehouse. He prayed it didn't come to that.

"What the fuck are we going to do with her?" a voice said. "She won't survive the trip."

Ashley moaned and Patrick froze.

"Leave her." It was Clark Grayson's voice. "We have two dozen blondes, they're not going to miss one. Are we ready? We need to roll fast. I'll take the decoy truck."

"No," a third voice said, "you're going to Los Angeles, Grayson."

Great, Patrick thought. Now there were three, and time was running out.

"Like hell I am."

"Your cover's been blown."

"I'll take care of Santana, and no one will know."

"Her boyfriend knows, and Lee said he's connected to the feds. They're not going to let you walk. It's L.A. or I kill you now, because no way am I allowing you to be arrested. The second truck is almost loaded, then we're out of here."

Grayson didn't argue, and they left the office talking about bypassing checkpoints, the door still open.

Elle was here, somewhere.

Ashley moaned, "Help."

Patrick crawled over to her. "Shh," he whispered. "Stay here for—"

He was cut off when the main doors rumbled open. The trucks started their engines, one by one.

Patrick heard a *pop-pop!* outside, then the lights went out. A second later, shouts and more gunfire.

He dragged Ashley behind the desk where he hoped she would be safe, then he flattened his body against the wall and looked out into the truck bays. The trucks blocked his visibility, but one of Lee's people saw him and fired. The girls were screaming from the backs of the big rigs, but it was clear that the middle rig was empty. The decoy.

Patrick leaned back, waited a beat, then, using the door-jamb as a shield, leaned out and fired three rounds. The guy who'd been aiming at him went down.

Where was Elle? He searched the other two offices. In the last, he found ropes, but no one was there. Had she escaped? Had they packed her up in the trucks?

The door burst open and Jack was there, in full SWAT gear. He motioned for Patrick to follow him.

"There's an injured girl in the third room," Patrick said. "Elle's here somewhere."

Jack didn't say anything. He was listening to something in his earpiece, and then opened the cab of one of the trucks and held his gun on the driver. "Turn off the truck," Jack ordered. "Hands where I can see them."

The driver complied. Patrick covered Jack while the driver stepped out of the vehicle. Jack searched him and then escorted him outside. Two ICE agents brought out the other two drivers. An FBI SWAT unit took custody of the three.

"Two down inside," Jack told Tucker.

"Three," Patrick said. "I don't see Grayson or Soldare's right hand, Jonny."

"Or Lee," Jack said.

"He wasn't here," Patrick said. "Jonny's giving orders. And they have Elle." But where?

More cops and FBI showed up, but it was clear Tucker was in charge. He motioned for two three-man teams to take each side of the warehouse. They searched, found no one else, and Tucker ordered Jack to open one of the trucks.

This one had the blondes inside, all young runaways like Ashley. Tucker called in an FBI team to escort them to safety. They opened the middle big rig. Empty.

The last was full of more than a hundred Chinese girls. They were sobbing and hysterical and started pouring out of the truck. Tucker fired a round into the ceiling to catch their attention, then he spoke to them in Chinese. Patrick had no idea what he said, but they calmed down and moved single file out of the big rig. ICE and FBI agents, all in full gear with automatic weapons, flanked them. As the young women reached the open door, they cringed at the sunlight. More cops led them away from the warehouse and out of sight.

"Where the fuck did they go?" Tucker said.

Patrick tapped Jack on the shoulder and motioned to the room the girls had been kept in. "We searched it," Jack said.

"They have to be in there. It's the only place."

Tucker nodded. He used hand signals that Jack understood, and the two entered cautiously, shining flashlights all around.

Patrick hit the wall. "They have to be here!"

Jack knocked on the wall and frowned. He then looked at the trucks. Patrick followed his gaze. He didn't know what his brother was thinking, but he definitely had an idea.

Jack put a finger to his lips and motioned toward the trucks. Tucker nodded, and Patrick wished he could read the minds of these former military guys, because he didn't know what they were communicating.

Patrick glanced at the plywood wall. It had sounded hollow. Was Jack thinking there was a false bottom or wall in the trucks?

Jack and Tucker walked around the trucks, inspecting the exteriors. Then Tucker motioned to the truck in the middle. The decoy.

"PK," Tucker said to Patrick, "watch the cab." Then he motioned to Jack and they shined their lights in the back.

Patrick walked around to the cab and stepped up on the running board. He had his gun trained toward the back. He heard knocking inside, but didn't know if it was Tucker checking the interior, or if it was someone inside the walls.

A large panel behind the passenger seat opened up and Patrick saw Grayson's face. He was stunned to see Patrick pointing a gun at him. He quickly disappeared from view and Patrick called out to Jack and Tucker.

Then Elle came out of the panel. Grayson held a gun at her temple as he pushed her through, holding her tightly. "I want a driver or she dies."

"You're not getting out of here, Clark," Patrick said.

"If I don't, she doesn't, either. Bring me one of my drivers. When I'm clear, I'll let her go."

"Don't make this worse."

"How can it get any fucking worse?" Grayson screamed.

Where were Jack and Tucker? Why hadn't they come around? There was a whole slew of FBI SWAT with their guns trained on the windshield, and Patrick was between them and Grayson. Great. But if he moved, that could put Elle in greater danger.

She was terrified. Her eyes were too bright, she had blood on her face and scalp. Her shirt was filthy and bloody. Patrick swallowed the rage that filled him. He closed off his emotions. When Elle caught his eye, she flinched.

"Get them out of here," Grayson demanded. "Now."

Patrick motioned to the SWAT team leader to go. He didn't budge. These guys didn't know who Patrick was from Adam, and they certainly didn't take orders from him.

"Tucker!" Patrick called out the door without taking his eyes off Grayson. "I need you to call off the FBI."

A moment later, Tucker walked past where Patrick was standing on the running board. He immediately called off the SWAT team, and they backed away.

Grayson nodded, excited that one of his demands had been met. "Good. Good. Now, a driver."

"Tucker, he wants a driver," Patrick called out.

"And put down your gun."

"I'll put my gun down if you put yours down," Patrick said.

Elle's eyes were focused on Patrick, and he was trying not to let her fear distract him. He glanced down. Her wrists were raw and bleeding and she couldn't stop shaking.

He wanted to shoot Grayson.

It had been a long time since Patrick had worked hostage negotiation. And he'd never had a personal connection with the gunman, or the victim, like he did now.

"I will kill her," Grayson said, his voice shaky.

"You'll be dead."

"So will she."

"Tell me what you want."

"Put the fucking gun down!"

Patrick slowly put the gun on the driver's seat in front of him. He glanced out the window and saw Tucker with a gun trained on Grayson. Where was Jack?

"Good," Grayson said. "Now tell that black guy to get me a car."

Patrick called out to Tucker, "He wants a car."

Tucker didn't say anything, nor did he move.

Patrick shrugged. "They don't take orders from me. I'm not a cop."

"Then get me someone in here who can make decisions!"

Patrick glanced at Tucker. He averted his eyes briefly, toward the back of the truck, then looked squarely at Patrick.

Patrick hoped he read him right. Now he had to figure out how to communicate with Jack.

Or maybe he really needed to communicate with Elle.

The most important thing was to get the barrel of the gun away from Elle's head.

"Okay, Clark, I'm going to be honest with you. That man over there?" He gestured toward Tucker. "He's not going to let you leave. He's kind of a hard-ass that way.

He saw what you left behind at the food processing plant. Four dead girls. He has a daughter. He wants blood."

Patrick had no idea if Tucker had kids, but he just rolled with the story.

"If I get out of this truck, he'll kill you. Notice, he's the only one around here with a gun."

"I have a gun," Grayson said, his eyes darting from Tucker to Patrick.

"Yes, you do. But I'm between you and Tucker. I leave, he'll kill you. No witnesses."

"Then she dies," Grayson said. "He's not going to shoot me. Not as long as I have her."

Grayson shifted his body and Elle's so that she was clearly between him and Tucker's rifle. That brought him closer to Patrick by several inches.

And gave Jack a clear shot. As soon as Patrick could get Grayson to lower his damn gun.

"Elle," Patrick said, "do you remember that kid in high school, Garrett something . . . he was in my graduating class."

"Garrett Brown," she whispered. She stared at him with a confused expression.

"Right. Garrett Brown. Remember that thing he used to do, freaked everyone out."

"Y-yeah." But she didn't. She looked more confused than ever. And terrified.

"What the hell are you two talking about?" Grayson demanded.

"I'm just trying to calm her down. Can't you see she's scared? She's shaking."

When he said "shaking," the realization of what Patrick meant showed in her eyes. Patrick nodded, just a fraction.

"It's about time. I've never seen her scared of anything—"

Elle started wildly shaking as if she were having a seizure, just like Garrett Brown used to do with regularity at their high school.

Immediately, Patrick grabbed Grayson's gun hand at the same time Jack put a gun on the back of his head and his arm around Grayson's neck. How Jack came that fast and quiet out of the back of the truck, through the same panel Grayson had used, Patrick didn't know, but the timing was perfect.

Patrick disarmed Grayson and pulled Elle away from him. He picked her up and carried her from the cab of the truck.

Her arms were tight around his neck and she was still shaking violently.

He said to Tucker, "The girl in the office. Ashley."

"We got her. She's on her way to the hospital. Looks like a broken rib and internal bleeding." He patted Patrick on the shoulder. "Good job, Kincaid. Ever want to go legit, let me know."

"RCK is legit."

Tucker snorted and went to cuff Grayson.

Patrick sat Elle down at the back of the SWAT truck. One of the guys brought her a water bottle. She drank greedily, then coughed.

"How—"

"Shh. I'll explain everything later." He looked her over. "Are you okay? Where are you hurt?" He touched the bruises on her face. Brushed away her dark hair, sticky with blood.

"I'm okay."

"You need to get checked out."

She shook her head and then started crying. "I didn't know. How could I not have known?"

He hugged her tightly and closed his eyes. "This isn't

your fault. Sometimes, people aren't who we think they are."

"But you knew. You knew the moment you saw him."

He looked at her and smiled. "Maybe that coma I was in made me psychic." He was trying to make her feel better, but it wasn't working.

"Or maybe I'm just a bad judge of character."

"No." He tilted her chin up. "Grayson fooled a lot of people. Not just you. I like that you see the good in everyone."

"Where was the good in him?"

"He helped some kids get off the streets. Tutoring them, getting them jobs—"

"While selling girls and drugs. No, nothing is going to make me think anything Clark did was good. He would have killed me. How did you do that?"

"You did it, too. You knew what I wanted you to do."

"But how did you know someone was behind us? That he was right there, that he could get him like that?"

"Trust."

"But *how*?" She was still confused and scared, and while Patrick had faced these situations before, this was a first for Elle.

And hopefully the last.

"How did you trust Kami? Why did you help her? Because you knew, in your gut, that you could. The man in the truck is my brother Jack. I trusted he'd know the exact moment to act. He would have killed Clark if that's what it took to save you."

"So much death. So much—" She stopped. "What about Lee?"

Kyle Tucker heard her, and approached. "Ma'am, we're already on our way to apprehend him. He attempted to flee the country, and they're detaining him at SFO right now. He won't be going anywhere."

Patrick asked, "What about Soldare?"

"She's my business. I have her right-hand prick Jonny, I will find her."

He walked away. Patrick had no doubt he'd nail Soldare.

Patrick said to Elle, "You need to give a statement, then I'll take you home."

CHAPTER 15

It was dark by the time the feds were done with Patrick and Elle, and Patrick could bring Elle to the hospital to visit Kami. They hugged and cried and Patrick let them catch up.

He stepped out into the hall to call Jack.

"Everything good?" Jack said.

"I don't know. I haven't brought her back to her apartment."

"Take her to a hotel."

"I need to be there when she sees it. Have the police cleared out?"

"Tucker said his people already wrapped up. But it's a mess."

"Maybe a hotel is better," he said, indecisive.

"I'm driving down to San Diego in the morning. I was going to leave at dawn, but Megan's flight doesn't get in until later in the evening, so I'm in no rush. You're welcome to join me."

"Do you think Ma would forgive me if I stayed here until this situation is cleaned up? I don't feel right just leaving Elle like this."

Jack laughed. "You're the golden child, Patrick. Ma

would forgive you forgetting to call on her birthday. I'll tell her."

"I'll call her to explain."

"That's why you're the golden child. Love you, bro."

"Back at ya."

He hung up and considered why he planned to stay with Elle. He loved his family, and missed them, but last night with Elle there was something different in him. He felt almost like his old self, before he lost two years of his life. Elle was so tactile and vibrant in everything she did. The passion that filled her job and her friendships filled her soul and spread to everything around her, including him. He craved it. He needed it. He couldn't go back to being the Patrick he'd been before his coma, but he could be better than he was today. He needed to let the anger and frustration go.

Dwight walked down the corridor to where Patrick waited, his expression more than a little worried. "You said she was fine."

"She is. She wanted to see Kami."

"Oh, right. That's why I'm here." He held up an envelope. "I need Elle to sign some papers for Kami. She might not need to testify at all on Wednesday. Lee will be arraigned tomorrow, and my office assures me he won't be given bail, especially since he was apprehended while attempting to flee the country. And then he's going to federal court where he's going to be arraigned on separate charges. My boss and ICE will fight over who gets to prosecute."

"The feds will win."

"On this, yes. But they have more on him than we do. You think Kami is going to be able to testify later?"

"She's a tough kid, and smart. She'll hold her own."

"How's Ashley?"

"Out of surgery. Her parents are flying in from Colorado, should be here soon. Kami asked me to check on her, so I'll do that while you talk to Elle."

As he started to walk away, Dwight said, "Patrick? Elle can be difficult. Don't let it stop you."

Dwight disappeared into Kami's room before Patrick could respond.

Patrick had explained to Elle on the drive from the hospital what had happened in her apartment, and she thought she was primed for what she would face.

But nothing he could have said would have truly prepared her for the destruction of her home.

She walked up the short staircase to the main room and stared.

There were bullet holes in her walls and kitchen cabinets. Her couch was overturned, the stuffing spilling out. More bullets? She walked to her windows. Shattered. Someone had boarded them up, but they hadn't removed her carpet, which was stained. Dark red.

Blood.

Someone had died here.

Three people had died here. Three people died in her apartment. Shot to death.

"Pack a bag, I'm taking you to a hotel," Patrick said.

"No."

"Yes."

Elle walked over to where the little Christmas tree she'd bought from a street vendor was crushed and broken on the floor. She picked it up. The small glass bulbs she'd hung—all cheap, nothing of value—were shattered on the floor. She put the tree on the table. It fell over. Tears burned behind her eyes.

"Elle," Patrick said from behind her, his hands on her

shoulders, "please. This was a bad idea. I shouldn't have brought you here."

"I would have seen it sometime," she said.

"But not tonight. Not tomorrow."

"How can you be so casual about this?"

"I don't understand what you mean."

She shrugged off his hands and walked away. She couldn't breathe. The whole day, from the moment Clark had held the gun on her until now, was surreal. The screaming girls, the gunfire, the tension in the big rig where she was certain she was going to die—it didn't feel real.

But it was. It was real and this was the proof. The blood on the floor. The violence that she saw with her own eyes.

"You killed a man. Here!" She pointed to the blood-stains. And then she saw more. So much blood. She had been blind, but she wished she didn't know. She wished she could be a Pollyanna, but she'd never be able to unsee this.

Patrick's jaw clenched and he looked as hard and un-feeling as he had in the truck when he confronted Clark. She really didn't know him. She thought she did, but he wasn't the fun-loving high school baseball player she'd had a crush on.

"I had to," he said. "I don't take it lightly, but I had no alternative. They would have killed both Jack and me to get to Kami."

He sounded so calm. How could he be calm? How could he talk about murder so matter-of-factly? Didn't he care?

"Oh, God, she saw this?" Elle's emotions were spilling over, and the more she felt, the more steadfast Patrick became. She didn't know this man.

"I secured her in the bathroom upstairs." Patrick reached out for her, and she flinched.

"Elle, let's go someplace else. You don't need to be here. I'll hire someone to clean it up. I shouldn't have brought you back." Jack was right, it was too soon.

"You can't clean it up. I can't forget what happened. I'll always see this blood."

Patrick took her hand. "You've been through hell. Give yourself time."

"Is that what you say to yourself? Give yourself time? How many men have you killed?"

Patrick stepped back. "I was a cop, Gabrielle," he said, his voice colder than she'd ever heard it. "I never killed except to protect another human being. I'm not going to apologize."

She shook her head. "Of course not." Oh, God, she'd hurt him. She hadn't meant to say that. Her head was about to explode, she wanted to run away. She'd never been so overwhelmed in her life.

"I don't understand any of this. I don't understand you. I don't understand what you do, or why Clark nearly killed me, or why three men died in my living room!"

She was getting hysterical, and she didn't want to be. She didn't want to sound ungrateful, because she was grateful. She just wanted to forget everything that had happened.

She took a deep breath. "Kami can't come back here with the place like this," she said quietly.

"I'll stay and help clean up."

She shook her head. "Go back to your family."

The buzzer rang on the door. She jumped, and hated that she was scared. Would she ever feel safe again?

Patrick had his gun in hand, at his side, and walked to the door. Was this how her life would be from now on?

She didn't know if she could live like this.

Patrick was talking to someone at the door. She kept picturing Patrick with the gun pointed at Clark. Pointed at her, because she was there in the truck, too. The risks he took to save her. Why would he do that? He could have died. She could have died.

Elle felt so confused she wanted to scream.

But she didn't see how it could have happened any differently.

This was a world unfamiliar to her. She'd seen violence, but always the aftermath. Stories from street kids who'd seen too much, too young. The court system. She'd never lived through it, not like this. She was so scared she couldn't think.

She sat on the floor and put her head in her hands.

"Elle?"

She looked up. Dwight was standing there.

"Where's Patrick?"

"He said he had to go. Come to my place."

"Patrick left?"

Why would he have walked out? What had she said to him? She could hardly remember. But she'd hurt him somehow. She wished she could take it back.

"You've been through hell. Patrick says you're in shock and he'll talk to you tomorrow."

"Shock?" What did Patrick know? Did he think that she'd just get over this, like she had dead men in her apartment every day?

She squeezed her eyes shut. He'd saved her life. She'd never faced her own mortality like she had today.

"Okay," she whispered.

Dwight extended his hand to her. She grabbed it, a life line, and he pulled her up.

"I like him," Dwight said, "but you always try to change people, Elle. You can't change him, like you couldn't change me. You either have to accept him for who he is, or walk away."

She slowly walked upstairs and stood in her bedroom crying. Feeling like she had just lost something she hadn't realized she had.

CHAPTER 16

Patrick sat in the hotel bar and nursed his beer. He'd already had a couple of tequila shots and was feeling the effect, but he considered having a couple more. He wasn't much of a drinker, so the hard liquor hit him hard.

Jack walked up and sat on the stool next to him and ordered another round. The bartender brought two shots of tequila and two more beers. They downed the shots together and slammed the glasses on the counter.

"Elle didn't take it well," Patrick said a few minutes later.

"Did you think she would?"

"I never should have brought her back to her place."

"I won't say I told you so."

"Shut up."

Jack remained silent.

"She had to see it with someone," Patrick said, trying to convince himself he'd done the right thing, even though he knew he hadn't. "If she'd walked in there alone—that would have been worse."

Jack drained his tequila and poured another.

"I've gone over the last twenty-four hours in my head and can't see where I would have changed anything,"

Patrick said. "Other than keeping a much better eye on Elle this morning so she couldn't sneak out."

"You're a good cop, PK."

"I'm not a cop."

"Being a cop is like being a soldier. Once a soldier, always a soldier. Shit happens. We're the people who clean it up. She'll either see it, or she won't. She's stubborn, but she's smart."

"We lead two different lives. And never the twain shall meet."

"Bullshit."

"She has this idealized view of the world. Even after this weekend, she doesn't see the bad. Except—when she walked into her apartment, I think it slapped her in the face. I tried everything I could, but I was getting so angry, I shut down. When her ex showed up, I let him take over." He sighed and sipped his beer. "I've been angry for a long time."

"I know."

Patrick glanced at him. "How?"

"Do you remember when I came to visit you in the hospital, when you woke up from the coma? You woke up as if it were the next day. All the pain and rage was still there. I knew it the minute I saw you. I don't think anyone else wanted to see it. And it won't go away overnight."

"It's been seven years."

"Five years for you. And you still haven't forgiven her."

"Forgiven who?"

"Lucy."

Patrick shook his head. "There was nothing to forgive."

"You blamed her."

"Shut the fuck up. I love Lucy. I never thought any of it was her fault."

"Not consciously, but she made a bad choice. And shit happened. And she feels it, because she knows you feel it."

"I've never—God, Jack, don't." Patrick loved Lucy more than anyone. His sister was all that made him whole. "She visited me. Read to me. I heard her voice all the time, in my head, when I was half dead."

Jack poured two more tequilas. "I shouldn't pretend I'm Dillon. I'm not good with this shrink shit."

"I don't need a shrink."

"You need to forgive yourself for all the shit that went down seven years ago. Your guilt for blaming Lucy, for being angry, for losing part of yourself. Let it go. That anger you have, Elle feels it, too. She might tell you that she has a problem with you taking down those men, but it had to happen. We saved lives today. What she felt was your anger that she went off on her own and put herself in danger. Yes, it was a dumb-ass move, but she did it for the right reasons. What she felt was your anger when all she wanted was justification for three dead bodies in her living room."

"I don't blame her," Patrick said. But maybe . . . maybe he did. He expected her to understand the situation that resulted in the violence at her apartment. He expected her to see the truth, but he hadn't known how to explain. He hadn't fought for her, forced her to see the truth.

But he wasn't a forcing kind of guy. It was there . . . or it wasn't. He didn't like emotional, personal confrontation.

Yeah, he could see how she might think he blamed her for putting herself in danger. He'd shut down because that's what he did so he wouldn't lose his temper. But maybe all she needed was to be held. A human connection. A reminder of hope.

"I'll talk to her tomorrow. What time are you leaving?"

"Whenever you're ready, bro. But you know, Ma won't mind if you're a day late."

"Right—the first Christmas we've all been together in nearly twenty years. She'll never talk to me again."

"She'll talk to you—like I said, you're the golden child."

"Maybe I can talk Elle into coming with us."

"Maybe you can," Jack said. He grabbed the bottle of tequila off the bar and motioned to the bartender. "Put it on my tab." Then he left.

Patrick called Lucy. It was three in the morning in Denver, but he had to talk to her.

She answered on the first ring. "Patrick?"

"You're awake?"

"We've had some excitement here," she said. "I heard you did, too. We'll swap stories when we get home."

Patrick was relieved to hear her voice.

"I'm really going to miss you when you leave D.C.," he said. In that moment all the anger, all the guilt, all the past blame, evaporated. She was getting on with her life, an agent with the FBI, in love with his best friend. He was so proud of her. Maybe, at one point, he had blamed Lucy for everything that happened seven years ago, but more than that, he blamed himself for not protecting her. Blamed himself for the feelings of anger he couldn't control. But now it was gone.

"What's wrong?" she asked quietly.

"Nothing."

She didn't say anything. That's what Lucy did. She waited. Patiently.

"Luce, I love you."

"I know. I love you, too."

"And—well, I'm going to miss you."

"Have you been drinking?"

He laughed. "I don't hold my alcohol as well as Jack."

"No, you don't. And for what it's worth? I'm going to miss you the most. Visit. Often."

"I'll see you in San Diego. I might be a little late."

"We all are."

The phone rang and woke Patrick up. His head ached. Jack was in the shower. It was eight in the morning—he must have gone out hard after two brutal days. And too much tequila.

"Kincaid," he grunted into the phone.

"Patrick? It's Carina."

She sounded panicked. "What's wrong?"

"It's Dad. He's in the hospital. He's had a heart attack."

"Jack and I will be there as soon as we can."

Patrick hung up. His dad—he had to go home.

He called Elle, but remembered that her cell phone was toast. He called Dwight. Voice mail picked up.

"Dwight Bishop, leave a message."

"Dwight, it's Patrick Kincaid. I have a family emergency in San Diego. Please tell Gabrielle that I'll call her as soon as I can. And—put in a good word for me, okay? I screwed it up last night, and I want to fix it." He hung up and hoped he hadn't made a mistake asking Elle's ex-husband for help.

But he couldn't have made the situation any worse than it was when he walked out last night.

Jack stepped out of the bathroom. "It's all yours."

"Pack up," Patrick said. "I'll be ready in five minutes. Carina called—Dad's in the hospital. We need to go home."

PART TWO

Denver

Saturday, December 22

CHAPTER 17

Lucy Kincaid stifled a laugh at the text message her brother Patrick sent.

> I wish I was stranded in Denver. When Mom found out I was in Sacramento, she sent me on an errand to San Francisco. You will not believe what she's asked me to do. See you at home!

"What's so funny?" Kate stretched and rolled over on her side. She was relaxing in one of the two queen beds in the Denver hotel they were stuck in.

Lucy held her phone out so Kate could read the message.

"At least he's in the right state," Kate said with an exaggerated sigh.

"You didn't even want to come," Lucy said.

"Only because your family terrifies me."

Lucy laughed. "Hardly."

"All those hugs and piles of food and constant noise. I was raised by my grandparents, who were the most soft-spoken people on the planet." And, as Lucy knew, they hadn't been affectionate. Kate could handle one or two

Kincaids at a time, but she usually avoided big family gatherings.

"You're lucky—you get to stay with Carina and Nick at their place. Sean and I are at the house, and Dad already made it clear that Sean has to stay in the room above the garage." Lucy didn't complain, however. It was the same for all her brothers and sisters; if they were involved with someone, they weren't allowed to sleep with them in the same bed under her parents' roof until they were married. Lucy was a bit nervous telling her dad that she and Sean were moving in together, but she wasn't the first in the family to do so.

"What are the boys doing?" Kate said. "If they're drinking in the bar without me, I'll shoot them."

After hours of weather-based delays, all flights in and out of Denver were canceled. The blizzard, which was being compared to the storm of 2006 when the airport shut down for nearly two days, was getting worse. Sean had reserved a hotel room in Denver while they were still back in D.C. as a precaution—he said he didn't like the weather patterns and thought the predictions were overly optimistic. Considering Kate and Dillon couldn't get their own room, Sean was enjoying being right—even though the four of them had to share one room.

"At least we have beds," Sean had teased.

Lucy sent Sean a text message. He and Dillon had dropped off their carry-ons, but Dillon had needed some things from the shop downstairs. "I'm sure there's a long line," Lucy said.

"If Sean tells me one more time that he didn't forget anything in his overnight bag, I'm going to beat him up."

Kate had next to nothing. She had packed light and checked everything at the airport. All she carried was a backpack that contained her laptop and wallet. Dillon was downstairs buying toiletries and a T-shirt to sleep in.

"He wasn't even a damn boy scout," Kate muttered and went back to reading her book.

Lucy grinned. Kate liked to give Sean a bad time, but for the most part, they got along. Kate once told Lucy that Sean was like the little brother she never had.

Sean responded to her text message.

Long lines, I'm in the bar. Join me.

She smiled and replied:

Don't tell Kate! I think she wants a drink.

Bring her.

All right. But stop gloating.

I don't gloat. ☺

Lucy laughed.

Kate said, "That was Sean, wasn't it? He's gloating."

"He said he's saving seats for us in the bar. Dillon is still in line getting the things you need."

Kate grumbled. "I need a beer." She sat up and slipped on her shoes. She stared at her feet and bit her thumbnail.

"Is something bugging you?" Lucy asked.

"Other than being stuck here?"

"It started when we picked you up this morning."

"No," she said in a tone that really meant "yes."

"Kate, something's been bothering you all week. Is it San Antonio?"

Lucy found out last week, before her FBI Academy graduation, that she'd been assigned to the San Antonio field office. She had two weeks before she had to report to her new assignment, and since those two weeks included Christmas she'd been able to promise her mom and dad that she'd be home for the holidays and they could finally meet Sean. But Kate had been moody ever since Lucy announced her location.

"I think San Antonio is lucky to have you. You're going to do great there. Dillon is a little upset."

"Dillon?" Lucy and Patrick had had a long talk last week before he left for Sacramento, and she knew he was upset not only about her move cross-country, but also about Sean leaving RCK. Still, they'd worked things out. But Dillon had seemed to be pleased with her appointment to San Antonio.

"Because he's going to miss you. So am I, but I knew you'd be assigned out of the area. Few agents, if any, work out of their recruitment office. I don't think Dillon quite understood that it meant you'd transfer two thousand miles away."

"I'll visit."

"Of course you will. I'll make you." She tried to smile. "Then what?"

"Are you taking Chip?"

At first Lucy was confused. Chip was her cat. "Well, yeah, I guess I didn't think much about it."

"Because I don't think he'll like the heat. And then there's the flight and you'd have to drug him, and I'm pretty sure that's not good for cats. The stress and everything. I just want you to know, if you can't take him, or if you find a place that doesn't allow pets, I don't mind keeping him. He can live with me."

It was clear as day that Kate wanted Chip. Now a bunch of other little things that she'd said over the last few weeks made sense.

But it was also clear that Kate didn't want to admit to Lucy that she'd grown attached to the orange and white cat that Lucy had adopted last summer when his owner was murdered.

Sean was attached to Chip as well. Though the cat had lived with Sean while Lucy was at Quantico, when both Sean and Patrick were out of town, Kate babysat.

Lucy thought Kate might need a pet more than Sean.

She said, "I'm going to be putting in a lot of long hours, and while Sean gets his business up and running, he might not be home a lot. Maybe it would be best if Chip stayed permanently with you."

"Are you sure?" Kate said. "I know you really like him."

"I do, but he knows and likes you. He stayed at your house as much as Sean's while I was at Quantico. It's settled, Kate, Chip can live with you."

Kate jumped up and hugged Lucy. Just a quick hug, but from Kate it meant something. She wasn't a huggy person.

"Why do I get the impression you would have missed Chip more than me?"

"Don't be silly," Kate said as she grabbed her wallet. "I'm going to miss you as much as Dillon will. Now I have something to remember you by." She winked.

A scream split through the silence and Kate pulled open the door, instinctively reaching for her gun, which she didn't have.

They peered into the hall, cautiously at first. Across the corridor, two rooms down, a man and woman stood outside a door propped open with luggage. The man was on his phone while the woman screeched in a high-pitched voice.

Kate approached first. "Donovan, FBI," she said.

The woman was borderline hysterical. "Ohgodohgod-ohgod—"

Lucy looked through the doorway. The room was just like theirs, only in reverse.

And the walls were streaked with blood.

At least, it appeared to be blood. And it smelled like blood, though there was no body that she could see. The bathroom door was closed, and she gestured to Kate.

Kate nodded. "You two," she told the man and woman, "go down the hall to the house phone and call security."

Both the man and woman were shaking, but they ran to the phone, leaving their luggage.

"I wish I had my gun," Kate muttered. "Watch the bathroom door. If you see any movement, let me know." Kate stood on the other side of the open door, out of sight of the bathroom. "We'll just have to wait," she grumbled.

If someone was in the bathroom, they'd be aware that the room had been discovered. Or the body was in there. Either way, they couldn't check without weapons, especially not knowing what they were facing.

"What's taking them so long?" Kate said.

"It's only been two minutes," Lucy reminded her.

"Feels like twenty."

It wasn't more than another minute before two security guards rushed down the hall. Both were young—not much older than Lucy—and when they saw the room, they both hesitated.

Kate introduced herself and Lucy as FBI and said, "Give me your gun and I'll clear it."

"No, ma'am," said the guard with "B. Decker" on his nameplate. "Stand aside, please."

The two guards quickly cleared the room—no one was hiding in the bathroom or closet. There was also no body to go with all the blood.

"Maybe it's paint," T. Bonny said.

Kate said, "Call the police and report a probable homicide. Get your manager up here. I'll stay until they arrive."

"Might be a while. I don't know how they'll get here in the blizzard." He glanced into the room again, pale. "And we don't know that there's been a murder."

"Were you on the job?" Kate asked. Many hotel security officers had been law enforcement, but Decker was a little young to have first been a cop.

"No, ma'am. I'm the assistant chief, Brian Decker. My boss is on vacation. But I don't think we should jump to conclusions."

The elevator doors at the end of the hall swooshed open and a young, fresh-faced woman with minimal makeup and blond hair pulled back into a severe bun rushed toward them.

"I'm Lynn Thomsen, the manager. What's going on here? We've had a dozen calls to the front desk about screams and—Oh, my."

"It could be a prank," Decker said.

"Yes, a truly awful prank," Ms. Thomsen concurred.

"We need Denver PD here to assess the scene," Kate said. "I'll talk to them, figure out what they want us to do."

"And you are?"

She flipped open her identification and badge again. "Special Agent Kate Donovan, FBI. My sister-in-law, Special Agent Lucy Kincaid. Agent Kincaid has the added credentials of being a pathologist, and she thinks someone was killed here."

Lucy hadn't said it, but that was certainly her opinion.

"Come to my office, we'll call the police and get to the bottom of this," Ms. Thomsen said.

"Lucy," Kate said, "stay here with security. No one goes in or out until we get the okay from Denver PD." She kicked aside the luggage and closed the door.

Kate had taken control easily, a testament to her personality and experience. Lucy stood with Decker, who didn't want to chat. Kate spoke to the two guests and asked them to come to the office to be interviewed; they left with her, after retrieving their bags.

Lucy called Sean. "We have some excitement upstairs," she said. "A room across the hall from us is covered in what appears to be blood spatter. Kate's talking to the Denver Police Department."

"Is this a joke?" Sean said.

"No."

"Where are you?"

"Guarding the door with hotel security."

"I'm coming up."

"You don't have to."

But he'd already hung up.

CHAPTER 18

Sean chatted with Decker about hotel security. At first, Decker was suspicious of Sean's questions and answered with vague, clipped responses. But within minutes, Sean had him talking details about their security system and where the security cameras were located, and recent security threats in the hotel.

Decker was in the middle of an elaborate story about how a local congressman had been caught on camera in a compromising situation with his mistress last year when Kate returned.

"I just got off the phone with Detective Harris of Denver PD," she said. "He's on his way, but it's going to take a while. He's across town, and apparently a twenty-minute drive is going to take two or more hours. Fortunately, the assistant chief of police went through my class as a LEO National Academy and vouched for me. We're cleared to run the investigation until Harris gets here."

"We shouldn't touch anything until forensics arrives," Lucy said.

"We might not have a choice. There's no team they can send out until tomorrow. Harris is trained as a criminalist as well, which is why they're sending him." Kate handed

Lucy a pair of blue latex gloves. "From housekeeping," she said. She glanced at Sean. "I told the manager to pull all security feeds and records. The room had been rented to a corporation for the past three days, and whoever was staying here checked out this morning. Denver PD can't run it because they're operating off a generator right now. No nonemergency work."

"I'll take care of it." Sean glanced at Decker. "Can you take me down?"

Decker looked like he'd been steamrolled. "Um, yeah, I need to talk to Ms. Thomsen first."

"You can introduce me," Sean said.

Kate added, "I overheard one of the security guys say something about a glitch. I don't like glitches."

"Trust me," Sean said with a wink. As he and Decker walked away, Sean asked, "Brian, are these glitches common, or was this a one-time thing?"

Lucy and Kate were now alone. Kate frowned and said, "I should have brought back the other security guard, but I have him working with the head of housekeeping to find out who cleaned the room, who was the last one in the room, and to see if anyone in the hotel knows who this guy was who checked out this morning."

Kate used a master key to open the door. She and Lucy stepped inside. Lucy drew in a breath. "I smell distinct biological matter, probably urine—but no hint of decomp. The body wasn't kept in the room long after death."

"No one could have survived losing this much blood," Kate said matter-of-factly, then glanced at Lucy as if to confirm her suspicion. "It *is* blood, right?"

Lucy nodded. "It smells like blood." What she wanted to say was that it smelled like violence, but that would sound silly. Though, looking at the room, violence certainly had left its imprint.

Kate let the door close as they visually assessed the

scene. There was nothing personal in the room. Lucy was careful not to touch anything; she wasn't even certain why Kate wanted them to go through the room, except to look for evidence that might point to the killer still being in the hotel, or evidence to identify the apparent victim.

The blood on the walls appeared dry, but there was a substantial pool on the carpet next to the bed that was clearly wet. If it wasn't blood, then someone had staged the room to look like a violent crime occurred. There were arcs of castoff across the walls and ceiling, suggesting the victim was on the floor while being stabbed repeatedly.

Lucy took pictures with her cell phone of the blood arcs and the pool of blood on the floor. She could almost picture the attack based on the angles and arcs of blood spatter, which disconcerted her. Not that she could see the violence, but because it didn't faze her. Her coolness at crime scenes made her good at her job, but it unnerved her too, the ability to calmly and without emotion dissect a crime.

"There are no personal effects here," Lucy said. "No luggage, no toiletries. The bed is made."

Kate checked her notebook. "The room was reserved to a corporation, but the hotel didn't have an individual's name to go with it. A corporate credit card was used at check-in."

"They're supposed to check ID."

"Supposed to."

After photographing the scene, Lucy checked the blood on the floor with one gloved finger. As she suspected, still wet. The arcs on the ceiling were tacky, some of the smaller drops dry. The uneven acoustic ceiling made visual analysis difficult, but the spatter on the walls was telling.

"Most of these arcs are castoff," Lucy said. She counted. "At least nine separate stab wounds." She walked back to the door. "The first stab wound was here, right near the threshold."

Kate concurred. "And the victim ran away from the attacker."

"So the victim was already in the room. A room that was supposed to be vacant."

"Housekeeping staff?"

"Possibly."

Kate said, "I'm already having security count heads of all housekeeping staff who were on duty today." She said, partly to herself, "Why didn't the victim scream? Why run into the room where she—or he—would be trapped?"

"Because the killer came in through the door—or the bathroom door—and the victim was already in the room."

"Using a master key."

"Or the room was open."

"Meeting someone?"

"Speculation at this point. But I can say fairly confidently that the victim was standing here for the first stab wound, ran back into the room, was stabbed here"—Lucy pointed to the large pool of blood—"and then collapsed. The stabbing must have been both deep and violent to render the victim immobile so quickly. There's no sign that he or she tried to move away while they were on the floor." Lucy gestured to arcs of blood on the bedspread and the walls. "Those are not castoff. If a carotid artery is cut, the heart will pump out the blood as far as thirty feet. I think the second or third blow definitely hit a major artery or the victim's heart."

"But you said there were nine."

"At least nine."

"That's a crime of passion."

"You could call it that."

"Meaning overkill. The killer stabbed the victim repeatedly even after he or she was dead."

"Yes, I think so."

Lucy stepped into the bathroom. The sink was tinged with red, and there were streaks of blood on the counter, mirror, and floor. "The killer washed up in here," she said.

"There's also something else," Kate said. "Something missing."

Lucy looked around and saw what Kate saw—or didn't see. "No towels."

They left the hotel room and stood outside the door. Kate called security and asked for a guard to meet up with them. She didn't want to leave the room unattended.

She then asked Lucy, "Theories?"

Lucy frowned. She didn't like to speculate. She preferred more information before formulating an opinion, though she had a theory. "The victim died quickly, but it was more violent than it needed to be. If theft was the motive, the killer would have stopped after the victim was incapacitated."

"But there's nothing personal in the room, which suggests that the victim might have been robbed."

Lucy considered. "What about if it was a guest who had already checked out? Put their luggage with the valet because they had to wait for a plane?"

Kate snapped her fingers. "Brilliant." She pulled out her phone again. "Decker? Call the concierge and get a list of all guests who have luggage in storage. Let me know when it's ready."

Kate grinned and turned back to Lucy. "I'm beginning to like that kid. I need a minion."

Lucy almost laughed. "Yeah, you do." She looked around the hall. "Now the big question is, how did the killer move the body?"

"Laundry cart. Easiest way to get it out unseen."

"Then are you thinking that a staff member is the killer?"

"They'd have a master key. A staff member could also be a victim." Kate considered. "What if two staff members are having an affair and using empty rooms to get it on, but this time something happened. Girl threatens to leave guy, guy kills her. Girl finds out guy is married and attacks."

"But this murder was premeditated," Lucy said. "A knife that size isn't going to be lying around."

"Except in the hotel kitchen."

"Good point."

"Okay, I'm going to talk to the manager and tell her to keep this all under her cap, though it might be too late for that. If it's a staff member, they may already know what we know, so everything else is going to stay between you, me, and Harris."

"When he gets here."

"Hey, maybe we'll have the case solved before he arrives."

Two security guards got off the elevator and Kate instructed them to not let anyone in the room until she returned with Detective Harris. Then she and Lucy walked to their room.

Kate pulled her phone from her pocket. "Dillon's calling." To Dillon she said, "Did Sean fill you in? Lucy and I are—" She stopped talking and her face turned even more serious. "Okay, we're coming." She closed the phone. "We have another body."

"*Another* body?" Lucy asked, her eyebrows raised. "Maybe it's our missing victim?"

"No, this victim hasn't been stabbed. But it's suspicious."

"How so?"

"A woman was found dead in the hot tub."

"And we're checking this out because?" Lucy questioned.

Kate shrugged. "We don't have anything else to do while we're stranded here. We might as well help the local police until they can take charge. It's like that game Clue. Here"—she gestured toward the bloody room—"we know that *someone* was killed with a knife in the bedroom. And in the hot tub. We have the person and place, but not the how."

"Dillon didn't say that the woman in the hot tub was murdered," Lucy said.

"No, but crime scene with no body and body with no crime scene? Makes me suspicious."

Me, too.

"We're a pair, aren't we?"

Kate grinned. "Yep. This could be the last time we work together. So, let's solve the case before Denver PD arrives."

CHAPTER 19

The indoor pool and connecting hot tub faced a wall of windows that, on a clear day, would have framed the Rocky Mountains. Now, all they could see was a sheet of white, glowing from external security lights. Guests were crowding the door, some obviously having been in the gym working out, others not dressed to exercise but here as spectators.

Lucy loved how Kate seized immediate command of every situation. She told the guests to give their names to the security officer at the door, including their room numbers, and then leave.

When no one moved, she pulled out her badge and said forcefully, "Now, people, or I'll have security detain you in the manager's office."

They moved. Kate was one of the most confident women Lucy knew, and she always learned something when they worked together.

Lucy whispered, "You should go back into the field."

Kate gave her an odd look that made Lucy think that she was either surprised at the comment, or had been thinking about it herself. Lucy hoped the latter was the case, because while Kate was an asset teaching at Quantico, she truly thrived as a field agent. Lucy hadn't realized that Kate didn't enjoy teaching until after Lucy had her as an instructor at Quantico.

Investigating was Kate's first love.

Kate said to Lucy, "Go do your thing."

"Thing?"

"You've seen a lot more dead bodies than I have. Tell me if this is a natural death, or if someone killed the blonde. If it's not a murder, I can go back to our crime scene upstairs."

"It might not be that simple."

While security processed everyone who had been in the adjoining gym, Lucy and Kate walked into the pool area. Lucy's brother Dillon, a forensic psychiatrist, was standing to one side talking to a petite gray-haired woman in a conservative business suit. A female wearing a one-piece black swimsuit was lying faceup next to the Jacuzzi, her skin red and slightly bloated. She was obviously dead.

Lucy approached the hot tub. Dillon introduced them. "Lucy, this is Abby Granger, the assistant manager. She's also certified in first aid and CPR. Security contacted her when the call came in."

Abby's short gray hair and wrinkled hands suggested she was in her fifties, but her face was smooth with a peaches-and-cream complexion.

"Two guests found her and pulled her out," Abby said, "but she was dead by the time I got here."

"Did the guest try to revive her?"

"Yes, but the gentleman said she wasn't breathing when he pulled her out."

"Where are they now?"

"It was a husband and wife, they're in Lynn's office. The manager."

That was going to be a crowded room. "No one saw what happened?" Lucy asked.

"No one was here when the couple arrived. The pool closes at eleven, they came in ten minutes to. The hotel card key should confirm the time."

Lucy looked over the body. The reddened skin and slight bloating suggested she'd been in the water, dead, for a while, but Lucy couldn't till if it was an hour, more or less.

Abby said, "She looks like she's been submerged for hours, but I think it's because of the heat of the hot tub."

"It is. See, her palms and the soles of her feet are already showing signs of maceration."

"Dear Lord, how long was she dead?"

"I can't say with certainty, I haven't recovered a body from water this warm before. And we don't know how long she was in the water before she died. In temperate water, like a lake in summer, it can be seen in an hour or two. In cold water and in winter, it can take a few days. So I'd say she wasn't in there for longer than an hour." But that was a guess.

"One time we had two college kids who nearly drowned when they got drunk and started playing in the pool," Abby said. "One hit his head and knocked himself out. Maybe she fell asleep?"

Lucy barely heard her. She was staring at the distinct discoloration on the woman's neck and shoulders.

"No, I'm pretty sure she was held under." Lucy's eyes settled on Dillon. "This woman was murdered."

Kate had Decker's security team seal off the pool room while Lucy covered the body. "We need an ID on the victim," Lucy said. "Did you find anything in the area? Her room key? A purse?"

Abby shook her head. "I didn't see anything when I came in."

"I looked when I arrived," Dillon added, "and the only thing was a hotel towel."

"How'd she get into the spa?" Lucy asked. "You need a card key, correct?"

Abby nodded. "Except a lot of people will come together. If she was with someone, she may not have needed her key. Or someone held the door for her."

Or the killer took her key for some reason.

"No one can leave the hotel," Abby said. "The roads are closed until morning, only emergency traffic."

Lucy understood what that meant, and by the fearful look on Abby's face, so did she.

"The killer *may* still be here," Lucy said, trying to keep the staff calm, "but we still need to ID the victim. That may point to someone else. Can you get a water sample of the hot tub, and a reading on the temperature, then shut everything down? The steam is going to compromise evidence."

"Certainly. The maintenance staff should have test tubes and a thermometer."

"Go ahead, we'll wait here until you return."

Abby left, and Kate started waving at Lucy.

Dillon said, "You go with Kate, I'll wait for Abby. Anything else?"

"Take a couple pictures, as good as you can get of her face. We can show it to staff and hopefully get an ID on the victim. We also need to get the body moved to a drier, cooler area."

"I have an idea," Dillon said. "I'll talk to security."

Lucy left Dillon with the body and approached Kate, who was waiting by the door. She said, "Sean has something, let's go to the security office."

They were alone in the elevator when Kate said, "I finally got through to Harris. He's a year from retirement and has more experience in his little finger than the two of us together, but he's never heard of anything like this. He doesn't know Decker, but says the head of security is a retired cop from Denver PD and there's never been any problems like this at the hotel. By Denver standards, it's a smaller facility and on the high-end side." She rolled her eyes as they stepped off the elevator. "I should have figured Sean would book us in a five-star hotel."

Sean was waiting for them and heard the last part of her comment. "Five-star hotel with a one-star security system," he said. "Whole system is down. Someone intentionally disabled it, but it was far too easy to do, and because the system goes down regularly, no one thought it was a concern when the system shut down at eight o'clock tonight."

That was only thirty minutes before they'd arrived from the airport.

"Do you know how? Are we looking for someone with technical skills?"

He shrugged. "Maybe, but not required. Someone went into the server room in the basement and literally pulled the plug on the internal cameras. All the other security is working just fine, but the internal cameras—no."

"Can you get them back up?"

"Of course," Sean said as if it weren't a question. "But it'll take a little time. I have to shut down the whole system, plug everything back in, run a couple tests, then reboot."

"Then maybe we can see who pulled the plug," Kate said.

"No," Sean said. "Someone destroyed the archive."

"What do you mean?" Lucy asked.

Kate said, "The cameras feed into a hard drive to store digital data. If there's a problem, security can retrieve anything that was seen by the cameras at a later date. So someone really is smart. As smart as you?" she teased Sean.

"Hardly. More destructive. Literally destroyed the hard drive. No technical skill needed to whack the box with a hammer. However, the culprit left the hammer. I asked one of the security guys to bag it for the cops when they show up."

"How long until you can get the cameras back up?"

"I'm working with their IT guy, we'll have them up inside thirty minutes. But that's the bad news."

"You actually have good news?" Kate asked.

"I wouldn't have called you for just that. I traced the company that rented the room. It's an architectural design firm based in Chicago. They specialize in high-end residences. The owner is James St. Paul, born and raised outside Chicago. Thirty-two, won a bunch of awards." He handed Kate a notepad. "His cell phone, home phone, secretary, associates. Plus, I took the liberty of running a quick background. There's no sign of him leaving Chicago, but his business credit card was used at the airport three days ago, and for food here in the hotel. I could find out if he was on a flight—"

"No," Kate said. "You wouldn't be able to legally. I'll have Denver PD run it and see where he went. Good work."

Lucy said, "I don't suppose you have a picture?"

Sean smiled. "Of course I do." He pulled a photo off a color printer in the security office. "There you go."

James St. Paul was blond and stunningly attractive—the kind of good looks that only get better with age, like Paul Newman's. The picture was from his Web site.

"Do you think there's a connection between the bloody hotel room and our Jane Doe in the hot tub?" Sean asked.

Kate and Lucy answered simultaneously, "Yes."

"Good to know you're both on the same page."

Lucy said, "We have a better timeline now. All the cameras went off at eight. The blood is more than two hours dry, and it could have been there for four hours or longer, but not all day."

Kate said, "The manager is retrieving all access logs into the room."

"Why didn't you just ask me?" Sean sat at a desk and ran a report. "Before the blood was discovered, the room was last accessed by a master key at eight-nineteen this evening. The key code sends a notation to the system every time the door is opened and by which key."

"What about St. Paul's key?"

"The last time it was used was today, early in the morning. He checked out at noon."

"Maybe he was able to get a flight out before they shut down," Kate said. "This might have nothing to do with him, but a staff member who knew the room was vacant."

Lucy said, "Can you run all card keys that were used to access the gym from the time the computer system went down until the body was found?"

"Yes, boss," Sean said.

"Are the master keys coded by staff member?" Kate asked.

"Unfortunately, no."

Kate made a note. "I'm going to have Decker find out who is missing a master card."

"I think the million-dollar question that we're all dying to know: where is the body?" Sean said.

Kate said, "Security is searching the hotel top to bottom."

"Unless someone used the incinerator," Sean said.

"Aha! I thought of something before you." Kate grinned and gave herself a point in the air. "I already looked into that possibility. The incinerator is in the basement and is separately monitored and regulated. The room is accessible only by a physical key, not a card key, which is in the possession of the head of maintenance and his assistant. Plus, it's on a separate security system."

"Okay, you win that round." Sean gave her a quick bow.

"My guess is that the body is still in the laundry bin," Kate said, more to herself than anyone in the room. Lucy agreed, which meant it should be easy to find the victim. But so far, nothing.

Sean handed Lucy a printout of everyone who'd accessed the gym during the time she specified. "You look a million miles away."

"I'm listening," she said, and she was. But she was also thinking. "Why move the body? They made no attempt to clean up the crime scene, only to make the body disappear."

"Forensic evidence," Kate said. "Maybe the victim fought back and there's evidence on the body. Or they didn't think the room was being used, and didn't want the body to start stinking up the place."

"Or," Lucy said, "they didn't want the victim's identity to be discovered. Maybe the identity of the victim points to the killer."

One of the security guards knocked on the door. "Agent Donovan?"

"Here," Kate said.

"Chief Decker said you wanted the list of all the luggage being held by the concierge." He handed her an envelope.

"Thank you," she said.

When he left, she opened it. She scanned the list, then hit it with the back of her hand.

"James St. Paul. His luggage is here."

"But he's no longer a registered guest," Lucy said.

"The hotel is allowing guests who checked out but couldn't get on their plane to stay in one of the ballrooms since the hotel is sold out," Kate said. "They brought in cots and blankets. I'll go to the ballroom and see if he's there. Lucy, check out his luggage."

"Do we need a warrant?"

"Not if it's been abandoned."

Lucy wasn't certain Kate was right, but she was more concerned about the safety of Mr. St. Paul than anything else. Kate walked out and Lucy said to Sean, "Can you find out, without hacking into any government agencies, if James St. Paul has any lawsuits, threats, restraining orders? I'd check both Colorado and Illinois."

"You think someone's threatening him?"

"Or maybe he's the threat. Maybe there's a restraining order against him, and he didn't like it. Denver isn't running anything that isn't an emergency because they are on generators."

"Got it." Sean rubbed the back of Lucy's neck. "You're tense."

"Just tired."

He kissed her lightly. "It won't be long until we're in San Diego."

"You looking forward to meeting my parents?" She smiled slyly.

"On second thought, the blizzard is looking better and better." He didn't sound scared. "They're going to love me."

"If you eat, my mom will love you. If you're respectful without being a kiss-ass, my dad will love you."

"Did you just say 'kiss-ass'?" Sean laughed. "I've rarely heard you swear, and I've never heard you say 'kiss-ass.'"

"A first time for everything." She winked at Sean as she walked out.

*   *   *

After reading the concierge ticket that all guests were given when they left their bags, Lucy felt better about searching St. Paul's luggage. Signing it, he'd given away the right to privacy, as the hotel claimed the right to search belongings under a wide variety of circumstances. The hotel was happy to let her access his solitary suitcase.

She wore gloves—again, disposable housekeeping gloves—and unzipped his quality bag. Inside she found neatly folded clothes. Jeans, slacks, sweaters. Toiletries. There was nothing in the suitcase that told her where he was or what he was planning. No day planner, no computer, no journal.

But something was missing. There was no coat. In this weather, and it had been below freezing when St. Paul flew in three days ago, he would have brought a heavy jacket. There was also no cell phone or any electronics.

"Agent Kincaid?" The valet stepped in. "This laptop was also part of Mr. St. Paul's belongings."

"But his ticket said he had one piece."

"Yes, but he returned later and checked his laptop. It wasn't on the same ticket."

"Thank you."

The valet left, and Lucy opened the laptop case. She slid out his MacBook Pro and opened it. She considered calling Sean, but she was computer savvy, and there were no security protocols on the laptop. It was already on, just sleeping, and when she opened the lid the screen lit up.

She first checked his calendar. He had only partial travel plans on his calendar—no exact times, no airline, and no destination. The only thing on his calendar that indicated that he'd been traveling was a car that had picked him up in Chicago at ten-fifteen the morning he departed. There was a confirmation number.

If he was paranoid—and it seemed that way to her

because of the lack of details in his calendar—then why would he include confirmation numbers? That would give anyone who wanted to hurt him valuable information. Many companies would share information if you had a confirmation number.

She went further back into his calendar and noted that it was about two months ago that he'd stopped adding any specific information and only made vague references to meetings and events. But there was nothing to indicate why.

She pulled up his e-mail.

At first she didn't see anything suspicious and, in fact, he had sent out very few messages of late. He'd sent a message to his staff that he was taking vacation time over Christmas and would be back after the New Year. No mention of where he was going, just that he would be available by cell phone only.

She focused on the messages during the week he'd changed how he managed his calendar. There she found the key: he had a series of messages to and from a lawyer about a restraining order. But it wasn't against him—he'd filed it against his ex-girlfriend.

The last message from St. Paul to his attorney was two months ago, almost to the day:

Joe, she's hacked into my e-mail again. She knows where I'm going, where I've been, she's calling my clients—if you need me, call my new cell phone. Don't e-mail me anything sensitive.

She dug a little deeper, into his social media pages and files. Two months ago he'd stopped posting on all the social media sites, except specific business-related topics. But he'd never deleted his archives. She found a heartbreaking message from a girlfriend sent four months previous.

James, I can't do this anymore. She keeps calling me, she keeps showing up outside my work. She's driving me crazy. I'm scared. I told you that you had to do something, that she's dangerous. I thought she was going to hurt you; but now I really think she wants to kill me. I've never felt so terrified in my life. I'm moving, because I don't want her to know where I live. I love you so much, but I don't know how to do this anymore. ~ Denise

Lucy found Denise's phone number and called her. It went to voice mail after several rings. She winced. It was late, after midnight, and she was calling a stranger. She left a message.

"Denise, this is FBI Agent Lucy Kincaid. I'm calling regarding your past relationship with James St. Paul, specifically an e-mail you sent him regarding threats you'd received. Please contact me as soon as you can." She left her number and hung up.

She then searched around on his computer for photos. He didn't have many, but she found one in his e-mail sent by Denise over a year ago. The message said:

James, I had such a wonderful time last weekend! I thought you might like this photo Tim took on the boat.

The man was James, looking happy and relaxed, in swim trunks and a T-shirt, sitting on a small yacht with a lake behind them. Denise was sitting next to him, smiling, her shoulder-length blond hair blowing out behind her.

Her cell phone rang. She thought it might be Denise returning her call, but the caller ID said Kate.

"I have some interesting information," Lucy said.

"And I have a dead body."

"You found our stabbing victim?"

"No. Security found a woman outside nearly buried in snow. No visible stab wounds, but she's definitely dead. Grab your coat, we're going outside."

CHAPTER 20

Kate was waiting for Lucy at the end of a long corridor in the back of the hotel, just inside double glass doors that led out to the courtyard. The ballroom where guests were staying who couldn't catch their flights was around the corner, but security managed to keep them out of this wing.

Kate was talking to an all-around large man in slacks and a thick black jacket with a bright yellow stripe around the chest. DENVER PD was printed in yellow under the stripe. He had a gray buzz cut, either former military or hiding a receding hairline, or both. While he was a big guy, he wasn't fat—in fact, he looked like 250 pounds of solid muscle.

"Lucy, Detective Howard Harris, Denver PD. I've filled him in while we were waiting for you. Howard, my sister-in-law, Special Agent Lucy Kincaid. Frankly, I'm relieved you're taking over because this situation has me scratching my head."

Harris laughed, reminding Lucy of a beardless Santa. He even had crinkly blue eyes. "I think you've done more in three hours than most cops could do in a day."

"I've found I like ordering around the security staff.

The power of being in charge," Kate teased. She gestured to the carpet inside the door. "A staff member noticed there was melting snow inside this door. He thought maybe smokers were going out here, instead of the main entrance where there is a roof and designated smoking area."

"Every winter I'm glad I gave up smoking," Harris said.

"You and me both," Kate said. "Because the staff has been alerted to contact security about anything out of the ordinary, security inspected the courtyard and found the victim."

Kate zipped up a jacket, which was much too big for her. Lucy looked at her quizzically. "Gift from security," she snapped. She turned to Harris. "I stuffed my jacket in my suitcase before I left. I didn't expect to be stranded in a blizzard on my way to San Diego." She handed Lucy another pair of disposable gloves. She kept her hands in her pockets.

They stepped outside and the driving snow made walking the ten feet to the body cumbersome. Already, the body was nearly covered.

Shouting to be heard over the wind, Kate said, "She was mostly covered, but the security guard saw the bright green jacket. He reached down and pulled up her arm."

Lucy squatted to inspect the body, the cold already seeping under her jacket. "Help me push the snow aside," she said.

The victim was a woman. She lay facedown wearing jeans and a heavy jacket. Her long blond hair was matted with blood.

"Could she have come out for a smoke and not gotten back inside?" Kate said.

"There's a significant amount of blood on the back of her head," Lucy said. She inspected the area around the skull. "I don't see a bullet hole, more likely blunt force trauma, but we'll have to inspect her inside. She was either knocked unconscious and died from exposure, or killed and left here. Do we have a place for this body?"

"At Dillon's suggestion, the assistant manager, Abby, took one of the conference rooms and put the AC on its coldest setting," Kate said. "It won't get cold enough, but it'll help."

They didn't have the proper supplies to bag the bodies and keep them outside, and they couldn't leave them exposed to the elements, which could destroy or contaminate any trace evidence on the victims.

Harris said, "The coroner should be here by morning. They can't get here sooner, not enough equipment or manpower and everything is running slower because of the blizzard." He pulled a small digital camera from his pocket. "I'm going to get a couple pictures. Stand back."

Lucy and Kate stood to the side while Harris snapped pictures of the body, the doorway about ten feet away, and the surrounding area. The security lights on the outside of the hotel gave the snow falling around them an odd, unearthly glow, but the courtyard was dark and the only sound was wind whistling past their ears.

"Okay, let's get her inside before we freeze alongside her," Harris said.

Kate stepped into the hotel and retrieved a stretcher, and the three of them lifted the unyielding corpse.

The designated room was directly off the back corridor, making it easy to move the body without any guests watching. Abby and Dillon were both there, cataloging external injuries on the body from the Jacuzzi.

"Put her over there," Abby said, gesturing toward a conference table covered by a sheet. "Leave her on the stretcher."

They did as she asked and Abby covered the body with

another sheet. Harris had a crime-scene field kit and took out vials and bags. "We need to collect as much evidence as we can from the bodies since the coroner is delayed. Bag the hands. I'm going to take better photos of the injuries on each victim."

Lucy took the paper bags and carefully put them around each victim's hands. Harris inspected the head injury to Jane Doe number 2. "You're right, Kincaid—no bullet entry or exit. Definitely not the stabbing victim from the hotel room. Something heavy and wooden did this damage. I see splinters, and if they're big enough for these bad eyes, they're big."

Lucy looked at them. She took tweezers from Harris's bag and collected several of the larger splinters from the wound and put them in a vial, then labeled it. "The weapon could still be outside," she said.

"And we're not going to find it tonight. It's buried, but I'll lead a security team tomorrow morning when there's light. Kate, can you call security and have them keep a guy on that door all night?"

Kate stepped aside to make the call. Harris gently turned the victim's head back, then pulled the sheet over her face. Lucy liked the older detective. Even though he was burly and a bit on the brusque side, he had gentle hands and took great care with the two victims in front of him.

He searched her body for identification. He found a hotel card key, but no ID—not uncommon. He bagged it and said to Kate, "I need the hotel to run this card key."

"Not a problem. At least it's more than we have on the first victim."

Kate introduced Dillon to Detective Harris, then said to Lucy, "You told me on the phone you found out something interesting about St. Paul?"

"Who's St. Paul?" Harris asked.

"We believe he used his company to rent a room in the

hotel, the room with the blood spatter. We can't locate him, but his luggage was checked with the concierge," Kate said. "I've also talked to staff who've interacted with him, and the only thing we've learned is that he spent most of the three days in his room."

"But he checked out, correct?" Harris said.

"Yes, noon today. I planned to contact Homeland Security to check his flight status, but since his luggage was left here—" She looked at Lucy. "Was it time-stamped?"

"Five hours after he checked out."

"So he could have gone to the airport, realized he couldn't get out, and returned, but they had no rooms available."

"What did you learn about St. Paul?" Harris asked Lucy.

"He was being stalked by an ex-girlfriend. I don't have her name, but I have his lawyer's name and number." She pulled out a piece of paper. "A recent girlfriend named Denise, no last name, broke up with him a few months ago because his ex was stalking her. She said in an e-mail that she was terrified for her life."

"Maybe St. Paul decided to take matters into his own hands."

"And kill two women?"

"Maybe they're not connected," Harris said.

Lucy said, "I couldn't help but notice these two victims are both blond and under thirty. And so is Denise, James's scared girlfriend."

"What, you think James St. Paul is a serial killer targeting blondes?" Kate said. She wasn't joking, either.

"I think we need more information," Lucy said cautiously. She didn't want to indulge in speculation that might influence how they investigated these two deaths.

Dillon spoke up for the first time. "I know what Lucy is thinking. She suspects the stalker ex-girlfriend."

"That makes no sense," Kate said. "Maybe if she went after St. Paul, but randomly targeting blondes?"

Kate needed facts. Everything had to make sense, and on the surface, nothing made sense about these murders.

"These two victims have very similar looks and builds," Lucy said. "The one photo I found on St. Paul's computer was primarily scenery. Denise was in the picture, but she was without makeup, casual, in the background. It was on a lake, and these blondes, at first glance, might pass for her. Especially if his ex-girlfriend had only looked at the picture and didn't have a copy." Lucy turned to Harris. "If it's all right with you, Detective, I'd like to turn over St. Paul's laptop to a computer expert who might be able to pull more information."

He said to Kate, "The same guy who found out that the hotel's camera system was compromised?"

"That's him," Kate said. "Do it, Luce, and send me the lawyer's information. I'll see if we can track him down and find out what's going on with St. Paul."

The door opened abruptly and a tall, lanky man stood stone-faced on the threshold. The manager, Lynn Thomsen, was behind him looking worried. "Sir—let me get the detective."

"I want to know if that's my wife!" His voice cracked.

Detective Harris approached. "Sir, what's your name?"

"Martin Katz. My wife was in the Jacuzzi and didn't come back to the room. I couldn't find her—and then I saw all the people, and the hotel wouldn't tell me anything! Is she okay? Is she in the hospital? Why won't anyone tell me what's happening!"

"Sir, I'm Detective Harris with Denver PD. Was your wife in the Jacuzzi at approximately ten-thirty this evening?"

"Yes! I told the manager that! She left for her workout, and then to relax in the pool. I wanted to sleep. We're driving to my parents' in the morning; they live in Colorado Springs, and with these roads . . ." His voice trailed off. "What happened?" he demanded.

Harris nodded to Abby to turn down the sheet on the strangulation victim. Katz rushed over and stared, then his knees buckled and he grabbed the table.

"No."

Lucy went to his side and helped support him, taking him to a chair lined up against the wall.

"No," he repeated. "No, no, no." His voice cracked. "Maggie's a great swimmer. How?"

"She was murdered, Mr. Katz," the detective said bluntly. He was watching Katz for a reaction—any reaction might indicate whether he was involved in his wife's death.

Katz looked up at the detective blankly, as if he didn't hear a word. "She's a terrific swimmer," he repeated. "Did she hit her head? Why didn't anyone help her?"

Harris went on and asked, "Do you have anyone who can verify that you were in your room this evening?"

Katz didn't react. Lucy realized the fact that his wife had been murdered hadn't sunk in. "I don't understand," he said.

"You said that your wife went to the gym this evening, and you stayed in the room."

"Yes, I said that. But—"

"What time did she leave the room?"

He blinked and said, "I don't know. After nine. I was half asleep. I'd been driving all day in this weather, and I needed to crash. Oh, God, I should have been there with her. I could have helped her."

"When did you realize she was missing?"

"I woke up at eleven-thirty, and she wasn't back. I called her cell phone. I thought she might have gotten something to eat. She didn't answer. I started looking around. I went to the gym. Security was there. It took me nearly an hour to get the manager to finally talk to me!" His voice was escalating. "Tell me what happened!"

"Your wife appears to have been strangled or intentionally drowned," Harris said. "We'll know more after the autopsy, but the coroner won't be able to get here until morning."

Lucy watched the information hit Katz and sink in. He shook his head. "Everyone loves Maggie. No one would hurt her. It was an accident. It had to be. An awful accident." His eyes closed tight and his body shook with emotion.

"As I said, we'll know more when the coroner arrives. In the meantime, I'll ask security to escort you to your room. Let them know if you need anything."

Katz didn't want to leave, but eventually Harris got him to go with security without resorting to threats.

"He didn't do it," Harris said emphatically. "Of course, we'll have to look at his background, money issues, but he seems genuinely in shock."

"I concur," Dillon said. Lucy had almost forgotten he was in the room—Dillon had an uncanny way of observing unobtrusively.

Harris said, "I'm going to talk to security and see what their resources are. I don't want to cause a panic, but we have to make sure that the guests know that they need to be careful, not go anywhere alone." He held up the card key he'd found on their frozen Jane Doe. "I'm going to find out what room this belongs to, maybe we'll get an ID on our second victim."

"First victim," Lucy corrected. "She definitely died earlier this evening."

"How can you tell? She was outside for a long time."

"I worked at a morgue for a year, I can extrapolate based on what I know about weather conditions and decomposition. I suspect she was killed before ten P.M., and we know Maggie accessed the gym at nine-thirty P.M."

"And," Kate added, "we have witnesses who saw her on the treadmill around ten in the evening."

"She knew the pool closed at eleven. She probably jumped in after her workout, then warmed up in the Jacuzzi." It was something Lucy did whenever she had access to a pool. "The killer was either in the Jacuzzi and didn't appear to be a threat, or came up to her after she entered. Another hotel guest, nothing to worry about," Lucy said, putting herself in Maggie's shoes. "Might have exchanged hellos or something innocuous. Kate, do we have the key cards yet that accessed the gym before and after Maggie?"

"Yes, there are only twenty-four, so we can run them down very quickly. We already interviewed those who were in the gym when we arrived. There are nine we need to track down and talk to."

"One of the flaws in the card key system is that anyone can walk in on a master key, or follow someone in who has a key," Harris said. "Most people in hotels, especially nice places like this, don't think about it, but if someone didn't want to be tracked, they could easily move around without having to use any identifying card key."

"Or steal a key," Lucy said. "Most hotels give two keys per room, even if there's only one guest. It's easy to misplace one, or think you lost it."

"It's easy to use anyone's key for public areas," Kate said.

"Any word on the missing stabbing victim?" Harris asked.

"Security has been searching the hotel, but so far nothing."

"Let's talk to them again. Dead people don't just disappear," Harris said with irritation.

Kate said, "Dillon, can you stay here with Abby? Make sure there's no trouble."

"Of course," he said.

"And, Lucy, let us know if Sean gets anything off St. Paul's computer."

Lucy left to bring James St. Paul's computer to Sean. He was leaning back in a chair in the security office, watching the monitors with half-closed eyes. "I just got the oddest call from your brother."

"Patrick?"

"Yep. He just sent me a message to be on call for something technical. But I haven't heard back from him."

"What's he doing?"

"I have no idea."

Lucy put St. Paul's laptop next to Sean. "I think St. Paul's ex-girlfriend is stalking him. He stopped using his e-mail for anything personal two months ago, and I read some of the messages that made me think he thought she was spying on him via the computer."

Sean sat up, wide-eyed. "This will be fun." He hooked up his tablet to the computer, then ran a program that examined St. Paul's hard drive. It took several minutes, and Sean chatted about Patrick and what he might be up to. "Do you know why he's in San Francisco?"

"He didn't say specifically, just that he was on an errand for Mom."

"She sent him to San Francisco on an errand?"

"I know, weird. But it's not that far out of the way, and he can just as easily get a flight out of San Francisco as he can out of Sacramento, maybe more easily."

Sean's eyes sparkled with discovery as he typed on St. Paul's computer. "The guy was right, he was being cyberstalked. There's a Trojan on here that records him when he's at the computer."

Lucy shivered. Being watched—especially by someone unseen—creeped her out.

"He disabled his camera two months ago," Sean said. "There are additional programs that forward all messages he gets to another e-mail."

"Can you track that e-mail?" Lucy asked, a wave of excitement running through her.

"Already did. It's shut down, but I can definitely get the host and basic account information. For account ownership you'd need a warrant, if you want to keep it legal." He worked quickly on the keyboard. "It's a freebie account with a national provider. I can't tell where the recipient lives, it's all routed through multiple servers depending on traffic volume."

Sean leaned forward. "Oh, shit. I think your theory's right, Luce."

"What?" She didn't see what he saw in the rows of code.

"He may have shut down the camera and stopped using his e-mail and run virus protection software and thought he was safe, but there's a boot code. Anytime he turns on his computer and hooks up to any Internet connection, a notice goes out to a public message board. The last time the notice went out was three days ago, when he logged in to the hotel network. Oh—this is good. I might be able to trace it."

"You can trace a public message board?"

"Not quite—but I can upload a virus to send me information about any computer that accesses that specific page and where that computer is—under most circumstances."

"Great. And can you find out if he sent any messages?"

"Yes, give me a little time."

For Sean, "give me time" essentially meant "I can work faster if you're not hovering."

She kissed his cheek. "You're the best."

He grinned. "I know." He glanced at her. "Go to bed. It's nearly three in the morning."

"What about you?"

"As soon as I crack this, I'll be up. Promise."

She left and went to the tenth floor. She found Kate and Detective Harris coming out of room 1080.

"You're right, Agent Kincaid," Harris said. "Definitely blood. I collected some samples and the crime-scene techs will be out here tomorrow, hopefully early." He closed the door. "The hotel blocked all electronic keys until they arrive. I'm going to crash in the security office—no way am I driving home in this weather."

"And we can get an early start," Kate said. "We have a guard on our makeshift morgue, and extra patrols in the halls. Sean got the security cameras back up."

"He also confirmed that St. Paul was being cyber-stalked," Lucy said.

"Do we have any real reason to think this is connected to St. Paul?" Harris said.

"We haven't been able to reach him, he left his luggage here, and we haven't found him in the overflow rooms," Kate said. "There's just something weird about the situation."

"He's the killer or the victim," Lucy muttered.

"What?" Kate asked. "I missed that."

"We're missing a body, someone who was killed in a room St. Paul had vacated. He's been stalked. He could easily be a victim. Or, he set it all up to make him appear to be the victim so he could get away with murder."

"Not on my watch," Kate said.

"Those two blondes could have been red herrings," Lucy said. "Killed to mask the real victim or the real motive."

"Or we could just have a psycho on our hands," Harris

said. He glanced at his watch and shook his head. "I can already tell I'm not getting much sleep tonight. Tomorrow, oh-six-hundred, I'm leading a search for the missing body. It's here somewhere, and I will find it."

CHAPTER 21

Lucy woke up at five-thirty after less than two hours of sleep. Kate and Dillon were still passed out in the bed next to her, but Sean wasn't there. He hadn't come back to the room at all. She picked up her phone and called him.

"Hey," he answered with a yawn.

"Where are you?" She tried to whisper so she wouldn't wake Kate or Dillon.

"I fell asleep in the security office. They have a comfy chair here."

"You should have come upstairs."

"I didn't want to leave my equipment running without me, and I needed the hotel servers."

"Find anything?"

Kate moaned and stretched. "Is that Sean?"

Lucy nodded.

"Whoever is tracking St. Paul did it from Chicago, but they're not online and I can't pinpoint the location until they get back online. I have his computer up and running and am waiting for the cyberstalker to ping it."

"Come upstairs and rest."

"I'm fine. I slept a couple hours."

"I'll bring you food."

"Great. I'm famished."

Lucy hung up. She'd showered the night before because it took too long to dry her hair in the morning, especially a morning that promised to be as busy as this one.

She left Kate and Dillon and went down to the coffee shop, where she bought two breakfast sandwiches, coffee for her, and orange juice for Sean.

Sean was talking to a young tech guy from the hotel, who seemed to be glued to everything Sean said. Sean winked at her when she walked in. "My savior has arrived," he said. "Gary, do you mind giving us a minute?"

"Go ahead. I'll download this to the main server, it'll take some time."

"Let me know when you're done."

"And you think this will really prevent anyone from messing with the system again?"

"No—but next time, your team will be alerted immediately. If the cameras go down, you'll know why. If someone's trying to piggyback on your system, you'll see it—and who. It would be better to upgrade the whole enchilada, but corporations are being stingy with money right now."

"Wow—this is really great. Thank you."

Gary left, and Lucy eyed Sean quizzically.

"Nothing illegal, promise," Sean said. "Their system is just so archaic, I couldn't help myself. I wrote them a program that should fix the worst of their problems."

"I love you." Lucy kissed him. "Eat, and tell me what you found out."

Sean slid over a piece of paper. "Here's St. Paul's attorney, his home phone and cell phone. I found St. Paul's cell phone number and it's completely shut down, either dead or the battery has been removed. No way to track it. Except that he made several calls from his cell phone in this hotel over the last three days."

"How do you know?"

"The hotel has an internal cell receiver, so all cellular calls route through it. Because it's owned by the hotel, and they already gave me permission to go through their system—"

"Understood."

"The last call he made was yesterday at noon, right after he checked out."

"To who?"

"Blocked number. The phone hasn't been used since."

Lucy frowned.

"But I found out more about Denise. Her name is Denise Vail, from a suburb in Chicago. She moved four months ago and left no forwarding information, so I'm doing a background on her and hope to find out where she might have gone. I also ran my facial recognition software on all the guests in the hotel. Most guests are recorded twenty to forty times a day on a variety of cameras—usually entering the elevator or in the lobby. Denise has been on camera only twice, both times yesterday morning. I don't know if she's a guest—but if she is, it's not under her name. Now I'm running a program reviewing all the guests who checked in yesterday morning. It's taking a while because there was an unusual number of check-ins due to the storm. And the two images I have of her are difficult to discern—my program didn't catch them as a hundred percent, but classified them as probable matches. She was wearing large dark glasses in one, and in the other had a hat on."

"Like she was trying to hide," Lucy said. "Did you compare her image to the Jane Doe we found outside?"

"I don't have a good enough picture, but Vail is five foot three—the victim is five foot six, according to Dillon. I'll let you know if I find her."

"Eat. I'm going to meet with Kate and Detective Harris and see what they want to do about the attorney."

"Do you want to know about the status of the airport?"

She'd almost forgotten. "Are we leaving tonight?" She wanted to leave—but at the same time, she had to admit that she wanted to find out what happened here. She didn't want to leave the case unsolved, even if it wasn't *her* case.

"Tomorrow morning. They're resuming flights this afternoon, but it's going to be a madhouse, and we'd have to get there early with no guarantee of a seat. I have the four of us booked tomorrow morning, first class."

"First class?"

"I have so many miles, they practically pay me to fly."

"Sean, I'm on a government salary. A rookie government salary. And you're no longer getting a paycheck."

"And I've told you before money isn't a problem."

He had, and she'd assumed RCK paid him well for his skills. She'd been raised in a big, one-salary family and had always been frugal, especially with things like clothing and airfare and luxuries. Sean had always been more than generous, but she had never thought about his finances before.

Sean eyed her oddly. "Luce, I don't need to work. Ever."

"I don't understand."

"I've written or fixed some of the best-selling software programs on the market today and was paid extremely well for it. I thought you knew that."

She shook her head, still not understanding what he meant by "I don't need to work."

"I work because I'd go insane if I didn't have something to do. Or find myself in deep trouble." He smiled, leaned over and kissed her. "It's nice that you fell in love with me before you knew I was rich."

"You don't act rich."

He laughed. "I buy the best electronic toys. I own a plane. I don't skimp when I travel commercially."

"Okay." Thinking back to all the times they went out and traveled, she realized that he'd never let her pay for anything. She hadn't thought much about it, because for all Sean's contemporary ways and state-of-the-art toys, he was a gentleman at heart.

"You're cute when you're confused." He kissed her and said, "Go find Kate and then tell me how fabulous she thinks I am."

"She'll never admit it. But I think you're fabulous." She smiled.

"And you, princess, are the only one I really care about."

Lucy tracked Kate down at the coffee shop ordering a large coffee to go. Kate said, "Harris wants to start in the basement and search every inch of the facility, including the immediate grounds outside, until we find the body. He's instructing the security staff now."

"Sean has information on St. Paul's girlfriend, Denise Vail."

"The one who broke up with him four months ago?"

"Yes. She's in the hotel. Or she was here, yesterday morning."

"Now that's interesting."

"What are you thinking?" Lucy asked as they took the elevator to the basement.

"That she shows up and St. Paul disappears."

"Sean's running facial recognition software against the hotel's archives to find out if she's registered in the hotel under a different name. I also have St. Paul's attorney's contact information."

"Good." Kate glanced at her watch. "It's seven in the

morning, and Sunday to boot. I'll give the info to Harris and see what he wants to do."

They found Harris talking to a large group of hotel staff members. Half were security. They broke off in five groups of two and went in different directions. "I have a feeling I'll be doing it again myself," Harris grumbled. He took a long gulp of coffee. "I also sent a team of four to canvass outside and in the garbage. There's been no garbage service for two days because of the storm, so it's possible the body could have been dumped there."

Kate repeated Lucy's information and said, "I can talk to the attorney."

"Do that," Harris said. "Agent Kincaid, do you want to join me on my own search? The crime-scene techs will be here between ten and eleven."

"You have us until tomorrow morning," Lucy said.

"Tomorrow?" Kate asked.

"Sean booked us on a flight early in the morning."

"Great," Harris said. "If the killer is still here—and I think he is because no one has left the building since before Mrs. Katz was killed—then we need all the people we can get."

Harris and Lucy walked through the basement, monitoring the progress of the security staff.

"So, what's your theory?" Harris asked Lucy.

"I don't have one."

"Of course you do. I could tell last night."

She said, "I don't like guessing. There are a lot of possibilities."

"I'm not going to shoot you if you're wrong."

Lucy considered what they knew. "I think all three murders are related. That even though there wasn't a body in room 1080, the killer had a reason for moving it. I think it might be James St. Paul."

"You think that this unknown stalker ex-girlfriend from Chicago tracked him down here?"

"Sean found evidence on his laptop that he was being cyberstalked, and two blond twentysomething women who resemble his girlfriend Denise are dead."

"Devil's advocate—what if that information was planted?"

"I don't understand."

"What if Denise is the psycho ex-girlfriend but is covering her tracks by making it seem that she left him because of someone else? You couldn't find a name on his computer; when Denise allegedly left St. Paul four months ago, then two months later he allegedly filed a restraining order against an unknown female."

"Then why kill two blond women?"

"To distract us."

"But it hasn't," Lucy said. "In fact, finding the missing body is at the top of our priority list right now—we have most of hotel security looking."

Harris frowned. "Maybe that was the distraction."

"What do you think?"

"I think the body is another blonde, and that James St. Paul is the killer. I've met a lot of psychopaths, and this whole setup is creepy. But I think that two of the three victims are the distractions. I think there is one primary target and the others are to make the target less obvious."

The radio Harris was carrying beeped.

"Harris here."

"Detective, we found a body. In the basement, outside the laundry. Go through the double doors at the end, down the corridor, and turn left."

Lucy and Harris walked briskly to the laundry. They found the corridor, and when they turned saw at least ten laundry carts and a dozen meal carts, many broken or in disrepair. One of the security guards, a young guy not older than Lucy, looked green as he stood at the front of the corridor waiting for them.

"Where's the body?" Harris asked.

The security guard was upset. "I checked here yesterday, but I didn't look inside the bins. Nothing seemed out of place so I didn't think—"

"Where?" Harris repeated.

He motioned toward the far end of the corridor. "Last cart on the right."

Harris and Lucy walked down the corridor to the end. Inside the last cart was a body.

It was a woman, in a maid's uniform so drenched with blood Lucy couldn't tell the original color. She was neither blond, nor James St. Paul. She was an anomaly.

"Now the million-dollar question," Harris said. "Why didn't the hotel tell us they had a missing maid?"

"I'm gone for an hour and you practically solve the case without me," Kate said when she caught up with Lucy and Detective Harris.

They'd moved the body to the makeshift cold storage. Harris was on the phone with his chief about the latest development.

"Hardly," Lucy told Kate. "Did you get an ID on the maid?"

"Monica Sanchez." Kate flipped open a small notepad. "According to the manager, Lynn Thomsen, Sanchez clocked out at four yesterday, so she wasn't on the staff list. I spoke to the head of housekeeping, who said she may have finished another maid's rounds—someone who had kids at home and didn't want to be stuck in the blizzard. When they called the staff who'd been on shift during our time window, they hadn't thought of calling Sanchez because she'd supposedly left earlier."

"And no one thought she was missing?"

"She's divorced, lives alone, her two kids are grown."

Lucy was saddened that someone could be missing for nearly twenty-four hours and no one thought to call about them.

Instead, she focused on what she could control—finding the killer before anyone else died.

"Whoever killed these women has a plan, and he—or she—is not going to stop until it's completed."

Kate zeroed in on the pronoun. "My money is on a she. Tessa Gilliam."

"Who?" Harris said when he got off the phone.

"St. Paul's stalker ex-girlfriend. I had a long chat with his attorney, who was unusually paranoid even for an attorney. He checked out my credentials while I was on hold. Apparently, Gilliam found out where he lived and poisoned his family's dog. The dog survived—mostly because it was an eighty-pound golden retriever—but it freaked him out."

"She went after St. Paul's attorney?"

"Because he's the one who spoke to the judge. She had to show for the restraining order hearing, and she was furious at how he portrayed her, as well as the fact that St. Paul showed up with a bodyguard. The girl is a nutjob."

"Was she charged in the poisoning?"

"No proof. It's one of those 'he knew it was her, but couldn't prove it' cases. Like the stalker psycho chick from the movies, the one who boiled the rabbit."

"Does he think she's capable of murder?"

"I didn't give him specifics on the victims, but asked if he considered her dangerous. He gave me a laundry list of reasons why he said hell, yes. It started with literal stalking—she'd show up at St. Paul's office, his house, when he was out to dinner with clients. She even had tea with his elderly grandmother in her nursing home, and that's what got St. Paul to finally file the restraining order.

She told his grandmother that they were engaged and she was thrilled to be part of the family."

"Were they ever engaged?"

"Not engaged, never lived together. He dated her for four months, and from what the lawyer said, it was hot and heavy until she started exhibiting irrational jealousy. He broke up with her after she confronted his personal secretary—a college intern—and said she'd slit her throat if she even looked at St. Paul the wrong way."

"Where's St. Paul now?" Lucy asked.

"His laywer won't tell me, not until he talks to him. But here's another interesting point—St. Paul and his girlfriend Denise never broke up. They pretended to split so Tessa would leave Denise alone, but they're getting married. They feared Tessa would try something if she knew."

Everything clicked together and made sense. "Denise is a petite blonde, like these two victims," Lucy said.

Kate snapped her fingers. "Bingo."

Harris shook his head. "What's Gilliam doing? Planning on killing every blonde in the hotel, hoping one of them is Denise?" He glanced at Kate. "You should watch your back."

Kate laughed. "I'm not petite, and I hit the big four-oh this year."

"You don't look it, and this woman is crazy."

Lucy said, "Denise is in danger until we find her. So is St. Paul. I was so certain he was the missing victim." This was why Lucy didn't like to voice her theories, especially with the limited information they'd been working with. "St. Paul is probably alive and in hiding. He must know that Tessa is in town. Maybe he and Denise aren't even in the hotel anymore."

"Other than the restraining order, Gilliam has a record— a stalking charge when she was in college, assault three years ago, two DUIs," Kate said. "And that's all local from

Chicago. There could be more. I have the local FBI office working on it and searching for Gilliam. We have her last known address, and two field agents in Chicago are checking it out now."

"My money is on Gilliam being right here in this hotel," Harris said, shaking his head.

"I'm certainly not going to take that bet," Kate said.

"I'll call my chief, see if he can get intel from the airport."

Kate pulled her cell phone from her pocket, glanced at the ID and grinned. "Hello, counselor." She listened. "Thank you. Let him know we'll be there in ten minutes. I'll identify myself by name, and show my badge in the peep hole." She hung up. "We got him. He's on the eighth floor, registered under a different name. They haven't left the room in twenty-four hours, not since St. Paul saw Gilliam in the hotel lobby yesterday morning."

CHAPTER 22

As soon as Lucy walked in, she felt the fear rolling off both James St. Paul and his fiancée, Denise. And it was very clear why.

Denise was very pregnant.

James motioned for them to sit on one of the two beds. "My attorney didn't tell me there were two federal agents and a detective looking for Tessa. What'd she do?"

They'd kept the information about the murders quiet, but there were rumors spreading through the hotel, mostly because too many people knew parts of each story. No one but security and the manager knew the whole truth, so the stories were wild, but guests weren't walking anywhere alone and many were staying in their rooms.

But it appeared that James and Denise were clueless. They hadn't left their room in twenty-four hours.

"We believe she's killed three women."

"Oh, God, James!" Denise grabbed his hand and squeezed.

James put his arm around his fiancée. "How do you know this?"

"Two of the victims resemble Denise," Kate said bluntly.

Tears welled in Denise's eyes and she buried her head in James's shoulder. "Where?" James asked.

"In the hotel."

"*This* hotel?" It was clear by his expression that the news was a total shock.

Harris said, "The first was a maid who was in the room your company had rented, room 1080. The other two were guests. We don't know where she is, but we believe she's still in the hotel, possibly registered under a false ID. We need everything you know about her, starting with why you've been in hiding."

"Isn't it obvious?" James said, his voice rising. "She's dangerous! You just said she killed three people, and I know she'd kill Denise if she found us. I can't—"

Lucy sat across from the couple and kept her voice calm but firm. "I know this is extremely difficult, but for Denise's sake you need to remain calm and focused. Anything you can tell us will help find her."

James took a deep breath and nodded. "I'm not good with all the secrecy. When we found out Denise was pregnant, we thought it would set Tessa off. She's been dangerous, but she never hurt anyone before."

"Except your lawyer's dog," Kate said.

"Well, I didn't want to believe it of her, but yeah. And then when she met my grandmother—but even the restraining order didn't stop her. So Denise and I staged a breakup and she came here, to Denver, to live with her parents for the past four months. We're getting married next weekend, at her parents' house. I stayed here, thinking if Tessa was going to follow, I'd know it. When I thought it was safe, Denise joined me, but stayed in a different room under her sister's name."

"Donna Jergens," Kate said. "The name this room is registered under."

He nodded. "But then I saw Tessa. Yesterday morning, in the lobby. I tried to get a flight out for Denise and me, a flight anywhere, but couldn't, so I checked my bags hoping she'd think I'd just disappeared. I got rid of my cell phone, Denise got rid of hers, and we decided to hole up in this room until we could get out. I even called Denise's parents and told them to leave their house. I didn't know what Tessa knew, if she knew about the Vails, if she was going to try to hurt them."

Denise cried out once, then buried her face again in James's shoulder.

"You know you won't be able to run from her forever," Lucy said. "If she wants to find you bad enough, she can. It's obvious she went to extreme measures to track you down. There were viruses on your computer that sent her information every time you turned on your computer."

He stared at her in shock. "I got a new computer four months ago! I don't do anything on it, except work. How did she do that?"

"You'd be surprised how easy it is," Lucy said.

"What are we going to do?" Denise said, her hands on her large stomach.

"You're going to stay in this room," Kate said, "and I'm going to put a bodyguard on you." She glanced at Lucy. "Think Sean's up for it?"

"Always," Lucy said. "Though he doesn't have his gun."

Harris said, "He can use my backup."

"Call him," Kate said. "I have a plan to flush Tessa out."

Lucy eyed her suspiciously. "I don't think Dillon is going to like it."

Kate blew out a sigh. "You can't read my mind."

Lucy raised an eyebrow. "I had the same idea when Detective Harris said you didn't look forty."

* * *

Sean seemed happy to escape the confines of hotel security. "I love my computer, but twelve hours straight is my max."

"You're a cop, too?" James asked.

"Better," Sean said with a half smile. "I'm a trained bodyguard."

Kate rolled her eyes. "Get over yourself, Rogan."

Sean feigned hurt. "At least I have you to keep my ego in check."

Lucy said to James and Denise, "Listen to Sean, and you'll be fine." Most of the time the friendly bickering between Kate and Sean put people at ease, but it was clearly making Denise tense. She was seven months pregnant—an early delivery would be dangerous for the baby, especially here without a hospital and the proper equipment. The most important thing was to keep her calm and comfortable until this was over.

Sean caught Lucy's eye. He didn't need to say anything, but she knew he was telling her to watch her back—and Kate's. She squeezed his hand in reassurance and left with Kate to join Detective Harris and Dillon in the manager's office.

"The crime-scene techs are here processing the hotel room and searching the courtyard for evidence," Harris said. "The coroner took the bodies an hour ago, through the freight elevator. I've asked my team to be discreet; better not to stir up any more rumors."

Dillon said, "A lot of guests have checked out and are heading to the airport—those that were stranded yesterday."

Harris nodded. "That was one of my concerns, that she could slip out much easier now."

Kate handed around copies of Tessa Gilliam's driver's license photo. "This just came in from Chicago. Decker in hotel security is passing it out to his team, and Harris's people already have a copy as well. Tessa is a natural blonde, but Mr. St. Paul said she's altered her appearance— she dyed her hair brown and may be wearing glasses. So you need to be extra diligent when looking at potential suspects."

Lucy added, "She knows St. Paul spotted her, and may have changed her appearance again—new hair color, even a new style."

"I have a team of four plainclothes officers in the lobby near the main entrance," Harris said. "Hotel security is covering the other exits and diverting guests to the front. If Tessa Gilliam is here, we will find her."

Kate had dressed in one of Denise's sweaters, something that Kate would never wear in a million years—it was bright pink with tiny blue hearts. Denise told them that she'd had the sweater for years, and she kept it because it was big enough to fit over her growing stomach. It might be something that Tessa would recognize. Kate wore a turtleneck underneath, which helped mask the wire she was wearing, as well as a Kevlar vest Harris had one of his female officers loan her. They didn't know if Tessa had a gun, but no one was taking chances.

"We have you covered," Harris said. He handed her St. Paul's suitcase. It was unique enough that they thought Tessa would know that it was his. They also had his computer, and Sean was working on a back trace—Kate would go to the lobby and log in. Sean would monitor the connection to see if Tessa was tracking it, and hopefully use that to locate her exact whereabouts.

Because Harris's large frame was noticeable, he opted to stay in the security room monitoring the cameras with Gary the IT kid Sean had befriended.

"Ready?" he asked Kate and Lucy.

"Let's catch the bitch," Kate said.

Kate, Lucy, and Dillon approached the lobby separately. Kate took the stairs, and Lucy beat her to the lobby by taking the elevator. She sat in the open, in front of the lobby's two-story-tall Christmas tree that dominated the center of the vast space. It was decorated in red and gold ornaments and white lights, too opulent for Lucy's taste, but when she sat down the pine aroma of the fresh tree made her smile. She reminded herself that this was Christmas, a time of hope and miracles. For her and Sean, starting their future in San Antonio; for James and Denise, putting the violence of their past behind them to start a family.

Lucy pulled out Sean's e-reader and pretended to read. From her angle, she could see Kate as she crossed the lobby and sat on the far side, the best place for the undercover cops and Lucy to keep her in sight.

Dillon agreed to stay out of the main lobby, but he staked himself out at the concierge desk. The added benefit was that it gave him a view of the elevator bank. Harris brought James down to the security room to monitor the cameras, while Sean kept Denise secure in her room.

As Lucy watched, Kate walked from the lobby to the checkout desk. They wanted to make her as visible as possible from all different angles. She stood in line for ten minutes before she got to the front.

Lucy couldn't hear the conversation with the clerk, but Kate would be saying that she was Denise Vail and was checking out.

Next, Kate went to the concierge to arrange for James St. Paul's luggage. She handed the clerk the ticket.

The concierge was closer to Lucy's position. The clerk asked, "Do you need a taxi?"

"Yes, but I have some time. I'm waiting for my fiancé." She made a show of displaying her ring.

"Beautiful! You're a lucky girl."

"I know." Kate beamed. Lucy almost laughed—maybe Kate should have been an actress.

The fake exchange took only a few minutes, then the clerk handed her James's suitcase and laptop case, which they'd returned to storage earlier.

Kate walked to the middle of the lobby, looked around as if searching for someone. Checked her watch. Pulled out her phone and sent a text message. It went to Lucy and the others in their group.

No sign of her. I'm going to run the program now.

Kate went back to her original seat in the lobby and pulled out James's laptop. She'd boot up and run a trace program Sean had installed so that Sean could monitor anyone who tracked James.

Lucy's responsibility was to keep eyes on Kate, and she wasn't going to let Tessa get close. She was in the best position to do so.

"It's running," Kate said into her mic, which was wired to the Denver PD network, and earpieces for Sean and Lucy.

Sean's voice came through. "I see it. Waiting."

No one spoke for several minutes. Then Sean said, "I got her. Third floor. She's on a smartphone. Give me a sec."

Harris said over the mic, "Beta Team, third floor. Await location of suspect."

Sean said, "I got her GPS. She's moving. In the elevator."

They all waited for the Beta Team from Denver PD to report in. They went radio silent on their approach, so Lucy couldn't hear what was going on. She kept her eyes on Kate and the immediate area. She didn't like that there was no word about Tessa.

Five minutes later, Harris broke the silence, "Negative. She's not on the third floor, or in the elevators."

"How can that be?" Lucy said.

Sean reported, "The trace isn't instantaneous. There's a short lag time. I'm trying to reestablish the connection; I lost it when she entered the elevator."

But for the next ten minutes, while they were all tense and waiting, Sean couldn't get the phone up again. "She shut it down. Maybe she realized there was someone piggybacking on her connection."

Kate snorted. "And I thought you were the best, Rogan."

"Touché."

Lucy was doubly tense. Tessa Gilliam wanted to kill Denise. She'd already proven she'd use whatever she had at her disposal—a knife, a blunt object, her hands. Lucy had the distinct impression of being watched. Not her, specifically, but as if someone were surveying the entire lobby. Waiting. She scanned the balcony but didn't see anyone who matched Tessa's description. She didn't see anyone who looked to be watching the room.

But this feeling was very familiar.

"Harris," Lucy said, "ask James if he'd be willing to come down to the lobby. We'll cover him."

"Too risky," Harris said. "She'll go after him."

"No, she'll go after Kate," Lucy said. "She's waiting—I can feel it."

"Don't tell me you're a damn psychic."

"No, I just have experience with psychopaths." *Far too much experience.* "Tell James to go right up to Kate and kiss her. I guarantee that Tessa will make her move."

No one said anything for a minute. Then Harris said, "He said he'd do it. Are you sure about this, Kincaid?"

"I'm positive. She's watching. But I can't see her."

"I'm putting a vest on him. Give us two minutes."

"Put a plainclothes officer right behind him, a man, not a woman. If it's a woman, Tessa will look twice to make sure they're not together. If it's a man, she won't notice him." Lucy hoped her instincts were right.

A moment later, Harris said, "He's on his way. Elevator four."

Lucy kept her eyes on the elevator. There were too many people in the lobby, too many people milling around waiting for shuttles or taxis, because it was too cold to wait outside. The snow still fell, but in quiet sheets, not with the driving force of last night.

Maybe this was a bad idea.

Don't second-guess yourself. Tessa Gilliam has killed three women. She'll kill again if she isn't stopped.

James emerged from the elevator. He hesitated, just a moment, then spotted Kate. He strode over. He looked nervous and scared, but didn't take his eyes off Kate. He gave her a large smile.

Ten feet behind him was a plainclothes cop. Lucy looked across the lobby, behind the cop, everywhere she could see without making it obvious. Checking faces, trying to see if anyone was giving James undue attention.

Harris said in her ear, "Suspect spotted on the second-floor balcony heading down the main staircase."

Lucy turned in time to see Tessa, walking with purpose down the stairs. She wore a black catering uniform, her freshly dyed hair pulled sharply back into a net and her face devoid of makeup.

"I see her," Lucy said.

To Lucy's left, James embraced Kate. As they kissed, Kate turned James away from the threat so her body was between him and the approaching killer. Then she whispered something in his ear.

Lucy turned back to Tessa. Her face was a mask of fury and purpose. She was so focused on James and Kate that she didn't see Lucy as she rose from her chair and walked right into her path.

Tessa bumped into her, but that didn't slow her down. She didn't even look at Lucy, her vision was so narrowed on the object of her obsession.

"James!" Tessa cried out.

Lucy turned quickly, kicked a suitcase into Tessa's path, and as Tessa tried to avoid tripping, Lucy grabbed her arm and pulled it sharply up in the back as she pushed her to her knees.

"FBI. Stay down."

Tessa squirmed and with her free hand revealed a knife, which she swiped at Lucy's leg, trying to get out of her grip.

Lucy stepped back to avoid a more serious injury, though the knife tore her jeans and cut into her skin.

She kicked Tessa's wrist. The woman dropped the knife and Lucy kicked it away as she pushed her face-first onto the marble floor.

Two Denver PD cops came out of the woodwork and held their guns on Tessa.

"I said stay down," Lucy told Tessa. Her thigh smarted from the cut, but she still cuffed the killer, then searched her for additional weapons. She found a nine-millimeter handgun and handed it to one of the cops.

Other cops ushered guests away from the lobby. Tessa suddenly stopped moving—she seemed to be in shock.

"We got her, Agent Kincaid," one of the cops said. "You need a doctor."

"I'm fine," Lucy said.

In her earpiece, Sean said, "What?"

"I'm fine," Lucy repeated. She looked down. Blood had seeped into her jeans.

"Tessa Gilliam, you're under arrest for murder and assault of a federal agent," the cop said as he pulled the woman into a standing position.

Tessa's face was completely blank. She looked at Lucy with no emotion, not pain or regret or fear.

Then, over Lucy's shoulder, Tessa saw James standing with Kate. Her expression changed immediately, from calm to pure rage.

"I'll kill her, James! I promise you, I'll kill you both!" She ended on a screech.

Harris came down and told the officers to take Gilliam to the station and book her. They left, though the suspect was no longer compliant. She fought and screamed while two strong cops ushered her out of the lobby.

"What a piece of work," Harris muttered. Then he turned to Lucy. "Good job, Agent Kincaid." He extended his hand. "I need to talk to my men, then I'll get a statement from you and Agent Donovan."

"We'll be here until tomorrow morning."

He looked at her leg. "You need stitches."

"It's a lot better than it looks," she said.

Kate and James walked over. James was shaking. "She will kill us. She's crazy."

"She won't," Lucy said. "She's going to prison for the rest of her life."

"But there's no evidence. You don't know that she killed those women. You don't know that she's done anything!"

Harris said, "I'm interviewing her. Did you see her hands when she fell?"

Lucy nodded. "Cut up."

"She nicked herself in the stabbing. That room is being processed carefully. We'll find her blood, no doubt. She's not going to walk away. We also have a hundred witnesses who heard her threaten you—she won't be getting bail, either." Harris put his hand on James's shoulder. "Go take care of your fiancée and your baby."

James nodded. "Thank you all for everything."

Lucy said, "I'll walk him back to his room."

Once upstairs, James and Denise embraced. Sean walked Lucy out. "Stitches?" he said and looked at her leg.

"A Band-Aid is all I need," she said. "I'd tell you if it was more serious."

"I doubt that." He kissed her. "You did good, Princess."

"So did you."

"We have all day, just to ourselves."

"And Kate and Dillon and giving our statements—sounds like a lot of fun."

Sean put his arm around her shoulders as they went into the elevator. "Dillon said he and Kate are eating in the restaurant. Want to join them?" He hovered his finger above the lobby button.

Lucy smiled and pressed 10. "They can wait."

CHAPTER 23

Home.

The wheels of the 747 hit San Diego at 10:47 A.M. Pacific time on Monday morning. What a whirlwind forty-eight hours! But it felt amazing to be here in San Diego, and to be here with Sean.

Lucy took Sean's hand and kissed it. "This is it," she said. Home churned up so many different emotions that Lucy didn't know whether to be excited or apprehensive. She'd had a wonderful childhood in many ways, but she always seemed to remember first the tragedies.

"I think you're more nervous about me meeting your parents than I am." He grinned. "How can they not love me?"

Lucy heard Kate snort from the seat behind them. "Don't pay attention to her," Sean said. "I promise, I'll be on my best behavior."

"I'm not worried." *Maybe a little.* "It's just—well, I know they'll love you, but we also have to tell them we're moving in together."

"We could elope," Sean said.

Lucy's heart skipped a beat. They'd never seriously discussed getting married, and right now she wasn't ready for anything else on her plate. Moving halfway cross-country to a city she'd never been to before, moving in with Sean on a permanent basis and not just staying with him a couple weekends a month, starting a new job as a rookie FBI agent—the idea that she'd have to plan a wedding had her nearly panicking.

"Hey," Sean said, and kissed her. "I was joking. I know now's not the right time." Then he smiled wickedly, his dimple deepening. "But there will be a right time, and I will know exactly when it is."

"Oh, you will?"

He kissed her again. "Of course I will. I love you."

Still smiling as the plane taxied toward the terminal, Lucy took out her cell phone and turned it on. Immediately, several messages beeped. She listened to them.

The first was from Carina.

"Dad's in the hospital. He had a heart attack last night—he's okay, but we're all here waiting for tests. Call me."

Lucy didn't check the rest of her messages. She immediately dialed Carina. "Dillon," she said, looking over her shoulder. "Dad's in the hospital."

Dillon pulled out his own phone and started dialing.

Carina wasn't answering. She tried Connor, and he didn't answer. She called her mom.

"Mom? It's Lucy. We just landed. Dad's okay, right?"

"Lucia, it's awful, baby. Come home." Her mom started crying and Lucy couldn't understand her.

"Mama, we're getting off the plane right now. We'll all be there."

Her mother started talking in rapid Spanish but with the sobs Lucy couldn't make out what she was saying. "Mama, Dillon and I are coming."

She hung up, fighting back tears. She turned to Dillon. He said, "I'm calling the hospital."

She nodded, and tried Carina's husband, Nick. She

thought he wasn't going to answer either, but then he picked up.

"Nick, it's Lucy. We just landed and I got Carina's message about Dad. Is he okay?"

"I just saw him, he's fine. They have him resting, and I don't know what the plan is, but his color is back."

Relief flooded through her. She said to Dillon, "Dad's okay. He's in the hospital, but he's okay."

To Nick she said, "I tried Carina and Connor, and neither of them are answering, and then I called Mom, and she was crying—I thought he'd died." She breathed an unsteady sigh of relief. She hadn't seen her dad in nearly two years. How could she have let so much time pass between visits?

"Lucy, your dad is going to be okay," Nick said. "We have another situation."

"What?"

He didn't say anything right off, and Lucy knew then that it was bad.

"There's been a shooting at the hospital," Nick said. "Carina has been taken as a hostage."

PART THREE

San Diego

Monday, December 24

CHAPTER 24

Carina Kincaid Thomas woke up Christmas Eve morning to a kiss. Her husband nuzzled her neck and whispered, "Do you know what today is?"

"It's not Christmas yet," she said with a smile. "Or my birthday."

Nick reached down and laid a hand on her stomach, which was still flat. "It's been fifteen weeks."

Carina had had three miscarriages over the last two years, and though all tests said she and Nick should be able to conceive, her body didn't seem to be able to carry a baby past the first trimester. Twelve weeks was the longest she'd gone. The last time she said she couldn't go through it again. It was as if with each loss, her heart broke and took longer to mend. She was thirty-seven. She might never be able to have a baby.

They weren't even trying anymore, but she'd conceived Labor Day weekend when she and Nick had rented a cabin in Big Bear. She'd spent the first three months waging an emotional battle against loving the tiny baby, but it was impossible. She wanted this baby more than anything else, and she knew Nick did, too.

She didn't think she was completely out of the woods,

but the doctor said if she made it through the first trimester, the odds were in their favor that the baby would come to term. So she and Nick agreed that they wouldn't tell anyone about this pregnancy until Christmas, because Carina couldn't handle the pain in her mother's eyes, or the sympathy from her sister-in-law Julia.

"We'll tell everyone tomorrow, at Christmas dinner," Carina said. Her phone rang. Then she noticed that it was after eight—she never slept in this late!

"Hi, Mom," Carina said. "I just—"

"Carina?" Rosa Kincaid interrupted. "I need you to come to the hospital. It's your dad."

Her heart raced. "Dad? What's wrong?" She swung her legs over the side of the bed. Nick immediately jumped up.

"They think it's a heart attack. They're running tests, but his doctor says he's going to have to have surgery. *Mi muñeca*, I need you."

"I'll be right there, Mama."

"Call Patrick, Lucy—they need to know, but I have to be with your father."

"Of course. Mama, Daddy's strong. He's going to be fine." As she spoke, tears leaked from her eyes. Her dad . . . she couldn't imagine her life without him.

She hung up. "Nick—"

"I heard. Get dressed. I'll drive."

"Your mother shouldn't have worried you."

Colonel Pat Kincaid tried to sit up in his hospital bed, but the nurse who was writing on his chart admonished him.

"Of course she should have," Carina said. She glanced at her brother Connor. *Tell him!*

Connor said, "Don't try to make Mom feel guilty for calling us."

"I'm just having a few tests."

"A few tests because you had a heart attack!" Carina exclaimed.

Nick put his hand on her shoulder. He could usually calm her down when she was agitated, just by his touch, but this was her dad. He'd been an army colonel, a military man for forty years before he retired. For the first fifteen years of her life she'd moved from base to base with her family. That's one of the reasons she was so close to her siblings, particularly Connor and Patrick. The three of them were born a year apart, with Carina in the middle, and they had done everything together. When you moved every two years—or less—you depended on your family. Your brothers. Your mother.

Your dad.

He was sixty-nine years old but had only retired a few years ago. He was still fit and strong. But seeing him here, in a hospital bed, with all the machines, she thought he looked older than she'd ever imagined he could be.

Carina couldn't lose him. Not now.

She caught his eye and realized that he was as scared as she was, but he was trying to be the tough soldier, to be strong for his family. Like when she was seven and they'd moved to Fort Bragg and almost immediately her dad was deployed to command a unit in Grenada. He'd been gone before, but this was the first time she understood that he was going to be in danger.

"Cara." He'd spoken her nickname, the one reserved only for her daddy, that last day before he left. "I need you to be strong for me. I have good men I serve under, and good men who serve under me. Trust that God will watch out for me just like He watched out for your mama when she escaped from Cuba. If I see you scared, I'll be scared. But if I see you're brave, I'll be brave."

"I'm brave, Daddy. I love you lots. I'll miss you so much."

He opened his wallet to reveal pictures of her and her brothers and sister. "I always miss you, that's why I keep these close to my heart."

Carina reached up and touched the small pendant around her neck. It was that deployment when he'd given her the pendant with his picture and hers.

She walked over to the side of the bed, leaned over, and kissed his cheek.

She whispered, "If I see you're brave, I'll be brave."

He squeezed her hand, recognition in his eyes. Carina kept the tears at bay until she left the room, Nick close on her heels. As soon as her father's door swung shut, she turned to her husband.

"Nick," she managed to whisper before the silent tears fell.

He held her tight; she needed him, but she also needed to pull herself together. For her mom, for her dad, for her family. She took a deep breath.

"I'm going to get some air," Carina said.

He inspected her carefully. "Are you okay?"

She knew he was worried about the baby, even though he didn't want to say it. It was almost funny—they had never seriously talked about having children, it was always "someday" in the future—until she discovered she was pregnant that first time. After the miscarriage, they realized that they both wanted a child. That knowledge changed them. That they wanted to create life together, share in the joy of a baby, had brought them even closer. When she never believed it possible to love Nick even more, she did.

"We're both fine," she told him.

"You're not in this alone, Carina."

"I know." She squeezed Nick's hand. He knew her better than anyone, and she loved him for it. He'd give her space because she wanted it, and he would be right here when she returned—because she'd need him then, too.

She left Nick by her father's door. He and Connor would talk, plan, and decide who would be responsible for what. Nothing pleased her more than the fact that her husband and her brother were best friends and business partners. They were both former cops who now worked private security and it suited them.

They'd have to make calls—something that Carina didn't want her mother to worry about. Juanita Santana, her mother's best friend, would help. She'd be there for them, cooking, driving, anything to ease the burden. When her husband died ten years ago, Rosa Kincaid had been her rock, and now—

Dad is not going to die.

Carina stepped out of the hospital, far from the smoking area where the smell of smoke made her want to puke. Her brothers and sisters were all en route to San Diego. Nelia was driving from Idaho to San Diego; she and her longtime boyfriend couldn't get here any faster. Jack and Megan—wait, hadn't Jack called and said Megan was flying separately? Why? Carina cradled her head. She couldn't remember. Lucy and Dillon were on a plane heading to San Diego—she hated to leave a voice mail for either of them, but what else could she do? Wait until they landed and tell them to head to the hospital instead of home?

She couldn't keep the information from any of them, but she didn't want them to worry—especially since they couldn't do anything to arrive in San Diego any faster. She would simply say Dad was in the hospital for some tests, and Carina would let them know when she knew more. All that was true.

She sat down on a bench and took a deep breath, then

made the necessary calls, leaving messages if no one picked up. When she was finished, she felt calmer, more focused. Her family would be together soon. Dad would be fine. She had to believe it.

Carina was surrounded by cops and alpha males in her work and family, but her father was the strongest man she'd ever known. He was firm, but loving; disciplined, but sensitive. He loved his country as much as his family, but when the rules stunk, he found a way around them. He saved the woman he would eventually marry from being deported to Cuba by claiming he found her on the beach, not in the waters off the Florida coast. He had taught Carina to never accept any man who didn't treat her with the respect she deserved. He had welcomed Nick into the family without hesitation and treated him as a son.

Thinking about her dad, the colonel, lying in a hospital bed reminded her that even the strongest of men, mentally and physically, could fall.

"I'm not ready to give you up, Dad," she whispered to no one.

Carina got up and walked around the pathway that circled the hospital. It rarely rained in San Diego, and she'd never had a white Christmas, but that was fine by her. She loved the sun and sand and climate of southern California. She needed the fresh air before she went back inside. She'd never been sensitive to smells, but since she became pregnant, scents were more noticeable—and usually unpleasant.

The hospital was designed as three towers connected by an open-air courtyard: the central building was the oldest and tallest of the three; the north wing included the cancer center, outpatient and laboratory services; and the south wing had the new surgery center and maternity ward. That was where her father was; that was where she would be in June if all went well with this pregnancy.

The walk revived her. She entered the main tower to buy a balloon for her dad—he wouldn't be happy if she brought in flowers, but because this was San Diego and they were close to a military base, there were plenty of military-themed balloons. She picked one that said GET WELL, SOLDIER! THAT'S AN ORDER!

There were small fake Christmas trees with cheap decorations, prewrapped presents, and a cluster of poinsettias to brighten up the rooms of those who would be spending Christmas in the hospital. Christmas was supposed to be a time of hope and rejoicing, of being with family without past regrets or personal disagreements interfering with the celebration. Carina ached for those who didn't have family, for those who were sick and wouldn't be able to be home for the holidays.

She would have moved anywhere to be with Nick, but Nick recognized that her family was the most important thing to her. She needed roots, she loved having a place to be home. She lived only blocks from her parents' house, and before Dillon moved to D.C., he lived within walking distance as well. She had lamented it when first Jack left, then Nelia moved, then Dillon and Lucy, then Patrick—until it was just her and Connor left. She'd always expected that her brothers and sisters would raise their families here, that their kids would grow up together, that Christmas and Thanksgiving and Easter and the Fourth of July and, heck, every Sunday meal would see the growing Kincaid clan enjoying family gatherings.

But that wasn't happening, and it made Carina unusually sad.

She found that her hand had drifted to her stomach and she realized that she had the only grandchild in her belly. Justin, her nephew, had been killed eighteen years ago, and this baby was the only future Kincaid. Her parents had seven kids, but no grandchildren, and why that bothered

Carina, she didn't know. Except that her family was living all over the country and she missed them.

She was about to call Patrick to find out his ETA when she spotted a man in khakis and a jacket—too heavy for the weather—leave the main building and head toward the north wing. She followed, her instincts telling her that he was too focused and walking too fast. His face was blank, a man on a mission, and his buzz cut and the way he held himself practically shouted military.

It's probably nothing.

But she still followed. It was part of being a cop; she couldn't ignore something that didn't feel right. She let go of the balloon, which would make her pursuit more obvious, then followed him into the north wing and the elevator. He pressed the Down button and didn't look at her. She watched his profile. His eyes looked straight ahead, but they were red and a bit swollen. He'd lost someone, it was clear as anything now that she was up close. She relaxed a bit, but decided to follow him when he left the elevator. He just wasn't acting right, though grief affected everyone differently. Soldiers often didn't know how to release the pent-up anguish. Grief was often postponed, buried under duty and honor.

He got off the elevator in the basement and walked straight, toward the morgue and the receiving rooms. A sign read AUTHORIZED ACCESS ONLY. He ignored it.

She got off as well and stopped, pretending to read the directory on the wall.

The soldier of grief turned the corner. She then followed. When Carina reached the fork in the hall, he abruptly turned and faced her.

"Why are you following me?"

"You look upset. Can I help."

"No."

He walked away and Carina hesitated, considering whether she should follow him. He was going to the morgue—possibly to identify a loved one—except why would he be unescorted?

She pulled out her phone to call security, but saw that she had no cell reception in the basement. She glanced around for a hospital phone and spotted one on the wall outside a set of unmarked double doors. She waited until the man rounded the corner at the far end of the hall, then ran over and picked it up.

A scream followed by a gunshot and a thud had her dropping the phone and reaching for her gun—except she wasn't carrying. She hadn't even thought to pack her side-arm because she wasn't on duty and had only been thinking about her dad's heart attack. She picked up the phone and dialed security.

"This is Detective Carina Kincaid from the San Diego Police Department. There's an unknown situation in the basement, shots fired, security needed."

A gunshot cut her off, aimed at the wall above her. Plaster rained down.

Carina slowly turned to face the man from the elevator. She dropped the phone and kept her hands up. The soldier pointed his gun directly at Carina's chest, center mass. He could kill her, but Carina couldn't ignore that the first shot was a warning. He'd missed on purpose.

The gunman had a nurse directly in front of him, easily restraining her with his muscular arms. Blood covered her hands, and her intense, fearful eyes sought help from Carina. But right now Carina was in no position to do anything but comply.

"Security is on their way," she said.

"I thought you were a cop. Detective Kincaid, you said, right? Walk slowly toward me. Any sudden movements, I will kill Nurse Browne." He placed the barrel of the 9-millimeter to Browne's neck.

Carina assessed the situation. There were sounds of shouts and running, but she saw no one in this hall. A red security light began flashing in the corner. Security would be down here any minute. SWAT would be called in. The soldier had to know that.

He glanced behind him and turned his body, Browne still in front of him, and fired. A woman screamed and Browne began to cry. "Now, Detective," he said. "I could use you to help me get answers."

While the shooter had looked aggrieved in the elevator, he now seemed in complete control. She slowly walked toward him.

"Release Nurse Browne and I will come with you."

"Do you have a weapon?"

"No."

"I don't believe you."

"I'm off duty. I'm here for personal reasons."

A flash of sympathy crossed his face, then it was gone. "Faster."

"Let her go."

"I can't."

Carina stopped walking when she reached the fork in the hallway. A woman in scrubs was crawling away. She was bleeding in the right calf. Carina immediately ran to her, grabbing towels off a cart next to the door. She applied pressure to the wound. It was a clean shot, but not fatal.

"Detective, in that room." He nodded toward the double doors in the morgue. "On three. One. Two—"

"Let Nurse Browne take this woman to a doctor. You have me."

He pushed Browne toward the door, his grip so strong

red marks were imprinted on the hostage's skin. "Go in," he ordered Carina.

Through the small window in the door, Carina saw three other hostages, one bleeding and the other two giving him medical attention. She pushed open the door and the three hostages jumped.

"Is everyone okay?" she asked.

"He's behind you!" one of the women said.

The shooter stepped into the room. He looked at Carina and nodded, pushed Browne out the door toward the victim in the hall, then pressed a button on the wall. The doors locked, and a blue light flashed both inside and outside the door. He looked at Carina. "I want answers, Detective."

He removed a device from his pocket and placed it across the threshold, unfolding it with care and confidence.

"What is that?" Carina asked.

"C-4." He pressed a button and the small bomb blinked. "My insurance. If anyone tries to walk out, I'll blow it. I'm not afraid to die. If you think you're willing to sacrifice yourself, think again. That's a load-bearing wall. There's not enough C-4 to take down the building, but it'll definitely do significant damage to this area and the floors above. Evacuating the patients will take time. Tick tock."

He looked at the black man lying on the floor with a leg wound similar to the one on the woman outside the door. "I don't want to kill anyone, but I will."

"We understand," Carina said.

"Good."

"What's your name?"

"Charlie Peterson. I'm sure security has already figured that out. Or will shortly. That"—he pointed to the blond nurse—"is Kristan Otto, LPN. The other"—he gestured to the brunette—"is Rena Lavagnino, RN. The orderly—what's your name?"

"Brian. Grover. Brian Grover. I—I'm an RN. Not an orderly."

"There, now we all know each other."

The three hostages looked at Carina as if she were the shooter's partner. Charlie said, "Sorry—Detective Carina Kincaid, right?" he said, then nodded to answer his own question. "I don't want to kill a cop, but I want answers, and if I don't get them, I will kill you."

Carina didn't know how to read Charlie Peterson. At first, she thought he'd just snapped, but he seemed sincere when he said he didn't want to kill anyone, just as sincere as when he said he would. He almost seemed to like her, which was odd, but she needed to use that. He didn't, however, like the three nurses in front of him sitting with their backs against the drawers which held the bodies of the recently deceased.

He said, "Detective, I don't trust you because I know what your job is. You want to take me down. I get that. Even respect it." He dropped a pair of handcuffs to the floor and kicked them over to her. "So I need you incapacitated. Sit down and cuff yourself to the table leg. Now."

She did as he ordered. The heavy stainless steel table in the middle of the room was bolted to the floor. He came over to check the cuffs and make sure she hadn't left enough room to wiggle out. He nodded. "Thank you. Don't attempt to pull anything over on me. I served in the army for six years. I don't need a gun to kill you."

"My brother was in special forces. Sergeant Jack Kincaid."

"Good. Then you know I can."

Carina was trying to build a rapport more than anything. Humanize his hostages to make it less likely he'd kill them. "My dad recently retired. He was a colonel. He had a heart attack last night and needs surgery. Which he's not going to get as long as this goes on."

Charlie nodded. "I don't want this to drag on any longer than necessary. If I even think you're thinking about screwing me over, I'll lock you in one of those drawers. I don't want to, but this isn't about you."

"I'll help you. Let Brian go. He's injured."

"No."

"Good faith. It'll go a long way—"

"I already showed good faith when I let the nurse and that woman doc leave. That's two fewer hostages, easier for me."

"If—"

"Stop trying to negotiate, Detective." He turned to Kristan. "Open it."

The young nurse, probably not more than twenty-four, was shaking. "You don't want—"

"Don't tell me what I want. Open her drawer."

Carina said, "Can you fill me in? They seem to know why you're here holding a gun on us, but I have no clue."

"My sister." His voice cracked and he took a deep breath. "She died. And one of them killed her."

CHAPTER 25

Nick tried Carina for the third time, even though he knew she would have called him if she could.

"Where is she, dammit?" Connor said through clenched teeth.

Nick shot his brother-in-law a narrow-eyed glance. The colonel was already worried as well as sick, and Connor needed to tamp down on his temper before they made a bad situation worse.

Connor's jaw tightened as he recognized Nick's unspoken admonition.

"Go," the colonel said.

"No, Dad," Nick said. "We're not going to leave you alone."

"It wasn't a suggestion," the colonel said. "Connor, find your mother and take her home."

"Dad—"

"Did you hear a question in my tone? Nick, find out what's going on and why Carina is not answering her phone."

Connor stood at the end of his father's bed. He wanted to argue, but he backed down. "Okay, Dad, but I'm coming back."

"I need to know my Rosa is safe. I'm not going any-where."

"I'll call you when I know anything," Nick told Con-nor.

Connor relented. "Call Will, and let me know what he says. Before all this happened, Mrs. Santana took Mom to the cafeteria. I'll take both of them to the house and have Julia stay with them."

Connor stared at Nick, but he didn't have to speak for Nick to understand his meaning. Then he left.

Whatever had happened—all they knew was that shots were fired—it had happened in the north tower. The colo-nel was in the south tower, and security had come around and told everyone to stay put. The south tower was locked down. Anyone who left would be funneled through the south exit.

Nick tried Carina for the fourth time, still no answer. He then called her partner, Detective Will Hooper. They'd been partners for years, since before Nick had met Carina, and the Kincaids treated Will like one of their own.

He kept his voice low. Even though the colonel could hear him, he didn't want to sound panicked.

"Will, it's Nick. Have you heard about the shooting at the hospital?"

"Yeah, I'm on call. I've been trying Carina. She beat me there? She'll never let me live it down." Will was late to nearly everything.

"We were at the hospital already."

"What's wrong?"

"The colonel had a heart attack last night. He's going through some tests right now. Carina went outside for air, but I haven't seen her in the last thirty minutes."

"She's probably running the show until SWAT arrives."

"She's not picking up her phone."

"I'm only five minutes out. I'll find her and get back to you."

"Do you know what's going on?"

"Shots were fired in the basement of the north wing of the hospital."

Carina would have no need to go into the basement. "If Carina calls you, just tell her to text me."

"Absolutely."

Nick hung up. Even if Carina was in the middle of securing the scene, why wouldn't she have responded to her partner? And she would have told Nick what she was doing, even with just a quick text message.

What Nick loved about Carina was also what worried him—she was good at her job, she loved her job, but she took risks every day. That was part of being a good cop. She never told someone else to handle a situation; she did it herself. People like him and his wife, if shots were fired, they went toward the conflict, not away.

Nick didn't regret leaving the sheriff's department in Montana to move to San Diego and become a private investigator with his brother-in-law, but right now, he wished he was a cop again.

From his bed, the colonel said, "She's fine, son."

"Of course she is," Nick said. The last thing the colonel needed was to be worried about his daughter.

"Go," the colonel said. "You don't need to babysit me. I sent Connor home; I'm sending you to find Carina."

Nick stood by the door and looked out through the narrow window. The hallway was deserted. He could see people in other rooms doing what he was doing. Guarding the door of their loved ones.

His phone rang. Immediately, he thought it was Carina—then caller ID showed it was Will.

"Nick, Tom Blade's team is staging outside the north

entrance of the hospital. Head down there. Tom is expecting you."

Tom was the head of SWAT for the city and Nick's closest friend. "What's happening?"

"I don't know," Will said.

"Don't lie to me, Hooper."

"I don't have a full report, I'm not telling you anything because I don't know anything, okay? All I know for certain is someone identifying herself as Carina called security from the north tower basement."

"Before or after the gunshots?"

"I don't know."

"What *do* you know?" Nick said in a rare burst of anger. He stopped himself. "I'll be there." He hung up and turned to Carina's father. "Dad," he said, "I'm going to check in with Will and SWAT. If you need me, call."

"Go, son."

Nick walked down the empty corridor. He was confronted by security at the elevator. "Sir, please go back into your room until we get the all clear."

Nick showed his ID and, even though it meant nothing, his PI badge. He did it fast enough and with enough confidence that the security guard didn't blink. "I've been called to check in with SWAT at the north entrance. What is the best way to get there from here?"

"We've sealed off that wing. Use the stairs, go to the first floor and talk to security. SDPD is on scene."

Nick went down the staircase. It took him five minutes and two more calls before he was waved through to SWAT. Tom's team was gearing up. Tom glanced at Nick and hesitated. Just a fraction, but Nick knew Carina was in trouble.

"Hooper said Carina called from the basement. Is that where the shooter is?"

"Yes. She identified herself when she spoke to security.

We have two witnesses, hostages that were released, who said a woman matching Carina's description is one of four hostages in the morgue. That's all I have right now. One of the released hostages was shot in the leg and is now in surgery, the other is being interviewed."

Nick's chest tightened. "Who's the shooter?"

"Charles Peterson. The ID is not confirmed. The witness thinks he's the brother of a cancer patient who died two days ago. We're on it, Nick. I'm telling you all this because we're friends and you were a cop. Don't do anything foolish. I'll take care of Carina, I promise."

"You know me better than that."

"And I know that when the woman you love is in danger, reason sometimes goes out the window. You can stay here, at the command center. If you leave, you will be on the other side of that line." He gestured toward the barrier that was being erected by uniformed officers.

He nodded once. "Keep me in the loop, Tom."

His phone vibrated. It was Lucy. What was he going to tell her?

"It's Nick," he answered.

"Nick, it's Lucy. We just landed and I got Carina's message about Dad, is he okay?"

"They have him resting, and I don't know what the plan is, but his color is back and they're running tests."

"I tried Carina and Connor, and neither of them are answering, and then I called Mom, and she was crying—I thought he'd died." Her voice hitched.

"Lucy, your dad is going to be okay." Nick hoped. "We have another situation."

"What?"

He had to tell her. She would be coming here anyway; she would find out soon enough.

"There was a shooting at the hospital. Carina has been taken hostage."

CHAPTER 26

Carina wished her brother Dillon was here. Dillon was a forensic shrink; he understood the twisted minds of people like Charlie Peterson. He'd know what Charlie really wanted even if the shooter wasn't sure himself about his plans.

Carina wouldn't want to see her loved ones' bodies after they died. Sitting by Patrick's bed while he'd been in a coma had been a living hell; if he'd died—she wouldn't have had to see the body to know the truth.

But maybe a soldier like Charlie did.

She glanced at Kristan who'd frozen in place, a deer-in-the-headlights gaze locked on Carina.

"Charlie, you don't want to see her like this," Carina said.

On the one hand, Carina understood the need for answers, the need to comprehend why something so unnecessary had had to happen. She'd lost people she cared about, and there was never a good reason. Seeing his sister's body might give him the peace of mind he required to get them all out of here before anyone was killed.

On the other hand, seeing his sister cold and dead might

send him on a suicidal path where they would all end up on a slab.

The phone was ringing. Charlie ignored it.

"You should answer it."

"Not now. Not until I see my sister."

"The police want to know that everyone is okay," Carina said. "You need to give them something, so no one dies."

Charlie said, "They wouldn't let me see her. By the time I got my leave, she was gone, and down here in the morgue, and they wouldn't let me see her. I don't believe the cancer killed her. Or a reaction to drugs. She was *fine* when I spoke to her an hour before she died. She told me she'd be home by Christmas, but if she wasn't, we were going to spend it here. She sent me to buy presents for the kids who wouldn't be able to go home." His voice trailed off, then he steeled himself and looked at Carina. "They said they aren't going to do an autopsy because she was under a doctor's care."

"You're family," Carina said. "You can request an autopsy."

He shook his head. "They said I'd have to pay for it because the doctor signed off on the cause of death. But it's not right. Something happened to Sarah and they're covering it up." He gestured to the three RNs.

"They just work here. They probably never even met your sister."

He shook his head. "All three of them were on duty on her floor the night she died. I'm not cruel, I don't want to hurt anyone who isn't responsible. Her doctor wasn't even in the hospital when she died, so how would he know how she died? Even he said that Sarah was just having a mild reaction to new medication and after being rehydrated and adjusting the dose she would be fine. I know doctors. If they thought there was even a small chance that something would go wrong, they wouldn't tell me she would be fine. They'd say, 'You know how these things are,' or, 'It's too early to tell.' Not 'She's having a mild reaction to the medication but she'll be fine.'"

That was the same as Carina's experience. Yet, doctors made mistakes. They were also busy. And if the doctor wasn't present when Sarah died, then maybe something had happened during the time between when Charlie checked and Sarah passed.

"There's no reason for any of these people to hurt Sarah. They were her caregivers."

"No one needs a reason to hurt people, it happens all the time," Charlie said. "And hospitals make mistakes. They screw up. One of these people is covering up something, and I will prove it."

"You don't know—"

"I *do* know!"

Carina couldn't lose this tenuous bond she had with Charlie. The best way to resolve the situation would be to keep him talking until he agreed to let the hostages go.

The phone started ringing again. Again, Charlie ignored it.

He gestured to Kristan. "Open her drawer now." He then said to Carina, "Stop talking."

Charlie motioned for Kristan to stand. Kristan looked at Carina, as if she wanted a second opinion.

"Go ahead, Kristan," Carina said. "He wants to see his sister."

Kristan slowly stood up. She said to Charlie, not looking him in the eye, "I . . . I need to see the chart on the desk. I don't know which drawer."

He nodded, keeping an eye on her.

There were sixteen drawers, eight across and two high. According to the chart, Sarah Peterson was in number 8, in the bottom corner.

Kristan walked over, then looked at Charlie again. "Are you sure?"

"Open the drawer."

Kristan did and then went back to sit with Brian and Rena. They were all watching Charlie, but trying not to be obvious.

Carina didn't care if she was obvious. She needed to keep an eye on him. If things went south, she had to act.

Charlie squatted next to his sister and stared. He didn't say anything; he didn't touch her. He just looked at her, unblinking.

Carina took that moment, when she was in his peripheral vision, to retrieve her cell phone from her pocket. She had one hand free, which had helped, but she still took care not to make a sound. She didn't have time to think, so sent a message to the last person who'd texted her, Nick.

Charlie Peterson, Army, sister Sarah deceased on 22nd. Minimum 2 guns. No fatalities, 1 injury. Explosives set at door.

She hit Send, needing to get that message out. She hoped it went, because she had one bar that fluttered in and out. Then she sent a second message.

I love you.

She slid her phone back in her front pocket. One of the hostages, Rena, had been watching her. Carina didn't give any indication that she'd done anything. No sense tipping off Charlie that he hadn't searched her.

Charlie's face was unreadable and he appeared as frozen as the corpse in front of him. Carina didn't know if that was good or bad. She could only see his profile.

He squatted there for a good ten minutes before he pushed the drawer back in with finality. Kristan stifled a scream. Charlie walked over to Carina, reached into her pocket and pulled out her phone. He read her message to Nick.

"Who's Nick?"

"My husband."

"Cop?"

"No."

"Doctor? What does he do?"

"He's a private investigator."

"He sent you a message. Tom's in charge, Will's here, Lucy and Dillon on their way. Hold tight." Charlie looked at Carina. "Who's Tom? Your partner?"

"Will's my partner. Tom is probably Tom Blade, SWAT team leader. He and Nick are friends." Carina knew enough about hostage negotiation to keep him talking, make it personal, but she wasn't trained in this. She was an investigator, not a psychologist.

"Lucy and Dillon? More cops?"

"My brother and sister."

"Special forces?"

"No. That's Jack. Dillon is a forensic psychiatrist."

"How many siblings do you have?"

"Two sisters and four brothers."

Charlie glanced at the drawer where Sarah lay. "I only had Sarah."

"You loved her."

"When I was in Iraq, she sent a care package every week. Every damn week, without fail. She was a teacher—third grade. She included pictures from the kids. She sent Oreos, because they were my favorite cookies when we were little. Letters telling me what she was doing, what her students were doing, her neighbors, my friends from high school. Normal stuff. She never forgot. Sometimes mail was delayed and I'd get four or five packages at once. She sent books—hundreds of books—that she bought at library sales. There were days—weeks—when we were bored out of our minds. The books helped.

"Then I was on base for a year, and we had dinner every week instead of exchanging letters. Our dad left when we were little, our mom died when Sarah was in college. I was already in the army. And now—she's gone, for no reason."

"She wouldn't want you to—"

"What's your sister like?"

"Lucy? I haven't seen her in nearly two years. She seems to be doing well."

"Why haven't you seen her?"

He was almost accusing her of something.

"She lives on the East Coast."

"That's no excuse."

"You're right."

"She's younger?"

"Yeah—eleven years."

"We're supposed to take care of our younger sisters," he said, though Carina didn't think he was talking to her anymore.

"This wasn't your fault, Charlie," Carina said.

"I know." He looked at the three nurses. "It's one of theirs."

Kristan was biting her nails. Rena had her head down. Brian was sweating.

Charlie said, "I want a private autopsy, right now, right here, where I can watch."

"If you want a cause of death, I can get an autopsy done for you. But it's not going to happen fast. There are tox screens they need to do, and it takes time to get the results from the lab."

"They can rush it."

"Charlie, if you let everyone go, I promise you, I'll make sure there is a full and complete autopsy on your sister. I give you my word." She doubted that it was as simple as that, but she could try. In the back of her mind, she knew that this was about more than an autopsy. There shouldn't have been a problem getting one, even if a doctor signed off on the cause of death. If the family asked, it would be done. It was standard.

The phone started ringing again, and this time it didn't stop. After a full minute Charlie walked over and answered.

"Yes, this is Sergeant Charlie Peterson. Everyone here is fine. Brian Glover, an RN, has a GSW to his lower calf, but the bleeding has stopped and he'll be fine . . . No, I'm not going to release him. I already released two hostages, and that's it . . . Just ask me about the explosives, I know Detective Kincaid already sent out the information . . . It's a pressure-sensitive switch. I also have a detonator that I can and will use if I suspect you're attempting to breach this room."

Charlie looked around the room and settled on Carina. "My demands are simple. I want what you want. A peaceful resolution."

Then he turned to the nurses. Carina didn't know what he was thinking, but if he thought that one of them was responsible for his sister's death, he wasn't going to let them leave alive. That had to be the final play here—vengeance.

"I want an autopsy on my sister. There's a reason I picked the morgue for this exercise. I want a medical examiner who doesn't work for the county or the hospital. Someone independent."

Carina had an idea. "Charlie," she said.

He frowned, but told the negotiator to hold on. "You have something to say?" He sounded irritated.

"Lucy. My sister. She's not an ME, but she's a pathologist for the Washington, D.C., medical examiner's office. She's a trained criminologist. You can trust her."

Carina didn't really want to bring Lucy into the middle of a hostage situation, but Charlie didn't know her background, that she was a criminal psychologist and a newly minted FBI agent. That could help them get the upper hand. Better, Lucy had dealt with hostage situations before.

Charlie considered. He must have seen honesty in Carina's expression, because he said into the phone, "Send down Lucy Kincaid, the pathologist. Have her wait outside the morgue. When I'm confident that no one is with her, that she is alone, I'll bring her in. No weapons, no tricks. Have a lab ready to run tests. If everyone does what they're supposed to do, this will be over before midnight and everyone will be home for Christmas." He hung up.

"Everyone," he continued, looking at the three nurses, "except the person who killed my sister."

CHAPTER 27

As soon as Lucy arrived at the hospital, two San Diego uniformed officers ushered her, Sean, Dillon, and Kate to the SWAT staging center on the north side of the hospital complex. Nick was there with Carina's partner, Will Hooper.

The scene around them was controlled chaos. There were two snipers at the top of the parking garage directly across from the north wing. Others were positioned at key locations outside each entrance. Lucy overheard that the entire north tower was being evacuated. Some of the patients were being moved to the south tower and main building, and others were being transferred to nearby hospitals.

Will immediately approached them. "I need Lucy," he said. He gestured to Nick. "Fill them in."

"Hold it," Kate said. "What the hell's going on? Why do you need Lucy?"

"Took the words right out of my mouth," Sean muttered.

Will glanced at the group. "We don't have a lot of time for a debriefing."

Lucy said, "Whatever you need from us, you know we'll help."

Tom Blade, whom Lucy recognized, stepped out of the SWAT truck. "Is she here?"

"Yes," Will said.

Tom sighed with obvious relief. "Great. Are you up to speed?"

"No," Lucy said.

Tom assessed the assembled group, then said, "The shooter is Charles Peterson, career army. We're still pulling his records, but I spoke to his commanding officer and he has a solid service record, multiple commendations, and a Purple Heart. A couple blemishes on his record for fighting, nothing out of the ordinary. His sister, his only family that we know about, died from cancer two days ago. We made contact with him fifteen minutes ago, but he broke it off after making his demands."

"What are his demands?" Kate asked.

"He wants a full autopsy by someone not affiliated with the hospital."

"Wasn't an autopsy done?" Lucy asked.

"According to her records, she died while under a doctor's care. She had an adverse reaction to a new medication and was admitted to the hospital. They changed her meds and thought she was responding, but she died that night. She's been in and out of the hospital for the past year."

"We need all her records, and her doctor—" Lucy began.

"Her doctor left on vacation before she died. He's unreachable. What Peterson wants is to witness the autopsy."

"He won't know what he's seeing."

"Carina told him you're a pathologist and could do it. He asked for you specifically."

"Why would Carina put Lucy in the middle of a hostage situation?" Sean said. "That makes no sense."

"It seems she told Peterson that Lucy was her sister and a pathologist, but made no mention that she's also an FBI agent," Will said.

"I'm not qualified," Lucy said. There had to be a good reason that Carina would bring her into this.

"But you know what to do," Tom said.

"Yes, I've assisted in dozens of autopsies, but it's been nearly a year since I left the medical examiner's office. And unless there's something visually noticeable, the lab work is what's important."

"We need to buy time," Will said, "and the best way to buy time is to go through the motions of performing an autopsy."

"You don't have to do this," Tom said. "We'll think of something else."

But even as Tom said it, Lucy couldn't think of another way. Carina was a smart cop. She had to have a logical reason for wanting Lucy down there—she wouldn't intentionally put her in harm's way. She might feel that this was the best way to talk the shooter out of hurting anyone else, if he thought someone was really listening to him and getting him the answers that he wanted.

"Carina wouldn't have told him I was a pathologist unless she had a plan. But I need to be fully prepared to perform the autopsy and take samples. There are protocols that need to be followed."

"Absolutely." Will squeezed her hand. "Let's get you geared up."

"Whoa," Sean said, looking from Will to Dillon. "You're okay with this? With sending Lucy down there with a gunman?"

"No," Dillon said. "Will, I need access to all Peterson's

files. I need to put together a profile quickly. But what you've said doesn't make sense. He took hostages because he wants an autopsy done on his sister's body? There's something more to this."

"Until we get him talking, we don't have anything other than what he's already said."

Tom said, "We have a tablet with wireless access. Lucy can use it as a resource for the autopsy, but its primary purpose is to give us an audio recording of everything in the room. That's going to give you what you need, Dr. Kincaid. I'm happy to have you consult, but we need eyes and ears in that room. We have blueprints, but he has a bomb on the door and we're moving ahead with caution before we try to access the vents. The ventilation system in the morgue and lab is separate from the main hospital's. This is good in that we may be able to send in a harmless sleeping gas, but if he suspects—and he might because he's special forces—he has a fail-safe. He's set a C-4 charge on the main door. We need to see the charge, get a good description, to figure out how to disarm it or interrupt his transmission."

Tom handed Lucy blue scrubs and a medical bag. "This should have everything you need. There's also a key to the supply cabinet in the morgue. Your job is to do the autopsy and get out. He's agreed to let you leave when you're done."

"And Carina?"

"Carina seems to have built a rapport with him. We need more information before we can decide a plan of action. But know that we will have a plan, and we will get you all out."

Will caught her eye. "Can you fake it?"

"Fake it? I thought we agreed I was going to actually do the autopsy."

"Go through the motions, but that's secondary to getting everyone out safe."

"Maybe," Lucy said, "if he gets the answers he wants, he'll give himself up without anyone being hurt."

"We can't count on that. We're going to run tests on the samples, but it's all for show—we'll give him nothing, but tell him whatever it takes to get him to release the hostages."

Lucy understood why, but she still wasn't certain it was going to work.

She caught Sean's eye. He didn't want her doing this, but he didn't say a word. He didn't have to.

She took his hand. His whole body was tense. "I hate this idea," he said.

"I know."

"But you have to do it."

She nodded. "It's going to work." She sounded more confident than she felt.

One of the uniformed officers approached Will. "Detective, the supervising nurse is here to talk to you." He gestured to a diminutive older woman standing just inside the barricade.

"Thanks, tell her I'll be right there." Will turned to Tom. "It's the floor supervisor. I need to talk to her about the hostages and debrief her."

"Go. I'll finish with Kincaid."

Will left, and Tom escorted Lucy inside the SWAT truck and gave her the supplies she'd need, then activated the tablet. "He won't be able to tell that it's recording. Even if he inspects it, it won't appear to be recording anything. The feed will come directly to me. When you leave the room, leave the tablet."

"All right."

She went through the medical bag and felt confident

that everything she needed was there. Then she stepped out of the truck and Sean was waiting for her.

He took her hands and pulled her to him. "Luce—"

She kissed him. "I'll see you in a couple of hours, okay?"

His jaw tightened.

She glanced around and saw Dillon but not Kate. "Where's Kate?"

"She's talking to the SAC in San Diego," Sean said. "Calling in the cavalry. You're one of theirs now."

"Really, Carina must have a plan, otherwise she wouldn't have mentioned me."

"Ticktock," Tom said.

"I'm ready." She hated leaving Sean angry and worried, but Tom said he could stay in the truck and monitor the audio if he kept out of the way.

Tom whistled to Will, who was still talking to the supervisor. Will rushed over. "Sorry—that was Marilyn Todd, the RN in charge of the cancer wing. She didn't have anything to contribute, except the identities of the three hostages. She also stated that Peterson was distraught when he found out his sister had died, but left the hospital before she had to call security."

"Did she know him?" Lucy asked. "Talk to him? Have anything to contribute as to what might have led him in this direction?"

Will shook his head. "She feels guilty, because she was scared of him but didn't tell anyone. You saw her; she's a small woman, Peterson is a burly two-hundred-pound soldier." He glanced at Lucy. "Ready?"

"Yes," she said. She glanced at Sean and gave him a smile. He wasn't smiling back.

"I'm going to walk you to the basement," Will said. "We have SWAT positioned at each corner of the hall, but you have to go to the door alone."

"Dillon," Lucy said, "walk with us, I have some questions."

As they walked toward the north tower entrance, she asked, "What do you think he really wants?"

"He wouldn't go through with this elaborate plan unless he had an idea of what the autopsy would find," Dillon said. "That's what I'm thinking, without more information. I suspect—and this is a guess, because I don't have any more information than you do—that he thinks the hospital made a mistake and his sister died because of it. He doesn't trust the hospital, which is why he feels the only way to get answers is for someone independent to come in. My primary concern is what he'll do if he doesn't get the answer he expected."

"If it was a hospital error, they have liability insurance, but if it was truly an accident, no individual is going to be punished, at least in his eyes."

"Do what you do best, Lucy—empathize with him."

They were at the top of the staircase leading to the basement. "I can't let you go any farther," Will said to Dillon.

Lucy hugged her brother, and whispered, "Keep an eye on Sean." She didn't have to explain why. Sean was a man of action; waiting for others was not in his nature.

"I will."

If Lucy was down in the morgue with a shooter and a room full of victims, she didn't want to think of the trouble Sean could get into up here with the cops. She didn't want him to be ejected from the hospital. Or worse—arrested.

Nick approached and was immediately stopped by two uniforms when he breached the line. Will frowned, but Nick said, "I need Lucy for ten seconds."

Will didn't stop him from pulling Lucy to the side. "Carina's pregnant," Nick whispered. "We haven't told anyone yet. I just wanted you to know before you go down."

She hugged Nick. "She will be fine." She gave him a stiff smile. She had to believe everything would be okay, even though she had no idea what she would face in the morgue. She couldn't let anyone know she was scared.

Then she went with Will down the cement staircase into the quiet north wing basement.

CHAPTER 28

It had been thirty minutes since Charlie last spoke to SWAT. He'd told them not to call again until Lucy was in the building. It was quiet. Too quiet for Carina. The three nurses were sitting together, heads down, resigned to the fact that they would be stuck here a little longer. Carina sat on the floor in the middle of the room, hand-cuffed to the autopsy table, and prayed she'd done the right thing. Charlie stood calmly by the phone, waiting, his ears pricked for sounds Carina couldn't hear. She knew SWAT would be coming in from all angles—they could be in the ventilation system for all she knew. But she heard nothing.

Carina hadn't seen her younger sister in nearly two years, and while she had reports from Dillon that Lucy was doing great, and she knew that she'd graduated from the FBI Academy, and had heard about all the other things she'd faced over the last year, Carina still remembered her as a traumatized rape victim. Lucy had intentionally pulled away from her family in the aftermath. Except . . . not the entire family. She'd lived with Dillon for the past seven years. She and Patrick were as close as Carina and Patrick had once been. And Jack had flown to D.C. to visit Lucy more often than he'd come to San Diego to visit her.

Dear Lord, that thought seemed like jealousy.

Maybe in the back of her mind she *was* a little jealous of Lucy. Not that she wanted her life, just that she wanted their family to be together in the same city. Nick had given up his career as sheriff in Montana to move to San Diego so Carina didn't have to give up her family. She wanted roots, and she had them in San Diego. She wanted family, and for a while they'd all been here, in San Diego. Now . . . it was just her and Connor. She wanted her child to have the same large-family upbringing she'd had, but instead of being an army brat, he or she would have cousins and friends and family a bike ride away. But . . . this little guy was going to be the only one for a long time. And when her brothers and sisters had kids, they would be far away.

Damn, Carina, your hormones are working overtime.

The phone rang and Charlie calmly answered it. "Good. When I see that she's alone, I'll bring her in. . . . No, I'm not disarming the bomb. She'll have to step carefully." He hung up and walked over to the door. He didn't disarm the bomb, but he adjusted the detonator so that when he opened the door it wouldn't go off. Then he pressed the lock release on the wall and the blue light turned off.

Carina didn't know if this calm was good or bad. He hadn't spoken more than half a dozen words after SWAT agreed to send in Lucy as a pathologist.

Rena, the older, dark-haired RN, slowly rose from her spot on the cement floor. "Please," she pleaded with Charlie, "let us go."

He turned and pointed his gun steadily at her chest. "Sit. Down."

"You have a cop and a pathologist, you don't need us."

"Sit."

Carina tried to catch the nurse's eye, but Rena was looking nervous, like she was going to make a run for it.

Charlie saw the same thing. "You were good for so long. It's not much longer. Unless you have something you want to confess?"

"We've done nothing!" Rena said. "None of us did anything to your sister. Just let us go."

"Rena," Carina said, hoping to calm her down, but the nurse wasn't listening.

Charlie strode across the morgue and grabbed Rena. He put the gun to her head. "What are you hiding?"

Rena sucked in a breath and closed her eyes.

Charlie easily held on to the nurse, moving the gun to the back of her head. He walked back over to the doors and looked through the window. "Ms. Kincaid, you may open the door on your left. Push it slowly. If you have equipment, toss the bag into the room in front of you. Watch your step. There is a detonator on your right. I also have a switch in my pocket that will set off the bomb. Understood?"

"Yes," Lucy said through the door.

"Then come in."

Lucy took a deep breath. There was no backing out now. She pushed open the door and threw her bag in front of her, then stepped over the threshold as Peterson had instructed.

To the left was a row of refrigerator drawers. Straight ahead was Peterson, holding a gun on a nurse. The woman, in her forties, looked terrified and angry at the same time. Peterson was dressed in khaki pants and a black T-shirt. He looked like any number of physically fit soldiers and cops that Lucy knew—clean-cut, tattoo on his biceps, experience sharpening his eyes.

Carina's right wrist was handcuffed to the autopsy table. Lucy breathed easier when she saw that her sister was okay.

"Lock the door, Ms. Kincaid."

She did. Blue lights over the door flashed again, and the windows darkened.

"Leave your bag where it is and walk over to the desk. Stand still and no sudden movements."

Peterson said to the nurse, "I'm going to let you return to Brian and Kristan. Don't do anything else but sit between them, exactly where you were before. Next time you get up without my permission, I will shoot you in the leg. Do you understand?"

She nodded and Peterson watched as she moved back to her spot and sat down. Kristan tried to take her hand, but Rena swatted her wrist away and put her head between her knees. Lucy assessed the three hostages. They were scared but, except for Brian's bandaged leg, appeared unharmed. Carina looked okay, too, other than being restrained to the leg of the autopsy table.

Peterson frisked her. "Good, you obeyed the first rule." He walked over to the door and moved the bomb so that if anyone opened the door, it would detonate. The bomb scared Lucy more than the gun.

Next, he picked up her bag and put it on the table. He dumped everything out and inspected the tools. He held up the tablet. "What's this?"

"I'm not a medical examiner. I'm a pathologist. I might need to look up information. I also downloaded a checklist for the autopsy. I don't want to forget anything."

"What's the difference?" he asked.

She didn't know if he was really interested, or if he wanted to catch her in a lie. "I'm not a physician. I have a pathology certificate, not a degree. That essentially means that I took a year of forensic biology in college and passed a qualification test. I assist in autopsies, I don't usually perform them myself."

"But you can do it."

"I've assisted in over one hundred autopsies back in D.C."

"Why are you here in San Diego?"

"It's Christmas," she said. "I came to be with my family." She looked at Carina. Carina gave her a very small nod. Good. They were on the same page.

He seemed to accept her answers and said, "I know you'll need tools, such as a scalpel. However, I still have a gun, and I have a detonator that will set off that bomb." To prove it, he held up a small black box, before putting it back in his pocket. "I promised Detective Kincaid that when you're done, you can leave. If you behave, I will keep my promise."

She nodded. "I need someone to help me. Usually, there are three of us, but I can do it with one person. Will you let Carina assist?"

He shook his head. "She's a cop. I want her to stay right where she is." He motioned to Kristan, the blond nurse. "Kristan will help you."

Lucy didn't argue the point. It was best to give him what he wanted, and then when she needed to have her way, she might have more leverage.

She said, "Where's the body?"

"Sarah," Charlie said.

Lucy said, "I try not to personalize the victim, otherwise I can't be clinical in my examination." This wasn't completely true for Lucy—she always saw the victims as people—but she wanted to show Charlie that she was here as a scientist and nothing more.

He stared at her and nodded, understanding in his eyes. He was a soldier; he knew what she meant.

"Drawer eight," he said, and walked over to the desk, far from the drawers, far from the autopsy table.

Lucy motioned for Kristan to take the portable gurney from its hook on the wall. She pulled open the drawer. Sarah Peterson had been in her early thirties. "I need her records," she said to the nurse. "Can you access the hospital files from here?"

"I don't know that I should," she said.

"Yes, you should. I can't do this without having as much of her medical history as possible."

"You mean this is for real? You're really going to do this?"

"Yes."

Kristan was confused, but Lucy didn't care. One step at a time.

They both pulled on latex gloves, then lifted the body onto the gurney. They rolled it over to the table, then carefully slid the heavy corpse onto the stainless steel table.

"Can you do this?" Lucy said to the nervous girl.

"Y-yes."

"How long have you been a nurse?"

"Almost two years."

"I need you to access her records." She glanced at Peterson. "Okay, Mr. Peterson? I need Kristan to access Sarah's medical records."

He nodded and moved away from the computer.

While Kristan did that, Lucy inspected the body. Sarah Peterson had been preserved almost immediately after death. The cold drawers slowed, but didn't completely stop, decomposition. But most medication that had been in the blood prior to her death should still be present in her tissues because it had only been forty-eight hours.

She opened the checklist application on the tablet.

"What are you doing?" Peterson asked.

"I'm making sure I don't miss anything." She showed

him the checklist. "I'm going to go through this step by step. If I have any questions that I think should be reviewed by an ME, I'll make note of it. I want to document this as best I can. Isn't that what you want?"

"Of course." He seemed surprised. Was he surprised that his demands had been met? He couldn't be so naive that he hadn't thought that this autopsy was also a way to bide time. "How long will this take?"

"It could take up to two hours," she said. "I don't know how long the lab work will take, but if they have a lab on-site and rush it, a couple hours maybe, for the basic tox screens. Some tests need longer to process than others."

Kristan printed out Sarah's file and handed it to Lucy. Lucy understood enough to get by. On the nineteenth, during a routine office visit, Sarah Peterson's doctor changed her medication. Two days later, she was admitted to the hospital with acute vomiting and dehydration. The on-call doctor put her on a different medication after consulting with her primary doctor, who was out of town. The conclusion was that she'd had a severe allergic reaction to the new meds.

Eighteen months ago, Sarah had been diagnosed with ovarian cancer. She had had surgery that removed the affected ovary, and it was considered a success. She'd gone through a round of chemotherapy and her last checkup had been cancer-free. But her body wasn't bouncing back as quickly as the doctor wanted, and she was put on another regimen of pills. That's what caused her vomiting and she was admitted and given an IV. "It says they drew blood when she arrived. That's good—if there are any anomalies they should be easy to detect."

"What do you mean?" he asked.

"If there is something foreign in her system that wasn't present when she was admitted, then we may be able to pinpoint when it was introduced and determine if it was the natural reaction of her body fighting off a medication, or if it was the wrong medication."

"Just do it."

Lucy continued her visual inspection and input her observations onto the checklist. Then she said to Peterson, "You might not want to look."

"I can handle it."

"This is your sister. There's a reason why doctors don't perform surgery on people they care about."

"I've seen men I served with blown up. My best friend lost his arm to an IED."

There was, sometimes, no reasoning with a soldier.

She began the incision and said, both to distract Peterson from what she was doing and to keep him talking, "My brother served in the army. Panama. Iraq."

"Carina told me."

Lucy glanced down to where Carina sat on the floor. Her skin was pale, and she had her head on her knees. Though the room was cold and the ventilation good, there were still fumes and smells that irritated, particularly someone who was pregnant.

"You okay, sis?" Lucy asked.

"Peachy," she muttered.

Lucy approached Peterson. He looked suspicious. She said, "My sister is pregnant. The smells are making her ill. Can you move her to—" She glanced around. "What about the chair? Cuff her hands behind her, through the chair?"

Peterson handed her the keys. "You do it."

"Thank you."

Lucy squatted next to Carina. "Nick told me," she whispered.

"Damn him."

"He's worried."

"I'm going to puke."

As soon as Lucy unlocked her cuffs, Carina stumbled over to a trash can and vomited. Lucy brought her a paper cup of water from the sink. "Here."

She waited until Carina had gotten some of her color back, then said, "I have to do this."

"I know."

She cuffed her, and then Peterson checked and tightened the cuffs. He looked at Carina oddly, and Lucy couldn't tell what he was thinking. She gave him back the key, and returned to the table.

There was no turning back now.

CHAPTER 29

"Everything is going as expected," Tom Blade said.

Hardly, Sean thought. Lucy was in danger, and nothing was how it should be. Worse, he felt impotent.

Charles Peterson had taken hostages over two hours ago. And now Lucy was down there with him. *Nothing* was going as expected.

"Dr. Kincaid, if you can work up a psych profile, it will help."

"I have a preliminary report," Dillon said.

Dillon was watching Sean closely. He expected him to do something, but while Sean could disable computers and hack into any secure system, he knew nothing about disabling bombs or hostage negotiations.

"And?"

"Charlie Peterson lost his only living relative who, by all accounts, he was very close to. Sarah Peterson was a third-grade teacher, well liked, with no enemies. She developed ovarian cancer and was treated, but there were complications and she died. A man like Charlie would naturally have a hard time accepting that her death was natural. He wants answers. He wants to understand. I think the plan you have in play is going to work, if we can get him to accept the autopsy report from Lucy. The big question is, what is Lucy going to find? And how will that impact him?"

"It doesn't matter," Tom said. "We've already printed out negative lab results, which should tell him she died because of an allergic reaction to the new medication—something that no one could have predicted."

Dillon frowned. "But how did she die?"

"According to the doctor, just that. They changed her meds and her internal organs shut down."

"I think the main question is why does he think one of the nurses had something to do with it?" Sean said. "Does he think gross negligence? That someone made a mistake and covered it up?"

"That's irrelevant."

"It's not irrelevant, Tom," Dillon said. "If we want to get the hostages *and* Peterson out of that room alive, we need to find out why he thinks one of the nurses is guilty of murder."

"Murder?" Tom shook his head in disbelief.

"Gross negligence at a minimum, but something set him off."

"He must have a reason for thinking something is wonky," Sean said. "We've all lost people we care about, but we don't take a bunch of people hostage."

"He's mentally unstable," Tom said.

"I don't think so," Dillon said.

"That's worse."

"He has a reason for doing this. Sean's right. Something set him off, something gave him reason to believe that his sister's death wasn't natural." Dillon turned to Will, who was listening to the exchange but not contributing. "We need his phone records for the last seventy-two hours. Re-create every step of the last three days, from when his sister was admitted until he took the hostages."

"We already have people working on it, but it's Christmas Eve, Dillon—we don't have the manpower right now. We're doing the best we can."

"I'm sorry—but those are my sisters down there."

"Tom and I know that," Will said. "We have every available man working on this."

Dillon rarely showed his anger—it was one of the things Sean admired about him—but right now he was slowly percolating. Did he have the same problems with the operation that Sean had? Did he see something no one else saw? "We need a thorough background check on Sarah, as well as the three hostages."

"I can do that," Sean said.

"Hold it," Will said. "I know you work for RCK and all, but we have a time issue here."

Sean didn't correct Will. If the cop knew he wasn't working with RCK anymore, he might ice him out. "I'm just offering my help."

Dillon asked, "Who spoke to the two women he let go after Carina confronted him?"

"First security, then two SDPD officers," Tom said.

"I'd like to talk to them," Dillon said.

"I'll take you," Will agreed.

"They might know more than they think they do."

Sean said, "I want to go."

"Sean, you should—"

"Dillon, if I sit here I'll go crazy."

Will reluctantly agreed. For some reason, this cop rubbed Sean the wrong way, and the feeling appeared to be mutual.

They couldn't speak to the doctor who'd been shot because she was still recovering from surgery, but they found RN Tammy Pence in a private office.

Will frowned at Sean. "We can't all go in there," he said. "We'll overwhelm her."

Sean said, "I'll wait out here."

Dillon eyed him suspiciously. Sean gave him an innocent look. "I'll stay right here," he said, and sat in a chair
next to the empty nurses' station.

Will motioned for Dillon to follow him. As soon as the
door closed, Sean rolled the chair over to the computer.

He hacked into the SWAT mobile computer. He considered sharing with SWAT ways to block people like him,
but he didn't like the way this operation was going. It
wasn't that they were doing anything wrong—on the surface they had set up a good net to catch the bastard who
was holding Lucy and Carina. But Blade hadn't been immediately forthcoming with his plans, and that made Sean
nervous. Lucy was at risk, and no way was Sean going to
leave her safety up to a bunch of cops he didn't know.

He also had seen Nick whisper something to Lucy right
before she went in. Not knowing what Nick said was driving Sean crazy.

It wasn't that he thought Lucy incapable of handling
this high-stress, dangerous situation; it was that they didn't
have all the information. Information was always the key
in circumstances like this. Without it, they were working
blind.

He scanned the recent files on the SWAT server.
They had blueprints of the hospital. Sean knew where
all the snipers were, potential exits, and bomb-diffusing
scenarios. What he really wanted was security footage—
why didn't they have it? Maybe they were using the hospital system and not downloading the data to their own
servers.

Sean pulled up the hospital's security network, glancing at the room where Dillon and Will were talking to the
nurse. He didn't know how much time he had.

He plugged his tablet into the computer and launched a
facial recognition program, the same program he'd written

and used to identify Denise Vail in Colorado. He input only the face of the shooter, and then had the computer do all the work, limiting the parameters to the last seventy-two hours. It could scan all the digital data much faster than the human eye.

Within two minutes, his program revealed all the instances where Peterson had been caught on camera. He made note of the time stamps, but one of the images caught his eye.

Last night, Peterson was talking to a young nurse in scrubs outside the emergency room. They were standing close together. The image wasn't crystal clear, but the nurse looked worried and Peterson had a rigid expression. She handed him something, as small as a flash drive, and then he hugged her and left. She watched him walk away, then went back inside the building.

The time stamp had the exchange happening just after midnight. Peterson wasn't seen on camera again until nine this morning, shortly after shift changes, when he entered the north tower. On camera, Sean watched as Lucy's sister Carina followed him. What had he done that triggered that cop sense in Carina? Had she seen or heard something?

Sean switched to the next camera to track Peterson's progress through the building.

"What the hell are you doing, Rogan?"

Will Hooper was standing over his shoulder. Sean had been so focused on the security feed that he hadn't heard him.

He rewound the digital file. "That woman—Peterson met with her at midnight last night. They clearly know each other. He then left and came back this morning."

"I should arrest you."

Dillon intervened. He gave Sean a disapproving look, but also a small smile. "Sean is tech savvy. We can use him."

"We have a pretty damn good tech department too—one your own brother developed."

"Patrick is my partner," Sean said. *Was my partner.* "I think this is important. Maybe this woman knows something. She handed him something, probably a flash drive."

"Print it," Will said. "I'll talk to Tom. But stay out of this, Rogan."

Sean was about to argue, but Dillon touched his arm as Will walked away. Dillon stopped Will outside the elevator. Sean followed at a safe distance after grabbing the printout.

"If Patrick were here, he'd be the first to vouch for Sean," Dillon said. "We have a lot of information and not enough manpower to sift through it, in a time-crucial hostage situation. Sean can greatly reduce the time we need to find what's important."

Sean handed Dillon the photo of the woman, and Dillon handed it to Will. "Like this."

Will turned around. It was clear that for some reason he didn't care for Sean, but Sean wasn't here to make friends.

He didn't talk to Sean directly. Instead he said to Dillon, "He's a civilian. He's your responsibility."

"I'm sure I have higher security clearance," Sean mumbled.

Will glared at him, then turned and walked away. Sean and Dillon trailed behind.

"That doesn't help," Dillon said to Sean.

"What did the witness say?"

"Pence was in the morgue doing paperwork. One of the hostages, Kristan Otto, came in and asked about a meeting. Pence didn't know about a meeting, and Otto said that she had a note when she came on shift to meet in the morgue at nine A.M. for a training exercise. Pence began to call around when the other two nurses, Glover and La-vagnino, entered for the same reason. Pence stepped out and ran into the doctor. Peterson came around the corner and the doctor immediately questioned him. He ignored her and went into the morgue. When he saw the three there, he pulled out a gun. The doctor was about to call security, and he shot her in the leg. Glover attempted to disarm him, and Peterson shot him in the leg."

"He didn't want to kill them."

"No—he wanted to disable them. That's when he heard Carina on the phone and grabbed Pence, using her as a shield to force Carina into the morgue. But the interesting thing is something Peterson said—he told Pence she wasn't involved."

Sean considered what that meant.

Dillon said, "According to the charts, all three RNs being held hostage had been on Sarah Peterson's floor within an hour of her death."

"And SWAT knows this and didn't tell us?"

"Sean, I know this is difficult for you—"

Sean ignored Dillon's attempt to diffuse the tension. The only thing that would help was when Lucy was back by his side. Sean said, "Does Peterson think one of them hurt his sister? Do any of them have a personal connection with her?"

"That's what Will is looking into now. It could be that Peterson needs someone to blame for what is really a senseless death. Sometimes, for soldiers like Peterson, it's the natural deaths, the things he can't explain, that are the hardest to accept."

Sean gestured to his copy of the photo of the woman talking to Peterson. "Why would she help him?"

"We don't know that she did."

"According to the timeline, he was given an early leave because of his sister's death. He didn't go AWOL, he wasn't acting impulsively. He went to the hospital and picked up her belongings four hours after he was notified, which fits the timeline from talking to his commanding officer and driving from base to the hospital. Then he returns late the next night to talk to this nurse?"

"How do you know this?" Dillon asked.

Sean didn't answer the question. It was probably better that Dillon didn't know he'd hacked into Tom Blade's account. "That nurse gave him something. We need to find her. She's the key to this, I feel it."

Lucy prepared all the blood and tissue samples and packaged them up. The autopsy had taken nearly two hours. It would have been faster had she not double-checked everything. Maybe, subconsciously, she was giving the SWAT team time to come up with a plan, but she also wanted answers. Her visual inspection of Sarah's organs didn't show any sign of cancer, but cancer wasn't generally present to the naked eye. She was missing an ovary, consistent with her medical records, but if there were any cancer cells present, Lucy would need to inspect the tissues under a stronger microscope than she had access to. She took samples of all organs and lymph nodes, as well as samples from Sarah's blood, liver, heart, and kidneys to run a wide array of tox screens. She didn't want to leave anything unexamined. Because though she knew this autopsy was on the one hand a delay, on the other she wanted answers almost as much as Charlie.

Not knowing the truth about the death of a loved one was worse than the answers that might be uncovered.

As per protocol, she put the organs back into Sarah's body and sewed her up. Kristan helped her put the corpse back in the cold storage, and they pushed the drawer closed.

Carina was pale, but she hadn't puked again. Still, the stress wasn't doing her any good. Lucy knew that she'd had at least one miscarriage two years ago, and her mother had commented that she thought Carina had had another but never told the family. She must be worried sick, but at the same time, she'd risked her life to save these three nurses, and convinced Peterson to release the other two hostages.

Lucy walked over to Peterson. "I'm done. These are the samples I need to get to the lab."

"I appreciate how professional you were with my sister. You treated her with respect. Thank you."

"I have a favor to ask."

"I'm not releasing a hostage."

"A trade. Me for Carina."

"No," Carina said. The handcuffs rattled as she straightened in the chair. "That's not why I told him you were a pathologist. I don't want to be traded."

Lucy ignored Carina and spoke directly to Charlie, looking him in the eye. "She's obviously ill. She's pregnant. This stress isn't good for her or the baby. I'll take her place in the chair. The tests will be done in a couple hours, and then we can all leave."

"You'd do that for your sister?"

"Yes," she said without hesitation.

He handed Lucy the keys to the handcuffs. "Let her go."

"Dammit, I'm not leaving!" Carina said. "Charlie, come on, this is my little sister—we were talking earlier about how important it is to protect our sisters."

Charlie said, "And you're pregnant. I don't want you here. Look, I appreciate everything you've done to help me get answers. Lucy will wait with me. And then I'll know what to do."

He motioned for Lucy to sit. "Don't move." Then he said to Carina, "Pick up the samples."

Carina complied. She caught Lucy's eye and shook her head. "Lucy—"

"I'm fine, Carina," Lucy said. She was scared, but she buried it with a deep breath. He hadn't put the cuffs on her, and that was a relief. She didn't want to be restrained; it might set off a panic attack even though she'd learned to fight them back. She could think more clearly if she didn't have to also fight her fears.

Charlie reset the detonator and told Carina to leave the same way that Lucy had come in. "Good-bye, Carina." He walked up behind Lucy. Lucy knew the gun was pointed at her head, but she didn't flinch.

When Carina hesitated, Charlie said, "If she does what I say, I will not hurt her. I owe you that."

Owe? That was an odd choice of words.

"Charlie," Carina said, "there is another way."

"Not anymore."

After Carina left and Charlie checked the bomb, he walked over to drawer 8 and put his hand on the outside, as if saying good-bye. He might have thought watching the autopsy would be clinical, but it had greatly affected him.

"Charlie," Lucy began, wanting to keep the conversation going.

He didn't look at her. Instead he stared at the three RNs sitting against the wall. "I'm done talking. Now we wait for answers."

CHAPTER 30

As soon as Will started toward the SWAT staging area, he was on his phone. He was several feet ahead of Sean and Dillon, but the expression on his face was stern.

Something had happened.

Will started running for the north tower, and Sean was right on his heels. As soon as they reached the main doors, Lucy's sister Carina stepped out.

Sean looked around for Lucy, but she was nowhere.

"Where's Lucy?" Sean interrupted.

Two uniformed officers approached Sean, but Will waved them away.

"Not here," Will said, his arm around Carina as he led her toward the SWAT truck.

"Where's Lucy?" Sean demanded as they walked.

"She's still inside," Carina said.

"What happened? Why is she still inside?"

Nick ran up to the group and hugged his wife. Sean stared at them as if they had all lost their minds.

Anger and a deep fear pulsed through Sean. Dillon put his hand on his shoulder, but Sean shook it off.

"What did you tell her?" Sean asked Nick. "You said something to her—did you do this?"

Carina stood between them, her hand on Sean's chest. "Lucy found out I was pregnant. I didn't want to leave, but she told Peterson and he agreed to a swap."

"No. No!" He turned to Nick. "You told Lucy to trade herself for Carina?"

"Of course not," Nick said.

Will pushed Sean out of the group. Sean was close to hitting him. He clenched his fists as Will jabbed his finger in his chest. "If you don't get it together, Rogan, I'll arrest you."

"Poke me again, and you'll have cause to arrest me," Sean said through clenched teeth.

Dillon stepped between them. "Let's figure out what's going on before we do anything. Sean," he said firmly. "Lucy knows what she's doing."

Sean didn't doubt that, but it didn't make him feel better to know that she was still in the morgue with an armed soldier who had nothing to lose.

Sean stayed behind the group to put his head together. He couldn't blame Nick, or Carina, or anyone but Charles Peterson. Lucy had her reasons, but Sean didn't have to like it.

Will and Nick walked Carina over to the ambulance that was waiting next to the SWAT truck. Sean trailed behind them. He needed to know what was going on, but Will was grating on him and it was best if he stood back.

Carina sat on a gurney, clearly frustrated by the attention as a paramedic put a blood pressure cuff around her arm. "I'm fine," she said.

Nick kissed her forehead and held her hand. Sean couldn't be mad at him for wanting to protect his wife and unborn baby. And it was exactly what Lucy would have done. Protect the innocent. Maybe Carina was a cop and willing to risk her own life, but the baby wasn't.

Lucy's been in worse situations. She'll be fine.

Sean had to believe that now.

Carina said, "So you heard everything?"

"Yes," Tom said. "The tablet Agent Kincaid brought with her has a one-way audio. We've been able to piece together from witnesses that Peterson has a vendetta against the three nurses down there, because of his sister's death."

"No," Carina said. "Just one. He thinks one of them killed her, and he lured them there."

Will said, "They thought they had a training exercise."

"How'd he get them down there?"

"We're working on it," Will said. "Rogan found something on the security feed. Peterson met with another nurse last night." He showed Carina the printout. "Recognize her?"

"No. But it makes sense that he has inside help. He knew his sister was in the morgue, and he knew which nurses had been on duty the night she died. He's positive one of them killed her."

Tom grabbed the printout. "We need an ID."

Will said, "I'm going to talk to the head nurse of the unit again. She pulled all the personnel files of the three hostages, and our people are going through them, but so far there's no connection between any of them and either Charles or Sarah Peterson. Let me call and have her brought over." He stepped aside.

"Carina, are you up for giving us a good visual of the bomb and where everyone is located?" Tom asked.

"Yes—get me the blueprints."

Tom unrolled the plans and said, "We're working on getting eyes into the room from the ventilation shaft, but it's a dedicated system and hard to access. We know he's expecting something, and so we're having problems—there's no quiet way to go in there. He shut down the security cameras from the inside—unplugged them. No way to get eyes in there."

Sean spoke up. "Is there a computer in the room hooked up to the hospital system?"

"Yes," Carina said. "Lucy had one of the nurses retrieve the victim's medical records."

"If there's a camera in the computer, I can get access," Sean said.

"We have our tech people working on it," Tom said.

"I can do it in five minutes."

Tom didn't believe him, but Sean didn't care. He stood his ground.

"Sean," Carina said. "I'm sorry we had to meet like this." She glanced from Sean to Dillon. "Lucy's not the teenager who moved away seven years ago. I didn't know what to expect."

"Why did you give him Lucy?" Sean asked.

"Hey!" Nick exclaimed, stepping up.

"I'm not accusing you of anything," Sean said, "I need to know the truth."

"Peterson caught me texting Nick. Read the message that said Lucy and Dillon were on their way. Peterson asked, I told him she was a pathologist. Didn't say she was a federal agent. Then when he was talking about the autopsy, it seemed like the expedient thing to do. I'm so sorry, I didn't mean to put her in danger."

"Lucy can handle the situation," Dillon said. "We need information. What is Peterson's frame of mind? He sounds logical, as if he planned this out."

"He did, but not as thoroughly as I would have thought. He seems to believe that if he went through proper channels to request an autopsy that the hospital would cover up the cause of his sister's death. He honestly believes that if he's not down there protecting her dead body, they'll do something."

"Paranoid?"

"Yes, I think so. Why he thinks he has to go to these

extreme measures, I have no idea. Something set him on this path, and he believes this is the only way to find out what happened to his sister. He is convinced one of those three nurses is to blame, and I had the distinct impression that he doesn't believe it was an accident."

Dillon said, "He could have made a broad attack against the hospital, but instead chose a focused attack. He only wants to punish the individual he thinks is responsible. Otherwise, he would have killed all three of them."

"Maybe he's not positive one of them is to blame," Will said. "Our plan will work then. Give him negative results and he'll see that his sister's death was simply a tragedy."

"Lucy thinks there's something warranting an investigation," Carina said. "Your guys, Tom, took the samples she collected, but she wrote instructions on what needs to be done."

"We can't let him control the outcome," Tom said. "We give him what he wants, every hospital will be vulnerable."

"Yes, but something killed that woman. It was probably just the change in meds—cancer treatment is hardly an exact science—and if he knows what it is, he'll let them go."

"You don't know that," Tom said. "He could plan on killing them when he gets the answers he wants."

Dillon asked, "Is he prepared to die?"

"Of course he is," Sean said. "Anyone bringing guns and a bomb into a public place and taking hostages is prepared for whatever comes. I don't think he expects to get out alive."

"Are you a shrink?" Will snapped as he came back to the group.

Dillon intervened. "I think Sean's right about this, but listening to Peterson talk with Carina and Lucy makes me believe that he sees Carina as an equal, and Lucy as a superior."

"I don't understand," Will said.

"Carina's a cop, and a lot of soldiers equate themselves in a similar role. They're equals, basically stopping the bad guys. He thinks Lucy is a scientist, a pathologist, and therefore has an education and background that gives her a unique and specialized skill set. He respects that." Dillon continued, "He also has no college education, and Lucy has an advanced degree—like his sister. He knows Lucy is Carina's younger sister, and would automatically be protective of her because of that. If she can keep him calm, I think she'll be able to talk him down."

Will shook his head. "She graduated from Quantico three days ago and is suddenly an expert on hostage psychology?"

"Not suddenly," Dillon said, and left it at that.

A uniformed officer popped his head in. "Detective?"

Both Will and Carina turned. Will stepped out to talk to him. While he was gone, Tom called in for a status on getting eyes in the room. He must have been disappointed in the answer, because he said, "I'm sending a civilian consultant in." He hung up and said to Sean, "Get me eyes into that room." He tossed him a temporary ID. "Don't abuse it."

"Yes, sir," Sean said.

Will came back and said, "We have an ID on the nurse Peterson was talking to last night. Wendy Parsons. She's off duty today and no one has seen her, so we're going to her house, which isn't far. Dillon, you can come with me."

"I want to go," Carina said. "I'm fine."

"Stay," Will said, "until the doctor clears you. You have a rapport with Peterson, you might need to continue working that angle." To the cop he said, "Tell the head nurse, um"—he snapped his fingers—"Todd, Marilyn Todd, that I'll be delayed, but not to leave. We still need her inside knowledge of the staff who worked on Sarah Peterson."

Sean wasn't pleased that he had two cops assigned to him— hospital security and one of Tom Blade's SWAT guys. It was clear Blade told his man to babysit Sean. But he'd worked around smarter tech guys and still gotten what he wanted.

Sean hated working on any medical system. They were often convoluted, and unless it was a state-of-the-art facility, they'd layer new systems on top of the old, ultimately spending more to force everything to work, rather than using that money on the front end to get a new, better system that would save time and money in the future.

This was one of those troublesome layered systems.

He plugged his tablet into the mainframe and rewrote a search program to pull down targeted information.

"What are you doing?" the security guy asked, suspicious.

"Running a program to locate the correct computer," he lied. He didn't need his tablet to do that. He needed the tablet to download the personnel files of the hostages so he could run faster background checks on them than SDPD could. While SWAT was looking into the hostages, their priority was the rescue, not the whys. He also told the computer to pull down everything on Wendy Parsons and the head nurse, Marilyn Todd. Parsons might be an accomplice, or she might simply have shared information with Peterson to help him with his grief.

It took him only a few minutes to identify the computers on the network and locate the specific unit in the morgue. Because he was on the mainframe and the computer was hardwired into the system, it was easy to access the hard drive and look at the specs. There was no active camera, but the computer had a dormant web cam built into the monitor. He first disabled the light on the terminal that indicated the camera was active, then he initiated the web cam.

He sent the feed to his tablet and the mainframe terminal, plus to the SWAT truck. Blade wanted the intel, so maybe he wouldn't be so irritated that Sean had hacked into the SWAT system.

SWAT had one objective: rescue the hostages. They didn't care, at this point, whether Sarah's death was natural or murder. They only cared that no one lost their life. He had to trust them to protect Lucy, and trust Peterson when he told Carina that he wouldn't hurt Lucy. But anything could happen—there were three innocent people in that room with his girlfriend, dozens of cops swarming the place, and a live bomb.

But answers . . . those Sean could find.

He informed the SWAT officer that Blade would have access to the computer feed in the truck. The officer seemed pleased—and surprised—and stepped out to call his boss.

Sean looked at the terminal in the security office. The morgue computer was on a desk in the corner, at an angle so the door couldn't be seen. The three hostages were partly visible sitting on the floor. Lucy was sitting in the chair. She wasn't handcuffed, which relieved Sean. Peterson was leaning against the desk, part of his arm visible but that was it. Sean had no audio because the audio had been disabled on the user's end. He would have had to be at the computer physically to turn it on.

He hit a button and the screen went blank.

"Hmm, I don't know what happened. Give me a minute." He made sure all the data and security logs he needed had downloaded to his tablet, then disconnected it, typed a code, and the feed came back.

"There we go," he said and winked. His phone rang. "Hold on." He answered the call.

It was Patrick.

"Where are you?" he asked.

"We just hit the L.A. County line. Jack is hauling ass, but it's going to be another two hours minimum. What the hell's going on? First it's Dad with a heart attack, now Carina is a hostage?"

"Lucy traded herself for Carina."

"What the hell?"

Sean filled Patrick in on the situation, as much as he could with the cop listening in.

"What aren't you telling me?"

"I can't really say, Patrick." He hoped his former partner understood.

"Oh. Are you in trouble?"

"No." *Not yet.*

"Do you have anything?"

"Just a theory, but I'll know more when Dillon and Carina's partner, Will Hooper, get back from interviewing a nurse who knows Peterson." Sean wasn't ready to share anything, not until he dug deeper into the three hostages' backgrounds and any deaths that might have occurred at hospitals where they worked previously.

"Why would Lucy trade herself for Carina?"

"Carina's pregnant." Maybe he shouldn't have said that. It wasn't his secret to tell, but then again everyone here knew.

"Oh God, I didn't know."

"Apparently, she hadn't told anyone, but Nick told Lucy before she went down to the morgue. Carina thinks that Lucy has a rapport with the bastard, and Dillon thinks that the guy looks up to and respects Lucy as a superior. Some damn shrink reasoning. The bastard has a bomb, he's special forces, and he's already ruined his career and his life—he doesn't have anything to lose. So I'm . . ."

Sean hesitated a second. "I'm doing what I can to ensure that Lucy gets out alive."

"Understood. Will's a good guy, Sean, we were close when I lived in San Diego. He knows what he's doing."

"He hates me."

"What did you do?"

"What I do best."

"Sean—I'll call Will, smooth things over. You rub cops the wrong way. Aren't you buddies with his brother?"

"Brother?" Sean snapped his fingers. "Dean? Will and Dean Hooper with Sac FBI are brothers?"

"Yes. Just—go easy with Will."

"I'll try."

Patrick hesitated, then said, "Peterson couldn't have thought this out."

"I have some ideas. Hopefully, this will all be resolved before you get here."

"Jack wants all the info you have on the guy. He'll talk to his commanding officer and friends, maybe get more insight."

"I'll send it to you now."

Sean hung up, shot Patrick a copy of his data, then turned to the cop. "I'm done here." He really needed to be alone so he could check his facial recognition program. "I need to use the facilities."

"Sergeant Blade wants you back at the SWAT truck."

"Do you have a bathroom there?" His lingering good humor after sneaking his downloads by the two cops disappeared.

The SWAT guy walked him down the hall. "Blade told me to keep an eye on you."

"I'm sure."

He went inside the restroom and closed the door. He immediately pulled out his tablet and launched his program.

It had finished running. And immediately, he found what he was looking for.

Wendy Parsons, the nurse who'd given Peterson a flash drive the night before, never left the hospital. She was supposed to have gotten off duty at eight A.M., but she wasn't ID'd on any security cameras thirty minutes after she met with Peterson. She went from outside the emergency room to the lobby to her desk, left—then never returned. From Sean's cursory examination of the hospital system, the lobby and main areas were well monitored, but the individual floors—other than the maternity unit in the south wing—were on minimal camera surveillance.

"People don't just disappear," he murmured.

Sean sent Dillon what he found. Dillon responded immediately.

Parsons isn't at home, and she doesn't appear to have come home after her shift ended.

Pounding on the door told Sean his time was up. "Rogan, Tom Blade wants us back at the truck now."

He burst out, "What happened?"

"Your girlfriend refused to accept the lab test results, said they weren't accurate."

"My *girlfriend* is a federal agent who knows what she's doing."

The cop snorted. "This could have been over ten minutes ago."

Sean followed him out of the building. If Lucy had refused the tests, she had a damn good reason for doing so.

But the stakes had just gone up, and Sean needed to find Wendy Parsons ASAP.

CHAPTER 31

Charlie's calmness didn't bother Lucy; in fact, she was glad he remained calm because it showed that he could be reasoned with. He was patient. He didn't talk to her, and she didn't push him, deciding that right now he was still processing all the information from the day, plus his reaction to his sister's autopsy.

But the silence disturbed the three nurses, and they'd been growing increasingly agitated as time ticked by. Kristan had jumped up three times and Charlie was upset with the young nurse's constant chatter. The third time she jumped up, Charlie went over to her and held a gun to her head. She slid down, against the wall, crying.

Charlie returned to his post at the desk. Lucy said, "Let me go over and talk to them, please. They're scared."

He eyed her cautiously. "Why aren't you?"

She looked him in the eye. "I am."

"You don't act scared."

"Honestly, I've faced things worse than death and survived."

He eyed her with interest. She'd spent the last hour slowly working on getting him to trust her. When the test results came back—too early, and he knew it—it was her idea to bring in the portable lab. If he thought he wouldn't get answers, he'd finally realize that his freedom was over. He was a soldier at heart, and while he could mentally put himself into the role of the attacker, he wouldn't be able to survive this way for long. He'd see what he was doing. She feared he would kill himself, or kill the hostages and then himself. In his mind, one of these three people was responsible for his sister's death, and if he had to kill all of them to see justice done, he would. She could practically see him working up the justification for murder.

She was the neutral third party, the one whom he viewed as impartial. It was clear that he admired her forensic skill, even though she was no more competent than any other trained pathologist who took pride in her work. It had been nearly a year since she left the ME's office, but she'd done so much during her internship there that the skills came back, just like riding a bike.

Medics in the military were in the middle of action, even when they weren't soldiers, and they saved lives. They earned the respect of the soldiers around them, according to her brother Jack. She had a sense that Peterson equated her with army medics, someone he needed to protect.

The problem was, she wouldn't be able to do all the tests. The basic tests were easy, but they'd need access to a high-end lab to run the sorts of tests for medications in quantities that could kill. What she hoped to do was show him that the tests that were returned were not falsified, and explain the limitations to testing. It was her only idea to buy them a little more time so that SWAT could make a move. Because had she told him the tests were fine, he would have known she was lying.

But the only way SWAT could act was if Lucy could get Peterson to dismantle the bomb.

He didn't say anything, and she didn't push him. The

silence actually calmed her. The ventilation system was purring. There were no sirens. No sounds of anyone attempting to breach the morgue. The one problem was Kristan's sobs. Just when Lucy thought she was relaxed, she started crying again. Brian would try to soothe her, then say something that pissed off Charlie, usually calling him a psycho and saying how SWAT was going to put a bullet in his head. Rena was the only one who had completely kept her head, after her initial outbreak at the beginning of the ordeal.

The situation had lasted well over five hours now, and Lucy had been in here for three of those hours. But the waiting seemed to keep Charlie calm as well.

"Go ahead," he said. "I'm watching."

"I know."

She walked around the autopsy table and kept her distance from the other hostages. "This is almost over. Kristan, I know you're scared, but it would help everyone if you could get yourself under control."

Rena stared at Lucy with an anger and hatred that surprised her. "Are you working with him?"

"I'm trying to get to a peaceful resolution."

"You're taking your sweet time. I didn't think Stockholm syndrome worked that fast."

Lucy wasn't going to explain herself to Rena or the others. "Kristan? Do you think you can do that for me? Be calm?"

Kristan nodded, her eyes red and swollen.

"Good." She turned to Brian. "How's your leg?"

"Numb."

Rena said, "We're nurses. We'll take care of our own."

"You know he's going to turn on you," Brian told Lucy. "He's a nutcase."

Hardly. He had a clean and logical methodology for

what he was doing. He wasn't crazy, and he wasn't going to turn on Lucy as long as she was honest with him.

"Just hold on a little while longer. We all want to be home for Christmas."

"If you really wanted to help, you would have gotten us out of here, not your sister," Rena said. "She's a cop, more capable of dealing with someone like him than you are."

Lucy wasn't going to reveal any of her training, outside of the ME's office. She didn't know if they would say something, and she'd already built a level of trust with Charlie that she didn't want to jeopardize.

She walked back to Charlie. "They're doing their best," she said.

"I don't really care."

"You do care. I understand how you got to this point. In your grief, you didn't see any other option. But there are always other options. We all do rash things sometimes."

Charlie almost smiled. "You're a cool cucumber. Have you ever been rash?"

"More than once."

"Name one time."

"I don't want to talk about me."

"You sound like some psychologist or something. Trying to get me to talk about my past. I already told you everything. There's nothing more to me. I doubt you've ever done anything without thinking it through—except maybe trading yourself for your sister. That you did out of love."

Partly. But Lucy had never worked with her sister. She didn't know how Carina would have handled the situation, and from the minute Lucy walked in, she had a feeling she could fix this without anyone dying. And Carina had thought so too, or she wouldn't have told Charlie that Lucy was a pathologist.

The phone rang and Kristan yelped. Charlie answered it. "Yes, sir. Thank you. You can leave the cart outside the door. I'll send Ms. Kincaid to retrieve it. I'll be watching, I want her back inside."

Charlie moved the bomb. Every time he got near it, Lucy's heart raced. She'd been stabbed and shot and knew what that felt like. She didn't want to know what it was like to be caught in an explosion. She didn't want to die. He'd asked why she wasn't scared, and she'd been honest with him. She was. But fear wouldn't help her resolve this situation. The panic attacks that had plagued her for so many years had almost disappeared. She still had claustrophobia, but had learned to control the physical reaction after years of practice and therapy with her brother Dillon.

Charlie looked at her. "I have to do this."

"We all have choices."

He pulled up Kristan and held her in front of him. The gun was at the back of her head.

"Go."

Lucy stepped out. Down the hall she saw several SWAT team members with guns pointed in her direction. A cop dressed as a lab tech wheeled over a cart. It had everything she needed to confirm the tests, except for the equipment that couldn't be moved. Basically, it was a microscope and some test strips.

She brought it inside and Kristan continued to sob. Charlie told Lucy to lock the door. She did. She set up the equipment on the autopsy table. Charlie ordered Kristan back to the floor, then replaced the bomb.

"Here's the printout from the lab," she said, and handed it to Charlie. "They tested for all standard toxins, and the tests came back negative."

"What about other things? Like overdoses of her medicine? A wrong medicine?"

"Labs have to know what to look for, then they are extremely accurate. But if they don't know they're looking for a specific type of drug, they'll never find it. Most drugs will still be present in the blood or liver even after a few days. Because I think she died of respiratory failure—though I'm not an ME and I can't swear to it—I asked them to run screens for any neuromuscular blocking agents. These are the types of drugs available in a hospital that have medical uses, but in the wrong person or in too high of a dose or mixed with the wrong medication, they can be fatal. But they can't run those tests in an hour, or even a day. The samples will need to be sent to an outside lab that has the capacity to run these specialized tests. The lab here in the hospital can't do anything beyond basic screenings."

"So what are you doing?" Charlie said. "Do you think I'm stupid?"

"I wanted to show you the process, so you understand."

"But you're telling me you can't give me answers."

"No. I can't. Not with the limited equipment. I thought you would want to see what a lab needs to do. I filled out all the paperwork, told them the types of drugs to screen for—" She stopped. Charlie was pacing and growing agitated. She didn't want him to think she was trying to deceive him.

"Hypothetically," she asked him, "if we could have tested for those drugs, and they came back positive, what would you do?"

"I would know how my sister died."

"But you're holding the three nurses who were on duty that night."

"Because one of them did it."

"And if the tests came back negative?"

"Then it would be a trick." He stared at her, and in his eyes she saw the truth.

"Charlie, what do you know that you haven't told me?"

He reached into his pocket and handed her a piece of paper with names and dates. It was written in flowery script, likely by a woman.

"Who are these people?"

"Women who died when they shouldn't have. The same way that Sarah died. When these three nurses were on duty."

"Why didn't you take this to the police?"

"Because they wouldn't have done anything! And it would have given the hospital time to cover it up." He was upset. "This was supposed to be easy. Why can't you just look and see?"

She had to remain calm to keep him calm. "Because only specialized lab tests can register most of the drugs that would trigger the asphyxiation that caused your sister's death."

"Then we'll wait for the results." He stared at her. "I don't like being made a fool of."

"That's not what I intended to do, Charlie. I wanted to show you what has been done and what still needs to be done." She pulled out the lab chart. She stared at it and frowned.

The lab had run all the tests. They'd just told Charlie everything came back negative. Had they even looked at the results?

She double-checked the name and numbers at the top and they correlated to Sarah Peterson.

"What's wrong?" Charlie asked.

"I think the police—who don't know how to read these types of reports—didn't understand what this meant." She pointed to a line item. "This is a standard screening. Her histamine levels were high. That indicates there may have been a neuromuscular blocker administered. Not for certain, but it's one indication."

"What are all these Xs here?"

"Those tests weren't run. They don't have the capabilities in this lab."

"Then I want those tests run. You asked for them, they run them, or we're staying."

Lucy put down the chart and looked Charlie in the eye. "I promise you, I will follow through on this. I will make sure all these tests are done. If anyone accidentally or intentionally poisoned Sarah, I will prove it."

He believed her. She could see it in his eyes. "You keep your promises."

"Always. You're going to need to face the consequences of your actions, but no one died here today. That means something. It means something to me, and it will mean something to the court."

"I just want to know the truth," he said quietly.

"I have a friend who works in the FBI lab in Quantico. I'll pack these samples up myself and make sure he gets them. We'll find out what happened to Sarah. I'm truly sorry for your loss."

Charlie reached into his pocket and pulled out the detonator. He typed in a code and the light went off. He put it down on the table. "Go."

Lucy nodded to the three hostages. They slowly rose. Rena helped support Brian's weight as he limped across the room. Kristan practically ran to the door. She opened the door without thinking, and Lucy cringed, expecting an explosion. There was nothing.

Kristan ran out, crying.

Rena and Brian stumbled and collapsed against the autopsy table. Lucy turned in time to see all the trays crash to the floor.

Charlie's eyes widened. "You did that on purpose. You destroyed evidence because it was you—"

He raised his gun.

"No, Charlie, it was an accident!" Lucy shouted. But she didn't know that. The autopsy table was heavy, it was bolted to the ground. They would have had to bump it extremely hard to cause the trays to fall. But Brian weighed over two hundred pounds, if he fell against it he could have . . .

Rena screamed as Charlie aimed the gun at her.

SWAT stormed in, guns pointing at Charlie.

"Drop your weapon!"

Charlie stared at the destruction in front of him. His sister's chart, the lab results, the slides and samples.

"Down, down, down!"

"Charlie, lower your weapon," Lucy said. If he would only look at her, she knew she could get through to him.

"They did it on purpose," Charlie said. He still held his gun, but his hand started to dip down.

"Give me your gun," Lucy said.

He stood there as if he didn't know what to do.

Rena screamed again.

Then there was gunfire and Lucy hit the ground as Charlie collapsed in a heap.

"No!" she cried. She crawled over to him. Tom Blade was at her side as another pair of SWAT team members got Rena and Brian out.

"Come now!" he ordered her.

"He has a vest! Get a medic, he's bleeding!"

He'd been shot in the upper torso multiple times. He was bleeding profusely.

There was chaos all around her. She tried to stop the bleeding. Charlie was mouthing something, and she felt his hand in hers. She squeezed.

The SWAT leader picked her up and carried her out, even as she fought him. She had to help Charlie. Save him.

"Put me down!"

Tom Blade put her down and pushed her against the wall. "Agent Kincaid, get hold of yourself! That man shot two people and would have killed you."

"He was giving himself up."

"He had a gun on the hostages."

"He was lowering it."

But he had been so shocked when the blood and tissue samples had been knocked to the floor. Would he have killed the hostages? Lucy didn't know for certain.

"I will not put the hostages or my team at greater risk. He was a threat, we took the threat out. If you have a problem with it, take it up with my superiors."

Lucy shook her head and closed her eyes. Tom was right. They had done what they had to do. But something was going on, something she was only beginning to see. She squeezed her hand and felt the paper in her grip.

So much loss, so much death, and all for nothing. She was going to find out what these names meant.

CHAPTER 32

Lucy washed her hands in hot, soapy water in the bathroom, tears streaming down her face as Charlie's blood flowed down the drain.

It wasn't supposed to have happened like that. He was going to turn himself in.

She kicked the tile wall, then put her forehead on the mirror and took several deep breaths.

Get it together, Kincaid. You need to give your statement. You need to be professional.

It seemed like such a waste.

The door opened, and she thought it would be Kate or Carina.

It was Sean. She didn't even tease him about being in the women's bathroom.

He went to her and wrapped his arms around her. She held on tight, crying into his shoulder.

"He wasn't going to shoot. His gun was coming down," she sobbed.

Sean didn't try to tell her she was right or wrong, or he was glad Charlie was down, he just held her. He gave her what she needed, his unconditional support.

It was several minutes later when she felt she could face Tom Blade and the debriefing.

"I want to see him," Lucy said.

"He's in surgery."

"It shouldn't have happened."

"Lucy, you did everything you could. The hostages are all alive, thanks to you."

But it didn't feel like she'd done everything she could.

Sean said, "Kate's here with the ASAC of San Diego. They need to talk to you. Are you up for it?"

"Yes." She reached into her pocket and handed Sean the paper Charlie had given her. "I need you to do something for me."

"Anything."

"After Peterson went down, when I was at his side, he put this paper in my hand. I have no idea who these women are, but he made it clear he wants me to have this."

Sean didn't say anything for a long minute. "I don't want you to get in trouble, Lucy."

"I have no idea how Sarah Peterson died. But I owe it not only to her brother, but to Sarah herself, to find out what happened. Charlie came in with a mission. A purpose. He's certain one of those nurses killed his sister. Accident or not, he knew something he didn't share with me or Carina, something that he believed an autopsy would reveal."

There was a knock on the door. "Lucy, it's Kate. We need you."

"I'm coming," she called.

Sean took the paper and pocketed it. "I have the security feed that shows him talking to a nurse late last night. Wendy Parsons. She gave him something. No one can find her."

"An accomplice?"

"Most likely." Sean patted his pocket. "Maybe this was it."

Kate said, "Lucy, now."

Sean opened the door and Kate frowned when he walked out. "We don't have time for games," she told him.

"This isn't a game," he said gravely, and walked away.

Lucy followed Kate to a conference room that had been taken over by security and SWAT. Will Hooper was there, and Tom Blade, and two people Lucy didn't know, a man and woman, both in suits.

They introduced themselves as SSA Ken Swan and Assistant Special Agent in Charge Danielle Richardson.

Lucy went through the entire afternoon from the time Hooper and Blade asked her to go in and perform the autopsy in order to buy time, to why she negotiated a trade with her sister, to her reasoning behind asking for the portable lab.

"He'd grown extremely agitated when the results came back negative. I wanted to show him that they did everything they could with the equipment they had."

"But he'd said if you did the autopsy, he would let everyone go," ASAC Richardson said. "Yet you fed into his delusions."

"No, he had information that made him believe that the lab tests were inaccurate. I showed him that not all tests could be run on-site."

"Again, he was delusional," Swan said.

"No, he wasn't," Lucy said. "He was grieving. He believed that his sister's death wasn't natural, based on information Wendy Parsons, the missing nurse, gave him."

"What missing nurse?" Richardson turned to Hooper.

Will seemed irritated with Lucy for revealing that intel. "We have a security camera showing that Peterson was talking to a nurse, Wendy Parsons, last night after midnight. We haven't been able to find her."

"An accomplice?"

"We don't know," Will said. "We haven't spoken to

her. But I have a warrant to search her house and bank records, and we're also checking airports, train stations, buses. Her car was found in the employee parking area, and records of her employee pass showed she arrived at work at eleven forty-five last night, but there's no indication that she ever left work. We're also checking with cab services."

"Did you find Peterson's vehicle?" Richardson asked.

"Yes, ma'am, we have it secure and will be taking it to impound for a thorough search.

To Lucy, ASAC Richardson said, "We've reviewed some of the audio and video footage from the morgue, and preliminarily we don't believe you acted inappropriately, but I need to send a report to your SAC in San Antonio."

Lucy nodded, though she felt like she was in a bad dream. She hadn't even started her new assignment, and her record would already be cloudy because of what happened here.

Except, she didn't see how she could have done anything different.

"My one concern was your interference with SWAT when they breached the morgue. You put your life in jeopardy."

"With all due respect, I was there, and Peterson was lowering his hand."

Tom Blade spoke up. "Kincaid, I was there, too, and he had the gun pointed at the two hostages who bumped into the table. He was indecisive."

"Yes, but he wasn't going to shoot."

"We don't know that. And as I said earlier, I wasn't going to risk hostages, or you, or my men, based on your psychological hunch that he wasn't going to discharge his weapon."

"I understand," she said.

"Do you?"

Blade was angry, but Lucy wasn't going to keep explaining herself.

SWAT did everything by the book, and there was no loss of life, which should have made Lucy happy, or at least relieved. But she kept going over the last few minutes of her time with Charlie, wondering what she could have said or done that would have resulted in a better ending.

Then Blade did a turnabout that surprised her. "For the record, Agent Kincaid convinced the shooter to disable his own bomb. If she hadn't done that, we wouldn't have been able to enter, and the outcome could have been a lot worse."

Richardson nodded. "Thank you. I'll expect a copy of your report as well, Sergeant Blade."

"You'll get it from my lieutenant, ma'am."

Lucy wanted to see her dad, but she needed one more thing. "I'd like Sarah Peterson's body to be sent to the county lab for a full and complete autopsy, including the tox screens that I asked for."

"You're not an ME," Will said.

"I saw enough to make me suspicious."

Richardson said, "You think there's merit to Peterson's claim that the hospital was negligent?"

"I don't know if it was the hospital, or one of the nurses, or if there is a personal reason that Sarah Peterson may have been a target. If there wasn't, then the nurse Wendy Parsons intentionally gave Peterson false information to lead him to believe that there was something unusual surrounding his sister's death."

"Look, Lucy," Will said, "we're doing what we need to do. But we can't follow the dictates of a terrorist, and that's what Peterson is."

"This isn't about Peterson, this is about a woman who died under suspicious circumstances."

"You're the only one who thinks that," Will said.

Lucy was getting angry and she didn't know how to pursue this.

"All I'm asking," she said with forced calm, "is for the county to claim the body and run tests on certain medications that would cause asphyxiation. Including the drugs she was known to have been given for her cancer therapy."

"That's up to the hospital and the D.A.," Will said.

"The D.A.," she said.

"You're not thinking straight," Will said. "Give us time."

Will knew exactly what she planned on doing, though everyone else was slower on the uptake, and the feds had no idea that Lucy's ex-brother-in-law was the district attorney.

Lucy said, "May I be excused? My father is a patient here; he had a heart attack last night and I haven't seen him yet."

"Yes, thank you for your time," Richardson said. She seemed to be preoccupied, and that was fine with Lucy. She wanted to leave.

Kate followed her out. "What are you up to?"

"Getting answers." She went outside and walked toward the south tower where her father had been admitted. There were still many police cars and the SWAT truck still staged around the north tower, and it would take time for them to clear the building. They'd brought in bomb-sniffing dogs to make sure that Peterson hadn't set any other charges.

Charlie Peterson was facing a minimum of twenty years in prison. He'd had a vendetta, but he wasn't a vindictive person. He wanted the truth, but she didn't know what he would have done had he had it. And she didn't think he knew, either.

She understood that SWAT had had no choice, but she'd promised Charlie that she would find out what happened to Sarah, and just because the samples were destroyed when the nurses knocked into the table didn't mean they couldn't get more samples. The problem was that time was crucial. Many drugs dissipated as the body decomposed. The cold storage slowed the rate of decomposition, but the longer they waited, the more likely it was that a poison would fade away. Many of the neuromuscular blockers would present in the liver for only a short time after death. After two days, there might be no more evidence.

She called the one person who could make it happen.

"Andrew Stanton."

"Andrew, it's Lucy Kincaid."

"Lucy."

Nelia's ex-husband was surprised to hear from her. She hadn't spoken to him in years—as far as she knew, her family's relationship with him was solely professional. But he had been Justin's father, and he had treated her more kindly than her own sister after her nephew's murder. He'd been the district attorney for the past ten years.

"Have you heard what happened at the hospital?"

"Of course."

"I need a favor. I wouldn't ask if it wasn't important."

He didn't say anything.

Lucy continued. "I don't know how to do it, but you're the D.A., so I'm sure you can figure it out. I need someone to order an autopsy of Sarah Peterson immediately, and specifically to look for neuromuscular blockers that would be available at hospitals. All the tissues and samples I took were destroyed during the SWAT action, but I think her brother was right to be suspicious. I think someone either accidentally or intentionally poisoned her, and then covered it up."

"Do you know what you're saying?"

"I'm not asking for anything that wouldn't be done under normal circumstances."

"If anyone thinks that the city or county can be forced in some sort of terrorist act—"

"Charlie Peterson is not a terrorist. He's a decorated veteran who made a huge mistake that's going to cost him for the rest of his life. But I think Sarah's death needs to be investigated. This isn't for Charlie, it's for the victim."

"Have you talked to Carina? Or your boss?"

"I don't think the police understand the timeliness factor for these tests. If she was poisoned, some poisons dissipate over time and there would be no physical proof. I think Sarah Peterson was poisoned with a neuromuscular blocker. Many of them are available at hospitals, and most dissolve to undetectable levels as the body decomposes. It makes sense based on the cause of death. If we're going to find out what killed Sarah, we need to act now. Not the day after Christmas or after the new year; tonight."

Lucy saw Sean run out of the south tower. She held her arm up to get his attention. He approached but didn't speak when he noticed she was on the phone. It was clear he had information.

"Andrew, I wouldn't ask you if I didn't think there was something here. I know you don't really know me anymore, don't know if you can trust my judgment. I'm just asking you—well, please trust me. I wouldn't have called you if I didn't believe in my gut that I'm right."

"I'll make some calls."

"Thank you. I mean it." She hung up.

Sean raised an eyebrow. "Was that who I think it was?"

"If anyone can get an autopsy done at four o'clock on Christmas Eve, it's Andrew." She took his hand, squeezed. "You have news?"

"Big news. Those names on that paper? They're all deceased cancer patients who died at the hospital over the last three years. Earlier, I hacked into—"

Lucy winced. "Don't tell me."

"Sorry. I have access to the personnel files for the three nurses. They were all on duty on the days these women died."

"They're all women?"

"Yes. I realized after the first two names there was a pattern. I wish I had the flash drive that Parsons gave Peterson."

"You're sure it was a flash drive?"

"Yes. And I zoomed in and enhanced the security video as best I could, and there was a piece of paper wrapped around the flash drive, which based on these folds could have been this."

"I need to get this information to the police."

"They're going to be furious you withheld evidence."

"I was in shock. I didn't realize I still had the paper in my pocket." She took the paper from Sean. "Thank you."

"I'm going to dig around into their previous assignments."

Lucy frowned. "Kristan Otto. She told me she was a nurse for only two years."

"Yes, but she was a student nurse here for the year prior to passing her test. Glover and Lavargnio were both here for three years and five years respectively."

"And Parsons?"

"She's new. Arrived six months ago."

"And maybe she saw something strange? Heard something?"

"And told the brother of one of the victims."

"Victims—that's harsh."

"There are eight names on that list. They have far too much in common to be disconnected."

"What do they have in common other than they were cancer patients who died in the hospital?"

Sean ticked off the similarities on his fingers. "All women under forty. All single, never been married, with no children. All cancer patients who had been in remission. All were admitted into the hospital because they had a reaction to medication."

"How do you know all of this?"

"They sort of gave me access to the hospital database when I helped them set up the web cam on the morgue computer. All the information is there when they look for it."

"You just gave me a victim profile."

"Seems that it would be hard to prove because they'd all been sick."

"But there's enough to make Wendy Parsons sufficiently suspicious to give it to Peterson." She frowned.

"What are you thinking?"

"Why Peterson? Why not her boss? An administrator?"

"Because she was worried about getting fired? Maybe she thought because Peterson was in the military he might know what to do with the information. He lost someone, he could ask the right questions. Or maybe she didn't know what she had, and Peterson did."

"He didn't know what to do with the information. He snapped under the weight of confusion and anger and grief."

"You're the psychologist."

"If I was any good, he wouldn't be in surgery right now."

"Hey, knock that off," Sean said. He took both her hands in his. "You did everything you could to save him and the hostages. No one died."

Yet.

"We need to find out more about these women and the

nurses who were on duty the night they died. Background information."

"What kind?"

"Can you find out if any of the nurses has had cancer, or had a close female relative who had cancer and died."

Realization crossed Sean's face. "You think one of them is a serial killer."

She didn't say anything at first, then nodded. "Maybe I do. I need to see my dad. I'm hoping Dillon is up there, and I can run this by him."

"Let's go."

While they entered the south tower, Sean took out his tablet and started a search program that would pull from multiple databases. "It'll run without me," he said.

"I certainly fell in love with smartest guy on the planet."

"That you did."

"Humble, too."

"Yes, right again." Sean grinned.

No one was in the colonel's room when Lucy arrived with Sean. Her dad looked like he was sleeping, and she didn't want to disturb him. But as she stared, tears sprang to her eyes. She had been an emotional basket case since the SWAT action, and this was so unlike her. She usually had her emotions under so much better control.

But this was her dad. And she hadn't been home in nearly two years. What kind of daughter was she?

He opened his eyes and smiled when he saw her. He looked pale and tired, but other than that he looked like her dad.

"Hi, Daddy."

"Lucia. I'm glad you're here."

She walked over and kissed his cheek, then sat on the edge of the bed. "Dad, this is Sean Rogan."

Pat extended his hand and Sean took it. "Patrick has talked a lot about you. More than my daughter."

"I'm sorry I haven't visited, Daddy."

"You've been busy. And I'm sorry your mother and I didn't come out for your graduation. We should have been there."

"You were recuperating from the flu."

"I could have made it. I should have."

"It's okay. Dillon and Kate were there, and Patrick and Sean—I was well represented."

"Carina was by earlier. She told me what you did," her dad said.

"I did my job." She sat on the edge of his bed and smiled. "I was worried about you."

"Now you know what it's like to be a parent. We worry, too." He squeezed her hand.

"What do the doctors say?"

"My doc thinks I overdid it at the gym after my bout with the flu and strained my heart, and coupled with my diet, my ticker rebelled."

"It could have been much worse."

"It is. I think your mom is going to make me eat fish and chicken for the rest of my life."

"Listen to her."

"I'm so proud of you, Lucy, of who you've become. You're not my little girl anymore. I think when you were growing up, I didn't know what to do with another baby, considering that Patrick was ten and playing in Little League. Everyone raised you, I can't take any credit."

"Daddy, don't be ridiculous. You were the best dad ever. I had a wonderful childhood."

"San Antonio isn't too far. When you're settled, we'll visit."

"I'd like that." She bit her lip and glanced at Sean.

"Lucy, I may be sixty-nine, but I'm not an old fuddy-duddy. I know you and Sean are moving in together."

"Who told you?" Her heart raced and she glanced at Sean.

"No one told me. But I certainly didn't think he'd be moving all the way to San Antonio and into a separate apartment."

"Oh." She hadn't thought about that. "We love each other, Dad."

"I know. I've already had reports from Jack and Dillon."

"Reports?" It was Sean who spoke, and his voice cracked. Lucy would have laughed if she wasn't also a bit nervous.

"Lucy's my baby girl. Of course I've been keeping tabs. Jack said only one thing, but it was enough. He said, 'He makes her smile.'" Pat stared at Sean. "You make sure my baby girl keeps smiling."

"Yes, sir."

Lucy's phone was vibrating, and she ignored it.

"Someone needs you," he said.

"No, I'm going to stay."

"Do what you need to do, Lucia."

"Are you sure?"

"Connor went to pick up your mother. The doctor wants to go over my test results and let us know what our options are."

"But you're okay, right?"

"Of course I am." But he didn't look her in the eye. He didn't know what the doctor was going to say. Maybe he needed surgery. That would be dangerous, especially for a man of his age.

"I'll be well taken care of."

"I know." But she didn't want to lose her dad. "I love you, Dad."

She kissed his cheek and left with Sean.

"Your dad is going to be okay," Sean said. "Believe that."

"I do." *I hope.* "Someone has been calling me repeatedly." She checked her phone. Carina had left her a message. She was just about to check it when she saw Nelia turn the corner.

Lucy froze. She hadn't spoken to Nelia in eighteen years, since Nelia's son, Justin, was murdered when he and Lucy were seven. Her own sister seemed to hate her, at least that's the way Lucy had always felt. If she and Nelia were in the same room, Nelia could have a conversation with everyone but Lucy, as if Lucy weren't even there. Nelia never spoke to her directly. Every family gathering was awkward. But they'd only been together a few times—after Patrick got out of his coma, again a few years ago when Lucy came home for one summer while in college. Nelia lived in Idaho, and while she seemed to have found a modicum of peace, she was still quiet, reserved, and carried a silent air of pain wherever she went. When Justin was killed, Lucy had lost her closest childhood friend. But Nelia had lost her only child.

Nelia caught Lucy's eye and hesitated. Then she approached. "Lucy. Hello."

"Hi." Her voice sounded like a child's. "This is Sean. My boyfriend. This is my sister Nelia."

Sean extended his hand, but his expression was cool. "Nice to meet you." Lucy had shared with him all the pain and frustration she'd felt over Nelia's attitude since Justin's murder, including Lucy's childhood belief that Nelia wished it had been her who'd died.

"How's Dad?"

"Good spirits."

"I, um, just arrived. We drove. Tom is downstairs talking to Jack and Patrick."

"I haven't seen them yet."

"Well, I'm going to tell Dad we're here."

"Okay."

Nelia hesitated, then turned into the colonel's room.

Sean had his arm around her shoulders and he squeezed. Lucy said, "That's the first time she's ever spoken directly to me."

"You're a forgiving woman, Luce," Sean said.

"It's okay, really."

It wasn't, but it had to be. She didn't know what to say to Nelia, and it was clear Nelia didn't know what to say to her.

Lucy didn't lose sight of the fact that she was much closer to Kate than she was to her two sisters, but now . . . she was beginning to realize that maybe that was okay. And that maybe she needed to make an effort with Carina. She was going to have a niece or nephew. She wanted to be an aunt, especially since she couldn't have children of her own.

Her phone rang again and she answered.

"Where are you?" Carina said.

"Outside Dad's room."

"Security found Wendy Parsons. She's dead."

CHAPTER 33

Wendy Parsons was found locked in a janitorial closet on the top floor in the north tower.

The locked utility rooms hadn't been checked during the immediate threat, because hospital security was more concerned with evacuating patients and there was no indication that Charlie Peterson had another shooter in the building helping him.

A criminalist from San Diego PD was processing the scene, and two doctors confirmed that she was dead with no visible sign of injury.

"He killed her?" Carina asked, shaking her head.

"No," Lucy said.

"Why do you say that?"

"Why would he?"

Carina shook her head. "Doc, how long has she been dead?"

"She appears to be in full rigor mortis. Twelve to eighteen hours. But that's a guess."

Sean said, "The last time she was seen on a security camera was at midnight. Peterson didn't go into the hospital, and didn't return until nine this morning."

Will Hooper turned down the hallway. "I need everyone out of here, except Detective Kincaid." He glared at Lucy. "You called the D.A.? Why would you interfere like that?"

Carina looked surprised. "You called Andrew? Why?"

"To get an autopsy on Sarah Peterson tonight. There are drugs that will disappear as the body goes through decomp, and if there's something there, we need to find it now. I'd like to inspect Ms. Parsons."

"Hell, no," Will said. "We have a damn good forensics lab in San Diego; this is my crime scene."

Carina pulled Will aside and spoke quietly to him. Will was angry, but he listened to her, said something, then walked away.

Carina told Lucy, "Five minutes. Will is a great cop, Lucy. We've been partners for ten years. Going over his head isn't cool."

Office politics was one of the areas where Lucy struggled. She always did what she thought was best, and sometimes she stepped on people's toes and didn't realize it.

"I'm sorry, Carina. It seems as though Will still sees me as an irresponsible teenager, and not a sworn-in FBI agent."

"And do newly sworn FBI agents normally call the district attorney for special favors?"

Sean couldn't keep his mouth closed. "Lay off," he said.

"I did what I thought was right. I'm willing to live with the consequences." Lucy paused. "Can you honestly tell me that you've never done something that wasn't technically by the book because you knew in your gut you had no choice?"

Carina couldn't answer that.

Lucy pulled on a pair of gloves and asked the criminalist to help her. "Did you get pictures?"

"Yes, ma'am," he said. "We're just waiting for the coroner."

The body was bent at the waist, suggesting that she'd been propped against the wall. No external injuries, except for bruising on her right arm, as if someone had grabbed her.

"Did you get these bruises?" she asked him.

"Yes. And there is a bump on the back of her head."

The doctor said, "It doesn't look serious enough to have knocked her unconscious."

Lucy carefully inspected the raised surface. "It's less than one inch in diameter, and about half an inch from the surface." She glanced into the closet.

Carina said, "She was found propped against the metal shelving. Her head was on the second shelf at an odd angle. At first glance, it appears that someone killed her and put her in the closet. No one found her because we'd evacuated this floor and the door was locked."

Lucy looked at Parsons's arms carefully, searching for any puncture wound. If she'd been poisoned, it could have been administered orally or injected.

Then she saw it. A needle mark on the back of her shoulder. "Get this," she said to the criminalist. "This is an injection site. See the bruising? She moved while the needle was inside, possibly trying to get it out."

"The timeline doesn't put Peterson in the clear," Carina said.

"I know, but he didn't kill her. She was helping him find out what happened to his sister."

"You sound just like Dillon," Carina muttered.

Lucy took that as a compliment.

"Luce, I have something," Sean said, and handed her his tablet.

Sean had finished with the backgrounds on the three nurses. None of them had lost a close relative to cancer who was a single female under forty. "I was wrong," she said.

"No you weren't. Peterson was wrong."

Sean swiped the screen and brought up another background search. "I ran all the employees—nurses, doctors, orderlies—in the cancer ward who started more than three years ago. There are eighteen who've been here for more than three years."

"You did *what*?" Carina exclaimed.

Lucy ignored her. She stared at the list. There were four employees on the list who had lost an immediate family member to cancer.

But one name jumped out at her.

She rose from her squat and said, "I need to talk to Will and Dillon. I have a theory, but we have no proof. And if we can't get her to slip up, she will kill again."

They were in a conference room in the north tower that SWAT and security had used during the hostage situation. It had been cleared out, but Tom Blade was in there writing a report and talking with the head of hospital security.

Lucy had asked Dillon to come because she didn't think Will would trust her instincts on this, but he knew and trusted Dillon. She was also glad Kate was there, but she was surprised Kate was sitting with SSA Ken Swan, who had been present in her earlier interview. Nick and Carina sat with Will. Lucy felt like there were two sides: San Diego PD on one, and the FBI on the other.

"I know who killed Sarah Peterson and eight other women in this hospital, but I have no proof. Unfortunately, if we can't get her to confess or slip up, she's going to get away with it."

"You're saying that nine women have been killed?" Will said. "That there's a serial killer?" His tone reflected complete disbelief.

"Yes," Lucy said with more confidence than she felt. She hated this part of the job, standing in front of colleagues and friends and explaining her theory. She'd done it in the past, and it always made her uncomfortable. She'd rather be at a crime scene than in an office. "Virtually all serial murders in a hospital setting are called mercy killings, but that's not what this is. This is a psychologically damaged nurse who is killing patients who remind her of her sister."

She took out the piece of paper that Peterson had handed her. "We know based on the security feed that Wendy Parsons slipped Charlie Peterson a flash drive and, I think, this piece of paper. He gave it to me and I didn't turn it over to you, Will, and I'm sorry. I didn't realize what I had at first, with everything that happened at the morgue, and then when I saw it I asked Sean to find out what the names had in common." She walked over and handed Hooper the paper that was now in a plastic evidence bag.

"You withheld evidence?"

"Not intentionally." *At first.* "All those women have died here, in the north tower cancer wing, in the last three years. This isn't unusual, except that all the women were single, under forty, had no children, and had been in remission but readmitted because of problems with medication."

"You are really going out on a limb," Will said. "We're here because a gunman took four people hostage and shot two people, and killed a nurse—"

"You don't have any proof that Peterson killed Wendy Parsons. There's no security camera on that wing where her body was found."

"How do you know that?" Will snapped.

"I told her," Sean said. He was getting angry with Will, and that wasn't going to do Lucy any good.

Carina intervened. "Will, just listen to the theory. I totally understand where you're coming from, but I think Lucy is right."

Will said through clenched teeth, "Explain."

"We know that Parsons gave Peterson information after midnight, and he waited for nine hours before he came back. Someone who knew those three nurses were going to be on duty during the same shift sent them a message about the training, and that tells me that Parsons knew what Peterson planned on doing."

"You're saying she's a conspirator," Will said.

"Maybe she didn't realize he was going to take them hostage, but thought he wanted them in the same room with him. Maybe she planned on being there herself to confront them with what she knew, and when she didn't show, Peterson did it his way. We can only speculate at this point. However, we know that she gave him something that made him believe that one of those nurses killed his sister, and I think her research on the drive she gave him was medical records of those deceased patients."

She glanced at the hospital security head. "Is there any way to find out if Wendy Parsons downloaded or copied patient data during the time between Sarah Peterson's death and when she handed Peterson the flash drive?"

"Yes," he said. "I would have to ask the IT department to research it."

Lucy knew that Sean could get it faster, but she'd already told him not to volunteer to do anything else, because they were pushing the envelope with what he'd already done.

"I think that was her proof, and because Peterson was a soldier she thought he might be able to get the information to the right people."

"If this is true," the hospital security chief asked, "why didn't she go to her supervisor?

"Because it's not proof. These were cancer patients. An investigation would have been started, but what if she was scared that the killer would go after her? She went to Peterson because he was an outside party."

"She could have gone to the D.A.'s office," Carina said, "or the FBI. Or any number of law enforcement agencies."

"We could ask her why she didn't, but she's dead," Sean said.

Lucy didn't want the meeting to deteriorate. She glanced at Dillon. He was listening, but he had yet to say anything.

"I asked Sean to run all employees who work in the cancer wing who'd been here at least three years. Not just the three nurses Peterson thought were responsible, but all employees. Then we took the list and ran a background to see who had lost a loved one to cancer. Four. Of those four, one name popped out.

"Marilyn Todd."

"The floor supervisor," Will said flatly. "The petite fifty-year-old nurse."

"Injecting someone with a neuromuscular blocker doesn't require physical strength," Lucy said, and realized she sounded sarcastic.

"But taking down a healthy, thirty-year-old nurse?" Will countered.

"Parsons was injected with something in her upper shoulder." Lucy walked over to the largest man in the room, the hotel security guard, and patted him on the shoulder. "It's that simple."

"Why wouldn't she have screamed? Called for help?"

"Because if the dose is large enough, she wouldn't be able to. Her killer injected her, pulled her into the janitor's closet, and left her there to die."

"It wasn't instantaneous?"

"Probably took a little time. She wouldn't be able to

move, her organs would shut down one by one, and she would die of asphyxiation. Endrophonium is an antidote for neuromuscular blockers, or atropine. There might be others, but it needs to be administered relatively quickly to stop and reverse the effect."

"What do these drugs do?" Swan asked.

"They're used for anesthesia. Common in hospitals, and I can think of at least half a dozen cases in the last fifty years where medical personnel used Tubarine or Pavulon and similar drugs to kill patients. This isn't coming out of left field."

"But they're closely regulated."

"Yes, but if you know how the system works, you can bypass anything."

No one argued that point.

"I believe that Parsons was suspicious, but didn't know who was guilty. She compiled information about these dead patients, but when Sarah Peterson died she panicked. Maybe she saw something, or sensed something, and she reached out to Sarah's brother."

"Why the supervisor?" Will asked. "This is a good theory, but there are no facts to support it."

"Fifteen years ago, Marilyn Todd's older sister Maureen died of breast cancer at the age of thirty-eight. She was diagnosed at the age of thirty-four, so she presumably fought it for four years. It wasn't in this hospital, and we'd need a warrant for her records. But Maureen had no other family; she died in Indio, and Marilyn was a nurse in the same hospital. From what Sean was able to find out through newspaper articles, Maureen had no children, had never been married, and Marilyn was her only caregiver. She'd been in remission, but the cancer returned and had spread before she ultimately died.

"I think in Marilyn's head, these women, even though they were in remission, weren't going to survive. They would be a burden on their siblings, on society, on the hospital staff—she saw her sister in each of them, and was repeating the past."

Dillon spoke for the first time. "She killed her sister. She justified it as a mercy killing."

Everyone turned to face Dillon. He always commanded respect whenever he spoke. And he'd clearly said what she'd been thinking.

"And she's killing these others who remind her of Maureen in order to continue to justify her actions fifteen years ago," Lucy concluded.

No one said anything for a minute, then Swan said, "But you have no proof."

Lucy shook her head. "It's a psychological profile. It's motive, but not evidence."

She looked at Will. He and Carina stared at each other, as if silently communicating. Then Will said, "We need her to confess."

"Why would she?" Swan said. "She got away with murder for years. If you're right, these eight victims in San Diego weren't her first."

"Once you go back to her previous employers, I think you'll see the pattern. It's all circumstantial, a difficult case to prosecute," Dillon said. "Will, I'd like to take a stab at interrogating Todd. I can break her, and it won't take long."

"Why do you think that?"

"Because once she realizes that she murdered her sister, the guilt will tear her apart."

"I don't know," Will said. "She's cold and calculating."

"But you thought she was sweet when you met her," Dillon said. "When you first interviewed her, during the standoff with Peterson."

Will reluctantly agreed. "How do you want to do this?"

The hospital security officer said, "I'm looking at the

duty roster. She's not on duty tonight. But with everything that happened, this might not be accurate."

"I'll send a patrol to her house to pick her up," Will said. "I hope you can do this, Dillon—because if we can't get a confession, we don't have enough evidence to arrest her."

"But we have enough to put her on administrative leave," Dillon said. "Can I get a ride with you to the station?"

Agent Swan approached Lucy after Dillon, Will, and Carina left. "That was an interesting deduction. I looked up your file after our meeting earlier, and it makes sense now."

"What makes sense?"

"I hadn't realized you had a degree in criminal psychology, or that your brother was Dr. Kincaid. I should have known, duh, the same name. Chip off the old block, right?"

"I learned a lot from Dillon," Lucy said.

"You should be there for the interview. With Todd."

She shook her head. "I don't need to be."

"I hope they get a confession, because that'll make this a lot easier." He glanced at his watch. "I need to get home. My wife is going to kill me for being late when I told her I was off at four. Good work, Kincaid."

Lucy hadn't realized it was already six. She and Sean walked back to the south tower to see her father before they left for her parents' house. Everyone was at his bedside, except Dillon, and Lucy felt at peace with her family. It wouldn't be the big Christmas Eve dinner they'd planned, but they'd be together, and that's what Christmas was about. Family.

Thirty minutes later, Dillon called her. She left her father's room and stepped down the hall so she could hear.

"Marilyn Todd isn't at her house," he said. "Will and I

are driving back from the station. Will just got off the phone with hospital security, and her car is in the garage. They're searching for her."

"What do you think she'll do?"

"I don't know. But she must suspect something. Or maybe Peterson's desperate actions made her realize what she's been doing. Maybe she can't justify it to herself anymore. Be careful."

"I think she's more of a threat to herself," Lucy said.

"And anyone around her." Dillon hung up.

Lucy looked around for Kate, but didn't see her. That wasn't a surprise, because Kate didn't like crowds. She grabbed Sean and told him what Dillon said.

"Charlie," she muttered.

"What?"

"Dillon said that maybe Peterson's actions caused Marilyn Todd to realize what she's been doing all these years. But I think when she killed Wendy Parsons, that was the first time she recognized herself as a killer. Before, she'd justified her actions as mercy killings. That she was doing good—it didn't matter that the victims were in remission, she was saving them from future pain and suffering like her sister'd had. But Wendy was a nurse, possibly a friend, who was researching these suspicious deaths, and Marilyn panicked. She killed her, hid her body, and the guilt of that—I think she may be going after Charlie Peterson next."

Lucy called Carina and told her they needed a guard for Charlie Peterson's room, because she thought Marilyn Todd was going to kill him. Carina said she'd call security.

But Lucy didn't know how long that would take. Charlie was two floors up from her father. She took the stairs, Sean at her heels.

She stopped at the nurses' station and showed her badge. "Charles Peterson?"

"I'm sorry, but Mr. Peterson died twenty minutes ago."

Lucy felt sucker punched. She was too late. He should never have died.

Sean showed the nurse a photo of Marilyn Todd. "Did you see her this evening?"

"Ms. Todd. Yes—she's a nurse here."

"In the cancer ward."

"Well, yes, but she's worked in ICU in the past. What's wrong?"

"Do you know where she went?"

"No. She didn't say anything."

"But she was in Peterson's room."

"I doubt it. It's a secure room, with a guard at the door."

"Security is going to want those camera feeds," Lucy said. She turned to Sean. "She's gone."

"You said yourself that she is breaking apart with guilt. She killed a nurse, and that would cascade, right? Where would she go?"

"The cancer ward."

Lucy ran from the south wing, across two courtyards, to the north tower where things were just now getting back to normal. She called Dillon and told him Peterson was dead, and that she was checking the cancer ward for Marilyn Todd.

"We're only five minutes away, and hospital security is on their way," Dillon said.

Lucy hung up. She got off the elevator on the eighth floor. The desk nurse told her visiting hours were over.

Lucy showed her badge. "Is Marilyn Todd here?"

"Yes. What's wrong? Is this about the hostages this morning?"

"I need to talk to her."

"She's in room 808."

"Is there a patient in there?"

"No, it's empty. We evacuated earlier, and not everyone has been returned to their rooms."

Lucy walked down the hall to room 808. She looked in through the narrow window in the door and saw Marilyn Todd sitting in the chair in the far corner. She was staring at the bed. "Sean, stay out."

"Luce," Sean began, then nodded. "I'm watching."

Lucy walked in. "Marilyn," she said quietly. "Marilyn, I'm Lucy Kincaid."

Marilyn looked from the bed to Lucy. "I know. You were one of the hostages."

Lucy nodded. "I did the autopsy on Sarah Peterson. This is where she died, isn't it?"

Marilyn didn't say anything. She looked back at the bed.

Lucy took a couple steps forward, keeping her hands visible. Marilyn didn't appear to have a weapon on her, but she had poisoned at least ten people. She didn't need a gun or knife to be deadly.

"Marilyn, you didn't want to kill Wendy. She was your friend. Your colleague. But she gave Charlie Peterson information that scared you. She knew Sarah's death was suspicious. And the deaths of eight other women. Women who reminded you of Maureen."

Tears slowly ran down Marilyn's cheeks. "It was an accident," she said slowly.

"Maureen was sick for a long time. You were with her every day. Through all her treatments. Through all her pain. You hurt when she hurt. When you found out she was in remission, you both rejoiced, but then the cancer came back and was worse than before."

"She wanted to die," Marilyn said. "She'd given up. Everything I did for her, and it wasn't enough."

"She asked you to help her commit suicide," Lucy said.

"I didn't want to. But . . . she begged me. They all begged me to stop the pain. So I did." She looked up at Lucy. "It was for the best. They would have suffered. Their families would have suffered."

"Sarah was in remission," Lucy said. "So were the other women."

"It wouldn't last. The cancer would return, bigger, blacker, more insidious. And the pain would be unbearable. Watching Maureen not even able to lift her arm after treatments. The vomiting. Wasting away. No one is safe. Cancer's a monster. It eats you up. I saved them all from years of suffering."

"And Wendy couldn't understand that."

"I followed her. I saw her give something to Peterson. She'd been acting strange all week. So I followed her and . . . I didn't mean to kill her, but she looked at me and she knew, just knew, and her eyes were scared, and she turned away . . . she would have called the police. I had to."

"But you didn't want to."

"I didn't know that man was going to take hostages, shoot my nurses, I didn't know!"

"It's going to be okay," Lucy said calmly.

Marilyn jumped up. "No! It's never going to be okay! Nothing is going to be okay. I—my sister—God. Dear God, I killed her!"

There was movement outside the door and Will Hooper was on the threshold. "Ms. Todd, remember me? Detective Hooper? Let's talk."

He stepped inside. Marilyn took a step back.

"Will, please leave," Lucy said. She'd been so close to getting Marilyn to give up peaceably.

"I'm done talking," Marilyn said.

She pulled a syringe from her pocket.

Will rushed her and grabbed her wrist as she was about to inject herself. A wild look crossed her face, fear and anger, and she jabbed the syringe into Will's shoulder. His muscles immediately went lax and he slumped to the floor.

The syringe was still in Will's shoulder. Lucy pushed Marilyn Todd to the ground and put a knee in her back. The woman froze.

Carina was at Will's side, while Sean rushed to Lucy. Will's mouth was moving, but no words came out.

"Get a doctor here with endrophonium stat," Lucy ordered. "I need handcuffs."

Carina handed her Will's pair, took the syringe out and rolled him over to his back.

Sean said, "The medics are on their way." He eyed Lucy, seemed to know she was okay without her having to speak.

Lucy cuffed Marilyn Todd and pulled her up, leading her from the room.

"I want to die," Marilyn said. "You should have let me die."

"Now you're going to have to live with the guilt," Lucy said.

Medics rushed into the room and worked on Will. Lucy turned Marilyn over to two uniformed officers, and turned back toward the room. She stood with Dillon and Sean.

"He's going to be okay, right?" Sean asked.

Lucy nodded. "They got to him fast enough. The blocker reacted immediately, but it's a process. Look."

Already, Will was able to move his limbs, though he was pale and unsteady. "He'll have to stay here tonight— there could be side effects."

"I heard most of your conversation," Dillon told Lucy. "You continue to amaze me, little sister."

"I learned from you, big brother."

Carina stepped out and said, "They're keeping Will for

a while. I need to call Robin, his wife, and tell her what happened." Carina smiled at Lucy, then gave her a spontaneous hug. "You're staying all week, right?"

"Yes," she said. "Through New Year's."

"Good. We have a lot to catch up on."

Carina and Dillon left, and Lucy said, "I'm exhausted. It's been a long weekend."

Sean draped an arm over her shoulders. "I would say we need a vacation—but really, I think we both need to get back to work. Then, maybe, we can have some peace." He kissed her. "Are you really okay?"

"Charlie—he should never have died. If I'd only seen this sooner—"

"Shhh," Sean held her close. She buried her face in his chest and let his love wrap around her.

He didn't need to say anything else.

EPILOGUE

Lucy stepped out onto the front porch on Christmas Day after dinner. Dinner wasn't the same with her dad still in the hospital, but they planned on doing it all again, since he'd be home tomorrow.

Andrew Stanton walked up the pathway, dressed in a suit and tie and looking more uncomfortable than she'd every remembered him. "You can come in," she said.

He shook his head. "I can take your family in small doses. All at once, not anymore."

"I'm sorry about that."

"You shouldn't be." He handed her an envelope.

"What's this?"

"Preliminary lab results."

"On Christmas?"

"I have a Jewish friend or two." He smiled, and Lucy almost laughed.

"You've really gone above and beyond." She opened the envelope. It was from a private—and expensive—lab. They'd run for all known neuromuscular blockers and found fatal levels of tubocurarine chloride in both Sarah Peterson and Wendy Parsons.

Andrew continued. "This is the evidence we need to

prosecute Todd. She's not going to walk. Will and Carina will be going through all of Parsons', files, but it seems that your and Rogan's suspicions were correct. She found what seemed to be a series of suspicious deaths and didn't know what to do with the information. When Parsons found out Peterson was asking questions about his sister's death, she gave him a list of names, the names he passed on to you. I don't know why she did it, whether she thought he could investigate, but it seems he decided to prove it himself."

"And you have evidence that Todd killed Peterson."

"We have her confession, and the hospital is working closely with my office. I think we'll get enough."

"Good." Even though they had stopped a serial killer, no one had won. Charlie was dead, Wendy was dead, Marilyn Todd would spend the rest of her life in prison. Lucy was filled with a dark sense of melancholy.

"Thank you. For everything." She took his hand. "Andrew, I'm sorry my family ostracized you after Justin was killed. I know now how much you suffered."

"We all did. So did you. I don't care that you were only seven; I don't think anyone realized that you were in pain." He tilted his head. "Has Nelia spoken to you yet?"

"Is it that noticeable?"

He nodded.

"At the hospital, when we were both at Dad's room at the same time. She really couldn't avoid it, but it's a start. Here—there's so many people around, she can avoid me. I'm okay with it. It is what it is, and I'm not going to plead with her to forgive me for something I didn't do. I know grief makes her hate me."

"She doesn't hate you, Lucy."

"Guilt? Because she thought I should have been the one to die?"

"Don't say that. Lucy—I don't have to explain loss to

you. We sometimes react in ways even we don't understand. It took me years to recover from Justin's death, but
I also had my career. I'm a workaholic. If I didn't have
this, I wouldn't have survived. I tried to help Nelia, but
we didn't have a marriage at that point. But she's okay
now, we've talked, she has Tom, and I'm putting bad
guys in jail, and you know what? That gives me purpose."

Andrew hugged her, then kissed the top of her head.
"Don't be a stranger, Agent Kincaid."

He left. Sean stepped out onto the porch. "Everything
good?"

"Now it is." She wrapped her arms around his neck
and kissed him. Out of the corner of her eye she saw Gabrielle Santana pass Andrew on the walkway. She hadn't
seen her drive over, so she must have walked from her
mom's house. "Gabrielle?" she asked, surprised.

"Wow. Lucy. I haven't see you since . . . well, since you
got taller than me." She eyed Sean, and Lucy made intro-
ductions.

"I go by Elle now. Is Patrick here?"

"Follow me."

Patrick sat on the back porch and stared out at the Christmas sunset. It didn't matter where he lived, where he ended
up raising a family—if he had one—this would always be
home.

Lucy stepped out and sat on the edge of Patrick's chair
and put her arm around his shoulders. "It's beautiful."

"Mom said you're staying for a week."

"I'm not going to make it home for a while. I thought it
would be a good time to reconnect with Carina, especially after yesterday."

"And Nelia?"

"I'll try."

Patrick took Lucy's hand. "Some things are broken and you can't fix them."

"She talked to me for the first time yesterday at the hospital."

Patrick frowned. "I don't understand."

"Nelia hasn't talked directly to me since Justin was killed."

"That can't be true."

"For eighteen years, it was true."

Patrick hadn't realized that. But he'd been a high school senior when his nephew was murdered, and he'd then gone off to college. Nelia had divorced her husband and moved away after a few years of no justice, but Patrick couldn't imagine that she'd never talked to Lucy. Except . . . Patrick couldn't picture a time they had.

"I understand," Lucy continued. "She sees me, she thinks about Justin. We were inseparable until . . . well, it's painful for her."

They sat there for a few minutes, then Patrick said, "I'm really going to miss you, Luce."

"I'm going to miss you. I was spoiled living so close to you for the past year. Sean's going to miss you, too. You two made a great team."

"We're bringing on two people to replace him."

"I know. He loves it." She laughed.

"I'll bet he does. So, he's really not coming back?"

"No, he's not. His brother needs to accept it."

Patrick sighed. "He has. He's just not happy about it."

"Sean's coming out with Gabrielle. They got waylaid by Mom in the kitchen. I snuck out." She put a hand on her stomach. "I'm stuffed."

Patrick almost missed the first part of Lucy's sentence. He must have misheard. "Elle is *here*?"

"Yes." She raised an eyebrow. "Want to tell me something?"

He was still wrapping his mind around the fact that Elle was here in San Diego, at his house. To see him? Or her family? He wanted to see her. He'd hated how they left things in San Francisco. He didn't know what was going to happen between them, but when he thought he wouldn't ever see her again, at least not unless he jumped through hoops to make sure they were in San Diego at the same time, he felt tense and sad. Elle was . . . amazing in so many ways. It was like she'd woken him up after a long sleep.

"There's nothing to tell," he said after a far too long hesitation.

She rolled her eyes.

"Being a psychologist doesn't make you psychic," Patrick said.

"I don't have to be psychic to read your expression. Jack caught me up on what happened in San Francisco."

"Jack has a big mouth."

Lucy laughed. "I don't think anyone has ever accused Jack of talking too much."

Sean came out onto the deck and took her hand. "Let's take a walk before your mom stuffs more food in me. She says I'm too skinny." He glanced at Patrick. "Why isn't she stuffing you with food?"

"Every time she walks into the kitchen I pretend I'm eating something."

"Sneaky. Your friend"—he smirked like a teenager—"is on her way out."

"Thanks, buddy."

Patrick watched Lucy and Sean walk around the house to the front. If anyone had asked him last year about Sean dating his sister, he'd have laughed or decked him. He hadn't thought Sean would be good for Lucy. But they'd both proved him wrong, and Patrick hoped that someday Sean would be his brother-in-law as well as his best friend.

Elle stepped out on the deck. She had a plate of food. She put it down on the picnic table.

"I didn't think you were coming."

"I told Lucy I would be right out, as soon as I could break away—"

"I meant, to San Diego."

"I wasn't," she said. She looked exhausted as well as nervous. "Patrick—I'm a bitch. I know it. I have nothing to offer you. I'm opinionated, independent, and I have a temper. I get overinvolved in everything I do, I work long hours for little pay, and I take risks I shouldn't take. I know that. I can't promise you I'll change—I tried to change for Dwight because I loved him, but it made us both miserable. But I can't stop thinking about you. You surprised me. You're not like anyone else I know. I lost hope that there were any heroes left in the world, and then you walked into my life and showed me I was wrong. I don't want to let you go—but I don't know what to do. I'm in San Francisco and you're in Washington, D.C., but just the thought of never seeing you again makes me want to cry—and I don't cry."

Patrick would have laughed if his own heart wasn't melting. Elle Santana was not an easy woman, but by God, she was a passionate one, and everything she did she did for others. Her passion and love for life and people was intoxicating.

"First, I don't want you to change. Trying to fit a mold that another person casts for you never turns out."

Her face fell. What had she been through that she thought she was imperfect?

"We're all flawed," Patrick said. "We all have demons we chase, and demons we run from. But you know what I love about you? You stand up for what is right. You say what you think. You care passionately about everything you do. Four days ago, I had a job and a family. I love both. But I had no life. I've dated a few women; no one ever inspired me. But you? God, Elle, you're an inspiration the minute you walk into the room." He got up and took her hands. "It's not going to be easy, living on two coasts, but I travel a lot—"

She tossed her arms around his neck and kissed him. He held her tight, but she was a bundle of energy. If they'd been alone, there was no doubt in Patrick's mind that they'd have been naked inside of a minute.

He really wished they were alone.

"I have ten days off," she said between kisses.

"Where do you want to go?"

She stepped back. "What?"

"Let's go someplace. Otherwise, we'll be here with family. And questions. And no privacy—"

"Anywhere. I don't care."

Patrick smiled. "Ten days? Really?"

"Really."

He took her hand and led her into the house. The Kincaids and Santanas filled the place. His dad was still in the hospital, but he would be home tomorrow. He loved his family more than anything, but for the first time he decided he was going to do something for himself.

"Mom," he said, "I have to go." He kissed her cheek.

The noise level was abruptly reduced by half.

"What's wrong?"

"Nothing. Elle and I have a plane to catch."

Mrs. Santana rushed to his mother's side. "What? Elle, are you still in trouble?"

"No, Ma." But she gave Patrick a quizzical look.

"No trouble at all, Mrs. Santana. We're just going to Hawaii for a little R & R. Elle earned it." He kissed her. Might as well show everyone in the room at once that Elle, the black sheep of the Santana family, was now taken.

Rosa Kincaid managed to control the huge smile that

threatened. She didn't want Patrick to know she was pleased. She'd be more pleased if they were married, but that would come.

Millie took Rosa's hand and pulled her to the kitchen as Patrick said good-bye to his brothers and sisters. It was so, so good to finally have all her children at home, even if it was only for a day. She needed this, now more than ever. Her husband would be coming home soon; she would make sure he ate properly—no more of those steaks he insisted on cooking every Sunday night. And her children— they were doing well. She was so proud of them. Not least of all Carina, who was giving her a grandchild. A grandchild would bring the life and love back into the house.

"You were right," Millie said, sounding surprised.

"I know my children," Rosa said. "And Patrick, he needed someone to pull him out of his shell. He will never be bored with your daughter."

"I hope he can handle her. She's so . . . wild."

"Oh, Millicent, you think about this all wrong. She's not wild, she's strong. She doesn't need to be handled, she needs to be loved. And Patrick has more love in him than he realizes."

"Do you want a wager? I suspect they'll be married in one year."

Rosa's eyes sparkled. "I suspect they'll be married before they return from Hawaii."

Read on for a Lucy Kincaid story

For the first time in print

RECKLESS

By Allison Brennan

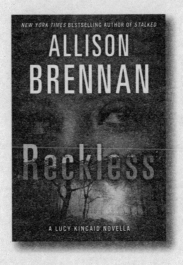

CHAPTER 1

Lucy Kincaid stood on the edge of a low cliff and looked out at the breathtakingly clear lake a hundred feet below. Waking up at dawn and the two-mile hike had paid off.

"Wow." It was all she could say.

Her boyfriend, Sean Rogan, grinned. "I told you this would be worth the journey."

"I really needed this time off."

He kissed her lightly. "I'm glad you could take a break."

Lucy hadn't realized how much she'd been looking forward to this weekend, the last in September. The late-night studying and early-morning physical training had taken their toll. They'd had two major tests, one of which Lucy had barely passed, earning the minimum 85 percent required. That had been in Warrants. She didn't want to cut her upcoming tests that close.

But for the next thirty-six hours, she would put aside her studies and focus on herself, something she rarely did. If it hadn't been for Sean, she'd never have learned to have fun again.

Yellow poplars and a variety of shrubs grew along the edge of a seasonal creek, now dry, which meandered through the tree-studded valley. To the south, the land was rich with maple and birch. The emerging autumn had just begun to turn the leaves from green to gold and red. Though the day was warm, a slight bite in the crisp air promised a chilly night.

"How wide do you think that lake is?"

"Less than a mile," Sean said. "It's probably cold—but if you want to go for a swim . . . ?" He sounded skeptical and Lucy laughed.

"No, I'm not that crazy. But it looks fresh. It'll be nice to have water to clean up."

"And I have a test kit to make sure it's safe to drink."

"Like a Boy Scout, always prepared."

She saw movement on the other side of the lake. "I think there's someone over there." She raised her eyebrows and teased, "I thought you said this was a *hidden* lake."

Sean frowned and took out his binoculars. "I see a woman. No tent. Probably just a hiker. Let's hope she goes away and leaves us alone."

"And here I thought you were the social half of our relationship."

He kissed her with several warm pecks. "Princess, I haven't seen you in a month. I'm not sharing you this weekend."

"So that's why you brought me out in the middle of nowhere—too many people in D.C.?"

"Too many people in my house," Sean grumbled. He lived and worked in a Georgetown town house with Lucy's brother Patrick. Though Sean lived on the second floor and Patrick the top floor, her brother's presence made romantic weekends difficult. "I figured an overnight camping trip in the backcountry would be different and fun. No responsibilities, no stress, just you and me and Mother Nature."

Lucy laughed as they walked along the edge of the

sloping cliff toward the south shore of the small lake. Sean had the area mapped, and though they had no cell phone reception, he had downloaded the maps and other information onto his tablet, and had brought a portable battery charger. His attachment to technology was almost obsessive. "I sure never pegged you for a back-to-nature type," she said.

"Camping isn't my first choice for a vacation, but on short notice and given less than two days to spend with you? I'll take it. We'll be settled and have the tent pitched by noon, then you're all mine."

Sean had picked up Lucy at Quantico at six that morning. She had to be back at the FBI Academy by six tomorrow night. The hike had stimulated Lucy's appetite—she was now used to eating a full breakfast after her morning workout. The muffin Sean had brought for her to eat in the car hadn't filled her up.

"As long as part of your plan is feeding me, I'm all yours," Lucy said.

She breathed in deeply and smiled. Growing up, her family had gone camping every summer, until Justin had been killed.

Justin was the son of her oldest sister, technically her nephew though he was a month older. He was Lucy's first best friend, and though they'd been seven when Justin was killed, Lucy still missed him. She realized now that she hadn't been camping—the "pitch a tent and cook meals over an open fire" type camping—in eighteen years. She didn't think her parents knew just how drastically they'd changed their lives after Justin was gone, above and beyond their grief.

"You're not listening to me," Sean said. He stopped walking and turned to face her. "What's wrong?"

"Memories."

"Bad memories?"

"No. It's just been a while since I've been camping. Since Justin."

Sean touched her cheek. "You okay? We can have a picnic and head back this afternoon. As long as we leave by three-thirty, we'll be at the car before dark."

She kissed Sean. He was always thoughtful and considerate of her feelings, which endeared her most of the time. But she didn't want to be coddled. "I'm okay. I used to love camping. I learned to swim in Big Bear Lake." Lucy had been a championship swimmer in high school and college. She'd had a chance to try out for the Olympic team but her heart hadn't been in it. Her coach had told her if she couldn't commit completely, then she needed to leave. She left.

They continued to walk around the lake, the cliff eroding to a wide expanse of flat land dotted heavily with birch trees. The forest was dense and cooler here than at the top of the cliff.

"This was a good idea," Lucy assured Sean.

"Our previous attempts to get away haven't been as successful."

She punched him lightly in the arm. "Bite your tongue. You want to jinx this?"

He laughed and shook off his backpack. He was carrying the tent with his pack; she had the food in hers. They each had a sleeping bag.

Sean took out his map. "About a hundred yards from here is an old campsite with a fire pit. This used to be a maintained camping area, but there was a flash flood a few years back that killed a group of hikers, so they close it off in the winter and after heavy rains. I guess they didn't think it was worth maintaining just for summer visitors."

"That's depressing," Lucy said.

He winked. "I'll protect you from the ghosts and goblins."

"If you—" She stopped talking. There was a rustling to her right, and she turned and looked. Nothing was there.

"I didn't scare you, did I?" Sean teased.

"No, I thought I heard something."

He looked in the same direction. "Could be a deer. There are some black bears in the park, but most are farther north of here or west in the George Washington Forest. Still, we should be cautious, especially after sunset."

"Great," she said, rolling her eyes. "We've both been shot by psychopaths, but watch, we'll be mauled to death by a bear."

"Ha, ha." Sean adjusted his backpack and they continued their hike.

Lucy wasn't overly concerned—she knew how to secure their food and how to react to wild animals. Her father, a retired army colonel, had always made sure the family was well prepared, though they had never encountered any serious dangers while camping.

Truth was, Sean couldn't have picked a better location. She'd missed so much of her childhood after Justin had been killed, and then her life had been irrevocably changed on the day of her high school graduation when she'd been kidnapped and raped. She wanted to reclaim some of what she'd lost. She could never go back—she didn't want to—but she could rekindle the joys of her youth with the appreciation of her new adult self.

"We should do this again," she said.

"Anything you want, if it means I get more time with you."

Sean was acting unusually possessive and Lucy wondered if it was because of the uncertainty of the future. They'd talked a little about what they were going to do after she graduated from Quantico, but so much depended on where she was assigned. Right now, they were in limbo, not knowing if she would be local or sent three thousand miles away. They couldn't make any decisions until they had those answers, which wouldn't come until December. She tried not to think about it.

"Are you and Duke still having a disagreement?" Sean and his brother Duke, who was a principal of Rogan-Caruso-Kincaid at their base of operations in Sacramento, had had some recent differences of opinion about the business, though he hadn't talked much about it. Sean had always done what Duke asked in order to keep the peace, at least that's what he'd always said. Lucy wondered if Sean's conciliatory manner toward his brother was more because he still sought Duke's approval. Duke had raised Sean after their parents were killed when Sean was fourteen and Duke was twenty-seven, and while Sean didn't talk a lot about his past, Lucy knew he'd been a wild teenager. Sean was open about most everything but whenever they talked about those years, Sean would make a wisecrack and change the subject. At first, he did it so smoothly that Lucy didn't notice. Lately, it was becoming more obvious. She was an open book, but Sean kept much of his past locked away.

"Duke's just being Duke." Sean sighed. "I really thought that when I moved out here to run RCK East that he finally accepted I was capable of making decisions. But sometimes, I think he'll never trust my judgment—or trust me without asking a dozen questions."

"He does," Lucy assured him.

"You don't know him like I do."

"Patrick trusts you."

"And Patrick is spending more time mediating between Duke and me than he should."

They stepped into a clearing, which included a fire pit just like Sean had said. It was evident that other campers had been in this spot earlier in the summer—brush had been cleared and the pit only needed a little cleanup to use.

He turned to her. "No more talk about my job, Duke, Quantico, nothing. Okay?"

"Okay." Lucy knew they'd need to discuss it eventually. It was eating Sean up inside, and she wanted to help. Sean had always been there when she needed him, even when she didn't realize she needed his support. She had to find a way to get inside what was really bothering him about Duke and RCK.

Maybe it had nothing to do with RCK. Maybe it was about what was going to happen to them when she graduated.

"I mean it," Sean said. He dropped his pack and faced her. "I can tell you're still thinking about the outside world. This is our time, Lucy. I don't want anything to interfere with us enjoying each other's company." He touched her face. "I really missed you."

She shook off her backpack and wrapped her arms around his shoulders. "I missed you, too, Sean Rogan." Smiling, she kissed him. "You'd better get that tent up quickly."

"I thought you were starving." He held her close and nuzzled her neck.

"Food can wait. I'll help you."

"This is supposed to be an easy tent to put up," Sean said.

"You've never used it?"

He shook his head. "You pegged me right, Princess. If I go camping, I usually have a cabin to sleep in. With running water. A mattress. Heat."

"Why don't I set it up?"

He raised his eyebrows in mock embarrassment. "Don't think I can do it?"

"All right." She sat on the ground. "Go."

"You're going to watch?"

She grinned.

Lucy wasn't surprised that the first thing Sean did was read the directions. Then he pocketed the instructions and put the frame together without a hitch. He spread out a footprint for the tent, clipped the tent onto the frame, and staked everything to the ground. Ten minutes later, he was done and grinning like a kid.

"You look very pleased with yourself," Lucy said.

"I am. I've never done this before."

Lucy stood and kissed him. "Good job."

"What's my reward?"

She knelt down and crawled into the tent. "Cozy," she said.

Sean followed her and pinned her beneath him. "I love you."

All worries about Sean and Duke, fears about their future when she graduated, disappeared as they kissed. All there was now was her and Sean, and she melted into him, completely at peace, this moment in time absolutely perfect.

A sharp male voice cut through the still afternoon, then nothing.

Lucy cringed, her body tensing. They'd seen a woman, now there was a man? Were they together? How many people were out here in the woods?

"They'll go away," Sean whispered in her ear, then kissed it.

"I know. I'm fine," Lucy said as Sean rubbed her shoulders. He was trying to make her comfortable with his touch and whispers, but she couldn't relax. She hated this part of herself. Wouldn't a normal twenty-five-year-old woman be able to ignore other campers when she was in a tent with her boyfriend? It wasn't like they were having sex out in the open for everyone to see.

But just thinking about it had Lucy's mind not focused on making love to her boyfriend, but rather on what the other campers would think. What they would imagine. On someone looking in the tent and seeing her. She couldn't unwind. She still had a hard time relaxing in Sean's bed when her brother Patrick was under the same roof. A lasting remnant of fear after being raped in front of an audience seven years ago.

"Dammit!" She sat up and hugged her knees.

Sean sat next to her, his head almost touching the top of the tent. "Luce, don't—"

"I hate myself sometimes." She squeezed back tears of frustration and despair. When was she going to get over this fear of being watched? These insane panic attacks that reminded her that she wasn't normal and never would be?

Sean squeezed her hand to the point that it hurt. In a low voice he said, "I *never* want to hear you say anything like that again. Do you understand me?"

"I just want to be normal."

"Stop. I know what you mean, but there is no normal. We've gotten this far, do you think I'm going to run away because the road isn't always smooth?" He took her chin in his hand and pulled her face close to his. He lightly touched his lips to hers. "I love you for you. End of story."

She breathed easier. "I'm so lucky to have you."

One side of his mouth curved up. "I know you are."

She wrinkled her nose and crawled out of the tent. "I *am* hungry," she said.

He followed her. "I'm sure the hikers will go away but after we eat we should explore the area, make sure no one else is around."

They spread a blanket on the ground and unpacked Sean's picnic. "We could feed an army," Lucy said.

"We're going to be here until noon tomorrow; I need to make sure you're well fed."

"We could be here a week."

"Not quite." But he looked pleased as Lucy took a bite of potato salad.

"You didn't make all this, did you?"

Sean laughed. "I'm a good cook but not *this* good. I went to that deli on M Street that you like so much, and then the brewery next door that has the lamb stew. We'll get the fire going before dark and warm it for dinner."

She grinned with appreciation. "You really planned this trip well."

"I did." He bit into his sandwich and looked around. "What did you do when you went camping with your family? I think I would have gone stir-crazy being in the middle of nowhere for a week with my family."

"My dad's best friend had a boat we'd borrow and take to the lake. We'd fish, have races with other campers, hike, play games—it wasn't quiet like this. It was a large campground with dozens of families. Justin and I had a lot of freedom." She drank some water. "We always found other kids to play with."

Two voices echoed through the trees. Clearly they were arguing, but Lucy couldn't make out what they were saying. Sean swore under his breath. Lucy felt bad for him because he had this weekend planned for the two of them, and now in his eyes it was less than perfect.

She said, "When we're done eating, we'll secure the food and take a walk. Maybe if they know we're also camping here, they'll tone it down."

Sean glared at the woods as if silently cursing them.

After they cleaned up, they walked east, in the direction of the voices. They no longer heard anyone arguing or even talking, but it was better to take care of the situation now. Maybe Sean was right and the couple was simply hiking for the day. Maybe they were lost and Sean could direct them back to where they needed to go.

Wishful thinking.

They trekked through a section of birch trees that went for as far as Lucy could see. "Are you sure you're going toward the lake?" she asked.

Sean glanced over his shoulder. "You doubt my sense of direction?"

"No, but—"

He held up his tablet. "Even if I didn't have this, I know where we are, okay?"

"Sorry for doubting you."

"Hrmph."

Lucy laughed. Sean turned left and a few feet later Lucy saw the lake through the trees. She crossed her heart. "I'll never doubt you again."

He reached over and tickled her. "See that you don't."

They walked along the edge of the lake, which was rocky and strewn with old, rotting branches and logs. Several pairs of geese were out swimming. One stuck his long neck under the water and, as Lucy watched, came up with a fish. From the north, six geese flew overhead, circled, and landed smoothly in the middle of the lake.

Lucy whispered, as if speaking too loudly would break the magic of the moment, "We should come back here before sunset. It's really lovely. Peaceful."

Sean nodded and gestured to a grouping of rocks about twenty feet high. "We'll climb up there. Good view."

She took his hand and kissed it. The spontaneous display of affection surprised both her and Sean. Lucy was acutely aware that Sean was the more romantic of the two of them. She appreciated it more than she could ever explain to him. He gave her not only what she wanted, but also what she needed. Things she needed that she could never ask for from anyone, he gave freely.

They walked around the rock formation and saw the campsite. It was a small camp, similar to Sean and Lucy's space with an old fire pit in the middle of a clearing. Instead of a tent, there was a small lean-to. A couple of back-packs and a rifle leaned against a tree next to the make-shift shelter.

The couple wasn't there, but their voices were close by. They were arguing again with an urgency that bordered on panic.

". . . find him . . ."

". . . lost . . ."

". . . can't go back . . ."

Lucy glanced at Sean. He'd heard the same thing, but he'd gone from curious to protective. He didn't like the tone any more than she did.

"Something's wrong," Lucy said.

The woman stepped into the clearing and saw them. She pulled a gun from her pocket and turned it toward Lucy and Sean. "Who the hell are you?"

CHAPTER 2

Sean took a small step in front of Lucy, his body tense. He made no move for the gun in his backpack, but hoped Lucy would go for it if the situation warranted.

He said, "Hey, what's with the gun? We're camping near here, just like you. Wanted to introduce ourselves. To avoid a situation like this."

The woman immediately lowered the weapon.

"You startled me." She stuffed the gun back in her pocket. It was a small .22, easily concealable.

Sean didn't relax but he offered a smile. "Sorry, we didn't mean to."

The woman was petite, her blond hair pulled back. The man also had light hair, and was both taller and wider than Sean. They were in their early- to mid-thirties and wore jeans and flannel jackets; both looked surprised— and suspicious—to find Lucy and Sean in their campsite.

"I'm Sean Rogan; this is my girlfriend, Lucy Kincaid. We're camping about two hundred yards southwest of here, on the south side of the lake."

The strangers glanced at each other. "Thanks," the woman mumbled. "We won't bother you."

"Is something wrong?" Lucy asked. "Is someone missing?"

The man narrowed his eyes. "Why?"

"I heard—"

The woman glanced over her shoulder at her male companion. There was some sort of silent communication going on, but Sean couldn't clearly see the woman's expression until she turned back to them.

"Our son," she said. "He wandered off this morning, maybe around six. Before we woke up."

It was just after noon. Might not be cause for concern. "How old is he?"

"Nine. We had an argument last night," she said. "I'm sure he's just trying to punish us."

The boy had been missing for several hours. He should have returned on his own by now. If he could.

"Do you have a radio?" Sean asked.

"No," the man grunted. "Don't worry about our problems; he'll come back when he gets hungry."

The father was probably right, unless the son was truly lost and couldn't find his way back. A boy that age might hide to scare his parents, but after this many hours? He'd be trying to find his way to camp. At least, Sean hoped that was the case. Unfortunately, when lost, the best thing to do was stay in one place so people looking could find you. But Sean had once been nine, and he'd always been curious. It had often led to trouble.

"We'll help you look for him," Lucy offered.

"We don't need help," the woman said. Then she added, "If he doesn't come back before dark, maybe—"

Sean interrupted. "That's too late. It's going to drop into the forties tonight. We need to get help. My car is only a two-hour hike away."

"By the time anyone gets here it'll be dark," the man said.

"I didn't catch your name," Lucy said.

Sean didn't like this situation at all. Lucy was also tense, and her voice held a hint of authority that told him she was suspicious of the situation.

"Sorry," the woman mumbled. "I'm Ann, this is Jeff. I'm just distracted by this whole thing."

"It's understandable," Lucy said with sympathy. "And your son?"

"Micah."

"Has Micah done this before?"

Ann nodded. "All the time. Once, he was gone for three days. He hid in someone else's basement. Everyone was looking for him. I thought the worst. But we found him sleeping."

Sean didn't know why he didn't believe Ann, but the woman's story, while it sounded plausible, had an air of falsehood. He glanced at Lucy but her gaze was fixed solely on the couple.

"The forest rangers need to be informed that there's a missing child," Lucy said. "They have substations, people who know where and how to search. I really think we should contact them as soon as possible."

"There's cell reception off the road where we parked," Sean said. "We can go back and call. Do you have a recent photograph?"

Ann shook her head. "I left my wallet in the car."

Jeff had his hand on his pocket, then dropped it. "Do you know how embarrassing it'll be if the rangers get out here and Micah walks into camp?"

"Do you know how upset you'll be if he doesn't?" Lucy snapped.

Suddenly Ann started crying and Lucy approached the woman, her compassion evident. Sean didn't like that the couple were armed. He shifted his backpack so he could easily reach his gun.

"I'm sorry," Lucy said. She put a hand on Ann's shoulder. "We'll help you find him."

"I know Micah better than anyone. I should talk to the rangers about him. I'll go with you."

"That sounds good," Lucy said.

Sean didn't let on that he didn't like that option. He needed to talk to Lucy alone. She seemed to pick up on that and said to Ann, "Why don't you pack up an emergency bag and we'll go back to our camp and do the same?"

Ann nodded. "We'll meet you there."

"Do you know where it is?"

"You said at the south side of the lake. We almost camped there yesterday instead of here, but Micah liked being closer to the rocks."

Sean had a sudden tragic thought. "Does Micah know how to swim?"

Ann looked at Sean as if she didn't know how to respond, then Jeff said, "Like a fish."

That still didn't mean he couldn't have been lost in the lake. Drowning was a silent death. The bottom of the lake could be polluted with debris—trees and mud and vines— where someone could easily get tangled. However, Sean didn't say anything. The rangers would dredge the lake if the boy didn't turn up in a couple days.

But that was in the future. It had been several hours since Micah disappeared. The father could be right— Micah could be watching and waiting for the right time to return.

Something still seemed off about the couple, though Sean couldn't pinpoint a specific reason why he thought so. Other than the fact that they had at least two guns, the .22 and the rifle against the tree. The father was gruff and didn't seem concerned about his son, but he was definitely angry about him running off. The mother seemed more worried, but it was like flipping a switch. One minute she'd been as angry as her husband; the next she turned on the waterworks. There might be a psychological reason for the response, but Sean thought they weren't telling them everything. Wouldn't the parents be in a panic by now? Sean didn't have kids, but he would be more worried—and far more proactive. What if Micah ran away for a reason? What if he had been abused?

Or maybe the parents were on the run. They hadn't been camping for long—the lean-to could barely fit two of them—but the weather hadn't turned yet, so it wasn't unsafe.

Sean broke the awkward silence that crept up. "I'll help Jeff search the immediate area again. Maybe we can pick up a trail."

Jeff shook his head. "We've searched everywhere. The kid will come back when he gets cold or hungry."

The kid?

Ann turned to her husband and put her hand on his arm. She spoke softly but emphatically. "Jeff, I *know* you're as worried about Micah as I am, you just don't know how to show it. Let these people help us, okay? Please?" Her voice cracked.

Lucy glanced at Sean. He shook his head slightly, hoping that Lucy understood that he didn't want to talk anymore in front of these two. And though he didn't like the idea of Lucy going back to the car with Ann, he didn't have a better idea to bring search and rescue here before nightfall.

Sean said, "Jeff, Ann, meet us at our camp in twenty minutes. Lucy can lead the way to our car."

"What's to say they won't get lost, too?" Jeff said.

"I have a map." Sean forced a smile. "No one will get lost."

The two seemed skeptical, but agreed.

As Lucy and Sean left the couple and were heading back to their campsite, she said, "I don't trust them."

"Neither do I. I think they're hiding something." He paused, then added, "What if there isn't a missing kid at all?"

"Why would they say there was?"

Sean shook his head. "I don't know. I just got a bad vibe."

"For what it's worth, I think Ann is worried, though she doesn't seem as concerned as I would expect. But Jeff seems the more volatile. I got the sense he would beat the poor kid when he returns."

"Maybe that's why Micah ran in the first place."

"Either way, we need to get help."

Sean pulled his gun from his backpack and tucked it into a holster in the small of his back. He put on a jacket to conceal it. "Do you have your gun?"

"I left it in the trunk. I didn't think I'd need it."

"Take mine—"

"No. I'm going with Ann; you're staying with Jeff and his rifle. Don't let him out of your sight."

"I don't plan to. But Ann also has a gun, and I'm not letting you go off into the woods with her unarmed." Sean handed Lucy his tablet and brought up the map of the area. "You can't go back the way we came—it's too steep in parts and will take longer. Go this way." He had the route already marked in blue. "It's about a quarter mile longer but it's a more gradual incline. If you set a good pace, you'll be back at the car in ninety minutes." He pointed to a red dot just off the trail he'd marked. "This is a peak, so you might get cell reception there."

"Good to know." She leaned up and kissed him. "Find him, Sean. He's probably scared."

"Be careful, Lucy. Keep her in your sight."

"I will." Lucy paused, then asked, "Did you find it odd that they didn't give us their last names?"

"Yes. If they're bank robbers or something, this would

be a great place to hide out, except that they don't have the supplies for a long stay. In fact, they barely have enough for the weekend."

"Maybe we shouldn't separate."

"I don't know." They walked in silence for a few minutes.

"If nothing else," Lucy said, "we need backup, right?"

"Agreed."

"And if they're telling the truth about their missing son, there's a lost kid out here who needs our help. The faster search and rescue starts looking, the better for all of us."

CHAPTER 3

Sean hadn't wanted Lucy to leave with Ann but it was the only real option they had. If there really was a missing boy—and Sean didn't see why the couple would lie about it—he was in trouble. His mother said he had a jacket but the cold was only one danger. Animals generally stayed away from people, but there had been known bear attacks in this backcountry, where there weren't many people around. Aside from the cold, lack of water was the number one danger. After three days, he would be severely dehydrated. However, if the boy walked straight in any direction, in less than three days he would find a road. Unfortunately, lost children tended to wander in circles.

After Ann and Lucy had left the campground, Jeff said to Sean, "We searched and called for him. He's not within earshot, or he's just hiding from us."

"He may have heard you but the echo disorientated your location." Sean assessed Jeff. "Why would he hide from you?"

"None of your business." Jeff rubbed his face. "Look, we had a fight. He's nine, he wants things he can't have."

Sean was generally a good judge of character, and he'd been on edge since meeting Jeff and Ann. But he didn't know why they bothered him. Now that Ann was gone, Jeff seemed to have relaxed a little. He was still border-line belligerent, but not as nervous.

His attitude could be any number of things. He could be abusive, or guilty of something that had nothing to do with his missing son.

"Do you have a picture of Micah?" Ann had said she'd left her purse in their car, but when she'd said that, Sean thought Jeff had been reaching into his back pocket. Sean's dad always kept pictures of the kids in his wallet—though often they were outdated. And while he might buy that a woman would leave her photos in her purse, no man left home without his wallet.

Jeff hesitated, then reached back and pulled a worn leather wallet out of his pocket. "It's a couple years old. He was in first grade."

Sean took the picture. It was a standard school photo with a blue background. Micah had a wide grin and was missing one of his front teeth in the picture. He was fair-skinned with dark hair and blue eyes and a light smatter-ing of freckles across the bridge of his nose.

"Cute kid," Sean said. The backside of the photo had Micah's name and the year the photo was taken, consis-tent with what they'd already said. Sean was marginally relieved—but his fear for the child grew. Six hours was a long time for a nine-year-old to be missing in the woods.

Jeff put the picture back in his wallet. "Yeah. Well." He cleared his throat. "How long do you think it'll take for Ann and your girlfriend to get back?"

"It's at least ninety minutes each way. Likely the rang-ers will want them to wait at the car until the search and rescue team is mobilized, so they know where they're go-ing." Sean glanced at his watch. It was almost one o'clock; the women had been gone for less than thirty minutes. "I wouldn't expect anyone back until four at the earliest. Probably closer to five."

"But they'll be back before dark, right?" Jeff asked.

"I hope so." This was getting them nowhere. "Did you hear anything this morning? When Micah left?"

Jeff shook his head. "Nothing."

"Where was he sleeping?" Sean looked around the camp. There wasn't much here. Two sleeping bags, the lean-to, two backpacks—

Two sleeping bags?

"Did Micah take his sleeping bag?"

Jeff frowned and turned, staring at the lean-to. He didn't say anything for a minute. "I didn't notice," he finally said.

This was sounding more and more like the kid had intentionally run away. If he had his sleeping bag and supplies, he could camp out in the woods for several days, maybe a week or more. Certainly until the weather turned. But why? When Sean was nine, he'd shown early signs of being the rebel he'd turned into after his parents were killed. He'd never run away but there were times when he'd snuck out of the house just because he could get away with it. He'd hide in the tree house his oldest brother, Kane, had built with their dad the year before Kane had joined the Marines. It was outside of the house, but still safe. Risky, but not dangerous. There had been an American flag and a Marine Corps flag hanging on two of the walls, and broken electronics that Sean would either get working again or refashion into something completely different. He always felt an odd sense of peace in the tree house, especially when Kane was deployed and he only saw him a couple times a year.

He always wondered if his parents knew he was in the tree house and that's why they never panicked. Or if they just didn't care.

What about Micah? Was he trying to figure out if his

parents really cared about him? Or was he running from them? Did he want to scare them, or was he scared of them?

"This changes things," Sean said. "Micah has the capacity to survive the night on his own. Do you know if he took food or other supplies?"

"I didn't notice," Jeff repeated.

Sean had the feeling again that he was missing an important fact. The honesty and connection he'd felt with Jeff a few minutes ago vanished.

"How far did you search?"

"I walked a good hour up the creek bed, then came back through the eastern ridgeline. I'd just returned when you and your girlfriend showed up."

"About the fight—"

"That's not important. He's a kid, for chrissakes. I'm the adult; he needs to listen and do what he's told."

Sean didn't comment on Jeff's reaction. Instead he said, "I'm going to circle around your camp and try to figure out which way he went."

"I told you—we searched all around here."

"I know, but I'm sure you and your wife were emotional and maybe you missed something."

"Whatever," Jeff grumbled. "I'm going to walk around the lake again. I gotta do something."

Sean walked along the edge of Jeff's camp slowly. Even though it was still daylight, he shined his flashlight on the ground, looking for signs of small footprints. Unfortunately, there were many footprints and none were distinct.

He walked deeper into the woods, sweeping back and forth, looking for any sign of Micah. A lost jacket. Food wrappers. Based on the disturbed earth, Ann and Jeff had retraced the same ground several times. With the poor sunlight that barely filtered through the trees and the falling leaves, a clear trail was impossible to find. Sean supposed a more experienced tracker might be able to identify whose tracks were whose.

About half a mile from the campsite, as Sean was considering turning around since he'd been gone nearly an hour, he saw something that seemed odd.

Tire tracks.

But these tracks were too narrow to be from a car or truck, not to mention that they weren't on a road. Sean had driven quads often enough to know that a small, four-wheel all-terrain vehicle had been here. The gouges in the earth were still fresh. On further inspection, it appeared that there had been two ATVs; the tracks couldn't have been here longer than a week and were probably made more recently. He saw no sign of the quads now. He hadn't heard any earlier, either.

Adrenaline fueled his urge to follow the tracks. But they could go for miles, and he needed to be back at the campsite by the time Lucy returned. Both Jeff and Ann had guns, Sean didn't, and they had possible access to ATVs that neither had mentioned, plus a missing kid. Was Micah even theirs? Would Jeff carry a photo of him if he wasn't?

Too many unanswered questions made Sean nervous. He didn't want to mention the tracks to Jeff, but at the same time he feared keeping quiet could jeopardize Micah's safety.

He followed the grooves for a hundred yards and determined that the tracks had come from the southeast, stopped where he'd first seen them, and returned the same way.

Why would they stop in the middle of the woods—not the lake, not a clearing—only to turn around and go back?

He'd given Lucy his tablet with the map but he drew out on a piece of paper the location of the tracks and a general indication of the terrain. He'd be able to find this place again. If he remembered correctly from the maps of this area that he'd downloaded, there wasn't much to the east except hills, trees, and a spattering of secluded homes miles away. It was certainly possible that someone had driven into the mountains to ride ATVs, but coming from the east or southeast added far more time than if they'd used the main highway. The riders might live in the vicinity—the closest residence was about four miles away, definitely within quad range.

Sean wished he had his map because he hadn't studied this part of the forest, focusing primarily on the route he and Lucy had hiked.

He pulled out his phone and hoped that Lucy was still in range to use the radio. He doubted it, but it was worth a try. Or, she may not have turned her cell phone on to save the battery.

There was no response.

"Luce, be careful," he whispered, then started back toward camp.

The first thirty minutes of their trek to the car was awkwardly quiet, so Lucy broke the silence and said to Ann, "I've been on search and rescue teams, and kids get scared. When they run away, at first they're mad and hurt and too scared to return because they think you'll be angry with them. It sometimes takes a while for them to realize that you're not going to be mad, that you'll be relieved when they return."

He could truly be lost, or injured, but Lucy didn't want to make Ann any more scared than she already was. Lucy thought if they kept up the pace she'd set, they'd beat the ninety minutes Sean predicted. The faster they got people out here searching, the better.

Ann frowned. "Are you sure that map is right?"

Lucy showed her Sean's tablet. "Sean downloaded the entire region before he left. He loves his gadgets. See here? We might be able to get cell reception on the knoll."

"So you have a phone?"

She nodded. "Like I said, Sean's into technology. Even though he knew we didn't have reception out here, he insisted we pack them. I have mine off right now, but I'll turn it on when we get to the knoll and see if we catch a signal. I can also communicate using the radio on the cell phone if we need it, but range is the problem there."

Though they were walking through trees that provided a natural canopy, the hike was making Lucy warm. She stopped to take off her sweatshirt and tie it around the strap of her backpack. She drank half a water bottle, then stuffed it back into her pack.

Ann said, "We should cut through here." She gestured to a slope that appeared to be a more direct route to the road, but it was also much steeper.

"We should stick to Sean's map."

"Is he some sort of expert?"

Her voice was snide but Lucy let it pass. "About some things he is. We know this route will get us to our car in ninety minutes; if we detour, it may take longer. Or there could be other hazards."

Ann opened her mouth to argue, then closed it, obviously frustrated. Lucy had to convince Ann to trust her.

"Ann, I know you're worried, and I want to help. I work for the FBI; I'm not an agent yet, but I have plenty of experience in search and rescue from when I interned with the Arlington County Sheriff's Department, and I know how to work with the authorities. We will find your son. We just need to bring in the right people for the job, okay?"

Ann was staring at her as if she'd just told her she was from Mars.

Lucy tried to ease the situation. "I just want you to feel

comfortable with Sean and me helping in the search for Micah. We'll find him. We're not going to leave until we do."

Ann nodded and turned away, walking in the direction Lucy had been going. Lucy followed. A few minutes later, Ann began to veer too far to the west. "Ann, this way," Lucy said, motioning to what appeared to be an overgrown path. Lucy wasn't surprised Sean had selected this route. It had obviously been used by hikers in the past.

The path led to a clearing ringed by maple trees. Not just a clearing but an old graveyard. Headstones had crumbled over time. This was an unusual place for a cemetery, but it could have been a family plot many years ago. She walked to one of the headstones that looked mostly intact.

WILLIAM OLDENBURG, III
Husband of ABIGAIL CUTTER OLDENBURG
1869–1914

The grave next to William's appeared to be his father's, though part of the name was cut off. The dates had nearly eroded away, but it looked like William the second lived from 1833 until 1889.

Lucy didn't particularly like cemeteries but she appreciated history. She wondered about the land they were on, who the family was, how long they'd lived here. Maybe tomorrow, before they went home—provided that they found Micah—she and Sean could explore the area around the cemetery. Maybe there was an old homestead or the remnants of a house.

Ann hadn't stepped from the edge of the clearing. "We shouldn't be here."

Graveyards often made people nervous and superstitious. Lucy said, "Go ahead and walk around the edge of the clearing. According to Sean's map, the path we're on continues over there." She gestured toward the opposite side.

Lucy glanced around and found the remnants of nine headstones. As she crossed the clearing, she saw recently disturbed dirt.

She stared at the mound. It had been covered with fresh leaves and they were piled higher than the leaves surrounding it. The dirt was darker and had definitely been turned.

As if someone had dug a grave, then filled it back in.

What if Jeff and Ann had killed their son and buried him, planning on telling people that he disappeared while they were camping?

Her heart thudded in her chest. The knoll where there might be cell reception was still a thirty-minute hike away. Her gun was in her pack and she would have to find a way to retrieve it without making Ann suspicious. She was going to have to fake it, pretend she hadn't seen this grave.

Lucy looked up, plastering a false smile on her face. "Ann, we should—"

Ann wasn't in the clearing. Lucy looked around but didn't see her anywhere.

For a moment, Lucy didn't know what to do. She was halfway to the car. Did she continue and get help, or go back for Sean? Was he in danger? Her urge was to go to Sean, but if Ann and Jeff were truly dangerous, she needed backup. She'd walk as fast as possible to the car, run when she could, call for help, and go back for Sean. It was a difficult decision to make, but it would take her nearly an hour to return to the campsite, and still with no way of contacting the police.

Maybe she was wrong—maybe Ann had simply walked ahead. Or had to find a private tree to relieve herself. Or . . .

Who was she kidding? Both she and Sean had been suspicious from the beginning, and now they were separated.

Lucy took off her backpack and retrieved her gun. She put it in her waistband, hoping Ann wasn't watching her, that she didn't see that she was armed.

Keeping her eyes open, looking for any movement, Lucy continued briskly down the path.

The split second after she sensed someone watching her, she reached for her gun. As her hand clasped around the grip, a sharp pain exploded in her head and she fell to the ground, unconscious.

CHAPTER 4

It took Sean nearly thirty minutes to walk back to his campsite, mostly because he was looking for signs that people or ATVs had been in the area. He didn't find any tracks that couldn't be explained as Ann and Jeff looking for their son. Lucy had been gone for over an hour. He tried the radio again but there was no connection. He tried different frequencies to see if he could ping a ranger in the vicinity, but nothing was in range.

Next time he went camping—if there was a next time—he would buy the best radio system he could find. That he hadn't thought they'd need a two-way radio didn't matter. What happened to being prepared? He had the map, the equipment, the food—but no communication.

Sean trekked over to Jeff's campsite to see if he'd returned from his excursion. He could lead Jeff into a question about the ATVs without letting him know he'd seen any tracks. He considered that they could have been rangers patrolling the area, but if that was the case why hadn't they come all the way to the campground? They'd know that people were still using the place, even if it wasn't maintained by the parks system.

As soon as he stepped through the trees he realized he'd been deceived.

All their equipment was gone.

The lean-to was there, but not the sleeping bags or back-packs. Sean stayed along the edge of the camp, looking for signs of where they'd gone. The only trail he could find led up near the stream. If he followed it, he'd be in the middle of open space, easy pickings if someone was looking for him.

Why had Jeff packed up and left? Sean hadn't heard anything; could he have simply been waiting for Sean to leave, then returned and grabbed his stuff? What about his wife? She was with Lucy; why would he leave without her?

The unease that Sean had felt since meeting Jeff and Ann grew to borderline panic that he'd sent Lucy off with someone who was dangerous. It didn't matter that Lucy could take care of herself or that she had a gun; she was in the middle of the woods with no backup.

He ran back to his camp and paced. He wanted to look for Lucy, but if he followed her trail and she returned via another route with the rangers, he wouldn't be here.

His only real option was to head back to the road the fastest way possible and call for help. Except that Lucy could very well be on her way back now, with help.

"Shit," Sean muttered.

Thirty minutes. He'd give her thirty minutes, then he'd go after her.

Lucy startled awake. She didn't know how long she'd been unconscious, but she'd been out long enough to be restrained.

She opened her eyes slowly, glancing around to see if anyone was there. As she adjusted her position she realized that she wasn't tied to the tree she was leaning against, but her hands were restrained behind her.

Her entire head hurt especially the lump where Ann had hit her. She assumed Ann was her attacker.

Dammit, she'd sensed something was wrong and hadn't reacted fast enough.

It was still day, and it appeared she hadn't lost more than ten or fifteen minutes of time. She was leaning against a tree in the old cemetery, close to the newly dug grave.

Lucy saw something sticking out from the ground. A cross, fashioned out of two sticks perpendicular to each other and tied at the center by a cord. The cord appeared to come from a hoodie. It had to have been put there recently because it wouldn't have survived any inclement weather.

Lucy cringed as she realized that Ann had her backpack—which included her phone and car keys. She didn't feel the weight of the gun at her hip. And the tablet with the map that Lucy had been holding was nowhere she could see.

She had looked at the map long enough that she could probably get out of here and to the car, but it wouldn't do her much good if that's where Ann went. She could flag someone down on the road, but it was at least a four-mile walk to the nearest ranger's station if no one drove by—or if no one stopped to help. And Sean was still back at the campsite with Jeff, not knowing that anything was wrong.

The back of her neck tingled. She was being watched. She tensed, fearing Ann had returned. Except she wouldn't kill her now, would she? Why tie her up if she planned to kill her?

She couldn't defend herself tied up. Her fingers were growing numb from lack of circulation. Then she almost smiled as she realized she was restrained with plastic zip-ties.

I owe you one, Jack.

Her brother Jack, former army special forces, had trained her in self-defense after her kidnapping seven years ago. She'd added to her skills through her FBI training, but Jack's survival training came in handy now.

She leaned against the tree and shifted so her feet were under her, then slowly pushed herself up using the tree for support. She stepped away from the tree, a bit unsteady on her feet. She took a couple deep breaths, then bent over, lifting her arms, zip-tied behind her back, as far up as she could. With all her strength she slammed her wrists on her butt. The movement made her dizzy, but she did it two more times and the plastic broke.

She rubbed her raw wrists and looked around. Movement to her left had her taking a step behind the tree. At first she didn't see anything, then a flash of black and white in the trees. Small.

"Micah," she said. "Is your name Micah?"

He hesitated, then stepped out from the trees. He had a gun in his small hands. It looked like a .22, similar to what Ann had been carrying.

"Micah, you don't need that gun."

He didn't answer and kept his distance from her. He looked like he would bolt at the slightest sign that she was going to move toward him, so she slowly leaned back against the tree. He was wearing jeans, a blue T-shirt, and a black hoodie. A hoodie without a string. His pale face had been scratched in several places, likely from branches. One was deep enough to have bled and should have been treated. It would definitely scar. With his dark hair and big blue eyes, he looked so much like her cousin Justin that her heart skipped a beat.

But he wasn't Justin. He was Micah.

"I want to help you," Lucy said. "Please—lower the gun. You're making me nervous."

"I'm not going to shoot you," he said in a high voice that suggested he would shoot if he felt like he had to. He was both brave and scared. But he put the gun at his side, still holding it tightly.

"My name is Lucy Kincaid. Your mother and I—"

"She's not my mother!"

"Shh," Lucy said, glancing around. "Micah, listen, I work for the FBI. I'm camping with my boyfriend. We can help you, but you have to trust me."

He looked skeptical but at least he didn't run.

"Who is Ann?"

His bottom lip quivered. "She killed my mom." His eyes shifted to the grave. Lucy's stomach flipped. His mother was buried there. "I think," he added.

"Micah, please trust me. Tell me exactly what happened."

He bit his lip, tears in his eyes, but he kept his emotions in check. Poor kid, he shouldn't have to hold back tears over his mother's murder.

"We were living with my mom's boyfriend. In a trailer. There were other trailers, too, and it was home, you know?"

It was home. Lucy doubted Micah had ever had a stable home.

"They make drugs. You know, meth." He said it matter-of-factly. "Mom used to have a problem, but not anymore. She cleaned up because she met Jeff and he told her she had to stay straight. For us."

Jeff. The man who said he was Micah's father.

"Where's your dad?" she asked quietly.

Micah shrugged. "I don't know," he mumbled. "I never met him."

"And your mom's boyfriend, Jeff, brought you to his home."

"Kinda. We had an apartment in Richmond for a while, then down in Charlotte—that's in North Carolina—and then he got a job in Baltimore. But—" He stopped talking.

"But he lost his job," Lucy guessed.

Micah nodded.

"What happened to your mother?" When he didn't say anything, Lucy pushed. "I can't help you unless you tell me everything."

It all came out in a rush. "We moved up here in July, just for the summer Jeff said, he got this great job. But it was making drugs, and Mom tried real hard, but she started using again, and Jeff was so mad—but he wanted to help her. Because it was against the rules to dip into the product, everyone knew it, and he covered for her until . . . until . . . well, it was just bad, and everyone knew Mom was using and they fought and Mom ran off. Jeff told me to stay, he'd find her, and he left, but so did the others. I followed them, and I heard . . ." His voice trailed off and he looked at the grave. "I heard gunshots. I ran away. Back to the camp. Jeff was already there and mad that I'd left. I wanted to tell him that Ann hurt Mom, but I couldn't. I just cried and he said everything would be okay. But when Ann got back, she told Jeff my mom died of a drug overdose and they buried her in the woods." His voice cracked and he couldn't stop the tears. "And I knew she was lying, that she'd shot her." He wiped his nose and eyes with the sleeve of his hoodie. "I ran away."

"To go to the police?"

He shrugged. "I don't know. Not the police."

"Why not?"

"Because one of the rangers is friends with Ann, he comes by all the time."

Lucy couldn't go to the rangers now, not until she knew who was on the take. And without her phone, she couldn't contact the FBI and alert them.

"I saw Ann hit you. I'm sorry."

"Where'd you get the gun?"

"I found it."

Lucy was skeptical. "You just found it. Lying around."

"I found it here." He looked over at the grave again, then quickly looked away.

The gun was evidence. Lucy needed to convince Micah to trust her—and give her the gun.

"We need to get you to safety, and I have friends—not rangers—who can help."

He shook his head. "They're going. They're going to leave and we'll never find them."

"Micah, listen to me."

"No! It's not just me, there's Tommy, and I'm not going to leave him."

"Who's Tommy?"

"My brother." His voice cracked. "He's six. I should never have left him, but I got scared. I went back and he was in Cynthia's trailer, but Cynthia saw me and I ran. But I can't leave him." He straightened his spine. Lucy knew if she said he had to go, he'd run from her.

"And that's why you haven't left." This brave nine-year-old was trying to protect his little brother.

"I don't know." He shrugged his skinny shoulders. "I don't know what to do."

Lucy did, but what she should do and what she knew she was going to do were completely different.

"Micah, I need you to give me the gun."

He shook his head.

"Have you ever fired a gun before?"

"Yeah." He didn't say it with conviction.

"I scored 98 on my last firearms test with the FBI. The only two guys who beat me had been in the Marines. They scored 100. I hit what I aim at."

He didn't want to give up his weapon, what he probably thought was his only protection. But he walked toward her, trust in his eyes, and handed it to her.

She took it and sighed in relief. Definitely a .22. The serial number had been filed off. She checked the magazine—the clip was missing two bullets. But a .22 wasn't much protection unless you were close or an exceptional shot. She put the gun in the small of her back and said, "Thank you."

"What are you going to do?"

"We're going to find my boyfriend, Sean. Ann and Jeff told us they were your parents, and you'd run off this morning."

He frowned. "I've been hiding from them for three days."

Lucy was surprised. "How?"

"I made a camp near here. They found it last night, but I hid."

"You've been out here alone for three days?"

He nodded. "I don't have anywhere to go. Yesterday morning, really early, I went back to the trailers to get Tommy and that's when Cynthia saw me. I think that's how they tracked me back to my camp."

Lucy knelt in front of the boy and put her hands on his shoulders. "Micah, you're not alone anymore. Stick with me, okay?"

"You're not going to let them take Tommy, are you?"

"We need to get help."

"I saw what Ann did to you. They're going to disappear, and, and . . ." He was at a loss, not knowing how to express himself, just knowing that if Ann and the others left the woods, there would be no justice for his mother, and his little brother would be in constant danger.

"We'll find Tommy and make sure that Ann and everyone else is punished for what they did."

He smiled for the first time. A tentative smile.

"I don't have a dad, and Tommy's dad is in jail. He's all I got, and I promised my mom I would always take care of him. I gotta keep the promise, Lucy."

CHAPTER 5

There had been complete silence for thirty minutes and Sean thought he was going to go out of his mind. He could no longer wait for Lucy; he was borderline frantic, and this kind of fear would lead him into making mistakes.

Lucy is fine, she knows how to watch out for herself.

The mantra wasn't working. He'd already searched the immediate area twice and found no sign of Jeff, other than fresh tracks leading away from the lake. He wanted to follow them but the first thing was to find Lucy.

"We should never have gone camping," he mumbled. It was like their relationship was cursed—they couldn't just go away and enjoy each other. Alone. Without something happening like this.

Next time, I'm sending Patrick on a vacation and keeping Lucy at home.

Sean had to make sure there was a next time.

He closed his backpack in the tent, taking his knife, cell phone, jacket, two energy bars, and two water bottles. He needed to hike unencumbered. If he reached his car before he found Lucy, and there was no sign she'd been there—well, he'd cross that bridge then. She had the keys, but he could hot-wire it. He almost laughed. It was a computerized engine, so the term "hot-wire" was so outdated. But he could get the car running without the key if necessary. He wasn't going to leave Lucy in the woods. He had his phone; he'd call in the cavalry.

He started walking at a good pace, retracing the path Lucy and Ann had taken. It was nearly four in the afternoon; he had two hours of daylight left, though already the quality of light was changing. He scanned the area, following their tracks while also looking for any other tracks to suggest they'd been followed or paralleled.

A slight movement ahead and to his right caught Sean's eye. He pulled his knife, keeping it at his side but ready to use.

Nothing.

Then a whisper. A slight rustle of leaves.

Sean hid behind an old oak that just barely blocked his frame. He peered around the side. A stick broke. Another rustle. A voice. Female.

Lucy came into view a moment later, and she wasn't alone. She had found Micah.

Sean stepped out of hiding. "Lucy."

Relief relaxed her face and she took Micah's hand and walked over to Sean.

"Micah?" Sean asked, though he knew it was.

"Yes. He found me." She hugged Sean tightly. She was shaking, just a little.

"What happened?"

Lucy stepped back and Sean saw her wrists were red and raw. He held up her arm. "What's this?"

"Ann was trying to get me to go another way, and I should have known there must be some reason why. We came across an old cemetery. Except"—she hesitated, barely glancing at Micah—"there was a fresh grave. Micah said Ann is one of a group of people who killed his mom and buried her there. They are living in trailers;

I don't know how far but Micah said it's an hour walk from the trailers to the lake."

"Trailers? How did they get them out here? There are no roads."

Micah was standing close to Lucy, his hand clenched tightly around hers. Sean softened his voice. "Do you know how, Micah?"

"We came from the other way. It's a service road, like for fires. It's locked, but the ranger let us in. He's one of them, too."

"Why?" Sean glanced around, worried about Ann's whereabouts and concerned that they were stuck in the middle of nowhere with no backup.

"They're cooking meth," Lucy said. "Micah's mother was living with Jeff. She tried to leave for some reason; they took her to the woods and killed her."

"Because she started using the product when she wasn't supposed to," Micah said in a matter-of-fact tone that belied his age, but also suggested that he was repeating something that he'd heard.

"Ann took all my stuff. And your gun. I'm sorry."

Sean hugged her again. "Don't apologize. I'm just glad you're okay."

Micah said, "Ann hit her on the head. I didn't think she'd wake up."

Sean squatted and looked Micah in the eye. "But you stayed and looked out for her. Thank you for that."

"She got out of the zip ties all by herself," Micah said, obviously impressed. "Broke them, just like that." He grinned. "She's really strong."

"In every way," Sean said.

"It's not strength," Lucy said, "you simply—"

Sean kissed her and she stopped talking. "You can teach the kid your trick later. For now let's get to my car and call the FBI."

"But you promised—," Micah began.

Lucy put her hand on Micah's shoulder. "Sean, they're packing up to leave. They have a ranger in their back pocket, involved with the drug network, and they know we're out here and we have contacts. I slipped up—I told Ann I was in the FBI when I was trying to get her to trust me." She laughed humorlessly. "As soon as Ann and Jeff get back to the trailers, they're going to leave. Micah has a little brother, Tommy. He's only six, we have to find him. Micah says that they use their cell phones at the trailers, so if we go that way we'll be able to call in help, and find a way to stop or delay them."

Sean wanted to help the kids, but they had no gun, one phone, and Ann and Jeff knew exactly where they were camped.

"Lucy, think about this—"

"I have." She tilted her chin up and Sean knew then that she would not back down. And could he blame her? There was an innocent kid at risk and a killer on the loose, and justice demanded action. It's why he loved her, and why he feared for her.

She handed him a .22. "Micah thinks that this is the gun they used to kill his mother. He found it near her grave. The magazine is missing two bullets."

Sean checked the weapon and handed it back to Lucy. "Keep it."

She sighed, obviously wanting to argue with him, but she didn't. "We need a plan."

"We'll go to the campsite and pack up," Sean said.

"What about Jeff and Ann?"

"While I was searching, Jeff grabbed his things and left. I know which way he went; we can follow the trail."

"I know a faster way," Micah said.

"He's been out here, alone, for three days," Lucy said. She had her arm over his shoulders.

"We still need to pack up—I don't know how long we'll be out here, and if we have to hunker down at night, we'll need our sleeping bags. But in case Jeff comes back, I don't want you anywhere near the site."

"We'll stay hidden," Lucy said.

Sean handed each of them a water bottle and energy bar. They ate while walking back to the campsite. Sean found a good hiding place a hundred yards into the woods where Lucy could easily see anyone approaching, but with a natural tree barrier to protect them from being seen. Then he went to pack up. He hid the tent, not wanting to be encumbered by the weight, but the sleeping bags were essential. Lucy's backpack was gone, and in it all her clothes. All she had was the sweatshirt tied around her waist. And the boy needed something more than the thin hoodie he was wearing.

Sean wasn't confident that they were making the right decision, but he understood why Lucy felt they didn't have much of a choice. A six-year-old was in danger, and if Ann and Jeff really planned to disappear, they didn't have much time to save him.

Micah said he knew a faster route to the trailers than either following Jeff's footsteps or the ATV tracks, but Sean was skeptical. Lucy said to Micah, "Can you give us one minute?"

The boy looked from her to Sean. The sadness and determination in his eyes broke Lucy's heart. No child should have to go through what he did. To be forced to grow up so fast.

He shrugged. "Okay." He walked thirty feet away and sat at the base of a tree. Lucy kept one eye on him while she spoke quietly to Sean.

"He's been hiding from the people who killed his mother for three days. He's *nine years old*. But he's a survivor. If we don't find the trailers right now, his brother will be gone. Tommy is all he has left."

"Lucy—why do I feel roles are reversed? You're usually the one demanding we call in the authorities. What's changed?" Sean glanced at Micah.

"Nothing's changed. This is a completely different situation. And of course we need to call, but if Micah is right and one of the rangers is helping them, we can't put out a blanket call for help until we get Tommy out of danger. We've got to find a way to delay them. But first, we get Tommy and Micah to safety."

"How many people are we dealing with?"

"Three men, two women. Jeff, Ann, Cynthia, and two guys Micah called their muscle. There are two ATVs at the camp. I need to see the layout but I think I have a plan."

"You want to rescue Tommy and steal the ATVs."

"That's about right."

Sean was thinking, and Lucy pushed. "Daylight is fading fast. We don't have time. Our car is in the opposite direction of the drug camp. Micah knows where he's going, Sean."

"It's not that I don't want to do it, but five against two with two kids in the middle?"

"They don't know we have Micah, and they don't know we're going after Tommy."

He took her hand and squeezed. "We'll go his way. But Luce—tell me you're on your game here."

She frowned and tensed. "I don't know what you mean."

"You're attached to him."

"I really don't know what you're talking about."

"Let's just say you bonded quickly with Micah. Don't be reckless, Luce."

"I'm not." Lucy didn't know what Sean was getting at,

but she definitely wasn't planning on doing anything stupid. "We're a team, you and me."

Sean rubbed his eyes. "All right, let's go." He motioned for Micah. "You're leading, kid. How long?"

He shrugged. "Less than an hour?"

"We have about an hour of light yet, and I don't want to have to bring out the flashlights. That might give us away. This only works if we can sneak up on them."

Micah nodded. "I can move fast."

"You're on."

They followed Micah in silence. The kid kept a good pace, and though both Sean and Lucy were athletic, they were doing their best to keep up over the uneven terrain.

Lucy realized why Jeff and Ann had chosen another way to their camp. They were maneuvering through dense trees and foliage. It was darker and colder in the woods and difficult to get a sense of direction since they couldn't see the sky except in brief glimpses through the treetops. A good place to escape, and to hide.

Sean was getting frustrated, however. Lucy could feel the tension in his body. He was worried about all of them, and not knowing what they would be facing, not having more information, and not having the ability to communicate was probably worse for him than for her.

He said, "How much farther?" It was nearly dark and Micah was barely visible ten feet in front of them.

Micah turned and put a finger to his lips.

Lucy listened. She heard a distant metal door slamming. A truck, maybe. A voice, but it was too far away to make out what it was saying.

He motioned for them to walk carefully. Fifty feet ahead, the ground nearly gave way to a sheer drop of three stories. In front of them was a wide, sloped clearing, a valley almost completely surrounded by a ring of trees. Some of the trees appeared charred. The ground looked too green and fresh. It was brighter here, as the setting sun cast the entire valley in colors. But the light wouldn't last long.

Three trailers were lined up twenty feet apart. She could only see two pickup trucks, each with an ATV in the bed. They would only be able to haul two trailers away, either because they planned to come back, or they didn't care that they abandoned the others.

A trailer with a metal attachment extending the entrance was distinctly separate from the group. The meth lab? Probably. That's where three men were talking. One was Jeff. Two went inside and Jeff walked across the clearing to the living quarters.

Lucy said, "We have to be careful there—the chemicals are extremely dangerous."

Sean turned on his phone. "No signal."

Micah pointed south. "Walk along this ledge. Ann used to go to the rock grouping down there to call people. Phones work in the valley, but they drop off all the time. The rock is higher. But you might be seen."

"Text messages can often get through as long as there is a minimal signal," Sean said. He handed his phone to Lucy. "You know who to call."

"I'm not going to leave you."

"We agreed—we need backup. We're going to sit here and keep an eye on the place. If they look like they're moving out, we'll change the plan. For now, we watch and wait."

Lucy agreed. "I'll be back as soon as I get through to someone."

Micah looked worried. "What if they see you? Ann is real mean."

Lucy rubbed the bump on the back of her head. "I know. But it's nearly dark, I'll be careful. You, too."

Sean watched Lucy weave through the trees to avoid

being seen by anyone below. He motioned for Micah to step back a bit and dropped his backpack behind a fallen tree. "We'll stay here for now."

"Is she going to be okay?"

I hope. "She's good. She won't be seen."

"I don't want Ann to hurt her again."

Sean glanced at him. "You saw what happened?"

He nodded, his eyes wide. "I thought she was dead. Ann hit her, then tied her up and took her stuff and left."

Sean wanted to deck that bitch.

A vehicle was approaching; it sounded like a truck. Micah moved forward, but Sean held him back. "Stay."

Staying low to the ground, he ventured toward the edge of the cliff. It was quickly getting dark, and all he saw were the headlights of a truck. Then it turned and Sean noted a seal on the door and emergency lights on the roof. U.S. Forest Service most likely. The corrupt ranger. There were loud voices, shouting, but Sean couldn't make out what was being said.

He pulled out his binoculars and looked at the scene. Ann and the ranger were arguing about something. It appeared that Ann won because the ranger looked pissed and stormed off into the meth trailer. Two men came out when the ranger went in and walked over to Ann. Damn, Sean wished he could read lips.

He looked around the camp. He hadn't seen any sign of Micah's little brother. But he spotted two dirt bikes, one small, one larger, next to the trailer closest to the cliff.

He went back to Micah. "Is your trailer the one closest to us? With the bikes?"

"Yes," Micah whispered. "Did you see Tommy?"

Sean shook his head. "You said Tommy's father is in jail?"

"That's what Mom said. They never got married. He was this guy my mom was seeing for a while. He left when she got pregnant. Just like my dad left." He frowned. "She said they didn't want kids, but she loved us enough for two parents. She always said that."

"Then believe it."

He shrugged. "We wouldn't be here if she hadn't brought us."

"She was under a lot of pressure." Sean didn't know what else to say to Micah. Lucy would know exactly the right words to make the kid feel okay about his mom and himself. Sean agreed with the kid: what mother would bring her young kids into the middle of this? But it couldn't have been easy for her, a recovering drug addict raising two boys.

Sean glanced at his watch. Lucy had only been gone ten minutes. It felt much longer.

"I hate drugs," Micah said.

"So do I." Sean glanced at him. Now that the sun had gone down, the temperature had dropped substantially. He pulled out his extra sweatshirt and handed it to Micah. Micah put it on. It went to his knees. Sean rolled up the sleeves for him. "My oldest sister, Molly, overdosed on drugs. I was little, younger than your brother, when it happened. I barely remember her, but my parents were so sad and angry and they blamed themselves." He paused. Like Justin's murder had forever changed the Kincaid family, Molly's overdose had a similar effect on the Rogans. "You've been strong for three days, Micah. I admire that. Your brother's going to need you."

Micah didn't say anything for a minute. Then, "Do you hate your sister?"

"Of course not. She didn't want to die. Drugs are addictive, they destroy people. She didn't know how to stop. Even with all the help my parents gave her, she couldn't seem to get out of the cycle. Sometimes—well, I was really small, but my parents were sad, and my brothers were sad and angry. I think they were mad at her but they also loved and missed her."

Sean motioned for Micah to stay hidden. "I'm going to check out what's happening. I don't hear anything."

He crawled over to the edge and looked down at the camp. The lights were on in all the trailers. He made out shadows and silhouettes but it was hard to discern how many people. Boxes were being taken out of the meth trailer and carried across the open space to the trailer on the far side. The ranger was still there, but Sean couldn't see him. Or Ann.

He crawled back to Micah. "They're definitely moving out," he said.

"Did you see Tommy?"

"No."

"We have to get him!" Micah's voice cracked.

"Shh, I know. I'm working on a plan."

"What?"

"I'm thinking." He had no idea how to get the kid. He didn't know if someone was in the trailer with him, or if he was even in the trailer Micah identified. Sean needed to get closer, but he wasn't going to leave Micah alone. When Lucy returned, he would find a way down to the camp. He didn't know how long it would take for them to pack up, but they didn't seem in too much of a rush. He suspected a few hours, then they'd leave. They might even wait until dawn.

"Ten more minutes," Sean said.

He heard the slide of a gun and a round being chambered. "You don't have ten minutes, Sean Rogan," Ann said behind him.

He kept his hands in sight and slowly turned around.

Micah leaned against Sean, shaking.

"Thank you for finding him. He's been nothing but a fucking pain in my ass."

"Don't. Touch. Him."

She laughed. "You should be more worried about yourself. I don't kill kids."

"Where's Lucy?" Sean raised his voice, hoping Lucy could hear and would stay away.

"She'll be fine. It'll take her a while to get out of the woods at night, but she'll make it. By the time she gets to the road, we'll be long gone." She stepped forward. "I'm not cruel. Micah, where did you hide my book?"

Sean frowned. "What book?"

"He didn't tell you he stole it from me. It has everything I need for my business."

Micah's voice cracked. "You killed my mom."

"The book, Micah."

"No!"

"I said I don't kill kids. But him?" She turned the gun on Sean. "My book, Micah. I'll count to three. One."

That's why she was looking for Micah—not because he'd run away, but because he'd taken something from her.

"Don't say anything," Sean said. "That book is what's keeping you alive, kid."

"I'll take you to it," Micah said.

"Just tell me where."

"I buried it. You won't be able to find it at night, but I can."

Ann motioned to the two guys behind her. "Take Rogan to the camp and secure him. I'll go with the kid."

"I swear if you hurt him—"

"You're not in a position to make threats," Ann told Sean. "I'm not going to hurt him. He knows these woods better than anyone, it appears. He'll find his way out soon enough."

"Where's Tommy?" Micah demanded, his voice cracking but holding his chin up.

"Don't worry about Tommy. If you take me to my book, I'll take you to Tommy. Deal?"

Micah nodded.

The two guys grabbed Rogan and zip-tied his wrists together, then led him along the edge of the cliff until it started to descend into the camp.

Sean looked over his shoulder and saw Ann, gun in hand, following Micah into the woods.

CHAPTER 6

Special Agent Noah Armstrong, Lucy's former training agent and a friend, wasn't answering his cell phone or his home phone. She sent him a text message, telling him it was urgent she talk to him immediately, then she called her sister-in-law Kate Donovan. Kate taught cybercrime at Quantico and was married to Lucy's brother Dillon.

"Kate, it's Lucy."

"Aren't you camping?"

"I need to reach Noah."

"I can barely hear you—are you whispering?"

"Yes. Long story, no time to explain. Sean and I found a meth lab."

"In the woods," Kate said flatly.

"There are two kids in jeopardy, a nine-year-old boy named Micah Sanders and his brother, Thomas." Lucy had gotten as much information from Micah as she could while they were walking to meet Sean. "Their mother's dead. There are three men and two women involved in the lab, and at least one forest ranger."

"Where are you?"

"Sean told Patrick where we were going, and I have

Sean's phone. I unlocked Sean's GPS signal and Patrick should be able to track it. We're on the eastern side of the Shenandoah National Park. There was a fire in the area a couple years ago; the meth lab is in a valley created by the fire. There's no obvious road going in and out that I can see, but there are three small trailers, two trucks, and a large trailer that appears to be where they're producing the drugs. They're packing up now."

"I'll call DEA. I have a friend who I trust. Just stay out of sight."

"We can't. One of the boys, Micah, is with Sean. His little brother is in danger. We need to get him out. He's a potential hostage."

"Lucy—"

"They killed his mother, Kate." Lucy lowered her voice. "I don't have time to argue. Tell your contact, and Noah when you reach him, that they are armed and dangerous. The meth lab is fully functional."

"I got it. I'll call Patrick for your coordinates, but even if there's a team in the area, it's going to take an hour or more to get to that location."

"We'll try to delay them."

"Don't do anything stupid!"

Lucy heard voices on the cliff—that couldn't be good. "I have to go."

"Lucy—"

She hung up and pocketed the phone. She hoped Patrick could pinpoint their GPS and Kate had the right contacts to get DEA or FBI out here as soon as possible. Because right now she feared that little Tommy was in the middle of the danger zone.

The best of all possible worlds would be to get Tommy from the camp and disappear into the woods until the cavalry arrived.

Voices again. Lucy scurried into the woods, stepping

lightly, keeping within the shadows of the trees, grateful she was wearing all black.

"Where's Tommy?" she heard Micah say loud and clear.

Lucy stopped. A female voice responded, but she couldn't make out what she was saying.

Ann?

Flashlights reflected an area about twenty yards in front of her and to the right. She stayed behind a tree and watched. In the circle she saw Ann holding a gun walking with Micah, then quickly lost sight of them. Remaining in the circle was a restrained Sean—and two armed men. They started walking toward her, then turned down the slope to her right.

How could she make this choice? Follow Sean or Micah? The man she loved or an innocent little boy?

They hadn't killed Sean, so it was likely that they wanted to keep him alive as a hostage or to interrogate him. Ann didn't know she had escaped her binds; Sean wouldn't have let it slip, and Lucy hoped Micah hadn't, either.

She didn't have time to ponder. She waited until Sean and the men passed by her hiding spot, then she pursued Ann and Micah.

Please, Lord, look after Sean.

She wasn't going to wait to act. She pulled the gun Micah had given her and followed Ann's flashlight through the trees. She was gaining ground.

She tripped once and bit her tongue to keep from crying out when her knee hit a rock. It took her a moment to get up and shake off the pain. She thought she'd lost them and scanned the area, looking for a light, listening for voices. They had stopped. She quietly drew closer.

Micah was kneeling on the ground, practically hidden within Sean's MIT sweatshirt, and Ann was closely watching him. What were they doing? At first Lucy thought that

Ann was going to execute the kid, shoot him in the back of the head, then she saw that Micah was digging in the ground.

She got as close as she dared, shielded only by the cover of darkness.

"You've got balls, kid, but I don't like games. That book is my life, and that means you screwed with my life."

There was an underlying hostility and superiority in Ann's tone. She'd already killed at least one person—Micah's mother—and had internally justified murdering a child. Lucy would stake her reputation—and her life—on it.

She pulled her gun, but kept it just behind her thigh, her index finger on the trigger guard. Shooting from the hip was primarily for closed quarters, and Lucy would feel more comfortable with ten feet between them rather than the twenty feet there were now. If Ann saw the gun, she'd immediately take Micah as a hostage. Or shoot Lucy without conversation. Lucy would try first to talk but she suspected Ann was in a panic. She probably had promised her product to someone who would kill if she didn't deliver, and that threat would put anyone in a dangerous mind-set.

Lucy circled as Micah dug in the dirt. He was quietly crying, but trying to stop. Lucy wanted him to see her, to know that she was there and would protect him. But how could she warn him without Ann spotting her first?

"Here," Micah said.

He held up a plastic bag with a black ledger inside.

Ann smiled. "Was that so hard, Micah?"

"Why did you kill my mom?"

"She was a liability, kid. And so are you." Ann pointed the gun at Micah's head.

Lucy stepped out of her hiding place and said, "Ann!"

Ann whirled around and aimed the gun at Lucy. "You fucking bitch," she said. "If you'd just stayed put, you probably would have lived."

"Let Micah go."

"Of course. I don't kill kids." Ann's snide tone said she was lying.

"Then let Micah walk away."

"No."

"Micah, run."

Ann turned the gun on Micah. "Don't move."

"You said you don't kill kids," Lucy said, delaying.

"There's a first for everything. Do you know what a big fucking headache he's given me for three days? And then you and your boyfriend waltz in, and I have to shut down my operation two weeks early? You cost me a hundred thousand dollars. Then you tell me you're a fucking fed."

"I've already called my partner. The FBI and DEA are on their way. It would be better to give up now, without anyone else getting hurt." Lucy focused on Ann's eyes and hands, trying to interpret Ann's next move.

Ann's arm went up and her eyes went to Lucy's chest.

Lucy fired her gun three times from the hip in rapid succession.

Ann got off a shot. The bullet whizzed by Lucy's left arm.

Ann fell to her knees. She fired again, but her hand was shaking and the bullet went into the ground.

Lucy ran over and easily disarmed her. She picked up the ledger that Ann had dropped when she fell and handed it to Micah. "Get behind me," she told him.

He was shaking, but did what she'd told him.

Lucy knelt next to Ann and searched her for additional weapons. She didn't have any. Ann couldn't talk. Though she was wearing a thick jacket, Lucy saw that all three bullets had hit her in the chest. She tore open the jacket to see if she could apply pressure. There was a tremendous amount of blood. Micah had the flashlight aimed at them, his whole body shaking. Ann grabbed Lucy's wrist, tightly at first, then lost strength and went limp.

She was dead in less than a minute.

Lucy turned her head away and closed her eyes. She hadn't wanted to kill her . . . could she honestly tell herself that? Had she simply wounded her, Ann would have shot Lucy—or worse, Micah. Her training had taken over and she'd gone for center mass. Three bullets to the chest, two center and one above the sternum, all hitting where Lucy aimed.

"Is . . . is she d-dead?"

"Yes." Lucy's voice was sharper than she intended. This wasn't the first time she'd killed someone to save herself or someone else, but the same surge of doubt and regret washed over her. Her mind instantly went to all the other possibilities. What she should have said or done. If she could have talked Ann down. If she should have waited longer before showing herself. But every way she sliced it, she couldn't see it going any other way. The loss of a human life, any human life, hurt Lucy deep inside, in a place she couldn't see or touch, but it itched. As if with each death, no matter how justified, a piece of her soul darkened.

"L-Lucy?" Micah touched her shoulder.

She let out a deep breath she hadn't realized she'd been holding, then turned to the boy and hugged him. His thin arms squeezed her neck, calming her, reminding her why she had to shoot Ann.

"It's okay. What about you? You okay? You're not hurt, right?"

"I'm not hurt." He didn't let go of her, his little body shaking uncontrollably.

Momentarily, she said, "We have to find Sean."

"They t-took him to the trailer."

"I know."

He stepped back and frowned at her, his brows furrowed. "Why didn't you help him?"

"Because you were in danger. But," she added quickly so the boy wouldn't feel any unwarranted guilt, "we're going to get him now. I have a plan. I don't know if it's going to work, but the FBI is on their way. I don't know when they'll get here, but we need to get Tommy to safety. That's our goal. Can you be brave?" There were a lot of unknown variables, but she didn't see another alternative.

His eyes flitted toward Ann. Lucy turned his face so he looked directly into Lucy's eyes. "Micah, I need you to do exactly what I say. Okay?"

He nodded.

"First, rebury the book. We need to keep it safe for the authorities. And then we'll rescue Sean and Tommy."

CHAPTER 7

Five distant gun shots echoed from the top of the cliffs. Sean's heart raced and his gut tightened.

Lucy. Micah.

He'd caught Lucy in his peripheral vision when he was being taken down to the camp, and he knew she'd go after Micah. He was an innocent kid and Ann was a major player in the drug wars. This setup proved it—this was no small mom-and-pop home lab, this was state of the art, as much so as any cartel would set up in a secure location.

Sean had to focus on his own predicament as well as finding Tommy. Five shots. Lucy must have gotten off at least one. She was an excellent shot—better than Sean—she wouldn't miss.

But his adrenaline was pumping, the blood rushing through his head, and he involuntarily jerked against his restraints.

"Take it easy, buddy." One of his captors—Jim, his partner had called him—checked Sean's restraints.

"Your boss said she wouldn't hurt the kid," Sean said.

Jim didn't look happy but he said, "We don't know what's going on. Ann's in charge. She knows what she's doing.

And that kid stole something that we need, or we'll all be dead. She probably fired in warning."

"Five times?"

Jim seemed to want to convince himself of that because he nodded emphatically and continued to pack up crystal meth into one-pound bags. There was well over a million dollars in product here. Probably more—Sean didn't know much about the meth trade. His brothers knew far more, and would probably know exactly how this operation worked and how much money was at stake.

Jeff walked in and glared at Sean. "Bastard." To Jim, he said, "Carl is getting antsy. We have to pack up now."

"What d'ya think I'm doing?"

"How long?"

"One hour, tops. But we'll have to leave the equipment behind."

"Forget the fucking equipment, we're blowing the trailer. Don't want to leave behind any prints." He stared at Sean. "Or witnesses."

"You're going to kill Micah and Tommy, too?" Sean said. "You had me fooled. I thought you actually cared about them."

Jeff punched Sean in the jaw. Blood filled his mouth. He spit it out. Damn, that hurt. Jeff shook out his hand.

"If it weren't for you, everything would have been fine. Micah would have come back. I would have explained what happened, he would have understood!"

"That you killed his mom?"

"I didn't kill Vicky! She OD'd."

Sean wasn't sure what had happened to Micah's mother, but Micah was certain that Ann had killed her. "So you just buried her in the middle of the woods and thought that her son would be okay with that?"

Jim said, "Jeff, take this box, it's ready. If you send Paul and Cynthia to help, we might get out of here faster."

"Cynthia is watching Tommy."

"I told you Vicky was bad news. A drug addict with kids."

"She was clean."

Jim snorted. "Not for long. If you weren't Ann's brother, she'd never have let you bring her."

"Shut the fuck up and do your job." Jeff ran his hands through his hair. "I'll send Paul in." He glared at Sean, then left the trailer.

"He didn't take the box," Jim mumbled. "Jerk."

Sean looked around and assessed the trailer. They'd shut down production, but they still had a lot of chemicals that were not only dangerous to inhale, they were highly combustible. The production line had been functional. The trailer had been gutted and divided in half, with one room—which Sean could only see through the open door—used for cooking the meth, and the other for filtering and packaging. They had a station to make individual doses but that was empty—it appeared that they were in the process of making doses when Ann decided to pack up. They'd have been out of here in a week or two no matter what.

Sean had thought most of the meth superlabs were in Mexico since the US had a tight control on pseudoephedrine. But it looked like Ann had gotten her hands on the raw materials. How? Through Mexico? A local pharmaceutical company? The DEA would have a field day with this lab, and shutting it down would definitely put a crimp in the supply chain.

They'd already distributed some of their product. Why keep it around if they had a great production system? Then they could shut down in winter and pop up back here or another backcountry hideout next spring.

Paul came into the trailer. Jim said, "Take those boxes to the truck. I want to be ready to go when Ann gets back with the book."

"I gotta talk to you." He glanced at Sean. "Outside."

"He can't do anything to us."

"Just come."

Jim swore and left with Paul. This wasn't good. They'd taken his wallet. The ranger probably ran his ID. They'd know he was a licensed private investigator. They'd assume he was up here on the job, and if they did the bare minimum of homework, they could easily find out about Rogan-Caruso-Kincaid Protective Services. RCK handled personal and cyber security—Sean and his brother Duke focused on the cyber end. The furthest thing from hunting down meth labs as there was, but they wouldn't know that.

How much time had passed since Lucy made the call to the FBI? Thirty, forty minutes? And Sean had no idea if she'd even gotten through, or how long it would take to mobilize a team. The lab was in the middle of nowhere, so even the closest FBI regional office was more than an hour drive. It would take time to mobilize a SWAT team. Would they be here in an hour? Two? Come in quiet or in helicopters? Sean hoped quiet.

They were on their own, at least for now. Sean had to get Tommy out of harm's way, then track down Micah and Lucy.

First he had to get out of his restraints.

They'd used zip ties on his wrists, which would be easy to break if he had any maneuverability—unfortunately, they'd also tied each of his ankles to the chair.

He looked around. Lots of corners. The closest to him that might work to sever the restraints was only a foot to his right, but he would have to turn his chair around to put his back to it, then twist in order to saw off the zip tie.

He jumped in the chair and turned it a quarter-turn. Did it again and it was almost in position.

The door opened and the ranger came in. Carl. His name plate read "C. Nelson."

"Sean Rogan, private investigator. Who hired you?"

"I was up here on a camping trip with my girlfriend. I already told Jeff that. And Ann. And I think I discussed it with Jim and Paul when they were tying me up."

The ranger backhanded him, then repeated, "Who hired you?"

Sean didn't answer. Carl Nelson was an ass, and it was clear to Sean that he wasn't just a bribed official—he was either in charge, or working closely with Ann. The others were hired help or, in Jeff's case, family. Carl was a leader.

Sean would fare better outside. If they moved him, they would have to untie his ankles. He'd have to time it right.

Or they might just shoot him here and burn the trailer.

Jim stepped in and whispered something to Carl. All Sean heard was "radio," and Carl scowled.

"Pack everything up, you have fifteen minutes and we're leaving the rest. I don't know what the hell's going on, but if Ann doesn't find that book she'd better not fucking come back because I'll shoot her myself. Where's my brother? I need to talk to him."

Brother?

The two men left, but Paul and Jim both returned with boxes for the crystal meth. They were loading the material up fast.

If Paul and Jim were here packing up, that meant Jeff was Carl's brother. Jeff, Ann, and Carl Nelson. Family operation. Which was why Jeff was able to bring in Vicky and her kids.

Sean wanted to believe Jeff wouldn't hurt the boys but he couldn't be certain of that, and Jeff might not have a choice. Carl was angry about something. It gave Sean hope that Lucy had overpowered Ann.

Except they hadn't said anything about Lucy. They hadn't asked Sean about her. That meant they didn't know she was here, and assumed she was still tied up in the woods where Ann left her.

Dammit, he didn't know what was going on, and without being able to communicate with Lucy or know where she was or what the gunshots were, Sean was going in blind.

There was a lot of commotion outside. The trucks had been started, there was the clang of metal on metal. Hooking up the trailers? It would slow them down. Sean heard an ATV roar into life, then fade off into the distance.

Someone was looking for Ann.

One less person. Great, one against four instead of five.

Sean waited until both Jim and Paul had left with two more boxes, then he turned his chair one more time, twisted his body to the side, and used a metal corner on the trailer frame to saw off the zip ties. His wrists were raw from straining, but in less than fifteen seconds the ties broke.

The knots on the ropes around his ankles were simple, and he quickly got one off before he heard voices. He took off the second and slipped into the adjoining room just before the door opened.

"Shit, where is he?"

Sean looked around and all he saw was danger. A tank of ether, ammonia, bottles of hydrochloric acid, butane—he was sitting on a bomb. He grabbed a bottle of hydrochloric acid. Then he saw his knife on the table. He quickly pocketed it.

"Put that away!" Paul said. "You fire a gun in here and we'll all blow up." Then, "Rogan, we know you're in the lab. You couldn't have gotten out. Step out slowly. Come out now and we'll let you get some fresh air."

They'd shoot him as soon as he stepped outside. But he'd have a chance.

"I'm coming out," he said. He stepped into the doorway between the lab and the packaging room. Jim still had his gun out but it was at his side. Paul stepped forward.

"What's in your hand?" he demanded.

Sean opened his fist so he could see.

"Put that down!" Paul said through clenched teeth. "Do you want to kill all of us?"

Sean shrugged. "Catch!" He tossed the bottle at Paul, whose eyes grew wide as he tried to catch it.

Sean rushed Jim. He brought his arm up to shoot, but not fast enough. Sean decked him with one fist and disarmed him with his other hand. Paul caught the bottle, then turned to Sean, panicked. "Don't—"

Sean jumped out of the trailer. Carl was standing next to his ranger truck, barking orders to a young woman. Cynthia, most likely. Carl saw Sean and drew his gun.

Sean didn't want a gunfight. He ran behind the meth lab, hoping Carl wouldn't be stupid enough to fire his gun into it. But he didn't have much time.

He checked Jim's gun. It was a nice little 9 mm—the guy had kept his gun well maintained, but it was completely empty. Why carry an unloaded gun?

There was nowhere to go.

The cliff was to the west, open space to the east, and south was the charred remains of woods coming back from a forest fire.

There was no place to run.

He was trapped.

He looked up. He didn't have the luxury of time. Without hesitating he jumped, and his fingers caught the edge of the trailer. The rush of adrenaline from his escape helped give him the strength to pull himself up and onto the roof. He hoped the shouts and confusion below would mask the sounds as he scrambled up the side of the trailer. He lay flat on the roof and waited.

And prayed they didn't figure out where he'd gone.

CHAPTER 8

At the sound of the approaching ATV, Lucy pushed Micah flat on the ground, then covered his body with hers. As long as the driver didn't turn around, his headlights should miss them. She couldn't tell who the driver was, but the silhouette appeared male.

As soon as it passed them, she helped Micah up.

"He's going to find Ann."

"But he won't find the ledger." She'd camouflaged the hole with leaves and sticks, blending it into the surrounding area. She'd considered taking it with them, but figured it would be safer hidden. If they got captured with it, Lucy wouldn't have any leverage to keep them alive.

She looked at her phone and was surprised there was a text message from Noah. The phone had no signal, but the message had come through thirty minutes ago—while she'd been tracking Ann and Micah through the woods.

FBI SWAT + DEA team en route ETA 2015 locked on Rogan's GPS. Team leader DEA Agent Alex Johnson. Confirm to all when possible. Four male, two female suspects. Two minor hostages.

She replied to all. The message wouldn't go through until there was a signal, but it would keep trying.

Sean has been taken captive, no confirmation on location. Minor child Tommy Sanders in one of the trailers. Minor child Micah Sanders with me. Operating meth lab on south side of encampment. Ranger at camp. They're shutting down fast. One female suspect dead. Confirm four male and one female suspects, two hostages.

She looked at the time. Twenty-five minutes before SWAT arrived, and that was assuming they knew exactly where they were and could come in quietly. Sound carried in the valley, and if Ann's crew knew they were trapped, Tommy and Sean became more vulnerable. SWAT wouldn't want a gun battle because of the meth lab.

"What's wrong?" Micah asked.

"It's okay. SWAT is on their way."

"Your forehead is all squishy. You're worried."

Smart kid. "They won't be here for nearly thirty minutes. We need to get Tommy to safety so he isn't a hostage. This is where I really need you to listen to me. We're going to your trailer. If Tommy's there, I want you to take him to the boulders where I made my phone call. Stay hidden in the rocks no matter what you see or hear. Got it? I need to know you and Tommy are safe so I can focus on finding Sean."

Micah nodded. "Okay."

"I will come back for you when it's safe."

"What if . . . what if something happens?"

"Stay at the rocks. The FBI will find you there."

He hugged her spontaneously. "Be careful, Lucy."

Lucy led Micah back down the path toward the camp. They stayed as low to the ground as possible, but the closer to the camp they got the less tree coverage they had.

She lay flat on the damp ground and surveyed the area. Micah lay next to her.

The ranger and the two men who had taken Sean were rushing around, shouting, and looking worried. As she watched, one of them was loading boxes into one of the trucks while the other two had guns out and were searching the immediate area.

He got away.

That was the most plausible explanation for why they were acting so worried. Unless there were more people involved and they knew the FBI and DEA were on their way through another source.

She didn't have time to contemplate the situation, but Sean was always resourceful.

There was no sign of the woman, Cynthia, who Micah had said was probably watching Tommy in the trailer. She also didn't see Jeff anywhere. He must have been driving the ATV.

She whispered, "We're going to be exposed for several yards. Stick close to the cliff—there's enough foliage there to partly cover us. But we're heading for your trailer, okay?" Fortunately, the door was on the side away from where the men were loading the trucks.

Micah nodded.

"Stay right behind me. When I slip into the trailer, stay outside the door. If anything happens to me, hide. I'm going to send Tommy out. Take him to the boulders, just like I said."

Again, he nodded.

She waited until two of the men were inside the lab, then she and Micah scrambled down the trail, where they were the most exposed. At the base she lay down behind some scraggly bushes. Micah followed suit. No one had seen them.

Staying as low as possible, she ran behind a new growth

of sassafras that framed the edge of the clearing. The ground was rocky and she nearly twisted her ankle. But she didn't want to slow down—it was now or never. She had to rescue Tommy before SWAT arrived, otherwise he would be a hostage.

Lucy pointed to a space near the trailer for Micah to hide. She then took a deep breath and opened the trailer door.

She didn't know what to expect, or whether Cynthia had a weapon. Lucy's gun was easily accessible in her waistband, but she didn't want to draw it with a child in the room, not unless it was absolutely necessary.

Tommy was sitting at a table, coloring. A voice from the bedroom in the back of the trailer called out, "Paul, is that you?"

Lucy put her finger to her lips and Tommy frowned. She approached slowly and whispered, "Micah is outside the door."

Tommy's eyes widened. "Really?" he said loudly.

"Shh." Lucy winced.

Cynthia said, "Paul, do we really have to leave tonight? I'm not ready."

Lucy held out her hand for Tommy, who willingly took it. She led him to the door and opened it.

"Who the fuck are you?" a voice behind her said.

"Go," Lucy said to Micah who jumped out of the bushes when he saw his brother.

"Tommy! Get back here!"

Cynthia took three long strides down the middle of the trailer toward Lucy. Lucy tried to follow Tommy out, but Cynthia grabbed her hair.

"Run," Lucy ordered the boys.

"Tommy!" Cynthia shouted, pulling Lucy back into the trailer. She tried to climb over Lucy to chase after the boys, but Lucy tripped her and the woman fell forward. She grabbed at the counter to right herself, and Lucy slammed her palm on Cynthia's hand.

Lucy didn't want to get caught, but Cynthia screamed at the top of her lungs. The woman reached back and tried to scratch Lucy, but Lucy grabbed her arm and pushed it high up behind her back. "Shut up," Lucy said through clenched teeth.

Cynthia screamed again and Lucy heard shouts from outside. Lucy jumped up and bolted from the trailer as fast as she could . . .

. . . right into the arms of the forest ranger.

"Hold it, little lady."

"Let me go," Lucy said.

He glared at her. "Who are you?"

"FBI Agent Lucy Kincaid."

He laughed heartily. "Right. FBI. All by yourself. You're the girlfriend of that PI. You should have stayed in the woods; he's long gone."

What did he mean by that?

He searched her and found the gun in her waistband. He stared at the gun, obviously recognizing it. "Where did you get this?" he demanded.

She didn't respond.

Cynthia scampered out of the trailer. Her nose was bleeding.

"You bitch!" She lunged for Lucy.

The ranger tried to fend her off, but Cynthia was wild-eyed and grabbing at Lucy.

The ranger's grip on Lucy's arms slipped, and Lucy took the opportunity to knee him in the groin and slam the side of her hand on his wrist. He dropped the gun, but Lucy didn't have time to pick it up.

She whirled around and ducked to avoid being hit in the face by Cynthia. She punched her in the gut and kicked her legs out from under her.

Then she ran. The ranger had pulled out his own gun and fired at her, but she'd already turned around the corner of the trailer.

Unfortunately, there was no place to hide. She had to take advantage of the dark, but to get out of here she'd have to run through the light cast from the trucks and meth lab, or go back the way she'd come.

Neither was a viable option.

She turned between the other two trailers and rolled under the one on the end. Then she froze and hoped they didn't figure out where she was hiding.

Sean heard a woman screaming from the boys' trailer and saw Micah and a smaller boy scrambling up the cliff. Lucy wasn't with them. It took all his self-control not to jump from the roof of the trailer and run toward the screams. He heard voices, but couldn't make out what they were saying, then he saw a woman run behind the trailers.

Lucy. There wasn't a lot of light on the far side of the camp, but Sean could tell by her shape and the way she ran. She slid under the third trailer and didn't come out.

Carl the ranger ran after her, but passed her hiding space.

"Where'd she go?" he screamed to Jim and Paul, who were coming out of the lab with more boxes.

"What?" Jim said.

"The girl Ann said she tied up in the woods. She obviously did a shitty job of it. Search these trailers. Shoot on sight."

Both trucks were idling, and Sean knew he could easily steal one if he could get to it—only problem was, he had no weapon. He needed a distraction.

He considered going back into the meth lab and grabbing the butane to start a fire, but he'd have to do it far from the lab. And the risk of burning down the whole forest after their dry summer was far too risky. He could maybe make a smoke bomb, something that would just divert their attention for a minute. But getting into the trailer was going to be next to impossible.

"She's not in the trailer," Paul shouted to Carl.

"Did you search both? Idiot."

The sound of the ATV returning from the woods distracted everyone. Sean had to take the risk. He slid down the back of the meth lab and ran to the closest truck.

Jim was loading a box into the back. Sean got the drop on him, covered his mouth with one hand, and pressed firmly into a nerve on his neck with the other. He was unconscious without much of a struggle. Sean was surprised himself that the pressure point on the back of the neck worked—his brother Kane had taught him the maneuver years ago but Sean hadn't even attempted to use it in practice because of the potential deadly side effects. As Kane had said, "It's a non-lethal attack, but it can still kill your target."

Sean let Jim's body slide to the ground and determined that he was still breathing. Sean then slid into the driver's seat and closed the doors. He drove the truck over to the third trailer, then rolled down the window and said, "Lucy! It's me! Get in!"

Lucy rolled out from under the trailer and jumped into the back of the cab behind Sean. Boxes of drugs nearly filled the back of the cab and she climbed over the center console and into the passenger seat.

Carl and Paul had seen them and were now running after the truck. Carl started firing.

Sean drove fast, dirt and rocks thrown up behind him.

"We have to get the boys—they're at the rocks where I made my call," Lucy said.

"They'll wait there, right?"

"I told them to. But what if they blow the lab? They're too close—"

"We'll get them. Look what I found in the lab." He tossed his tablet in the backseat with Lucy. "Wish I'd found my gun there, too."

"The ranger got mine."

"We'll be okay." Sean glanced behind them. "They're following."

"Good," Lucy said.

"Good?"

"FBI SWAT should be here any minute."

"What's any minute mean?"

"Noah sent me a message that they'd be here by eight fifteen." She pulled out the cell phone. The face was smashed, but she could still use it. "Sorry about your phone—I think it broke when I was fighting with Cynthia. There's a signal; I'm going to try and reach Noah."

Sean glanced in the rearview mirror. "I couldn't care less about my phone, Luce." The other truck was gaining, which meant they either knew what they were doing, or were reckless, or both.

Sean stepped on the gas. The rough terrain made maneuvering at this speed difficult.

Lucy was talking loudly on the phone. "We're cutting out—they're chasing us. We're in a black truck. . . . Black. . . . I don't know. . . ." She leaned forward and looked at the dashboard. "Chevy. They're pursuing in either another black Chevy or a forest ranger truck, a Bronco."

"How long?" Sean asked. He had his high beams on but he had no idea where he was going. He couldn't see a road—he was following what he assumed was the worn path that they'd used to get in and out for supplies.

Lucy said, "They're staging—Noah's patching me through to the team leader."

"We don't have time."

A bullet shattered the window behind Lucy.

"Sean! Something's burning in the back of the truck."

Sean had seen that.

"We have to dump this and take our chances. I don't know what could explode. Get ready to jump, Lucy."

Sean had one hand on his door, and with the other, he made a sharp right turn with the wheel while braking.

"Now!"

They both jumped out and rolled away from the truck. The truck pursuing them slammed on the brakes, but the crash of metal on metal made Sean clench his jaw.

Where was Lucy? He'd jumped first. She had to have made it out. He'd seen her door open.

The fire in the truck bed was growing. Sean had no idea what was back there, could be suitcases of clothes or could be something more dangerous. The drugs were in the cab, and when those burned there would be toxic smoke.

"Lucy!"

He couldn't hear if there was anyone pursuing them.

"Over here!" Lucy was scrambling toward him. "We have to get out of here."

"When will the feds arrive?"

"They'll be staging somewhere nearby."

"Staging?" Sean understood the necessity of planning, but this was a damn emergency.

"Sean—I'm worried about the boys. Is there any way we can circle around and find them?"

"We have to get out of here before the truck explodes."

"But—"

Sean grabbed her by the shoulders. "I looked at the map while I was on the roof. We can get to them from another angle. Trust me. We can't go back the way we came."

Lucy shook her head. Of course Sean was right—and

Micah promised to stay hidden in the boulders. She hoped he listened to her. She hoped no one had followed them up the cliff trail. "I'll follow you," she said.

Sean grabbed her hand and they ran fast, away from the burning trucks. She didn't see anyone pursuing them but they could have disappeared into the night. The fire was building, casting a bright, orange light around them. At first she didn't see anyone, then she spotted a lone male running back toward the camp.

"Sean," she said, "someone is heading back to the camp."

"Good, they're not following. We're going to—"

"FBI! Put your hands behind your head, get down on your knees. Do it!"

Lucy complied immediately as three SWAT team shooters came out of the darkness and spread out in front of her. Sean hesitated.

"Sean!" she shouted.

He dropped to his knees.

She said, "I'm Lucy Kincaid, new agent at Quantico. I'm the one who called this in to my training officer, Noah Armstrong."

While one cop had his gun on them, the other two came over and handcuffed both Sean and Lucy. Lucy knew it was standard protocol, but it still terrified her. She hated being restrained, a deep fear, borne out of being held captive seven years ago. In a drill at Quantico they had to get out of a variety of restraints and she was good at it, but she always had to battle the beginnings of a panic attack first. She was grateful she wasn't in full panic mode now—she'd learned to control it only through hundreds of hours practicing.

Sean was angry but fortunately complied.

"Two young boys are in jeopardy," Lucy said. "I need to get to them."

She was thoroughly searched and her hint of panic

turned to anger. She had no ID on her; it had been in her backpack. No proof of who she was. There was precious little time.

An explosion not far from them rocked the ground. The pickup trucks.

Sean said, "The trucks were full of crystal meth."

The leader spoke into his radio as the three of them put on breathing masks. They'd been prepared, so someone had informed them of the hazard.

"Up," the other two said, and helped Lucy and Sean stand.

"I need you to take these cuffs off me," Lucy said. "The boys are in danger. If they blow the lab, the boys won't be able to get away from the smoke."

"You can talk to the agent in charge."

"DEA Agent Alex Johnson, correct?" Lucy said, remembering the name Noah had sent her. "My training agent is Noah Armstrong out of the D.C. office. He sent me a message that he was on his way and that Agent Alex Johnson was in charge of this op."

The team didn't say anything, and Lucy wasn't surprised.

Out of the dark, six SWAT team members with masks passed them, heading toward the camp. Another group of three came and escorted Lucy and Sean to a tactical van and a Hummer with a tac team loading. They had a full contingency of SWAT—both FBI and DEA.

Alex Johnson, a six-foot-tall black man who looked like he was solid muscle, had the air of a man used to being in charge. "Team Delta is getting in place. Team Alpha, on Delta's command move in."

A HazMat truck was parked and a team in HazMat suits was getting ready.

"Sir," the team leader who had captured Lucy and Sean said as he approached Johnson.

After Johnson finished giving orders, he came over. He looked at his phone and then at Lucy. "It's her. Release them. Report?"

"Micah and Tommy Sanders are hiding up on the cliff in a grouping of rocks southwest of the camp. We need to get to them quickly," Lucy said.

"Map," Johnson ordered one of his men.

"I know how to get there," Sean said.

Sean didn't sound like himself. He glared at the SWAT team that had handcuffed them. "We'll take over from here," Johnson said.

"Time is not on our side," Sean said. "If they blow their lab, the boys are in immediate danger."

"Please," Lucy said, "you need to trust us."

"This isn't about trust, this is a tactical operation." Johnson was listening to something. He said to Lucy, "Do you have confirmation that the boys are at the rocks?"

"I told them to go there."

"That's not good enough."

He said into his com, "Whereabouts of two children unknown."

"I know where they are!" Lucy said.

Johnson turned his back on them and Lucy was livid. Micah trusted her to get them out, and he would do what she'd told him. The only reason they would not be there is if they'd been captured.

"Rogan, show me the layout," Johnson said. He had a satellite map of the valley. The Nelsons had done a good job finding a location that had enough tree cover to make it difficult for air surveillance, but the map was recent and showed two trailers plus the meth lab. Sean pointed to the lab. "That's where they cooked meth—they just shut down production; the equipment and raw materials are still inside." He pointed. "This is about fifty yards, from the lab to the trailers. There are three, not two." He pointed to an empty space. "That's where the Sanders kids stayed. This trail"—he traced it—"is not as steep as it looks in the picture; it's how we came down the cliff. There's also more foliage—what is this, two months old?"

"Ten weeks."

Sean nodded. "That's in line with Micah's statement that he came here in July. Here are the rocks—that's where Lucy called Noah."

"Can you confirm four males, two females?"

"One female," Lucy said. "I shot one."

"Is she immobile?"

"She's dead." Lucy looked at the map. She estimated the location and pointed. "Micah had buried a journal of hers here. I reburied it in case of capture. I wanted the leverage. It's the only reason Micah's still alive; he stole it after they killed his mother."

Sean traced with his finger. "This looks impassable, but we can get to the rocks from here. It puts us close to the meth lab, but it's the fastest and most direct route. As long as your people know we're coming through and don't shoot at us."

"We don't randomly shoot at people," Johnson said.

"Just cuff them?"

Lucy put her hand on Sean's arm, but said to Johnson, "Sir, we need to go."

Johnson looked at the map and their location and said, "North, get vests for Kincaid and Rogan. Take them with your team to find the boys. You'd better know what you're doing. Armstrong is on his way, said you both have good instincts."

Sean raised his eyebrow. "I'll have to thank him."

"Don't know about that. He also said you both attract trouble like a magnet."

Lucy and Sean donned Kevlar vests. Sean and North led the way while Lucy stayed close behind with the other two SWAT team members, Montes and Kershaw.

The rocks were over half a mile away. They circled around and heard action at the camp, but Lucy was focused on locating the boys.

The slope was a steady incline, but soon they were at the same elevation as the boulders, and Sean motioned for them to turn north. The truck fire, though half a mile away, was still visible. The camp below was surrounded by SWAT—they'd come in at all angles.

A moment later North held up his hand. His men stopped. North scanned the area through night-vision binoculars.

But Lucy didn't need binoculars to identify the ATV parked just outside the rock cluster.

North motioned that there was one hostile suspect at their target location. Lucy's fears were realized. Jeff.

One of the boys cried out, and Jeff shouted, "Shut up!"

Sean whispered to North, "His name is Jeff Nelson. His girlfriend was the boys' mom."

North called out, "Mr. Nelson, this is the FBI. Stand down."

Silence.

Then Jeff made his demand. "I want the woman who killed my sister. Then I will let the boys go."

CHAPTER 9

North ordered the team to take a secure position. No one had a clear shot at Jeff Nelson since he was holding Micah close to him, a gun to the boy's head.

Lucy knew, intellectually, that trading herself for the boys was foolhardy. But emotionally, she wanted to. She'd promised them they'd be safe. Micah had trusted her every step of the way, never questioning her, doing exactly what she'd asked of him, all to help his little brother.

Now both of them were in danger.

North called in the report to Alex Johnson.

"Hostage situation at target location." He gave the exact coordinates.

Lucy watched Jeff closely. He was distraught and his hand was shaking. He didn't want to hurt the boys. Of that, Lucy was certain. Except that he was grieving and trapped, everything in his life falling apart. He'd had a situation that was working for him, and now his girlfriend was dead, his sister was dead, his brother was likely in custody, and he knew he wouldn't get out of this situation a free man.

Tommy was huddled on the ground next to a rock, his eyes big and terrified.

"Tell him to let Tommy go," she told North.

"You're not in charge, Kincaid," he said.

"In good faith, tell him to let Tommy go."

North said, "Mr. Nelson, I'm Lee North. I just want to talk."

"You heard what I want!"

"Let the younger boy go. I know you don't want to hurt him."

"I heard her voice—Kincaid. She killed my sister. It had to have been her."

North glanced at Lucy and she nodded.

"Let me talk to him," she said.

"No," North said. "He's unpredictable and fixated on you."

"I know what's going on with him. I can talk him down."

"It's an order, Kincaid. Or haven't they covered those at Quantico yet?"

She bit back a response. Of course he was right, and he didn't know her or what she'd done prior to joining the FBI. But she was a criminal psychologist and knew enough about Jeff Nelson and his situation to help fix this mess.

North said to Jeff, "Let Tommy go. Then we will talk."

Jeff clutched Micah and hunkered down behind a rock, out of their sight. He was saying something to the kid, but Lucy couldn't make out what it was.

"Jeff, I need to keep communication open between us. Talk to me, buddy."

Jeff didn't say anything, and Lucy shifted uncomfortably. Sean put his hand on the small of her back, sharing his strength and confidence, but it didn't help like it usually did.

North said quietly, "The hostage negotiator is coming up from the tactical truck. ETA fifteen minutes. Team Alpha has the other suspects in custody and is securing the camp." To Jeff he called out, "Jeff, your brother, Carl, and everyone else is in custody. You don't want to be the only one who ends up on a slab."

Lucy winced. That was the wrong thing to say. Ann was already dead, and Jeff knew it.

Jeff laughed. "Right. Then I have nothing to lose and nothing to gain!"

"You can gain our trust by letting Tommy go."

Lucy wished she could see Jeff and Micah. She could see part of Tommy huddled in the rocks but not his face.

North motioned for his men to fan out ten feet in either direction and said they were cleared to take a shot if they could get it.

Lucy prayed it didn't come to that. Tommy and Micah would never forget the sight of Jeff getting his head blown off.

North called, "Jeff, you there?"

"I'll send Tommy out if you send Lucy Kincaid in."

"You know I can't do that," North said. He glared at Lucy and motioned for her to stay put.

"I can do this," she whispered. She glanced at Sean. His face was hard and unreadable, but his eyes understood. He didn't want her to go, but he knew she had to.

North stepped away from them and talked into his com. Lucy couldn't hear what was being said, but he turned around a half minute later and looked her in the eye. "Are you ready for this? Tell me now if you're not up to it. That child's life is at stake."

"I know." Her heart pounded, but her mind was clear. "I'm ready."

North called out to Jeff. "Jeff? I'll let you talk to Kincaid if you send Tommy out first."

There was silence, then frantic whispering from inside the rock circle. Tommy started crying, and Micah said, "It's okay, Tommy. Go. I'll be there when I can, okay?"

His small voice was so brave and Lucy bit back a cry

of rage over what was happening to him right now. He should never have to go through something like this. No child should.

Tommy climbed over the rocks, then stopped and glanced back toward his brother. North motioned for one of his men to grab the boy. It happened fast and Tommy was being carried down off the rocks and away from the scene.

North nodded at Lucy. "You're on, Kincaid."

"Micah?" Lucy called out. "Are you okay?"

"Yes." His voice was so quiet and tentative, she almost didn't hear him. He spoke up. "I'm okay."

"I'm glad." She took a deep breath, forced her heart rate to slow down. "Jeff, Micah told me how good you were to him and Tommy. I know you don't want to hurt him."

"You killed Ann. All she wanted was that damn book."

"Jeff, you're not going to want to hear this but I'm telling you the truth. Ann was going to kill Micah. I had to protect him. Just like you've been doing ever since you came into his life." She'd pieced together things that Micah had told her and the little she'd learned about the Nelsons from listening to the communications between Alex Johnson and Lee North.

It wasn't much. Carl was the oldest, Jeff was the youngest. Their parents had been career criminals—the mother was now dead, the father's whereabouts unknown. Carl had no record, but his sister, Ann, did, and Lucy suspected she'd always taken the blame, but that Carl was the ringleader. Jeff was the only one who'd graduated from a community college and held down a regular job, but the economy hit his industry—construction—hard.

They were still piecing together addresses, financial information, and the like, but according to Johnson, Ann Nelson had been on the DEA radar for years. They'd never caught up with her but had suspected she had a large distribution network in the east.

"You were just trying to provide for Vicky and her boys, weren't you? Trying to do what their fathers never did. Micah said he never knew his dad, but you were the closest thing he had."

Jeff wasn't talking, and Lucy wasn't sure that was a good sign.

"I would never have shot Ann if Micah's life wasn't in immediate danger. But I am sorry."

"She wouldn't have hurt him."

"I didn't know her like you did. All I saw was a gun pointed at that little boy and I acted." That wasn't the entire truth. Ann had threatened Micah but she'd aimed at Lucy. Judicious lying was warranted here.

As long as Micah didn't contradict her.

"Jeff, you've been protecting Micah for the last two years. You're the only one who can protect him now."

"This was all supposed to be easy. Micah, why didn't you just give Ann the book?" Jeff's voice cracked.

"She killed my mom," Micah's little voice said. "You told Mom you loved her."

"Ann said she overdosed." A sob escaped Jeff's throat. "I wanted to protect you, Micah. God, this is all fucked up."

North moved as if to speak and Lucy put her hand up. Jeff was going to let Micah go, she was certain of it.

She prayed she was right.

"I'm so, so sorry, Micah. Don't hate me."

"I don't hate you, Dad."

Silence fell among the boulders. Lucy feared she'd been wrong, that Jeff was going to do something very bad, but then Micah scrambled over the rocks and ran right over to her. He hugged her tightly.

North and Kershaw rushed in and Jeff stood up without resisting.

"He wouldn't have hurt me," Micah said. "He was crying."

Micah was crying, too. Lucy knelt down and hugged him tightly. "You were so brave."

"Is it over? Can I go see Tommy now?"

"Yes. Tommy is waiting for you."

North and Kershaw had Jeff cuffed and on the ground. North said, "We have another team coming here to take custody of him so we can secure the rest of the area. Where's this book?"

Lucy didn't want to leave Micah. Sean said, "I'll walk back with him. You need to show them the book and the body."

"I'll take you." She said to Micah, "Stay with Sean, okay? I won't be long."

Micah said, "Will they go get my mom, too? Does she get a real grave?"

"Yes. She most certainly does."

Lucy watched Sean and Micah walk off, and she sat down to catch her breath. Not because she was tired, but from the stress.

North looked down at her and said, "You did good, Kincaid. What'd you do before the FBI?"

"A lot of things," she said. "But this is where I'm supposed to be."

CHAPTER 10

Lucy woke up in Sean's bed, light streaming through the two narrow windows. Light? What time was it?

She stretched and looked at the clock. One? *In the afternoon?*

Chip, her cat, whom Sean was caring for while she was at Quantico, meowed loudly when she got up. She scratched him behind the ears and he purred and stretched.

She rolled her neck around a couple times. Her entire body ached. Sean wasn't there so she rose slowly from the bed and went into the bathroom. She had bruises everywhere, her wrists had been taped, but nothing was broken.

Sean was sitting on the bed petting Chip after she finished brushing her teeth. "You okay?" he asked. "I heard you moving around."

"I can't believe you let me sleep in so late."

"We didn't go to bed until after dawn." He took her hand and pulled her down next to him. Chip jumped down with an annoyed meow, knowing he was no longer the center of attention.

Sean kissed her. "We have visitors downstairs."

"Who?"

"The boys."

"I thought they were in the hospital."

"They were fully checked. A little dehydrated and malnourished, but otherwise healthy. Micah insisted on seeing you. I'm lucky he's only nine, or he'd be some stiff competition for me."

She laughed and kissed him. "You have no competition, Sean." Then she frowned. "What's going to happen to them?"

"I don't know. Maybe the fed who brought them over has information."

"What fed?"

"The DEA agent from last night, Alex Johnson."

"I'm glad he's here—I have some questions for him."

"He has some for you. Noah's also here—you have to go to Quantico to face a panel on the shooting."

She leaned against his shoulder and sighed. "I thought we'd have more time together this weekend."

He held her face in his hands. "I love you, Lucy. So much."

He seemed unusually emotional. She leaned forward and kissed him lightly on the lips, then touched her forehead to his. "Following Ann and Micah was one of the toughest decisions I've ever had to make. You were only feet from my hiding place, I wanted to go to you—"

"We're partners, Lucy, in every way. You have to save the innocent first. I can take care of myself, and if they didn't shoot me on the cliff, they weren't going to shoot me in their camp."

"That's what I was thinking, but that didn't make the decision any easier." She didn't know if she could handle these life-threatening decisions. How could she choose? In the line of duty, would she have to make such a choice again? Between her partner and a victim? Between two innocent people? She didn't want to think about it, but it would haunt her.

Sean took her hand and together they went downstairs.

Micah and Tommy were playing on Sean's air-hockey table in the large family room that opened up into the kitchen and dining room. When Micah saw Lucy, he missed blocking his goal and little Tommy scored.

"Point!" Tommy said.

His eyes followed Micah's and he burst out in a grin. "Lucy!" He ran over to her and gave her a tight squeeze. "Sean has an air-hockey table! He said we could play! Do you want to play with us?"

"Of course," she said. She glanced at Agent Johnson and Noah who were sitting at the table. Both looked at her with serious expressions. "If we have time." She walked over to Micah and gave him a hug. "How are you guys doing?"

He nodded. "Alex said we have grandparents. My mom never talked about them. I thought they were dead."

He was putting on a brave front, but his voice cracked at the end and she saw how scared he was of what was happening. Though the situation he endured over the last three days was far more dangerous, it was this limbo that terrified him. Tommy, on the other hand, was bouncing around and didn't seem to be affected by any of it. At least not yet.

"Families are complicated," she said.

"They live in Florida."

Lucy smiled. "Florida is very nice. Sunny and tropical."

"Alex is taking us. I've never been on a plane before." He frowned and glared over Lucy's shoulder, then whispered, "I wanted you to take us, but he said no."

"I have to go back to my training. But you'll have my

address and you can write me and send me pictures of your new house."

"I have to come back in a couple weeks to talk to a judge about everything."

She nodded. "That's good. I'll find out when and we can have lunch or something."

"What if Alex says no again?"

"If you want it to happen, I'll make it happen. You're my friend, Micah, and I always make time for my friends." She glanced over at Tommy who was now running around the small backyard, chasing squirrels up the trees. "You're a good brother, you know that? Tommy is very lucky to have you."

He hugged her, then went outside to join his brother. Lucy watched them through the windows.

Alex cleared his throat. She sighed and sat down at the table where she could also watch the boys play. She hadn't thought much about the fact that she couldn't have children of her own—she'd had emergency surgery when she was eighteen and her uterus had been removed. It was a loss she'd dealt with, but now, watching the two dark-haired boys, she imagined what it would be like to have her own boys, to watch them grow and run and laugh. To love and protect them.

"Social services thought it best to unite the boys with their maternal grandparents as soon as possible," Alex said. "I'm flying with them to Miami tomorrow after Micah gives a preliminary statement to the judge. I'll stay overnight to make sure everything is kosher. I have an agent there who'll check on them periodically, as well as the court-appointed counselor until the guardianship is finalized. The grandparents are young—in their early fifties—and both working. Mr. Sanders is a high school science teacher and Mrs. Sanders teaches second grade. Victoria was their only daughter. She left home at eighteen and hadn't contacted her parents in nine years. They think she was pregnant with Micah by then, and they think they know who his father is. The guy never knew he had a kid, according to them."

"You learned a lot in just one morning," Lucy said.

"When young kids are involved, I think it's best to move quickly."

"Thank you."

"I wouldn't be here except Micah insisted." Alex glanced out the window and smiled. "He's a hard kid to say 'no' to. I'll make a visit happen."

"I appreciate it." She then asked, "Did you find his mother's body?"

Noah answered that. "The FBI evidence response team has been out there all night, using Sean's map, and yes, we found her body. They're exhuming it now for autopsy, then proper burial. But you were right—two bullets to her head."

"And what about the others?"

Alex spoke. "DEA is handling the investigation into the drugs and distribution. Ann Nelson has been leading this dog-and-pony show for several years. She moves each season to a new location—either in a warehouse or the open space—bribes someone, or in this case involves a family member, and produces hundreds of pounds of meth. Based on the waste found in the forest, they probably manufactured thirty pounds of meth this summer in that one trailer. It was far more advanced a setup than your average garage meth-house."

"Is that a lot?"

"A superlab, which is usually a permanent lab run by the cartels, produces about one hundred pounds annually, about twenty-five dollars a hit, a hundred thousand hits"—he did the math in his head—"so Ann's operation, which is a third of the size of a superlab, was probably putting close to a million dollars of meth on the street. Not bad for a few months of work." Alex leaned forward, almost giddy. "We think, after examining the burned-out trucks and what remained in the lab, that they had it all with them so it hadn't hit the streets yet, which is good. Jeff Nelson is going to talk. His lawyer is working out a deal with the U.S. Attorney and I think we're going get their entire network. This is hugely important because meth is relatively new on the East Coast—we haven't been dealing with the problem as long as the West Coast, but we have seen an increase in mom-and-pop labs over the last couple years. This is a major blow to their network."

"Good," Sean said.

Lucy was happy with the results but Noah looked unsettled. "Noah, what's wrong?"

"I don't know where to begin."

Noah was very angry and Lucy became confused. She didn't know what to say, why he was so deeply irritated. "I didn't plan this," she said. "It's not like Sean and I knew they were there."

Noah rubbed his face. "I don't see where you could have done anything differently than you did, but you'd better be clear and straightforward when you give your official statement."

Lucy's confusion turned to worry, like she was missing something important. She said, "Last night you said the shooting was justified."

"It was. But you're still a trainee. You're not supposed to be carrying a gun. I know it wasn't yours, but it seems every time you slip under the radar, when things are working out for you, something like this happens and you're in the spotlight again."

Sean leaned forward. "What are you getting at, Noah? Spit it out, because you sound like a jerk."

Lucy winced. Sean and Noah had never liked each

other, even though for her sake they had been trying to get along.

"Dammit," Noah muttered. "I'm not supposed to tell you this, but Paula called in the Office of Professional Responsibility to conduct the hearing tomorrow. It's not going to be a breeze—not like the hearing after what happened in New York last month. You were following orders then. This was something that happened on your own clock."

"I would do it again," Lucy said. Her stomach turned queasy and had she eaten anything today she would have been ill. "Ann Nelson would have killed those boys. She killed their mother."

"All I'm saying is, trouble finds you, Lucy. Stay on guard."

Sean was going to say something, but Lucy took his hand and squeezed it. She didn't need him to defend her. "Noah," she said softly. She looked at the boys again. They were sitting on the swing out back, rocking, and Tommy was talking a mile a minute, pointing at everything. Micah was the strong, silent type, listening to and protecting his brother. Lucy suddenly wished she could keep them both, raise them—but that was a ridiculous thought. She and Sean weren't married, she was embarking on a new career, and she was only twenty-five. She couldn't give them what they needed. Not now.

"I can't live my life constantly worried that what I do is going to jeopardize my career," Lucy said. "I have to do what's right and be confident in my decisions—otherwise I'll never be a good agent. I'm not apologizing for the choices I made yesterday, no matter what the risk was, because they were the right choices at that time. If I hadn't shot Ann, she would have killed Micah or me. And they teach us to shoot to kill, remember? I used my training appropriately. I don't feel good about it but I don't feel bad about it, either. Not when those boys now have a chance at a normal life."

Normal. Maybe Tommy. He was still very young, and while he'd remember what happened, he had his older brother to look out for him.

But Micah would never forget the three days he was alone in the woods. He'd never forget finding his mother's grave or watching Lucy shoot his mother's killer.

But it didn't matter in the end because all the things that happened to land them here were not their fault. Ann and her crew had made the choice to manufacture and sell drugs. Vicky Sanders had made the decision to bring her kids into that life. How they got out wasn't as important as the fact that they were out, and had grandparents who loved and wanted to raise them.

Noah was torn because he wanted to protect her from facing the hard questions that OPR would give her. But life was hard. Lucy wasn't going to run away or bury her head or beg for forgiveness. There was nothing to forgive.

"I understand," Noah said. He stood up. "I'll see you tomorrow morning. Chief O'Neal wants you in her office at seven to talk before the panel convenes at seven-thirty. She's given you a pass tonight. She likes you, a lot more than Paula Dean."

"I planned to be back by six tonight, I don't want any special treatment—"

Sean put his hand over her mouth. "I'll have her back at Quantico tomorrow morning."

Alex stood as well. "For what it's worth, I've already given my statement and your actions were appropriate, Agent Kincaid. You and Mr. Rogan not only saved the boys, but kept nearly a million dollars of drugs off the streets. And my SWAT team captain Lee North had similar things to say in his report. I've known Lee for six years. Praise from him is rare. You earned it." He walked out to the backyard to get the boys.

"Thanks for the heads-up, Noah," Lucy said.

"Just watch yourself tomorrow. Going up in front of OPR is never fun, even if you have the truth on your side."

After everyone left, Sean made Lucy lunch. She picked at it, and he told her, "You must be starving."

"My stomach is in knots."

"About the panel tomorrow?"

"That. And Micah. He's a brave kid. I wish—" She stopped herself. This wasn't a conversation she was ready to have.

Sean took both her hands and kissed them. "You wish you could take him home with you."

She squeezed back tears and shook her head. "I'm not ready to adopt a child. I'm just worried about him. What he's going to be living with, inside, for the rest of his life. He's brave, but he's still a nine-year-old boy."

"Micah and Tommy are going to be okay. They're going to have a real home. That's what they need. And that DEA agent, Johnson, seemed to be on top of things. I'm sure the grandparents will get Micah help if he needs it."

"You're right." She looked at their joined hands. Her future had once been so bleak she didn't know if she would ever really have one. "I guess I was just thinking that when the time is right, I want to take in kids who need a home."

"Kids like Micah and Tommy."

She nodded.

"And when the time is right, I'll be there with you. I've told you before, I'm not going anywhere. You're stuck with me." He pushed her plate in front of her. "Now eat. Then we're going to take a shower."

She raised an eyebrow. "We?"

Sean grinned. "Yes, *we*. Together. We have a free night, and we're not leaving this house. In fact, after we finish eating, we're not leaving my bedroom."

"Afraid that if we leave the house trouble will find us?"

"Afraid? No. Confident that trouble is outside that door? Hell, yes."

And keep reading for an excerpt from
Allison Brennan's exciting new series debut

NOTORIOUS

A Max Revere Novel

Available in April 2014 in hardcover
from Minotaur Books

CHAPTER 1

Going home was a bitch.

Maxine Revere had flirted with the idea of flying in solely for Kevin's funeral so her perfect and dysfunctional family wouldn't hear about her visit until she was already on a plane back to New York City. Three things stopped her.

Foremost, Max did not run away from uncomfortable situations. She recognized that she wasn't the same nineteen-year-old who'd defied her family.

She'd also get a kick from walking into the family mansion unannounced and watching a reboot of *Dallas*, set in California. The Sterling-Revere family could take on the Ewings and win without breaking a nail or going to jail. Being the blackest sheep in the herd was more fun than taking two cross-country flights in one day.

But the primary reason she was staying for the weekend was for Kevin's sister, Jodi O'Neal. Kevin had been Max's former best friend and confidant. He'd killed himself, and Jodi had questions. Max had no answers for the college coed, but she understood why Jodi sought truth where there had only been lies. Max had survived grief, she'd been a close acquaintance with death, and maybe she could give Jodi a modicum of peace.

Traveling first-class had advantages, including prompt disembarking. Max strode off the plane at San Francisco International Airport, her long legs putting distance between her and the other passengers. Her two-inch heels made her an even six feet, but her confident stride and stunning looks caused heads to turn. She ignored the attention. Her cell phone vibrated and she ignored that, too.

Her full-time assistant and as-needed bodyguard, former army ranger David Kane, easily kept up with her. He turned heads as well, mostly from fear. When he wasn't smiling, he looked like he'd kill you with no remorse or pleasure. He didn't smile often. But as Max had learned, looks were a form of lying. David's steel core protected him as much as her pursuit of truth protected Max.

"I don't need you," she told him. "We settled this yesterday, or were you placating me?"

"All I suggested was that I drive you to Atherton before I head to Marin."

"It's foolish for you to drive an hour out of your way. I'm not incapable of driving myself." She ignored David's subtle smirk. "And I need a car. This isn't New York where I can walk everywhere or grab a taxi. Go. Emma is waiting."

"If you're sure."

She glared at him. "She's your daughter."

"She comes with her mother."

"I'm not the one who screwed Brittney in a failed attempt to prove I wasn't gay," Max said, "and I will not let you use me as an excuse to avoid the selfish bitch." Tough love. David adored his twelve-year-old daughter, but her mother made their relationship difficult. Brittney wouldn't let David spend a minute more with Emma than the court mandated, and the flight delay had already cost him two hours.

They wove through the crowd at baggage claim without slowing down, and stopped at the carousel where their luggage would be delivered.

"Emma wants to see you," David said.

"The funeral is tomorrow. You'll be on a plane to Hawaii Sunday morning. Enjoy your vacation—when you get back, if I'm still here, we can meet up in the city for lunch and I'll take Emma shopping."

David grunted. "She doesn't need more clothes."

"A girl can never have too many shoes." Max doubted she'd have kids of her own, and she enjoyed playing aunt to David's daughter when Emma visited him in New York.

Max parked herself near the carousel opening because she didn't want to be here any longer than she had to. Airports were part of her life, but she grew tired of the waiting part. Before leaving Miami, she'd shipped one of her suitcases back home to New York; the second, smaller bag of essentials she'd brought with her to California. She didn't plan to stay in town long.

"Ms. Revere?" an elderly voice behind her asked.

Max turned and looked down at an older couple. The man, at least eighty and maybe five foot four in lifts, stood with his wife, who barely topped five feet. They both had white hair and blue eyes and would have looked like cherubs if their faces weren't so deeply wrinkled.

Max smiled politely. "Yes, I'm Maxine Revere." She expected them to ask for autographs or question what investigation brought her to California. The true-crime show she hosted every month on cable television had been moving up in the ratings. When she only wrote newspaper articles and books, few people outside of the business knew what she looked like. Now that she was on camera, people approached her regularly.

There were pros and cons to being recognized. She was on a tight time schedule today, but the couple looked sweet.

"I told you, Henry," the woman said to her husband. "I'm Penny Hoffman." Mrs. Hoffman extended her hand nervously. It was cold, dry, and fragile, like the woman in front of her. "This is my husband, Henry. I knew it was you." She gripped her purse tightly with both hands, the straps worn and frayed. "Do you believe in divine providence?"

Touchy subject. Max answered, "Sometimes."

David was standing to the side, watching the situation. He was always on alert, even when it was wholly unnecessary. Ever since the incident in Chicago last year when Max had been attacked in a parking garage by someone who hadn't wanted to hear the truth on her show, David was suspicious of everyone.

Even little old ladies.

"We just flew in from Phoenix," Henry said.

"For our granddaughter's wedding," Penny added. "Last year, we were here for a funeral."

"My condolences," Max said.

Penny blinked back a sheen of tears and smiled awkwardly. "Our other grandchild. Jessica's brother, Jason."

"Penny," Henry said, taking his wife's hand, "Ms. Revere doesn't want to hear about this now."

Penny continued. "The police say they have no leads."

The way she said no leads had Max's instincts twitching. The police might have no leads they shared with the family, but there was always a lead—and it was obvious by her tone that Penny had her own theories.

In Max's experience, murder was almost always personal. There were stranger murders and serial killers, but they were few and far between.

Most victims were killed by those they trusted most. A friend. A spouse. A parent. A child.

David cleared his throat. He grabbed Max's red case from the conveyor belt. He'd already retrieved his smaller khaki bag. He wouldn't have checked it at all, except he'd packed a gun.

"They need to go," Henry told Penny. "It was very nice to meet you, Ms. Revere. Very nice. You're even prettier in person."

"Thank you," Max said. "If you'd like to write me a letter about your grandson's case, here's my office address and e-mail." She pulled a card from her pocket.

She received hundreds of letters and e-mails a week from families wanting her to do any number of things, from proving a loved one innocent to a killer guilty. Most dealt with cold cases and contained few leads. She didn't have time to investigate all the unsolved murders she heard about, and she couldn't always solve the ones she investigated.

But she always gave the families whatever truth she found. For better or worse.

She took a pen out of her pocket and wrote on the back. "Here's my personal e-mail."

Henry took the card, but Penny looked upset. "I have written. Twice."

By the sound of her voice, she hadn't received a response. A sliver of anger ran up Max's spine. Her newest assistant was going to have some explaining to do if she wanted to keep her job. All e-mails and letters must be responded to within a week. Max had drafted four form letters that fit most situations, and what didn't fit she was supposed to review.

Henry said, "We thought you might be interested in the case since Jason was killed at Atherton Prep."

Max was speechless—a rarity. She'd graduated from Atherton College Prep thirteen years ago, but no one had told her about this murder.

The second in the history of the campus.

"When?" she managed to ask.

"The Saturday after Thanksgiving."

Nearly five months ago.

"I'll be in town all weekend," Max said. "I'd like to hear your story. I can't promise I'll investigate, but I will listen."